HEALING SANDS

HEALING SANDS

A Sullivan Crisp Novel

Nancy Rue and

Stephen Arterburn

THOMAS NELSON
Since 1798

NASHVILLE DALLAS MEXICO CITY RIO DE JANEIRO BEIJING

Published in Nashville, Tennessee. by Thomas Nelson. Thomas Nelson is a registered trademark of Thomas Nelson, Inc.

Published in association with Alive Communications, 7680 Goddard Street, Suite 200, Colorado Springs, CO, 80920, www.alivecommunications.com.

Page design by Mandi Cofer.

Thomas Nelson books may be purchased in bulk for educational, business, fund-raising, or sales promotional use. For information, please e-mail SpecialMarkets@ThomasNelson.com.

Library of Congress Cataloging-in-Publication Data

Rue, Nancy N.
Healing sands / Nancy Rue and Stephen Arterburn.
p. cm. — (A Sullivan Crisp novel ; no. 3)
ISBN 978-1-59554-428-5 (pbk.)
I. Arterburn, Stephen, 1953– II. Title.
PS3568.U3595H4 2009
813'.54—dc22

2009036772

Printed in the United States of America

09 10 11 12 13 RRD 6 5 4 3 2 1

For Dale McElhinney, who has the heart of Sullivan Crisp

CHAPTER ONE

I did not, as my ten-year-old son described it, "freak out over everything" back then. It took something big. The problem was, something big happened daily. At times hourly.

That particular hour it was a waste-of-time photo shoot. I told my editor at the *Sun-News* that before I even pulled away from the movie set at White Sands. I was still ranting about it into my Bluetooth as I pulled out onto Highway 70 and headed across the Chihuahuan Desert toward Las Cruces, straight into the eyeball-searing sun.

"Why anybody wants to make a film in the middle of a gypsum dune field is beyond me," I said. "Two hundred and seventy-five miles of nothing but white."

"I know shooting there in the middle of the day is a nightmare," Frances said. "I thought they were going to let you take inside shots of rehearsal."

"Evidently, 'they' didn't know what they were talking about. Or they just said that to get us there, with no intention of giving me access to the set."

I took a long drag out of my water bottle and attempted to stick it back into its holder on the console. I missed and the thing tipped over, still open, onto the floor on the passenger side. Right into my unzipped camera bag.

"So—what happened?"

"After they discussed it to death," I said, "they finally decided I could interview Darnell Pellington."

"Who?"

"Exactly." I kept my eyes on the highway and groped on the floor to retrieve the bottle. "He's one of the co-stars."

"You were supposed to get—"

"I know, okay? I wasn't going to break out the 400 and do the paparazzi thing."

The typing stopped, and Frances sighed into the phone. "So what did you get?"

"Ten minutes in Darnell's trailer while Ken interviewed him. In light so low all the people tromping through needed miners' helmets to see where they were going."

"So you're telling me it was a bust."

I finally got my hand on the water bottle and fished it out of my bag, empty. "Look, I'll send you what I got as soon as I can get Internet access. There's probably something salvageable."

Frances gave me the short grunt she delivered when she could take the time to laugh. "I'm sure it's more than just salvageable. Anyway, no big deal. It's just a secondary story."

Oh. That made me feel infinitely better. I abandoned my attempt to assess the damage to my camera and focused ahead on San Augustin Pass, rendered invisible by the afternoon sun on my Saab's dirty windshield.

"At least you got to see White Sands," Frances said. "That your first time?"

"Yeah," I said. And hopefully my last. Everyone had raved to me about the mile upon mile of pure white sand in the middle of a New Mexico desert, its unique beauty, blah blah blah. Personally, if you've seen one sand dune devoid of vegetation, you've seen them all. I'd been too busy crawling around with a light meter on the floor of what could have passed as a FEMA trailer; I couldn't exactly appreciate the splendor. Besides, the silence out there made me nuts.

"Well, sorry about the assignment," Frances said. "You're on till three?"

"Yeah. I'm headed back to the paper now."

"I'll see what else I can come up with."

That was Frances Taylor's version of good-bye. I climbed the pass and fumed.

If she gave me another city official's daughter's wedding or the fiftieth fiesta of the year, I was going to have an embolism. I'd lost count of how many times in the last six weeks I had questioned the wisdom of taking this job instead of . . .

There was no *instead of.* Photography was all I knew, and I was lucky to get a position when most newspapers were downsizing. It wasn't the kind of photojournalism I was used to, but it served my only purpose: to be close to my boys.

The Saab chugged over the pass that cut through the gargoyle peaks of the Organ Mountains. As I began the drop into the Mesilla Valley, I punched in Dan's number. I was in a borderline foul frame of mind already. What better time to call my ex-husband?

"What's up?" he said, in lieu of hello.

The hair on the back of my neck, I wanted to say.

"I thought I'd come by and see the boys when I get off work at three."

His silence was long and, in my view, calculated to set my teeth on edge.

"Alex will be here," he said finally. "He'd probably like to see you."

"Which means you don't think Jake would."

"Did I say that?"

"You didn't have to."

I could imagine Dan running the back of his hand across his forehead to wipe out me as much as the dust of whatever thing he was creating. I knew he wasn't smearing off sweat, despite the eighty-five-degree September heat. Dan Coe never got worked up enough to perspire.

"Look," I said, "how is Jake going to get past this thing he has about me if we don't spend any time together?"

"I can't force him."

"He's fifteen—you're thirty-nine. Who's the grown-up here?"

"So I make him see you. You think that guarantees he's going to talk to you?"

"If he doesn't see me, that's going to guarantee that he *won't.*"

"I wish you'd just give him some time. Wait him out."

I squeezed the steering wheel. That was Dan's solution to everything. You're going broke? Give it time. You see that your marriage is disintegrating? Wait and see.

"I think it's a good idea for you to see Alex today, though," Dan said. "He starts soccer practice after school tomorrow, so a lot of his free time'll be taken up after today."

"He's playing soccer?" I tried to imagine my sprite of a ten-year-old doing anything athletic. All I could conjure up were his wiry arms and legs and his enormous brown eyes. And the charm-your-Nikes-off smile I missed. So much.

"He played last year too," Dan said. "He's good. So is Jake."

The message was clear: if I had been around for the last twelve months, I would have known my boys played soccer, and now loved tamales, and . . .

"Look, I've got to get back to work," Dan said. "You want me to tell Alex you'll be by?"

"Tell him I'll take him out for Chinese. Jake too."

"They hate Chinese," Dan said.

I bit back a *Since when?* I knew the answer. Since I'd left their father and they'd chosen to live with him. Since I had become *mama non grata.*

My phone beeped. "I have another call coming in," I said. "I'll be there around three thirty."

It was Frances.

"Okay—get over to Third Street," she said. Her tone brought me up in my seat. "It's in about the worst zip code in the city, but—"

"What's going on?"

"A Hispanic kid was mowed down by a white guy in a pickup truck—looks like it might have been a hate crime. If that's the case, it could be A-1, three-column, possibly four, so shoot looser than you would otherwise."

"I'm on it," I said.

"You know where it is?"

"Yeah," I lied and veered into the parking lot of an abandoned pottery shop. "I can get there in ten."

When she hung up, I punched the address into the GPS I'd dubbed Perdita, which means "lost." Frances had a tendency to make assignments sound bigger than they were, probably because nothing much happened in a city whose marketing hook was "One of America's Top 100 Retirement Towns." My six months in Africa had made me something of a cynic about what we Americans consider picture-worthy.

With a map on Perdita's screen, I pulled back out onto 70 and pushed the speed limit toward town. This could be a chance to do what I loved, which was to make pictures that moved people to think, got them to feel unexpectedly. Or at least wake up from a siesta long enough to see that life was not all about prizewinning jalapeños.

"God," I said, "give me the story I'm supposed to tell." It was what I prayed en route to every assignment. I wasn't always sure God particularly wanted me to tell the story of the Chile Festival or the mayor's son's confirmation, but it worked often enough to keep me showing up.

Frances had exaggerated about the zip code, I decided, as I pulled in behind a Las Cruces Police Department cruiser. What qualified as a bad part of town here would have been upscale to some of the people I'd photographed. The address was a few blocks over from the Downtown Mall, a six-block interruption in Main Street, which, except on Wednesdays and Saturdays when the Farmers and Crafts Market convened, was little more than a ghost town. This was Thursday.

The area that surrounded me as I climbed out of the Saab was just as ghostly and a little more run-down. Every other storefront stared vacantly onto the street, while the rest listlessly advertised shoe repair and beer/cigarettes and homemade Mexican food. The only one with clean windows and a freshly painted sign was an establishment that promised to cash paychecks.

As I crossed to the passenger side to pull out my camera bag, I still couldn't see where the actual accident had taken place. An ambulance was parked on the corner. Its lights flashed in alarm, and its engine waited impatiently at high idle, yet there was no sign of the paramedics. I had more gear in my trunk, but for the moment I decided to take only my bag from the floor. The bottom was damp, but the camera itself was dry. That bottle, thankfully, must have been emptier than I thought.

I hung the camera and my press badge around my neck and slung the bag containing another lens over my shoulder. Only when I got around the ambulance did I see that there was an alley behind the row of stores. A police cruiser blocked it, but I walked past like I belonged there. It was always easier to ask for forgiveness than permission.

A quick scan told me I was the first photographer on the scene, although even as I maneuvered my way around a line of reeking trash cans, I saw the van for the only local television station cruise past. Right now the police were too occupied to notice the media, but they would once the TV cameras got hauled in. I had a few opportune moments.

The alley was lined with one of those thick adobe walls New Mexicans loved, and I pulled myself up onto its rounded top. I squatted to maintain a low profile and surveyed the scene.

It was hard to tell what the damages were, with people in uniforms swarming like ants around what I made out to be a faded blue pickup truck. Its fenders were dented, but the rust in the creases told me that hadn't happened today. Even the bumper hanging off the rear looked as if it had settled into its off-kilter position some time ago.

The swarm of officers sorted itself into two groups. One

concentrated on the cab of the truck, the other hovered on the ground behind it. That clump suddenly rose as a gurney came to life and was pushed off through the gravel in the direction of the ambulance with a sense of urgency that pulled at my camera. I took a shot I knew I wouldn't use. The paramedics around the gurney shielded the form they carried, and I didn't even try to get a glimpse of the face.

The siren wound up, a sound that never failed to slit my heart, and I turned my attention to the truck again. The group around the cab was intent on whoever was inside. Two policemen stood in the bed, plastered to the rear window. Three more manned the front from the alley, and one guarded each of the two side windows. I snapped a few shots and zoomed in on the officer on the driver's side, who was talking in that too-calm manner I'd seen negotiators use when they were trying to defuse a hostage situation. Whoever the perpetrator was, he wasn't giving up easily.

With the victim gone, the area behind the truck was momentarily clear. I slid from the wall and got as close as I dared. What I saw sucked the air from me. Blood spattered the tailgate and clung to a clump of dark hair on the bumper. The ground was soaked with more of the same.

It didn't matter how many horrendous crime scenes I saw, I was always surprised at how cruel human beings could be to each other. The only way I kept going was to remember my mission: to keep people from becoming desensitized to violence.

I took one shot before I shivered away from the bumper and focused on the gouges that had been dug into the dirt-and-gravel alleyway by the truck's tires. There was something aggressive, even brutal about them, as if the driver had used his pickup as a weapon. I managed to get several pictures before I heard the inevitable.

"I'm going to have to ask you to step behind the tape, ma'am."

I clicked once more before I lowered my camera.

"I'm sorry," I said. "There wasn't any tape when I got here."

"There is now."

The officer's face was so grim, I didn't argue but dutifully followed his pointing finger to the yellow tape he'd just strung across the entrance to the alley. When the action was as important as his expression suggested, the *re*action would be more so. The better pictures were always of the moments after.

He lifted the tape for me, and I ducked underneath. By then the TV crew was calling out inane questions, and Ken Perkins from the *Sun-News* was right in there with them. I looked for another vantage point from which I could take readers where they themselves couldn't go.

The question was, where? The wall was too obvious now, so I took stock of the back entrances to the stores that formed the alley. People were stuffed into the doorways of some, including the restaurant several doors from the corner. If I joined them, I could get a full frontal of the truck, and none of the officers seemed to care that the doorway folk were technically in front of the tape.

Nor did those folks themselves care when, after hurrying through the now-empty restaurant, I squeezed my way among them into the back opening to the alley. The aura of fear and shock surrounded them like a shell of ice.

I was farther away from the truck than I'd been before, which meant switching to a longer lens. The group of cops still flattened against the vehicle didn't seem any closer to extricating the driver, so I had time.

The brittle conversation among the people I was crunched in with took place in Spanish, of which I knew little beyond *Como esta usted?* Fortunately, their faces were telling the story.

Two round-cheeked girls about Alex's age clung to the doorframe, their brimming dark gazes volleying between the truck and the adults they stood with. The hands of a sturdy middle-aged woman shook as she pressed them to her mouth. Another rocked her body, eyes squeezed shut. A square man in a stained white apron showed no emotion at all except in the tightened stare that never wavered from the faded blue truck.

I opted against the longer lens and stepped back from them, quietly raising my camera. This was the reaction. I cursed the click of the Canon as I shot their pain and their prayer, but none of them even flicked an eyelash at me. I was glad. I wasn't sure that even in English I could say what I wanted to about the shock they were trying to claw through.

A cry from one of the women jerked us all back to the doorway. I crowded in behind them and looked over their heads. Even at five-two I was tall enough to see that the door on the driver's side of the truck was open and someone was being encouraged to climb out. I raised the camera again and made a guess about where to focus.

One of the officers pushed the door closed with his foot. Two others pulled the driver clear of the truck. Below me, the praying woman cried out again, *"Solo es un nino!"*

Was that "only a boy"?

The arms being handcuffed had the lanky, awkward look of a young teenager. He couldn't have been more than fourteen or fifteen years old, and although I watched through my lens, I debated whether to take the shot even if they turned him to face us.

But when the officer put his hands to the narrow adolescent shoulders and twisted him around, I let the camera fall against my chest. Already screaming, I shoved through the huddle in the doorway and tore across the alley.

"Get back!" one of the officers yelled back at me.

"No—"

"Come on, lady," said another, who thrust his arm out to block me. "No press."

I knocked the arm aside and pointed at the boy in the handcuffs. "I'm not the press! I'm his mother!"

CHAPTER TWO

White walls. Gray metal table. Glaring fluorescent light. And a police detective who probably hadn't smiled since his swearing in as a cop in 1987.

It was exactly the way it looks on those real crime shows. Only when you watch it on television, you can't feel the anxiety coursing through you like barbed wire in your veins. Especially when the accused is your fifteen-year-old son, slumped like a comma in the chair between you and his father, hiding behind his hair, grinding his terror with his teeth.

Detective Levi Baranovic sat across from us, boring his greenish eyes into Jake as if he were trying to drill out his thoughts. It hadn't worked in the forty-five minutes we'd been sitting there, and I had to grind my own teeth to keep from screaming.

He leaned back in the chair, and the light glared on the high forehead created by his neatly receding line of otherwise thick, coffee-colored hair. "Let's go over this step-by-step, son," the detective said, "because I don't think you understand the position you're in."

He leaned on the table again, long face close to the top of Jake's bowed head.

"You were found behind the wheel of the vehicle that backed over a sixteen-year-old Hispanic boy. That vehicle belongs to the boy's mother, and we found both it and you behind the restaurant where she works. From our first examination of the scene, we've determined that the truck backed over this boy with excessive force for reverse." He cocked his head at Jake. "Of course, since you don't have a driver's license or a learner's permit, you aren't familiar with how a motor vehicle operates. Am I right?"

Jake's dark, chin-length hair remained in motionless panels on either side of his face. He didn't appear to be breathing—until Detective Baranovic slapped his hand on the table. We all jittered on our seats, including Dan, who pulled his fingers through his shorter version of Jake's hair and let out a long, slow sigh. I wanted to slap him. Sighing—hand-slapping—reviewing the same information until I could have recited it myself. Why didn't somebody try something that worked? I would have voiced that, but I'd already been threatened with exclusion from the room if I couldn't keep my mouth shut.

"We only need one parent present," Baranovic had informed me when I told Jake five minutes into this to sit up and look at the detective and explain what had gone down out there in that alley. Since then, I'd sat silently wearing down my molars and tracking the sweat that rolled straight down my back.

"Have you ever driven a vehicle before today?" the detective asked.

Jake shook his head and kept his gaze on the table. With his hands in his lap, he began to pick at a mole he'd always had on his wrist.

"The truck struck Miguel Sanchez and then pulled forward and stopped. Did you just sit there while he was unconscious on the ground?" Detective Baranovic reached his fist across the table, and for a mother-bear instant I thought he was going to punch my son, but he used it to lift Jake's chin.

Jake's dark blue eyes were blurred with fear, and moisture had gathered beneath them, though from sweat or tears I couldn't tell. Otherwise, he was as pale and still as one of his father's statues. So was Dan.

Jake tried to pull away, but the detective's fingers held his jaw.

"I just want to look at you, son." He dropped his hand. "You don't strike me as racist. But you see, we have a pigmentation situation here. Miguel Sanchez is a U.S. citizen. When a white boy comes in and deliberately runs him down, people start making noises about something racially motivated. Now—" He gave a tight shrug. "I can't do much about the fact that all the evidence points to you as the perpetrator of this crime, which I see as attempted homicide—"

He put his hand up to me before I could get my mouth open, but I grabbed Jake's arm anyway. Jake pulled away, leaving me with a vise grip on the sleeve of his black sweatshirt.

"Talk to him, Jacob!" I said. "You're being accused of murder!"

Jake shrugged.

Baranovic stood up, hands on the table, and loomed over Jake. He wasn't big, but his presence was. "So you're telling me you don't give a flip about this kid, is that it?"

Jake shook his head.

"That's not it, or you don't care?"

"That's not it." Jake's voice shot up into the hormonal, adolescent atmosphere and disappeared. He was so frightened I could hardly stand it.

"Jake, please," I said.

"Mrs. Coe—"

"He's terrified! *I'm* terrified! Why don't you let me talk to him alone—"

"No." Dan put his hand on the back of Jake's neck as if he were retracting him from a brood of vipers.

"Am I going to have to ask you both to leave?" Baranovic didn't raise his voice, but his tone had an edge that could have sliced a rock.

I put my hand over my mouth and waved him on.

"If this was somehow an accident," he said to Jake, "or Miguel provoked you in some way, you need to tell me. That will make it a lot easier on you when I take this to the juvenile prosecutor. She's going to decide whether to file formal charges, and if she does, then a fitness hearing will determine whether they try you as an adult in regular court. If you go in there like this—showing no remorse, with no explanation . . ." He pulled up from the table. The muscles on the forearms below his rolled-up sleeves were taut. "It's going to go as badly as it can possibly go."

Jake said nothing.

"So what happens now?" Dan said.

"We have the option of sending him to county juvenile detention until his hearing, but normally we only do that with youth who are at risk for re-offending or for nonappearance in court. I can release him into parental custody." He looked back and forth between us. "You folks decide who I'm releasing him to. I'm going to need some paperwork filled out."

I stared at Dan until he let go of Jake and got to his feet. "I'll take care of that," he said. He patted Jake's shoulder. "You okay, buddy?"

Was he *okay*? Who was *okay* when they were being charged with attempted homicide in a hate crime? Did he look *okay*? The boy was sweating so hard he was about to evaporate, and probably wished he could.

At least Jake didn't assure him he was just fine, which was what Dan always wanted. Say you're okay, and then I can go on making art and making nice and making believe all's right with the world. Say you're not, and I will still go on making art and—

"I'll be right here if you need me," he said to Jake and followed Detective Baranovic out.

Silence frosted the room that had moments before been a sauna. Jake didn't look at me until he suddenly seemed to realize we were alone. His face came up, ashen and twitching and no longer able to hide the fear that obviously raked at him.

"I'm taking you home with me," I said, "so we can talk this thing through."

"I'd rather go to detention," he said.

His words kicked me in the gut. "You're in serious trouble, son."

"I *know*!" He dug the heels of his hands into his eyes, and I watched his bony shoulders shake, sure they'd grown smaller and more gaunt in the last two hours.

"All right—we won't go there right now. Let's just go home where it's quiet and try to sort this out."

"I'll go home." He turned the stormy eyes on me. "With Dad. That's my home."

"You bet, buddy," Dan said from the doorway. "Hey, it's going to be okay."

Jake collapsed onto his arms on the table, and I stormed out the door. In the hall, Dan stopped beside a drinking fountain and assumed the position: back against the wall, arms folded across his chest, crossing me out as his brown eyes surveyed the floor tiles. Jake had learned it from the master.

"'It's going to be *okay*, Jake'?" I said. "What's going to be okay, Dan? The food in detention? Those cool shackles he gets to wear around his ankles when they drag him into court? What are you *thinking*?"

Dan dragged his eyes up to me and held them there. "I'm thinking you hate to lose, Ryan. But for once, it isn't about you."

I was stunned, and I must have shown it. Why did he choose now to grow a spinal column?

"I know it isn't about me," I said. "It's about what's best for Jake. If I can get him away from here, I can get him to talk—"

"Since when? He won't even have a pizza with you and tell you about his day."

I didn't notice until then that Dan was covered in white dust up to his elbows, and the front of his jeans was streaked in it as well, as if he had been rubbing his hands up and down his thighs. He'd obviously torn out of his studio without even stopping to wash off the plaster.

Something dawned on me. "Where's Alex?" I said.

"He's with Ginger."

"Oh."

Ginger was Dan's "significant other," Alex had informed me. If my ten-year-old had used that term for anybody else, I would have been amused. I'd only seen her once, from afar, when I'd dropped

Alex off one evening. She'd struck me as a candidate for *Deal or No Deal*, one of those women who stood around with suitcases.

I shoved my hair off my face, though it tumbled back immediately onto my forehead and left several chopped-off, dark strands in my right eye. "Look, you have Alex to be concerned with, and this is going to be huge for him too. You can't deal with both of them, so—"

"Why not? I've been doing it for a year."

"Right," I said. "And now one of them has been arrested for attempted homicide."

"You're saying this is my fault?"

I could only stare at the man whose voice teetered on the edge of anger. Dan usually left the anger to me.

"Jake wants to come home with me, so I'm taking him," he said. "Otherwise he's going to detention, and I don't want that, and I don't think you do either. I already signed the papers."

I charged across the hall to the interview room and looked through the wire mesh glass in the narrow window. Jake still had his head on his arms, almost as if he'd fallen asleep.

It was impossible to fathom that my son had tried to kill someone, even in light of the sullen wall he'd built between us. He was angry with me, but in that maddeningly passive way that had driven me away from his father. Surely not angry enough to take it out on—whom? Who was Miguel Sanchez?

I pressed my forehead to the glass. Did it mean something that he was Hispanic? We had never been racist. The boys had been growing up in Chicago before Dan moved them here. Their birthday parties had looked like junior United Nations summits.

And yet Jake didn't deny it, no matter how menacing Detective Baranovic made it all sound. He didn't try to pin it on someone else. He wouldn't even confess that he'd done it.

And I knew why.

I watched him now as he pulled himself up from the tabletop and once again dug into his eyes with his fists while his mouth contorted.

He didn't confess, because Jake Coe had never been able to lie. Alex could get away with a fib until he was caught dead to rights, and even then I usually had a hard time believing his little prevarication hadn't been the gospel truth. But Jake had never even tried it. When I broke up brother fights that rivaled WWE, Jake clammed up and let the chips fall where they may. And that's what he was doing now.

He wouldn't confess, because he hadn't done it.

I tried to turn the door handle, but it didn't budge. When I whirled around to go for the detective, I saw a petite woman with impossible breasts running down the hall, mahogany curls bouncing as she half stumbled in kitten heels toward Dan. When she reached him, he bent over to allow her bronzed arms to fold around his shoulders. She pushed his face into her neck, where I was certain he'd be bruised by the barrage of necklaces that dipped heavily into her cleavage.

"Are you all right?" she said into his hair.

This was Ginger. She pulled back and cupped Dan's face in her hands, which I was surprised she could lift with the number of rings she was wearing.

"It's bad, isn't it?" she said.

"It'll be okay. Where's Alex?"

"He's with Ian. It's bad. You're just so strong about stuff like this."

Stuff like this? She'd seen Dan faced with his son's possible incarceration before?

I turned back to the window to see that Jake had gotten up from the table and was standing in the corner with his back to me. A mental picture formed, what I had come to know as a God-image because it emerged whole and unbidden. It was Jake at five, putting himself into time-out before I even knew the balloons had been tied to the cat's tail, before I'd even pinned the deed on him. He was now a lopey five-foot-ten, but he was the same little boy who would take a punishment he didn't deserve if it meant he could avoid a confrontation.

I slapped my hands against the door on both sides of the window—but that was as far as I let my anger go. I had to have a plan, and as I stood there absorbing my son's pain through the glass, I arranged it, shot by shot, in my mind. I would get to the bottom of this for him.

CHAPTER THREE

The juvenile prosecutor did indeed file formal charges against Jake that afternoon. Although the fitness hearing wasn't until one o'clock Friday, I took the day off so I could find a lawyer. I didn't even have a dentist or a hairstylist yet in Las Cruces, much less an attorney. Locating someone in criminal law had not been on my to-do list.

The only people I knew to ask were my colleagues at the paper, and I didn't want them to know about this. Because Jake was still a juvenile, at least for the moment his name wasn't released. I turned to the Internet, where a Uriel Cohen sounded good on her Web site and even better on the phone—sharp and intelligent. She promised to meet Dan, Jake, and me at the courthouse at twelve thirty.

"I wish you'd lawyered up before they interviewed him," she'd said.

"Don't worry," I said. "He didn't say a word."

Until noon, I poured coffee I didn't drink and made the bed I hadn't slept in and studiously avoided the front page of the *Sun-News*. I'd told Frances I didn't have anything worth sending her. In truth, when I looked at my shots on the laptop the night before, they told a clear story of a vicious attack on a young man that left his family and friends seized with horror.

I finally relented around eleven that morning and skimmed the text of the front-page article. Miguel Sanchez was in serious but stable condition at Memorial Medical Center.

Señora Sanchez probably hadn't slept any more than I had. I could see her in my mind, where God put her—pressed to her son's bedside, trying to push life into his forehead with her hand, whispering the will to survive into his ear. It was everything I wanted to be doing with my own son.

But I didn't see Jake until he and Dan slipped into the courtroom at the Third Judicial District Courthouse a mere fifteen seconds before the bailiff called our case. It might have been by design, so I wouldn't have a chance to speak to him, but then, Dan was always late and, like today, always seemed surprised that it made any difference.

"Didn't you get my message?" I hissed to him. "We were supposed to meet with the attorney first."

I jerked my head toward the fiftyish woman with limp white hair I'd just spent thirty minutes stalling with.

She gave Dan a quick assessment through black-framed rectangular glasses and said, "We'll talk later. This is only a fitness hearing."

Only a fitness hearing? I wanted to scream. *They're going to decide whether to handle our son like the young boy he is or treat him like a career criminal.*

I looked past Dan and drank Jake in. He evidently wasn't that long out of the shower. The dark hair was only now starting to curl out of his apparent attempt to slick it back, and his face looked raw, as if he'd tried to scrub off any visible signs of fear. But he'd had no success with his eyes, which had the same frightened sheen I'd seen the day before. Except for the manly Adam's apple that moved painfully with every swallow, he could have been twelve.

He sat so that I was left next to Dan, who smelled vaguely of Irish Spring soap and gasoline and had tried the same approach with his hair that Jake had. Except for their eyes—Jake's were blue, like mine—they were so alike, I used to joke that I'd merely been an incubator for the child. I didn't find it that amusing anymore.

The judge, the Honorable John Hightower, was a boxy, humorless man with more eyebrows than hair. He cocked one of them at us from the bench.

"This is a fitness hearing to determine whether"—he glanced

down—"Jacob Coe is to be tried as an adult in the vehicular assault of Miguel Sanchez.

"What do you have for me, Ms. Hernandez?"

He cocked the other brow at the representative from the DA's office, a large woman with mocha skin and enough dark hair for six women, which she tossed over her shoulders several times as she stood up, making her long, beaded earrings dance. The image of a Hispanic matriarch was completed by the command in her stride as she approached the bench.

"Your Honor, I would like to read a note that was found on the seat of the truck where Jacob Coe was apprehended."

I hated the way she said his name, as if he were a newly discovered disease.

Hernandez perched a pair of red half glasses on her nose. *"To whom it may concern—that would be you, Sanchez, in case this strains your English vocabulary."* Hernandez gave the words a sarcastic twist. I crossed and recrossed my legs.

"Whereas you are a lowlife immigrant loser, and whereas I am an American-born citizen with certain inalienable rights—therefore, you are going down, dude. Way down. When I'm finished with you, you'll be licking the dust."

Hernandez looked over the top of the paper, directly at Jake. He stared at his hands, which shook where they dangled between his knees.

I leaned into Uriel Cohen. "Jake didn't write that," I whispered to her.

She didn't answer. Hernandez was handing the note to her, which she studied for an interminable moment. Dan tugged at my sleeve.

"What?" I said between my teeth.

"Leave it alone."

"I'm going to tell her Jake's dyslexic. There's no way he wrote that."

"Just leave it."

Uriel put her hand on my arm and stood up.

"This is typed," she said to the judge. "And it's unsigned. I don't see a strong link to my client."

"Except that it was on the seat next to him with his fingerprints on it." Hernandez drew herself up. "This vehicular assault was clearly not an accident, or even an impulsive act. It was planned. That alone indicates that he should be tried as an adult."

"He's fifteen years old, Your Honor," Uriel said.

"I don't care if he's ten—this is a premeditated crime with racial features. That sounds pretty adult to me."

Judge Hightower smeared his hand over his lower face. "What else do you have, Ms. Hernandez?"

My pulse raced. There was more?

Hernandez swept to her table and then to the bench, wafting yet another sheet of paper in his direction. "Your Honor, phone logs have also revealed that a call was made from Jacob Coe's residence to the home of Miguel Sanchez one hour before the incident."

"Which proves what?" Uriel said.

"It doesn't have to prove anything, Ms. Cohen," the judge said. "It only has to give me a reason to bind this case over to regular court."

The courtroom fell silent as he worked his eyebrows over a file in front of him.

"Is there a history of problems at home?" he asked.

"The parents are divorced, Your Honor."

"As are 50 percent of the parents in this country," Uriel said.

"The defendant's father has sole custody," Hernandez said, as if that alone was reason to lock Jake up indefinitely.

"Any evidence of lack of parental control?"

"He was driving a vehicle without a license. He—"

"I mean prior to the incident."

Hernandez folded her arms. "None that has been reported."

The judge looked up at us. "What about family support?"

"You see that both of his parents are here," Uriel Cohen said.

"However, the detective who interviewed the accused reported that they argued—"

Uriel grunted. "What couple doesn't—especially in a situation like this?"

The judge put up his hand. "There are three things here that I don't like." He bored his eyes directly into Jake. "One—the severity of the crime you have allegedly committed. Two—the strength of the evidence. And three—your attitude, young man."

My heart stopped.

"According to the interview report, you were uncooperative, refused to answer questions or defend yourself in any way. And I myself am not seeing much remorse." He shook his square head. "You will be tried as an adult. However, because of your age, your case will be expedited according to Juvenile Justice Commission recommendations."

Hernandez didn't hide a look of triumph. "The people would like to revisit bail at this time, Your Honor."

I turned on Uriel, but she was already getting back to her feet. "We ask that the defendant be released to the custody of his parents, Your Honor. He has no priors. He is not a flight risk. He doesn't even have a driver's license."

"He doesn't seem to need one." Ms. Hernandez didn't look at Jake this time. She turned her eyes on me, lip curled as if she could smell how much I reeked as a mother.

I wanted to spit at her.

"I'll leave custody as it is," the judge said. "Young man, you are to adhere to the restrictions that apply, or you will find yourself behind bars."

With a bang of the gavel, we were done. Papers were shuffled and new names were called, and Uriel Cohen was herding the three of us up the aisle and out into the hall where she nodded us to a long bench none of us sat on.

"What was *that*?" I said.

"Just a hearing." She turned to Jake, who held his hands together in front of him as if he were still in handcuffs. "Don't let that scare you."

"How can that not scare him? They wanted to put him in jail!"

"We all heard it, Ryan." Dan shifted his gaze up and down the hall and once again hung his hand on the back of Jake's neck.

I lowered my voice. "That just wasn't fair. You didn't have any time to prepare—"

"It wouldn't have made any difference. I knew going in they had enough. If he'd been a year younger, it might have gone differently. Over fourteen they consider them to have the 'guilty mind' required to be accountable." Uriel pulled her mouth into a straight-line smile. "We didn't want to show our hand. We'll save it for—"

"Save what?" I said.

"Look, I'm going to take Jake home." Dan put out his hand to Uriel. "Nice meeting you."

"Dan, we need to talk about this!"

"No, actually, why don't you let me get my ducks in a row, and then we'll all sit down together and sort it out, hmm?" Uriel let go of Dan's hand and gave Jake a quick nod. "You guys go on, and I'll call you."

I dropped my forehead into my hand and listened to Dan and Jake's retreating footsteps across the tile to the front door. They all but broke into a run.

"I know that all sounded grim for Jacob."

I looked up at Uriel Cohen. "Jake. We call him Jake."

"Jake. Nina Hernandez made it sound like we might as well cart him off to Springer right now, but I feel positive that I can get straight probation for him."

"Probation," I said.

"He has no priors," she said. "Never been in trouble with the law before?"

"No!"

"Is he a decent student?"

"He has to work at it, but he does fine. Unless his grades have slipped in the last year."

She looked at me.

"He hasn't been living with me," I said. "I was out of the country until six weeks ago."

"I should have no problem getting him two, three years' probation max. All that stuff about premeditation and racial features was just to make us think—"

"Are you saying Jake's going to be convicted?"

She tucked a lanky strand of white hair behind each ear. "I need to go in with a defense that plays up the impetuousness of youth—"

"You don't understand," I said. "There is no way Jake did this. I've watched him carry a black widow spider outside on a sheet of paper because he can't stand to kill anything."

"We can definitely use that."

"I don't care what the evidence is, things are not what they look like here." I shook my head hard. "I don't want probation for Jake. I want him acquitted."

Uriel's eyes took on a glint. "I see you're a woman who's used to getting what she wants."

"I'm used to getting to the truth. Aren't you?"

"I'm used to getting the best possible deal for my client."

When I opened my mouth to protest, she put up a hand. "That could mean an acquittal. It could mean probation. In any case, I don't think it's going to mean any jail time for Jake. In fact, I can almost promise you that."

"If I can get the true story of what happened out of Jake, will you use it?" I asked.

"It depends—"

"No, will you use it? Because if you won't, I'm finding another lawyer."

She blinked. "Girlfriend, you are tough. You want to come work for me?"

"That doesn't answer my question."

I was already turned toward the exit.

"Okay—I will try to use anything you bring me that will hold up in court. That's the best I can do. And there's not another lawyer who can do any better than that."

"You'll hear from me," I said.

Her mouth twitched. "Oh, I don't doubt that for a minute."

I careened out of the courthouse and crossed Picacho Avenue without bothering to check for cars. I licked at my dry lips as I headed for the lot where I'd parked the Saab. Evidently I was the only person in existence who didn't think Jake had turned into a racist killer overnight. Fine. I was used to doing it all myself.

I didn't see Levi Baranovic until he reached out an arm to keep me from plowing into him. Even at that I didn't recognize him at first. He was wearing a crisp shirt and a conservative tie and a pair of sunglasses. He *wasn't* wearing the grim expression he'd had on the day before. At least until he registered who I was.

"Mrs. Coe," he said.

"Detective." I straightened my shoulders. "I'm glad I ran into you. How is the investigation going?"

He looked at me blankly. "What investigation?"

"The vehicular assault."

"There isn't much to investigate," he said. "We have a smoking gun."

"It looks like one. It's not. I know my son didn't hit that boy, and I want you to keep looking."

"For what?"

"For witnesses."

"There were none."

"For other possible explanations, then. That's your job, isn't it?"

He took off the sunglasses and rubbed at the bridge of his nose. "Let me tell you about my job, Mrs. Coe. I just came from Memorial Medical Center because Miguel Sanchez can't go to a free clinic or some Mexican *farmacia* to be treated for what's going on with him. I had to talk to his mother, see if she knew any reason why your son or anybody else's son would want to run over hers."

His eyes hardened on me, and my stomach turned over. He was going to say she'd seen it happen.

"She couldn't tell me anything," he said. "All she could say, over and over, was that her boy is in a coma. That both of his legs are broken. That he has serious internal injuries and a fractured skull. If he ever regains consciousness, he will probably be in a vegetative state. That's what she told me."

I could see the face of the woman I'd never met, and I could feel the pain that ripped through her. Only *that* stopped me from pinching the detective's head off.

"I grew up in Las Cruces," Baranovic went on. "It's a good town, and I don't want to see it sucked up by youth crime the way places like Atlanta and LA have been. I've got two kids myself, and I want them to think 'race issues' means who can run the fastest."

"I'm right there with you."

"So I have given every scrap of evidence we have to the DA, and if I find more, I'll give that to her too." He slid the sunglasses back onto his face. "Because I'm all Miguel Sanchez has to provide closure for his family. That's my job, Mrs. Coe."

I stood there long after he disappeared around the corner, grasping for sanity, until my cell phone rang. I fished it out of my bag, ready to tell Frances to either get off my back or fire me. But it was Dan's number.

"Yeah," I barked into it.

"Hi, Mom," said a boy-husky voice.

I closed my eyes and reined myself back in. "Alex," I said. "Hey, guy."

"You wanna come to my soccer practice?"

"Oh—yeah—I heard you were a little jock now."

"I'm a superstud. It's at four o'clock. Can you come?"

"Try and stop me. Where?"

"Burn Lake. You know where that is?"

"Yes," I said, though I didn't. "See you at four."

"Oh, and, Mom?"

"Yeah?"

"Could you bring the snacks?"

"Snacks?"

"For the team, for after practice. All the moms do it, and it's your turn."

"Then I'm on it," I said.

We hung up without my asking how many snacks to bring. I didn't want him to know I had no idea how many kids were on a soccer team. Or anything else about his life.

But I was determined to find out.

CHAPTER FOUR

Since "snack" was the only thing he'd asked of me, I wheeled up to a mini-mart and loaded up on everything I knew Alex loved, which was anything with peanut butter in it. With several gallon bags of Reese's in one sack, two family packs of PB crackers in another, and four liters of Gatorade in a third, I careened out of the store, and with the help of Perdita headed for Burn Lake.

As I pulled into a parking space between two cars with orange Las Cruces Youth Soccer bumper stickers, I had to admit that it was a pretty impressive little sports complex. It took me a good five minutes to discover which soccer field was Alex's, and when I got there every boy was dressed in the same floppy shorts and baggy T-shirt and plastic guards up to his knees. I only picked mine out when somebody yelled, "Good tackle, Alex!"

That someone was Dan.

I stifled a groan and looked up into the stands, but I saw only a knot of women in visors and sunglasses, most of them on cell phones. When I heard him again, I turned toward the field. Dan was out there running with the kids, wearing a ball cap that said *COACH* on it.

A fact Alex and Dan had both neglected to mention. Since when did Dan know anything about soccer?

"You must be Alex's mom."

I turned and had to look immediately down, at a tiny woman with dark straight hair that was almost as long as she was. She shook back girlish bangs and smiled almost shyly at me.

"I'm Poco Dagosto," she said. "Felipe's mom."

I hoped I looked like I knew who Felipe was. "Nice to meet you. I'm Ryan." I tried to put out a hand to shake hers, but I was too encumbered with grocery bags.

Her deep-black eyes lit up. "Alex said you were bringing snacks. He promised me he gave you more than two minutes' notice. Well, here, let me take some of that."

She tried to extricate two of the sacks from my arms, and one of them tumbled to the ground and spilled out the Reese's peanut butter cups, just in time for two more women to join us. One of them leaned over to retrieve them and was instantly lost in a blonde tangle of her own hair. The other one lowered her sunglasses and stared.

"You brought candy?" she said.

"I hope it's for us." Poco giggled like a nervous twelve-year-old. "We could always use the chocolate."

"No, seriously." Anti-candy Woman took the shades completely off and surveyed me with cool blue eyes the shape of apostrophes. Straggles of hair had escaped her ponytail and were wagging in the breeze. They'd once been a mousy brown. Turning gray wasn't going well.

"I see peanut butter crackers," the blonde woman said. "That works."

She had stood up and was peering into the bag I was holding. I still couldn't see her face for the mass of hair the wind continued to have its way with. All I could tell was that she wore round glasses and had a voice like a yoga teacher.

"Alex probably didn't give her the memo about what to bring." Poco gave another random giggle. "We don't usually like to give them sugar," she said to me.

"Or preservatives." Anti-candy looked pointedly at Blondie.

"It's okay. I'll run to the store." Poco tied the top of one bag and started on the second. "You can take these home for later. Oh—you guys, this is Ryan Coe. This is Victoria West."

Blondie finally managed to get her tresses out of her face and give me a spacey smile before it all went wild again. Had no one ever told this woman about barrettes?

"And this is J.P. Winslow."

I expected her to add *and associates.* The name was perfect for the unsmiling woman who was obviously running some kind of assessment on me based on my snack snafu. The blue apostrophe eyes didn't leave my face.

"Victoria is Bryan's mom," Poco was saying, "and J.P. is Cade's."

"I hope there isn't going to be a quiz," I said.

No one seemed to find that amusing, except Poco, whose response to everything so far was a fretful laugh. I got the distinct impression I had failed some kind of test already.

"Okay, so, I'll be back," Poco said, and she took off to get what I was supposed to have procured instead of the ill-gotten booty J.P. Winslow was still giving the death stare to.

Victoria pointed up the bleachers. "You want to join us?"

J.P. didn't echo the invitation, which was my incentive to say that, yes, I would love to. I followed Victoria's hair five rows up, where we sat in front of another group of women who nodded and waved.

"What's Cade doing?" J.P. said, pointing to the field. "How is he ever going to get control of the ball if he can't keep his balance?"

"Maybe he's just trying to trap the ball out of the air," Victoria said on the other side of me.

J.P. shot her a look that assured me I wasn't the only one flunking out today. I leaned on my knees and tried to find Alex among the scattered ten-year-olds below. Once they started to move, it wasn't hard. He was smaller than most of them, for starters, and scrawnier. He had both Dan and me to thank for that. Although I had never had a weight problem in my life, I couldn't claim to have a good figure. Everything about my body was flat. Everything.

Alex's diminutive size seemed to be working for him at the moment as he skittered down the field after a much bulkier boy who was hogging the ball.

"Tackle him, Alex!" I yelled, standing up. "Take him down!"

I heard some titters behind me.

"Do you even know what 'tackle' means in soccer?" J.P. said.

It evidently didn't mean what it meant everywhere else.

"It means steal the ball, not take him down." She pulled in her chin. "Sit, before you make a complete fool of yourself in front of your kid."

I didn't sit. I wasn't used to being given orders, and I sure had no intention of taking them from the Soccer Nazi.

"I think I'll get a little closer," I said. "Excuse me."

"She's not going to be able to tell what's going on from there," I heard Victoria say as I trotted down the steps.

"Like that's going to matter," was J.P.'s answer.

Welcome to your son's soccer league, Ryan. We hope you'll feel right at home—as soon as you get a clue.

I sat on the bottom bench like I knew exactly what I was doing and realized right away what Victoria was talking about. All I could see were the backs of the boys who weren't currently on the field and, of course, Dan.

He stood on the sidelines among them, long, lean legs hanging out of the adult version of the same baggy shorts the kids were wearing, hands parked on the negligible hips that barely held them up. Beneath the shadow of the ball cap, all I could see of his face was his mouth, lips separated as almost-always in an attitude of surprise. Dan was like a cat. Every day was a new wonder to him, as if he hadn't seen and done it all before. It was the thing I had fallen in love with, and the thing that had driven me into rage I didn't even know I was capable of . . .

What was I *doing*?

I stood up and forced my eyes away from Dan and onto Alex, who now had the ball between his feet. He used them to get it past a boy who seemed determined to get it away from him with his own size nines. That seemed to delight the mothers in the stands as well as his father, who held up a hand to high-five Alex when he scooted by. I was definitely going to have to brush up on my soccer. I didn't know what was good and what was going to win me a sneer from J.P. Winslow.

Not that I cared.

Except, from the glow on Alex's face and the confidence that danced his feet down the field, I knew this was a huge part of my son's life, so it had better be part of mine.

I glanced up at the women above me, the full-time mothers who, ten to one, drove minivans and had something simmering in the Crock-Pot at home and were still married to the fathers of Cade and Bryan and Felipe. I had more hope of fitting in with an Amish community.

Soccer practice ended at five, and I forced myself to observe the snacks Poco supplied for the boys—baby carrots, apples, string cheese, and bottled water. Personally, I would have wanted a Snickers bar after a workout like that, but I slid the information into my mental Mom file and pulled some cash out of my wallet.

"Take this," I said to Poco when I was sure J.P. was out of earshot.

Her eyebrows knitted together. "For what?"

"For when it's your turn to bring the snack, since you had to bail me out."

I didn't mean for my tone to take on the edge it did, but Poco untangled the eyebrows and moved closer to me. The top of her head was at my chin.

"Don't let J.P. get to you," she said, almost without moving her lips. "She'll warm up once she gets to know you."

I was about to tell her that it was not my life's desire for J.P. to get to know me, when I felt something warm and moist beside me.

"Hi, Mom," Alex said. "Dad said could you drive me home because he has a meeting."

"Soccer league board," Poco said.

As if I didn't know. Which I didn't—but it seemed to be

common knowledge that I was playing catch-up with my family. I mean, gosh, I didn't even have a bumper sticker.

"I absolutely could," I said. "Get your stuff."

"I'm goin' with Mom, Dad!" he yelled across a dozen kids and, of course, their mothers. "We'll see you at home!"

I could almost hear the thoughts. *What? You told me they were divorced. Somebody find out and get back to me . . .*

Alex and I left them to gossip it out for themselves. He was grinning from one earlobe to the other when we climbed into the car, and it dawned on me as I pulled out of the parking lot just what that had been about. I held myself back from saying, "No, son—your father and I are not getting back together, no matter what you do."

I sagged a little. His invitation to come to practice probably had less to do with me seeing him play soccer than with me seeing his father. Why else wouldn't he have informed me that Dan was the coach?

But going to Dan's right now played into my plan to talk to Jake as soon as possible. This had to be a God thing. It screamed for the prayer, "Please give me the words I need to say."

Or the words Jake needed to say. I'd wrestled with it during the long hours I'd lain awake the night before—Jake's refusal to talk about any of this—and it had come to me that it wasn't all that unusual. Jake had always been one to bottle things up—who was being mean to him on the playground, what unfair thing was happening in the classroom, which fear was haunting his nightmares—until it all poured out in a burst of little-boy angst. And just to me. The only person he would ever share those secrets with was me.

Until he turned twelve. That was normal, I'd thought. His voice was changing. His legs were getting hairier. He was showing all the signs of starting the painful trek into manhood, so why wouldn't he switch his confidences to Dan? I was wistful about it, but not disturbed.

Except that he didn't go to Dan, who was at that time hiding in his studio, busily making me think he was filling orders for customers of the business I helped him start. The shop that was slowly going under and would finally sink before I knew where it was headed—when it was too late to stop it.

Jake went to his room and did some hiding of his own. Which, I had to admit, I didn't see as a problem until the day in court when he informed the judge that he wanted to live with his father. The day he wouldn't even look at me.

I turned onto the dirt road that led from Lakeside Drive back to Dan's place in the southern part of Las Cruces. Though it was only a few miles from the house I'd bought, it might as well have been on a different planet. Yet I was barely aware of the copse of apple and pear trees gone wild that we rode through, their branches entwined overhead like a feral canopy of fruit. God was giving me a different image—of the bond I'd had with Jake before the divorce. It had to be there still. I thought when I came here to mend it that it might have to happen gradually. But there was no gradual now. There was only right now—or there was prison.

We stopped in a cloud of dust in front of Dan's L-shaped, tile-roofed farmhouse. It was pleasant enough, swathed in shade trees and reminiscent of pictures I'd seen of New Mexico's territorial period, even though it was only about twenty years old. I still wasn't sure how Dan had afforded it. He knew as much about handling money as I did about soccer, and of course *What money?* was always the question. He played the role of starving artist well.

Motion caught my eye in one of the front windows as I got out of the car after Alex, who was already disappearing around the back. All the windows were wide, with three paned panels framed in cornflower blue against salmon-colored adobe walls. A face disappeared from the glass, but not before I recognized curls and a set of unnaturally white teeth. I wondered if Ginger and Dan had ever discussed their views of Rembrandt—an artist for him, a toothpaste for her.

She opened the door for me before I got there. What—did she live there?

One would think so, the way she ushered me into the open,

cream-tiled entranceway with an air of ownership. I didn't ponder that, however, because Jake was there, too, standing in a shaft of fading sun that striped through one of the skylights between the ceiling vegas. The light seemed to go through him, as if he weren't wholly there. The downward cast of his eyes told me he wasn't.

"Danny called and said you were coming," Ginger said.

Danny? I would have pondered *that* longer if I hadn't seen her rest her hand on Jake's back.

"I knew you'd want to have some alone time, so I've got you set up in the den. Alex is always hungry when he gets home, so he'll be out here demanding food any minute." She rubbed Jake's back. "Won't he? And Ian's due in from practice in thirty minutes. It gets a little wild around here after school." She nodded her head of full, fat curls toward the back of the house. "You two get settled, and I'll bring you some snacks and make sure everybody leaves you alone."

She couldn't have been more accommodating, but all I could think of when she dropped her hand from Jake's back was that he'd never flinched while it was there. And that now, when *she'd* set it up, my son was going to give me some "alone time."

Jake led the way halfheartedly through the open, airy living room and kitchen, all of which carried the mixed aroma of apple-cinnamon potpourri and cayenne pepper. French doors, painted the same cornflower blue as the window frames, opened into a room I hadn't been invited into before.

The floor was covered in terra-cotta tile, and an adobe window seat was piled with pillows in patterns I'd only seen on Navajo pottery. The furniture was cozied around an adobe kiva where a small fire crackled.

None of it took the chill off of Jake, however. He fell onto one of the sofas and sat there, flattened against burnt-orange cushions and yet at the same time crouched for flight back to his cave, where I wasn't welcome.

I perched on the window seat facing him. "Thanks for seeing me."

"It's not like I had a choice."

"You don't, because we have to get this worked out. Let's just walk through it, okay?"

Since he didn't hurl himself from the room, I cut to the chase.

"All right, so how did you get downtown yesterday?"

"I just did."

I sucked in a breath. "All right, so, you're there. How did you wind up in somebody else's truck? Did you steal it?"

"No!"

He glanced at me for a flicker of a second and looked away.

"So somebody let you get in the truck."

"I guess."

"You're not sure, or you don't remember?"

He shook his head. I wanted to shake the rest of him. No wonder cops wound up smacking their suspects.

"What about the note? I know you didn't write that, Jake. I mean, unless something's changed."

"Don't say I'm not smart enough to write like that."

I stared at him. "I wasn't going to say that. When have I ever said you weren't smart?"

"I just don't want to talk about this." This time he did hurl himself from the room, nearly mowing down Ginger, who was entering with a tray.

"You want me to bring this to your room, Jakey?" she said.

He didn't answer. When she looked at me, I got up and went for the back door.

"I guess nobody's hungry," I heard her say.

The door opened onto a wide-planked deck overlooking a surprisingly neat area of brick walkways and stoned circles and cable-spool tables holding pots of red geraniums. Alex was in a far corner, batting at a soccer ball with his foot. I sat on the low step and tried to stuff my rising anger. It was a lot like pushing toothpaste back into a tube.

But I hadn't seen anger in Jake just now. He was irritated—sick of being questioned and threatened and advised of his rights. But I didn't see the kind of rage it would have taken to break someone's legs and fracture his skull and throw him into a coma.

Or was it just buried under the shruggy shoulders and the snipped-off answers? I'd seen boys do that in Chad, boys who had more to bury than Jake did. But even as the idea came to me, I dismissed it. They interred their anger under faces that showed nothing. I could see something in Jake, a shadow of—what was it? Fear? Guilt?

I stood up, sending a pair of fallen yellow cottonwood leaves scurrying. It couldn't be guilt. But Jake wasn't going to help me prove it. I was going to have to do that on my own.

I looked at Alex, who was bouncing the soccer ball on his lifted knee with surprising accuracy.

Or . . . I might get a little help.

He stopped and grinned as I strode toward him, hugging my arms around myself against the gathering chill. "So," I said, "are you going to teach me about soccer, or what?"

His grin widened. He was unarguably the most charming child ever created.

"You wanna learn?" he said.

I nodded at the ball he had parked on his hip. "Show me how you move it around with your feet."

"It's called dribbling, Mom," he said with exaggerated patience. "You just do this."

I watched him tap the ball with his insteps in a circle around me.

"How did you get so good at this?" I asked.

"Practice. Jake helps me."

The ball escaped, and he had to chase it under the bank of creosote bushes that separated the yard from Dan's outdoor sculpture gallery beyond.

"Are you and your brother still close?" I asked when he emerged.

"Kind of." He went back to juggling the ball off of his knee. Apparently that was his latest very-cool skill. I showed the proper appreciation.

"Jake hangs out with his own friends mostly," he said. "But me and him play soccer, like, every day. Or we did."

"Until when?" I said.

"Until yesterday."

The ball got loose again, and this time I stopped it with my foot.

"Good trap, Mom," he said.

"Alex."

He looked at me, brown eyes round.

"I don't think your brother ran over that boy, and I'm going to prove it. Will you help me if you can?"

His gaze dropped to the ball, and he pried it away from me with his toe. It wasn't the reaction I expected.

"Are you and Dad gonna fight about it if I do?"

I expected that even less. "No! Why would we fight about that?"

He put the ball in motion again. "You guys fight about everything—and then I don't know whose side I'm supposed to be on."

I couldn't even go there, not with a screaming fit starting in my head. I was going to have to save that one for Dan. Meanwhile, my ten-year-old continued to dribble a ball in a circle that probably matched what was going on in *his* head.

"Let me give it a try," I said.

He pushed the ball to me with the inside of his foot, and I trapped it again with mine, since that had impressed him the first time. I had less success with dribbling. Two kicks, and the thing was in the koi pond. Alex retrieved it, snickering happily.

"You got a long way to go, Mom," he said.

"Alexander—don't you want a snack?"

We both looked up at the figure standing in the back door with the tray of goodies nobody seemed to want.

"I'm good," Alex called to her.

When Ginger disappeared, I said, "Does she live here now?"

"No. But she's gonna homeschool Jake since they won't let him back in the school. That's why she's here."

I detected an edge in his voice, and I went for it.

"So—she calls you Alexander?"

"She puts a *y* on the end of everybody's name. Danny. Jakey. It doesn't work with mine."

"You can't exactly say Alex-y."

"Yeah, but it's like she has to do *something* with it, so she calls me Alexander. She's just weird."

Well. His loyalties to me and to his father might be divided. But there was no place in there for Ginger.

At least there was that.

CHAPTER FIVE

Dr. Sullivan Crisp pulled his feet off the desk when he heard Martha Fitzgerald coming down the hall, and stuck them back into his Top-Siders. There was going to be enough eyebrow raising during this conversation as it was. Why give her a reason to shoot them all the way up into her hairline when she saw his Road Runner socks?

"Come on in, Martha," he said before she could tap oh-so-primly on the door. That always made him want to do something un-prim in return.

"Are you sure this is a good time?" she said, even as she headed straight for one of the red-padded client chairs in front of the desk, leather portfolio in hand.

"A good time, but not a good place," Sully said. "It's too nice out to be stuck in here." He wiggled his own eyebrows at the French doors opening onto the patio. "Step into my outer office."

Martha smiled a tight, automatic smile. Sully had figured out within two weeks that Martha seldom frowned, but she had a broad selection of smiles, some of which made great substitutes for a scowl. She nodded her head of smooth, bottled-but-attractive blonde hair as she followed his extended arm through the door he opened for her.

She positioned her self-consciously middle-aged self in one of the Equipale leather-and-wood bucket chairs at the table, ducking to miss the long bunch of chiles Sully had hung there. Those things were all over Las Cruces right now, and he loved them. If Martha didn't, she was careful not to show it.

"Can I get you anything to drink?" Sully said.

"I'm fine. We have a lot to cover—"

"Do you mind if I suck down a Frappuccino while we talk?"

Sully could tell she was forcing her eyebrows to remain in check. He pulled a cold Starbucks bottle out of the small fridge and sighed into the chair facing her. "Thanks for humoring me," he said.

"It's no problem, Dr. Crisp."

"When are you going to start calling me Sully?"

"Sully," she said.

He knew she'd be back to "Doctor" five minutes from now, even though she, too, had a doctorate in psychology and fifteen years more experience than he had. His being the founder of the Healing Choice Clinics seemed to make it impossible for her to lighten up.

"What's first on the agenda?" he asked.

She flipped open the leather portfolio. "The Hillman issue," she said.

"Bring me up to speed."

"I reported suspected child abuse when I was working with the Hillman girl, but CPS found no evidence."

"Oh, right, so Mr. Hillman has threatened to sue us."

Martha nodded stiffly.

"You still maintain there was abuse?"

"Yes, I do. I saw evidence of—"

Sully put up a hand. "No need to explain. You wouldn't have gone that far without good reason. Has Mr. Hillman's attorney contacted you yet?"

"No."

"Then let's just file that one away. If and when the time comes, the ministry will back you up." He fished a small voice recorder out of his pocket and said into it, "Put Hillman on the back burner and hope he doesn't scorch his buns." He grinned at Martha. "What else you got?"

"Bob Benitez," she said.

"Ah—Bobby the Blogger."

Martha twitched an eyebrow. "A lot of people think everything they read on the Internet is gospel."

Sully crossed one long leg over his other knee and propped the bottle on it. "What's his beef again exactly?"

"His niece came in for counseling—she was one of Carla's clients—and he says her ethnic background was not taken into consideration in her counseling."

"Was it family therapy?"

Martha consulted her notes and shook her head.

"So how did he know whether her counseling was ethnically appropriate or not?"

"I couldn't tell you."

"Do we care about what ol' Bobby is blowing smoke about in his blob?"

"Blog," Martha said—and then gave him a quick look.

He grinned at her again, and both her cheeks went pink to match her perfectly professional blouse. He'd caught her giving his Hawaiian shirts and chinos the eyebrow more than once since he'd arrived to get the clinic back on its feet.

"Bob Benitez and his wife are influential in the social justice circle here in Las Cruces," she said.

"So—what is it he wants?"

"From what I can tell, he just wants a case he can use to prove that the mental health care of Hispanics is inadequate for their special needs."

Sully refolded his legs and took another swig. Martha waited.

"Well," he said. "We could post a comment on his blog, explaining that at Healing Choice we show our clients that God loves them and can lead them to healing whether they are white, black, brown, or blue. Or we can refuse to dignify it with a response, and he'll find somebody else to pick on. What say you?"

She cleared her throat. "I suppose we should go for the latter."

"I like the way you think. Ignore Bobby," he said into the recorder, then turned to Martha. "Anything else?"

Martha glanced needlessly at her list again. "Carla Korman."

"I'm still not sure I understand what gives with that. I've read the file, but it doesn't fit together somehow. You want to try to unmuddle it for me?"

"I don't even know if I understand it," she said.

"Give it your best shot."

"She had been working here as a therapist for two years when I came on board, and as far as I could tell, her clients thought highly of her."

"Except for Bobby Benitez's neice."

"But he never filed a complaint. There were none until that flurry about two months ago. All of a sudden, four different people came out of nowhere saying she gave them counsel that led to this or that disaster. All of them complained to the Healing Choice head office—they're the ones who removed her."

"That happened while I was out of the loop," Sully said. "Rusty Huff was handling things then—and I don't think he would have let her go without the juice to back it up." He tilted his head at Martha. "What's your take on it?"

"She was completely devastated, and I can't say I blame her. It just seemed to happen so suddenly."

Sully nodded and muttered, "Talk to Rusty about Carla Korman," into the recorder. "So what's the situation at this point?"

"The PCMFT board is trying to decide whether to completely revoke her license. They want us to fill out some paperwork. You're familiar with them, of course."

Sully nodded. He knew the Professional Counselors and Marriage and Family Therapists all too well. Part of his reason for being in Las Cruces, besides getting this particular clinic off of its ear, was to investigate the possibility of getting someone else's license revoked by that same board. Until he'd found out she didn't have one. He drained the Frap bottle. Just thinking about it made him want to bite the top off of it.

Martha was still giving him the curious version of her smile. "How would you like for me to proceed, Dr. Crisp?"

"Why don't you follow up on the complainants if you will, see if you can get to the bottom of this. If Carla was struggling with something herself, I'd rather see her get help than the boot."

"I'll get on it."

"Have Olivia help you. You already have a double client load until we can hire someone to replace Carla."

"That's okay. Olivia is . . . I can handle it."

Sully felt a grin spread across his face. "Issues with our Olivia?"

Martha glanced at the open French door. Sully nudged it closed with his foot.

"Dish," he said.

"I don't mind the chitchat and the burned popcorn in the microwave," Martha said.

She did, of course, but Sully just nodded her on.

"But I caught her in a lie, and I don't think we can have that."

"Seriously."

"I waited a half hour for a client yesterday, and when I went out to check with her to see if he'd called to cancel, she swore he hadn't. I called him later, all concerned about him, and he said he'd notified Olivia two days ago. I confronted her, of course, and she melted like a pat of butter."

"Tears?"

"Beyond. She said she was afraid to tell me she'd messed up." Martha blinked at him. "I just don't understand that."

Sully bit back the explanation that Martha could be as intimidating as a boa constrictor and tapped his recorder. "You want me to say something to her?"

"No. I've got it handled. This is just FYI."

"And not a moment too soon." Sully nodded at the French door where Olivia herself was approaching, hand already poised to tap on the glass. He stifled a grin when Olivia looked Martha's way and turned a little green.

"Come on out," Sully said as she pushed the door open only far enough to speak through. "We were just talking about you."

Olivia's eyes, which bore a strong resemblance to Bambi's,

widened as if she were staring into the proverbial headlights. Her face, already a powdery shade, went paler, leaving every fine freckle on her nose in bas relief. Sully could have predicted that both hands would go up to her brown straggle of hair and shove it behind her ears. Then they clutched at the long string of beads she wore with what Sully thought they called a peasant blouse. The lace on it had the same chewed-on-by-a-goat look as the ends of her hair.

"Am I in trouble?" she said. "I am, aren't I?"

"Nah," Sully said. "You're just on a learning curve."

"Oh," she said. "Okay—well—you said to tell you when it was almost time for your appointment—you know, with that guy who's applying for the job. And it is. Almost time."

"Good, then," Sully said. "Just show him back when he gets here."

She skittered out without a glance at Martha, who closed her portfolio and stood up.

"What I want to know," Sully said, "is who hired *her*?"

"Carla," she said. "She was a rescuer."

And Martha, clearly, was not.

When Martha was gone, Sully went into his office, propped his feet on the desk again, and pulled out his cell phone. There was just enough time for a quick check-in with Porphyria before she left for Nashville.

The connection to the Smokies was faint at best, but Porphyria's voice was still as rich as molasses when she answered. He closed his eyes; he knew she'd have hers closed too. She did that with him, as if, as his mentor, she was shutting out everything else to give him all the space.

"Don't you ever work, Dr. Crisp?" she said.

"I'm working right now. I'm calling for advice."

"You're calling to check up on me, and I'm fine. I told you this is just my annual physical."

Sully chuckled. "Nothing gets by you."

"I didn't get to be eighty-one years old by being a fool."

"Winnie's driving you down to Nashville?"

"You know she is." Porphyria paused. "Sully?"

"Yeah?"

"I am fine. You worry like an old woman."

Sully let out a guffaw. "Just have your niece call me when you get down there."

"Mm-hmm."

"And when you get done with the exam."

"Mm-hmm."

"And when you get back home."

"You don't have anything else to do out there in New Mexico?"

Sully imagined the dark face smoothed out like the countenance of an African queen.

"Now that I'm here, I think I'm putting it off, Dr. Ghent."

"Your search for Belinda Cox."

"Yeah." Sully dropped his feet to the floor and swiveled the chair around, his back to the door. "The trail led me here, and I don't think it's a coincidence that this particular clinic needs me at this exact time."

"God doesn't do coincidence. So have you looked her up, or are you just wallowing?"

Holy crow. Even from thirteen hundred miles away she read him like a picture book.

"The last place she worked as a counselor was at a church a couple of miles from here," he said.

"You've gone there."

"Not yet."

"And why are we dragging our feet?"

"Because I'm still not altogether sure why I'm doing this."

"Well, I guess you better find out."

"You're not going to cut me any slack, are you?"

"None whatsoever. But I will say this."

Sully held his breath, in case the sound of his own air should cover even a syllable that came from those marvelous lips.

"Just be sure you aren't trying to out-God God. You know God won't have that, now."

"And neither will you."

"Mm-hmm. Well, it's not me you have to answer to, is it?"

"Since when?" Sully said.

"Mm-hmm," she said again.

When she hung up, Sully looked wistfully at the phone. If it weren't for Porphyria Ghent, he might be in a psychiatric hospital or tucked, by his own choice, into a coffin. He wouldn't be taking steps back into the life he'd had to leave behind for months while she helped him face his demons.

His wife hadn't been so blessed. She hadn't had a Porphyria Ghent. She'd had Belinda Cox, and Sully had to find the woman and make sure she never did to another human being what she had done to Lynn. And to their baby girl. At least, that was the reason he'd given himself, until other possibilities had begun to muddy the waters.

A tap on the door signaled Olivia and—what was that applicant's name? Sully dropped the phone into his pocket and stood up.

"Come on in," he said.

Olivia poked only her head in. "He's waiting in the conference room."

"I think I'll see him in here, Olivia."

She pressed her lips together until a deep dimple appeared on either side of them. "He's cute," she said.

"That being one of the major qualifications, things are already looking good for Mr.—"

"Kyle Neering," she said.

Sully didn't know from cute in other guys, but the tall, slender, thirtysomething man Olivia showed in a moment later was definitely a sharp dresser. He also had a neat haircut and a firm handshake, and he looked directly into Sully's eyes when he introduced himself.

"It is a pleasure, sir," he said.

"It would be a pleasure for me if you wouldn't call me sir," Sully said.

Neering shook his head as he took the chair Sully offered him. "Sorry. I just have a lot of respect for you and your work. I've wanted to meet you for a long time." He gazed around the room as if he'd just entered the Oval Office. "So this is where it happens."

"Where what happens?"

"The amazing things you do with people."

"I don't see clients in here, if that's what you mean." Sully sank into the other client chair, which fit him the same way a necktie would. "In fact, I'm not seeing clients at all at this clinic. I'm just here to make sure it's going in the right direction."

"And I'm here to convince you I can help with that." Kyle leaned forward. "I've read everything you've written, studied your podcasts—I even caught your seminar in Little Rock a couple of months ago. I'm a total admirer of your work." His face glowed from handsome jaw to dark brown hairline.

"Well, don't stop now," Sully said drily. "You were just getting warmed up."

"Look, I'm not trying to pump up your ego. I mean, I would love to have this job, but I couldn't pass up an opportunity to tell you what your ministry has meant to me."

Sully slid Kyle's file from his desk and opened it. He was already familiar with Kyle Neering's fairly impressive credentials. He just needed an excuse to get away from that practically idolatrous gaze.

"That your family?"

Sully's head came up. He followed Kyle's point to the photo on the shelf behind his desk, and he felt the familiar cave in his chest.

"My wife and baby," Sully said.

"They're both beautiful. You're obviously blessed."

Not by a long shot, pal, Sully wanted to say to him.

Instead, he crossed one leg over the other knee and said, "Let's talk."

CHAPTER SIX

By the Sunday after Jake's hearing, I had discovered that soccer can eat up your life the way termites consume your woodwork.

I was at Burn Lake all Saturday morning and all Sunday afternoon. So, unfortunately, were the other soccer moms. I wasn't sure at first whether Victoria and J.P. were there to watch their respective sons practice or to scrutinize my lack of understanding of team-motherhood.

I got the snacks right, and I'd made a vow not to yell anything until I'd had a crash course in soccer terminology. But J.P. didn't hesitate to tell me that Alex's shin guards were too big for him and that she saw him picking his nose when he was supposed to be watching the ball. If it hadn't been for Poco continually changing the subject while we sat, interminably, on the bleachers, I probably would have told her to take a look at her own kid.

Because even with my uneducated eye, I could see that Cade wasn't doing so well down there. He was a pudgy boy, for starters, and his cheeks remained an almost neon shade of red at all times, as if just walking were an exertion. He never had the ball longer than two seconds before someone else snatched it from him, and when one of the other boys yelled, "To you, Cade!" he was usually gaping off in the other direction and missed the thing completely.

By Sunday, even J.P. was admitting he was a mess. "I think he's starting puberty," she said.

"At ten years old, J.P.?" Poco said, more gently than I ever could have.

"I don't know what else would cause him to suddenly turn into a complete klutz." J.P. shoved the trickles of graying hair back from her forehead. "It could be his weight, I guess."

Whatever it was, it hadn't improved since the day before. Halfway through practice, J.P. fretted that Dan was going to eliminate him from the team. I laughed out loud.

"I don't see what's funny," J.P. said.

Poco put her hand on J.P.'s arm. "I think Ryan was just—"

"I can speak for myself," I said. "Dan would keep a quadriplegic on the team if it meant he could avoid a conflict."

"I don't think that's funny either."

"Anybody want a drink?" Poco said. "I brought a cooler."

J.P. shook her head and gazed dismally at the field. Victoria ordered a water. Poco grabbed my hand and pulled me with her. My plan was to tell her when we got to the bottom that I didn't need her to play mediator—that J.P. could bring it on as far as I was concerned.

Poco opened the cooler, thrust an icy bottled water into my hand, and had me sitting with her several sections over on the bleachers before I could protest.

"I thought a little space would be a good thing," she said.

"Thanks," I said, "but if I need space, I'll make some."

"I wasn't talking about you. I was talking about J.P. You intimidate her."

I grunted. "I don't think she intimidates that easily."

"She doesn't."

"So are you the protector of the psyches in this group?"

"Yes," she said simply.

I found myself staring at her. She was a tiny thing, but there was something big about her spirit.

"You're probably right," I said. "I'm spoiling for a fight."

"Is it because of Jake?"

I homed in for signs of gossip gathering, but Poco's black eyes were soft. As if she truly did give a flip.

"How did you know?"

"Dan asked a few of us to pray. I'd already read the article, but of course they didn't mention Jake's name."

"Yeah, well, it's not what it sounds like in the paper."

"It never is. No offense."

"None taken. Working for the *Sun-News* is not my lifetime goal, trust me. I'm just doing it so I can be near my boys."

I took a long drink from the water bottle. Why was I telling her all this? I didn't normally open a vein for perfect strangers, or anyone else.

"Jake's fortunate you're here right now," Poco said.

"He doesn't think so."

"He *would* be pretty upset. Alex too."

I looked out on the field, where Dan had the boys gathered around him. Alex was standing a little apart from the group, ball parked on his not-there hip. He looked small and lonely.

"I'm sure you and Dan will do a great job walking them through this," Poco said. "But in case they—or you—need another ear, I can totally recommend the Healing Choice Clinic."

I pulled in my chin. "You're talking about therapy."

"It's not like you think. When I was going through a bad time, I saw a woman there—Carla Korman—and she was amazing. I think I would have become an alcoholic or something if it weren't for her."

To avoid any further disclosure, I said, "If it's warranted, I'll give her a call. Thanks."

Poco formed a fine frown line between her brows. "She left, unfortunately, but I can guarantee you anyone you see there will be wonderful. Are you familiar with Sullivan Crisp?"

"I've heard his radio show once or twice."

"He's the founder of the clinics, and the therapists all use his principles."

"Thanks," I said. "Really, if I see a need, I'm there." I craned my neck toward the field, where the group was setting up a howl. Even as I watched, Dan quelled it and pulled the team in tighter. Even Alex pressed into the knot.

"What's that about?" I said.

Whatever it was, J.P. was already taking the steps two at a time, with Victoria sailing behind her. By the time Poco and I reached them, J.P. was practically on the phone to her attorney.

"You'd better be right," she said, looking straight at me. "Dan better not be making cuts."

As if I had anything to do with what Dan decided.

"What about it, team?" I heard Dan say.

Some kind of tribal shout went up, and this time the players looked a little less hostile. Dan gazed over their heads at the mothers.

"I've chosen a team captain. J.P., you ought to be real proud of your boy."

Of course. Make the worst kid on the team the captain, or watch his mother file a lawsuit. A typical Dan choice.

As the boys diverted their allegiance to the moms with the snacks, Dan came over to us.

"You know," J.P. said, "Cade doesn't need to be patronized."

Could this woman not make up her mind?

"If he's going to be captain, I want him to deserve it, and right now he's playing horribly. What he needs is some help with his skills."

"He's just suffering from a little lapse in confidence," Dan said. "I think making him captain is going to give him a boost. Besides . . ." He smiled his slow, crooked smile. "Just because he isn't David Beckham doesn't mean he isn't a leader. I gave him the opportunity. He'll make himself a captain."

No, his mother will. If it kills him.

Dan went off to join the boys, and I turned in search of my purse. Somebody touched my arm. I looked back at J.P.

"I have to ask," she said. "Why did you let that man get away?"

"*He* didn't get away," I said. "*I* did."

I chewed on that all the way to Dan's, while pretending to listen to Alex go on about how cool it was of Dad to make Cade captain and how Dad wouldn't let the other guys boo when he announced it and how all the guys were saying he was the most awesome coach ever, except the ones that thought they should be captain but they would get over it because Dad was going to figure out a way to make them feel like they were something big, too, because that was what Dad did. I felt like Alex was filling out a profile on Match.com.

When we arrived, Jake and a boy I didn't know were kicking a soccer ball around in one of what Dan called his "sculpture parks." Could I not get away from this game to save my soul? But at least Jake was outside rather than in self-imposed exile in his room. Out where I could get to him.

At least that was my plan. He took one look at my car and headed straight for the backyard. I left my door hanging open and went after him.

"Jake," I said. "Just stop."

He'd gotten as far as the gate that led to the yard off the back patio. He did stop, hand on the latch, but he didn't turn around.

"I know you think I'm going to ask you all these questions," I said to his back, "but I just have one. I promise."

He turned with all the enthusiasm of a root canal patient.

"Just tell me *why* you won't talk to me about what happened. That's all I want to know."

His reply was swift, as if he'd been expecting me to ask. "Because Dad says I don't have to."

Without waiting for me to go back on my word, he slipped through the gate almost without opening it. I felt every blood vessel pump as I stomped back to the front of the house where Alex was still pulling his gear out of my car. Dan's 4-Runner was now parked beside it.

"Where's your father?" I asked.

"I think he went out to the studio."

Why had I even bothered to ask?

I hadn't been to his studio here, but it was obviously the long, low adobe building toward the back of the property, and to get there I had to make my way through another sculpture park. It had always been a dream of Dan's to build his pieces as massively as he wanted and then simply plant them where they would be "discovered" by anyone who happened by. That dream had obviously come to fruition.

I charged past giant banjo players welded together from hubcaps and bicycle pedals and less easily identified scraps of metal. Around baseball players fashioned from railroad ties and hunks of stone. Between two stoneware masks that were taller than I was. Every piece fed my fury, until by the time I reached Dan's doorway I could have disassembled his kiln brick by brick with my teeth.

Dan was already in baggy jeans and the same white muslin too-big shirt he'd worn to work in ever since I'd known him—back when I thought what he did was romantic. I had grown to despise it, just as I had every bucket filled with broken pieces of tile and every stack of unpaid bills. He stood back from a tall swirl of metal, hands on his narrow hips, as if he were waiting for it to speak. I spoke first.

"Why did you tell Jake he doesn't have to talk to me about this?"

His eyes traveled up the metal structure that nearly reached the ceiling. "Because there's nothing to talk about."

"There is *everything* to talk about. He's going to go to prison if we don't find out what happened."

"How do you know that what happened isn't exactly what it looks like happened?"

"*What?*" My voice screeched higher than the structure he was still looking at.

"What if he did run over that boy? For some reason we can't even fathom?"

"Are you *serious*?"

"If he did, Ryan," he said, tears brimming in his voice, "don't you think he needs help, instead of a lawyer or a private investigator or whatever else you have going?"

I was stung by the piece of that which was right, the piece I hadn't thought of. I sucked in air. "Okay, we'll get him help, too, somebody that can get him to talk. Poco just told me about a clinic here in town we can take him to. It's Christian, supposedly the best."

"I wasn't talking about professional help." Dan ran his hand along the metal. "I was talking about family. He needs the people who love him to guide him."

I spewed out all the air I'd just sucked in. "No, Dan—you just don't want to fight it. It's easier to let Uriel Cohen try to get him probation than go after this thing."

"It isn't that."

"Then you actually think he's guilty! What could possibly make our sweet son capable of something that heinous?"

"I think I'm looking at it."

I could only stare at him as he turned back to his metal—thing—and picked up a square of sandpaper.

"You were wrong when you said it was *my* fault Jake got into trouble," he said. "I think it was you. You and your anger made him 'capable.'" He pressed the paper to the metal, rubbed with it, let it drop to the floor. The tears had reached his face. "I think that's why you can't allow him to be guilty—because if he is, you'll never recover from your *own* guilt."

"You are out of your mind!"

"Am I, Ryan? Or would that be you?"

He jerked his chin toward my hand. My fingers were clenched around a shard of metal that teetered atop a pile of pieces waiting to be chosen. My arm was drawn back to hurl it.

"I have supper ready."

The late afternoon sun formed a halo on Ginger's curls before she stepped in and sparkled her eyes and her teeth and her skin at Dan. She was absolutely carbonated until she took in the scene.

"Baby, are you all right?"

She cast me an accusing glance. I let go of the metal and listened to it smack against the rest of the pile on its way to the floor.

"He doesn't need to be upset," she said in a voice higher than anything I could aspire to. "He has an important project to complete."

"I'm sure the world is waiting with bated breath," I said.

"New Mexico State is." Ginger wafted an arm toward the towering hunk of metal. "They commissioned this and five other pieces. They're going up all over the campus." Her eyes narrowed to well-calculated slits. "Or didn't you know?"

"That's just wonderful." I dug my fingers into my temples. "But I'm a little more concerned with my son right now."

"It seems to me that you should have thought of that before."

"Ginger."

Dan put his hands on her shoulders from behind. She grabbed onto both of them, chest heaving as if she and I had just gone at it with the boxing gloves.

"How about we continue this conversation at another time?" Dan said to me.

"Like in about ten minutes—alone," I said. "I'll wait at the house."

I stormed out of the studio and stepped almost straight into the arms of the boy I'd seen playing soccer with Jake. He seemed larger than he had among the lumps and humps of adobe forms. A shock of rich hair fell over his forehead like an ad for Abercrombie and Fitch.

"Is everything all right out here?" he said in a voice that was deep and take-charge. He looked over my shoulder into the doorway to the studio and then back at me, eyes concerned. "Jake thought he heard somebody arguing."

"You stay out of it." I snapped myself past him.

Jake was there, arms folded across his chest.

"Listen to me, son."

"No," he said. "I'm sick of listening to you. You have nothing to say that I want to hear, so just . . . just . . . shut up."

"Excuse me?"

"Just leave me alone. That's what you're good at, isn't it? Leaving?"

For once I was too stunned to speak.

"Jake, dude, you might want to lighten up," said the boy behind me.

"It's okay, buddy."

The kid fell silent at the sound of Dan's voice. I found mine.

"Dan," I said through my teeth, "this is out of control."

"I think you're the one who's out of control," Ginger said. "You come in here all—"

"Bag it. I'm going." I turned and stabbed a finger toward Dan. "But we're not done."

My heart slammed as I made my way through the ranks of the all-metal band, and so did the voice in my head. When did Jake go from monosyllabic grunts to a stream of obnoxia? How did that Ginger person insinuate herself into my boys' lives? And when did I get kicked to the curb as the one to blame for it all? I was almost to my car and halfway to a stroke when an outside voice overtook me.

"You just stay away from him—are we clear?"

I turned around in time to see Ginger snatch a piece of irrigation hose from the base of a soaptree.

"What are you *doing*?" I said.

She brandished the hose at me. "I want you to stay away."

My anger teetered toward laughter. "I don't know what you're going to do with that—wait, let me get a garbage can lid so I can defend myself."

She looked at the hose as if she'd just realized it was there. She let her arm drop to her side. "I just can't stand to see them all hurting like that. I get a little crazy."

"Ya think? Does Dan know his girlfriend is a nutbar?"

"They're so upset anyway, and then you come in here and stir everything up."

"It needs to be stirred up," I said. But I put up my hand. "I'm not going to discuss this with you, of all people."

"All right, then, I'll talk." She took a step toward me, out of the shade, where despite her lowering her weapon, I could still see a trace of wildness in her eyes. "Don't ever talk to my son again the way you just did back there."

My urge to guffaw disappeared, and a fire went up my backbone. "Jake is *not* your son."

"I'm talking about Ian."

"I don't even know who Ian is."

"You told him to stay out of it!"

"Oh—that Ian. He doesn't have any part in this."

She took another step. "No, see, you are so wrong there. Ian is the only one who's going to get Jake through this. He's the only one Jake talks to—because he *cares* about him."

"What is he, seventeen?"

"Sixteen—and more mature than most grown men I know."

"I don't care if he's a child prodigy, lady—he's not part of this family."

"And you are?"

"Oh, please." I turned and clawed for the car door handle.

"No, see, you're done here," she said. "You're never going to have a relationship with any of them, so why don't you just let us handle Jake, the way we've *been* doing for the last—"

"Forget about it." I yanked the door open. "I'll be back."

"Didn't you just hear a single thing I said?" With a heave she hurled the hose across the sculpture park, barely missing a metal monster strumming his ukulele.

I slammed the door and fishtailed the car out of the driveway.

I was shaking so badly I only drove around the bend in the dirt road, out of sight of the house, before I stopped to put my forehead on the steering wheel.

Five minutes ago I'd been almost amused by the woman waving a piece of garden hose. Now all I could see was myself, with a shard of metal in my own hand. Her mad-woman tirade couldn't outshout the words Dan had put on me.

You and your anger made him capable of this.

Was he right?

What if he was? What if I had?

The only thing I knew was that I didn't want Jake to look at me—or himself—and see a woman throwing pieces of art in uncontrollable rage.

I dug in my purse for Poco's phone number.

CHAPTER SEVEN

Sully was passing the break room late Monday morning when an aroma pulled him in.

"When did we start a gourmet restaurant in here?" he said.

Martha looked up from the table where she was parked with a salad and a magazine and pointed wordlessly to the microwave. Kyle pulled out a plate of something bubbly and expensive-smelling and wafted it onto the table across from her.

"Seriously," Sully said as he strolled to the table. "What is that incredible smell?"

"Veal Florentine," Kyle said. "Get yourself a plate."

Sully shook his head. "There's too much green in there for me."

"And nothing in it is fried." The corners of Kyle's mouth twitched. "Don't you people from Alabama like everything breaded and boiled in grease?"

"You're not that kind of Southerner, are you?" Martha said.

Sully eased into a chair, still studying Kyle's lunch. "I'm the kind of Southerner who likes to know the ingredients in what he's eating."

"But if it smells this good, who cares?" Kyle took a forkful and smiled, close-mouthed, as he chewed. Martha looked expectantly at Sully.

"How's it going so far, Kyle?" Sully said.

"I'm settled in, ready to work. Now all I need are some clients."

Kyle looked at Martha, who looked at Sully, who had never seen such smooth triangulation.

"I've given Kyle two clients to start with," Martha said.

"A seventy-two-year-old man grieving for his wife who died two weeks ago. He'll need me for about three sessions before every widow at the senior center starts baking him pies."

"Or you start baking them," Sully said, eyeing the dessert Kyle was unwrapping.

"I don't cook," Kyle said. "I just order out."

Martha folded her hands neatly on the tabletop. "The other client is an unhappy woman who I think will respond to Kyle."

"She's a schoolteacher. Of course she's unhappy. Look—" Kyle chipped at a flake of tissue-thin pastry with a tine of his fork. "I know every client deserves full attention no matter how small the problem may seem to us . . ."

"And that small problem may only be the tip of a much larger iceberg that has been forming for years," Martha said.

"I just want something a little more intense. That's the way I like to work, you know? Get in there and make a difference."

"You'll get your chance, tiger," Sully said.

"When you've shown what you can do with the less-intense cases." Martha glanced quickly at Sully. "I hope I'm not stepping on your toes."

"Listen, we're a team—and since I'm not going to be here more than a couple of months, you two are the core of it." Sully looked from one of them to the other. "So I think your first session ought to be with each other. See if you can work this thing out."

"Is there a 'thing'?" Kyle said.

"We'll deal with it, Dr. Crisp," Martha said. "Right now I need to look over some files."

She tucked her Tupperware into a zippered insulated bag and showed remarkable restraint when she clicked the door closed behind her.

"She doesn't think I have enough experience," Kyle said.

"Did she say that?"

"No, but—"

"Then that'll be a good place to start with her." Sully grinned and nodded at Kyle's shirt. "Now, where *I* want to start is with this getup you're wearing. Dude, you don't have to wear a tie and cufflinks around here."

Kyle laughed. "You think I oughta loosen up? Go for the Top-Siders and the Hawaiian shirt like you?"

Sully shook his head, still grinning. "Nah. Wear a three-piece suit if you want to. Eat sushi. Just work out your deal with Martha."

"Got it. You sure you don't want some veal?"

Sully stood up. "I was thinking about a bean burrito from Chihuahua's."

"You're killin' me," Kyle said.

Sully actually downed *two* burritos, picked up a Grande Frap with whipped cream from Starbucks, and sat in his parked Mini Cooper and called Porphyria. She should be done with her physical by now.

"Here's the scenario, Dr. Ghent," he said when she answered. "I have an experienced, highly intuitive therapist who plays by the book and a young hotdogger with less experience than enthusiasm, but a whole lot of potential."

He waited for the mm-hmm so he could fix the twinkle on her face in his mind.

"Could you hold on for one second, Sully—just one second now—"

Sully heard another voice in the background, as if someone were being paged on an intercom.

"I apologize. What were you saying, Sully?"

"Porphyria, where are you?"

"I am in a hospital room with people who will not stop fussing over me. I am just before running every one of them out of here."

Sully felt the smile in her voice, but he couldn't come up with one of his own.

"Hospital room?" he said. "Since when do they admit you for a physical?"

"Since they decided my heart isn't tapping out the rhythm they want to hear."

Sully set his cup in the console. "What's wrong with your heart?"

"I think that's what we're about to find out. It's probably just a malfunction in the pacemaker." She gave a deep-throated chuckle. "I never have liked the idea of being fitted with spare parts. Now, how are you doing with your motivation question?"

Sully shook his head. "That can wait if this is serious. I can get a flight tomorrow."

"It's going to get serious if I see your face in this hospital. Do what you have to do—one God-thing at a time. Now, I mean it."

You didn't argue with Porphyria Ghent, not when she took that tenor. So Sully hung up dutifully and put the car in gear and headed for the Pichaco Hills Community Church as if Porphyria were in the seat next to him, floating a hand toward the windshield, making him go where the answers were. The fact that she wasn't . . . that she was in a hospital room with doctors frowning over her EKG . . . He couldn't go there, in body or in mind.

According to MapQuest, he had about a fifteen-minute ride ahead of him across the Rio Grande to the western skirts of Las Cruces, which gave him a chance to experience the same sensation that had come over him anytime he'd ventured out since his arrival in New Mexico.

It was as if he were drifting in a space where the sky took up more room than the tireless desert, which itself ended in distant purplish mountains without ever seeming to reach them. Even as he drove, the light changed and the shadows shifted across the land, and it became a different place than it had been moments before.

It was good to be noticing those things. Large as they were, he would have missed them a year and a half ago when this journey first began. In the process of working with Porphyria for three months and working with his own client in Nashville for a number of weeks before he started a year-long speaking tour, he had become myopic. That, he hoped, was about to change.

He tried to settle back in the seat, not an easy task in the Mini Cooper with his long legs and tall torso. The guy at the used-car lot had all but told him he was going to look like a clown climbing out of a circus car, but it was cheap and temporary, and its frog-green paint job wasn't hard to find in a parking lot the way his eighteen months' worth of rental cars had been.

Unless Kyle Neering was at the same location. Sully had been amused when he pulled up to the clinic that morning to find that Kyle's car was almost identical to his. Gourmet lunch and cufflinks notwithstanding.

Sully made a turn off of Route 70. With five minutes to go, he needed to focus. If he had been preparing a client for an errand like this, he would have suggested rehearsing what he might say when he got there. So far that exercise hadn't been productive.

I'm looking for Belinda Cox. She's the quack who called herself a counselor, the one who fourteen years ago told my postpartumly depressed wife she needed to renounce her demons instead of taking medication and getting real therapy, even though she knew she was suicidal. Yeah, as a result, my wife drove off a bridge and took our infant daughter with her, and now, after a near-breakdown, I'm just getting around to locating Ms. Cox and finding out if she's still using those same methods. I don't want to throw her in front of a train. I can't even see that her license is revoked, because she doesn't need one for her kind of "counseling." I just want to expose her so she can never allow another woman to go so far into her nonexistent guilt that she can't find any way out except to kill herself. At least, I think that's why I'm doing it. So—have you seen her?

Sully almost missed his turn and squealed the Cooper's tires into a freshly resurfaced parking lot. His hands ached from clutching the wheel. As he licked tiny points of sweat from his upper lip, he decided on a simple *I'm looking for a woman named Belinda Cox. I believe she has an office here?*

Although he suspected she had moved on. When he called the number listed for Belinda Cox, he got a message saying it had been disconnected.

Sully smoothed the front of the Hawaiian shirt with his palms and strode toward the door marked *Office.* His Google trail had ended here. Maybe someone could help him pick it up again. Someone like a church secretary. They knew everything.

A bell tinkled cheerfully as Sully entered a sunshiny office that smelled like breath mints and furniture polish. The woman at the desk smiled before she even looked up at him, as if everyone who walked in blessed her and Sully was going to be no different, no matter who he was. When she did raise her head, the smile reached her eyes.

"How can I help you, my friend?" she said in a voice as dimply as her chins.

"I'm looking for someone," Sully said. "Someone who I believe has an office here, or did have."

"And that would be—?"

"Belinda Cox."

Sully had never seen a smile evaporate that way, chilled out of existence by the steely gaze that took its place.

"She no longer rents office space from us," she said. "She left here four months ago."

"I suspected as much," Sully said. "Did she leave a forwarding address?"

"No, sir."

Sully waited. Ten years of working with clients hadn't been wasted on him. There was more she wanted to say.

"Are you a family member?" she asked.

"No."

"A friend of hers?"

"Not by a long shot."

The woman melted a few degrees and nodded toward a rocking chair situated catty-corner to her desk. If experience served him well, she was working up to a good vent.

"I'm Sarah Quinn, by the way," she said.

"Sullivan Crisp," Sully said. "Sully."

"Well, Sully, I don't know why you want to find that woman,

but I hope it has something to do with the IRS or unpaid parking tickets or some such thing."

"I take it you weren't fond of her."

Sarah sniffed. "I just want to make it clear, first off, that she was never affiliated with this church. She only rented office space from us, until the pastor asked her to leave."

Sully's raised eyebrow seemed to be sufficient encouragement for her to elaborate.

"She never paid the rent on time," she said, ticking that off on a plump finger. "She said she was running a counseling business, which I never saw the need for in the first place, since Pastor does such a good job of that himself. The first time I saw her, I knew I'd never go to her with a problem."

"Why was that?"

"She dressed like she just came off the reservation, beads and shawls and feathers hanging from her ears. But there isn't a drop of Native American blood in that woman's body—blonde hair, freckles all over the place. I mean, honestly . . . right off the bat I knew she was trying to be something she wasn't." She doubled the chins. "Now, who wants a counselor who doesn't even know who she is?"

"I hear you," Sully said.

"And the way she talked to me, loud, like she thought I was either deaf or stupid or spoke a foreign language. There's no doubt in my mind she saw me as the hired help."

Sully stifled a smile.

"And then the goings-on in that office. She was two doors down from here, and I could hear her in there just yelling and raving, telling the devil to get out and screaming at people to renounce him."

Sully's hands froze to the arms of the rocker.

"And here was Pastor, trying to hold Bible study with all that going on. The people she was seeing would cry, and some of *them* would yell too. They'd come out of that door sobbing—it's a wonder some of them made it out of the parking lot."

"We are definitely talking about the same woman," Sully managed to say. "So you have no idea where she relocated?"

Sarah shook her head. She had her hand to her neck, which had turned an angry shade of fuchsia. "She finally made her last rent payment, and all that was printed on the check was *Zahira*."

"Was that the name of a company or something?"

"I have no idea." She looked over her shoulder at the door behind her and lowered her voice. "It wouldn't surprise me if it was some kind of cult or something."

It was another twenty minutes before Sully could extricate himself from Sarah. When he left, she made him promise to call her if he found "that woman."

The day had drawn out to three thirty by the time Sully turned onto Union Street and pulled into the clinic parking lot between Kyle's matching Mini Cooper and a red Saab he didn't recognize.

He strode through the clinic's turquoise double front doors with every intention of going straight to his office and Googling *Zahira*. But Olivia practically vaulted over her desk in the corner of the reception room and planted herself between Sully and the hallway.

"We have a situation," she said. The doe eyes had obviously been stricken by headlights.

"What's up?" Sully said.

Olivia curled her fingers around his wrist and tugged him away from the hall.

"Okay, so, this woman comes in and she is, like, about to freak out, you can tell."

"Define 'freak out,'" Sully said. "Are we talking mobile unit?"

Olivia shook her head, and the eyes continued to enlarge. "She's just, like, mad, and I thought, uh-oh, another lawsuit, but she said she wanted to see a counselor and I asked her if she had an appointment and she said she didn't know she needed one. The way she said it, it was like it was my fault nobody told her. I mean, you can't just walk in here, right?"

"Liv," Sully said, "what did you tell her?"

"I didn't know *what* to tell her, 'cause you weren't here. And Kyle and Martha were in the break room having it out—they still are."

"Olivia," Sully said. "Did you get a name?"

"Um—it's like a guy's name, only she's a woman."

"Where is she?"

"I put her in the green counseling room—she didn't seem like the yellow type—and I gave her the papers to fill out. I don't think she's happy about it."

"How long has she been in there?"

Olivia looked at her wrist full of bangles, among which Sully did not see a watch.

"About five minutes," she said. "But I don't think she's going to last much longer. I turned up the music and offered her some water, but she still wanted to rip my lips off, I could tell."

Olivia finally seemed to run out of information. "Did I handle that okay?" she asked.

"I'm sure you were amazing," Sully said and headed for the counseling room to survey the damages.

Judging from the expression on the face of the woman who turned on him from the window, they were considerable.

"Hi," Sully said. "I'm sorry you had to wait."

"So am I," she said. "You have no idea."

CHAPTER EIGHT

I didn't catch your name," the man said.

Of course not. I was sure that ditz at the front desk didn't either. She alone made me want to beat a hasty retreat out of there.

He was still waiting, obviously in no hurry to fill up air time.

"Ryan Alexander-Coe," I said. "And you are?"

"Sullivan Crisp," he said. "Sully."

So this was Dr. Crisp himself, the one Poco referred to in hushed tones as if he were the pope. He approached me, holding out a lanky arm and tilting his head like an overgrown kid. Except for the graying hair at the temples, he could have been loping onto a high school basketball court. Somewhere in the South.

"Can I get you anything?" he said. "Water? Juice?"

"No, thank you."

"Frappuccino?"

"I didn't come for the beverages," I said.

"Then maybe we should get to why you did come." He folded more than sat on the green club chair that angled toward the one I was sitting in. I supposed the cozy arrangement was designed to promote the baring of souls.

The rumpled chinos, the worn deck shoes, the shirt straight out of Waikiki all bordered on sloppy, but there was nothing careless about the way he moved. Or the way he waited.

Good. I had no problem taking charge of a conversation. I'd practiced this one all the way over here.

"I have a serious family problem," I said, "and I want to fix it. I know this is Christian counseling, and I'm good with that. I'm a

Christian. But I don't want to be preached at. I don't want Ephesians thrown in my face or any of that—which, I assume, from looking at your Web site last night, isn't going to happen."

He nodded, face solemn, but I got the distinct impression he was smothering a smile. If he was amused by me, he was going to get un-amused fast, or I was out of there.

"Do you mind if we unpack some of that before we go on?" he said.

"I wasn't clear?" I said.

"Oh, absolutely. You know why you came. A lot of folks have no idea."

"So what's to unpack?"

He scratched the top of his head as if he were puzzled. I was sure he wasn't.

"You've come to us with a family problem," he said. "Do you want family counseling, then? We can definitely do that here."

"You mean bring my sons and my ex-husband in? No."

I thought I saw his forehead twitch. I hadn't meant to let the ex-husband thing slip just yet.

"So it would be just you working on a family problem," he said.

"Yes. That's what I said, wasn't it? I can't see my—any of them joining me. This is something I need to deal with." Oh, Ryan, shut up. You're babbling like an idiot.

He let me seethe at myself for a minute before he said, "Am I hearing you say that you want us to show you how to go back to your family and fix the problem?"

That was exactly what I was saying, but coming out of his mouth, especially in that Southern drawl, it sounded ridiculous. I hated to sound stupid, no matter whose mouth my words were coming out of.

"Let me ask you this," he said. "Just to clarify."

I nodded.

"Did something specific happen that made you decide to come see us?"

My breath caught in my throat. He waited and watched. Must be nice to make $150 an hour saying nothing.

"I almost lost my temper," I said. "I mean, really lost it. I can get mad and speak my piece, but this time I felt like I was going to lose control. I can't afford to do that." I stopped and tried not to shift my eyes away from his, which were so obviously seeing what I wasn't saying.

"Are you under a lot of stress?" He bumped his forehead lightly with the heel of his hand. "Of course you are. You said you had some difficult things going on at home." He tilted his head at me, looking again like a boy with an old soul. "You're thinking being on the brink of losing control was more than just a normal reaction to an abnormal situation?"

I was tempted to say, *Sure, that's it,* then run from this man-child who was quoting my thoughts. But then he leaned forward and rested his forearms on his thighs like a catcher waiting for my fastball. "If someone else reacted the way you did when you lost your temper," he said, "would you recommend that she seek help?"

All I could see was Ginger, hurling that hose across the sculpture garden. Ginger's body, my face . . .

"In a heartbeat," I said.

He nodded. "That's something I may be able to help you with if you'd like to work with me."

"You? I thought you didn't see patients yourself. Aren't you the Mac Daddy in this outfit?"

"I don't usually see clients myself," he said. "But there are exceptions."

"Why am I an exception?"

His face broke into the grin I knew he'd been holding back the entire time I'd sat there. I was prepared to lash out at it, accuse him of making fun of me. But once it made its full way from one earlobe to the other, the thing was so big, so easy, I would have looked like Kate-the-Shrew if I'd attacked him for it.

Instead I said, "What?"

"That's why you're an exception," he said. "Because nothing gets past you. We'll keep each other on our proverbial toes. That is, if you—"

"All right," I said. "So how does this work? I can't start now—I have to get to my son's soccer practice."

"How about tomorrow?" he said. "Is this a good time for you?"

"I get off work at three, so I'll come straight here. But I have to leave by four."

"Not a problem." He grinned again. "I think an hour is about as long as you're going to put up with me at a time."

It was the last thing I expected a therapist to say, especially Mr. Man, King of Christian Counseling. But then, what did I know?

About, it seemed, anything?

All the way to Burn Lake, I said out loud all the things I wished I'd said to Sullivan Crisp's face. *I am not going down a bunch of bunny trails with you. And that includes my ex-husband, our divorce, my potty training . . .*

When I pulled into the shade of a cottonwood in the parking lot, I was still asking myself why I had agreed to see the man. I was hoping I could give myself a different answer than the only one I could settle on: it had to be somebody, so it might as well be him.

And it did have to be somebody, because if Jake was not acquitted, there probably wasn't enough metal in that studio for me to throw.

I hiked the zippered bag full of bananas and granola bars and juice boxes over my shoulder and headed for the knot of mothers on the bleachers. All I wanted were some coping skills. I was an intelligent woman. A few sessions with Sullivan Crisp should do it. He was right about one thing: I wasn't going to be able to put up with him for much more than that.

It was after four, and practice was already under way when I joined Poco midway up the bleachers. J.P. and Victoria were sitting behind her, and I got the distinct impression I'd just happened on a conversation I wasn't supposed to hear.

"Ladies," I said. To Poco I said, "I brought the snacks. All healthy."

"I knew you'd catch on." The signature giggle was even more nervously frayed than usual.

"Did I interrupt something?" I asked.

"No, no."

"You know what?" J.P. said. "I'm not good at dicky-doing around. I think we should just get it out in the open."

"Dicky-doing?" Victoria said faintly.

Poco put her hand on J.P.'s knee. If that was the signal to back off, J.P. didn't get it.

"We were talking about your son Jake and his situation."

I whipped my face toward her so hard my neck crunched.

"I know," she said. "But I want to make sure our kids don't find out about it."

"Why would they, unless you tell them?" I said.

J.P. lowered her sunglasses and peered over them down onto the field. "Alex knows, doesn't he?"

It hadn't even occurred to me to ask Alex not to share this whole thing with anyone outside the family, but I still bristled.

"You think he's going to make an announcement to the soccer team?" I said.

"Of course not." Poco still had her tiny hand on J.P.'s knee, and it still wasn't working.

J.P. sighed impatiently. "Something could slip out, and I don't want Cade or any of the other boys upset."

"So what's your point?" I said.

"I just wanted to make sure you've spoken to Alex about not discussing this thing with the other kids."

I looked down at the field.

"You have, haven't you?"

"Look, how I handle this with my boys is my business and mine alone."

"Not when it affects *my* boy, and Victoria's and Poco's and everyone else's." J.P.'s blue eyes drew together like a snake's. I had an image of her tongue forking out at me next. She all but hissed, "I would no more handle it that way if it were me—"

"It's not you, though, is it?" I said.

She stood up, capris bunched into wrinkles at the bend in her legs, and huffed off down the steps. I waited for Victoria to follow her.

She just gazed after her, however, eyes in their usual trance.

"I think you made her mad," she said.

"Ya think?" I ran a hand through my hair, which I knew was already standing up in spikes from the raking I'd been giving it all afternoon.

"You have a lot on your mind," Poco said. "If Alex lets something slip, so be it. We'll deal with it." The faint line appeared between her brows. "But if he does, how do you want us to handle it with our boys?"

I looked at Victoria, who was nodding vaguely.

"Tell them that we don't know exactly what happened," I said, "but that Jake is innocent until—" I couldn't say it. I couldn't even let myself think anything that involved the word *guilty*. "Just tell them we're working on finding out the truth."

"And that Alex needs their support."

Our heads swiveled to Victoria. Her face was still so unfocused I wasn't sure she'd actually said it, until Poco breathed, "Right."

What had just happened? Whatever it was, I was confused. I chalked it up to the fact that I had no experience with groups of women. I'd always avoided them the same way I eschewed sales and fad diets and department store makeup counters.

And intended to continue doing so.

The temperature had dropped to the low sixties by the time Sully stretched out on his back deck on a chaise lounge that left his feet hanging over the end. God had just treated him to a psychedelic sunset, and the sun was now sizzling on the top of the thick adobe wall that surrounded his backyard, preparing to reduce the two gnarled Mexican elder trees to mere silhouettes.

Sully liked the wild tangle that overtook not only the backyard but the front of his rented house as well. It gave the place a funky look that matched the chipped tile on the porch overhang and the patinaed pink stucco. Every faded blue window frame and gap between the floorboards reminded him of himself at this point. Put together in the past in pieces and trying to come together as a comfortable whole in the present.

Sully propped his laptop on his knees and turned it on. While it loaded, he sipped at a Frappuccino and studied the long bunch of brick-red chiles hanging from an open beam over the nearby table piled with his files. What was it about them that he got such a kick out of? Maybe because they were so deceptively cheerful looking, and then you bit into one and got the spicy surprise of your life.

The computer announced that it was ready, but now that he stared at it, he had no idea what to Google. Zahira's Devil Renouncement / New Mexico? Some kind of Internet 411 for Zahira Cox? What did that mean, anyway . . . Zahira?

For lack of a better direction, Sully Googled the word. He skipped Zahira's School of Belly Dance and the Zahira Primary School in Hambantota and went to a list of baby name meanings. He snorted out loud. Zahira was Arabic for "brilliant and shining."

He went back to Zahira's School of Belly Dance and searched the faces for anyone even remotely resembling Belinda Cox, but the photographs were such poor quality, everyone in them looked as if they'd been blurred for a reality cop show. Sully clicked the site off and dug in the pile for a folder. He opened it and pulled out a photograph whose subject was all too clear, even from fourteen years ago.

She had too-blonde hair, bleached of any natural color and shine, and it lay in thin, flat layers around a face flecked with freckles. There was nothing ingenuous about Belinda Cox. Her eyebrows were too tweezed, her lips too glossy. She wore a practiced expression, as if she'd worked in front of a mirror to align her features to say, "I'm only trying to help you."

Help? She hadn't helped Lynn do anything but lose her beautiful mind. And she was going down for that if he had to tear Las Cruces apart . . .

Sully stared at his fist, now crumpling the picture into a ball. He let it bounce to the table where it rolled against the laptop and waited.

Sully closed his eyes. *God, don't let me do this. Don't let me turn this into revenge.*

He'd had himself convinced this was about ethics, about protecting other innocent people. But there was no denying now that it was intensely personal. Porphyria was right. He had to get this done so he could put it to bed and get on with his life. If he didn't, it was going to take over.

He looked at the crushed ball on the table. If it hadn't already.

CHAPTER NINE

Sully always prayed before a session. That was the one thing that still came naturally. The rest might not, seeing how it had been a year since Nashville and his last one-on-one client. He hadn't even intended to work with this one, but he didn't think Kyle was ready for Ryan Alexander-Coe, and Martha already had a full load. Besides—Ms. Coe was something of a time bomb, and even Olivia had spotted her as a potential lawsuit.

He pretzeled his legs into a bow in the butterscotch corduroy chair-and-a-half. Face resting in his hands, he breathed in God. And Light. And Christ, Light from that Light. Light on the only path he'd found he could follow.

God-in-Christ . . . shine through me . . . help me to lead her to make some sense of herself . . .

Sully breathed into the prayer until he came to a level place where perhaps Ryan Coe's new path could start. Then he opened his eyes and reached for the folder on the trunk between his chair and the identical one Ryan would sit in.

He grinned as he glanced over the paperwork she'd filled out the day before. To use a psychological term—she was a pistol. Small woman with a big mind. Gunned you down with her shotgun eyes. Wasn't going to put up with—how did she say it?—having Ephesians thrown in her face.

She also said—both in yesterday's interview and on her form—that she wanted help controlling her anger. *I need coping skills,* she'd written. There was no doubt that she had a short fuse, but Sully didn't think just anything lit it. Whatever got her going came from someplace deep. The trick was going to be letting *her* find the God-path, but getting her to let *him* lead for a while. She must be something on the dance floor.

He perused the form for her occupation. Photojournalist. Formerly employed by the Associated Press, but currently working for the *Las Cruces Sun-News.* He salivated mentally. That might be a road worth going down.

A tap on the door was followed by Olivia's head. He'd heard her staccato laugh in the reception area earlier, punctuating Kyle's urging her to go back to school and get her degree. Martha was going to have to assign Kyle more clients before he started having sessions with the receptionist.

"She's here," Olivia whispered.

"Who?" Sully whispered back.

"Mrs. Coe."

"Okay. Why are we whispering?"

"Because she scares me."

Sully stood up and strode to the door. "Is she armed?"

Olivia's eyes popped, and Sully smiled at her.

"You're teasing me," she said.

Sully followed her out to meet Ryan noticing on the way that Olivia looked less like she'd caught the latest sale at the Goodwill than she had previously. Her hair was up in one of those messy bun-ish things, but at least it wasn't dangling in her face like left-over goat food. He wondered if Kyle had counseled her on that too.

"Here he is," Olivia said to Ryan and then skittered to her desk.

Ryan's bright eyes were focused completely on Sully, as if she expected him to begin the session right there. He ushered her back to the counseling room before she could start firing questions at him.

As it was, she was barely seated in the oversize chair, which held her like a big hand, before she had the first one out. "Do you do cognitive therapy?"

They were obviously dispensing with the pleasantries. He'd go with that for now.

"You're familiar with it?" he said.

"It's where you give the patient alternative ways of thinking and reacting—in my case, to anger."

If he had to guess, Sully would say she'd looked up anger management on the Internet the night before.

"That's basically it," he said.

"Good. That's what I want. I already tried watching football and screaming at the ref and throwing pillows at the television. That only makes me want to tear the rest of the living room apart."

Sully was impressed. Innumerable expensive studies had shown that angry people who already knew they were ticked off didn't feel better after they punched something out. That only worked for people who weren't in touch with their anger—and that didn't describe Ryan Coe.

"And I don't want the relaxation training, which I know is another method." Ryan squinted as she shook her head. "That sounds too woo-woo to me."

"Woo-woo," Sully said, grinning.

Ryan gave him a hard look. "Look, can we get something straight, Dr. Crisp?"

"Absolutely."

"If you find me amusing, this isn't going to work out. At all."

Sully settled back in his chair, hands folded at his waist to keep from rubbing them together in anticipation.

"I think you have an intelligent sense of humor," he said. "I appreciate that. If you say something funny, I'm probably going to at least smile." He did. "You'll have to cut me some slack here."

"Fine. Sorry."

Sully let out a *buzz.* As he expected, her face went deadpan.

"What was *that*?" she said.

"That's my signal that you've broken one of the few rules I have. No need for apologies. We're just getting to know each other here."

The small pointed chin lifted. "What are the rest of the rules, then?"

"We'll discover those as we go along."

"No," she said.

Sully felt his eyebrows rise.

"I don't want to hear that obnoxious buzzing sound again, so give them all to me now, and I won't break them."

Sully considered arguing the point and thought better of it. If she was going to come out of this session still speaking to him, he'd better not antagonize her in the first five minutes. Although from the right-angle way she was sitting in a curl-up chair, he judged it might already be too late. Game Show Theology was going to be a hard sell with her.

"Fair enough," Sully said. He spread a hand and ticked off his fingers. "The rules of the game, as it were. One, what we just discussed. Two, I won't judge you, and you won't judge yourself. Three—"

"Define *judge*."

Sully let his hand drop. "Example. You came in with anger issues. I'm not going to tell you that you're an evil person because you break a plate or scream obscenities. By the same token, you don't get to say that about yourself either."

"So you're saying it's okay to smash crockery and cuss."

"No. I'm saying doing that doesn't make you a monster. Our job is to find out *why* you do that—or whatever it is you do when you're angry—and figure out a way to use that knowledge to give you the control you're looking for."

She nodded, eyes still on him as if she were trying to soak him in. There was no doubt she wanted to fix this. He just wasn't sure how patient she was going to be with the process.

"Back to the rules," she said. "And then I have another question."

With the strange sensation that he was the one being led down a path, Sully put up three fingers. "Number three, if we get to the end of a session and one of us is angry, we don't leave without at least talking about it. We may not come to an agreement, but we don't walk out muttering under our breath, either one of us."

"I didn't think therapists got angry at their patients," she said.

"Yeah, we get our hackles up, same as the next person."

She gave him another blank look.

"What?" he said.

"You're just not what I expected," she said.

"What did you expect?"

She opened her mouth, then shook her head. "It doesn't matter. What are the rest of the rules?"

"That's it," Sully said. That was, in fact, more than it. He'd made up the last one on the spot, just for her. "But you know, your expectations of me do matter. This isn't just going to be about me giving you tools and you going out and using them, although we'll do some of that. That's the cognitive therapy you were talking about." He recrossed his legs as he warmed up. "This is going to be more about a relationship—you getting to know me so that hopefully you'll come to trust me, and me getting to know you so I can decide how best to help you."

Sully waited. If his instincts were right, this lady *was* in touch with her anger. What she wasn't in touch with was the hurt that made it happen. Getting her to talk about that might be a feat right up there with the loaves and fishes.

Finally she said, "All right. What do you need to know about me?"

"Let's start with your current situation," Sully said.

Ryan squinted again before she began. "My current situation is that I've been divorced for two years because my husband—ex-husband—was great at sculpture and terrible at marriage." She pointed her eyes at him. "And we won't be getting into that."

Sully nodded her on. They *would* get into that. But not today.

"I have two sons, ten and fifteen. When Dan and I got divorced, I assumed the boys would live with me, but they surprised me in court by announcing to the judge that they would prefer to live with their father." She smiled without humor. "He was terrible at fatherhood, too, but they didn't see it that way." She took in some air. "Anyway, I took an assignment in Chad—Africa—and when I came back, Dan had moved them from Chicago, where they'd always lived, to New Mexico. He was in some artist-in-residence program in Roswell, and then he just migrated with the boys to Las Cruces. If I wanted to be near them, I had to come here, too, so I resigned from the AP and got a job with the Las Cruces paper."

She stopped for another breath. Some of the bravado had gone out of her eyes, but she plunged back in with let's-get-this-over-with energy.

"I've tried to let my boys know that I love them and I want to be part of their lives, and my younger son, Alex, is coming around. But the older one, Jake, basically won't have anything to do with me. And now he's been arrested for allegedly backing over a Mexican boy with a pickup truck, on purpose. Which, although Jake was found at the wheel of the vehicle, I know he did not do."

She stopped and looked hard at Sully, as if she were daring him to disagree. He wasn't about to.

"But his father thinks he did," she said. "The police aren't investigating further, because for them this is a slam dunk. The lawyer is talking about getting Jake off with probation. And my son won't tell me what happened so I can help him. Which all frustrates me to no end, and then I get . . . furious. And on Sunday I picked up a piece of scrap metal in my husband's studio and almost threw it at him." Ryan's face had grown ashen. "I'm afraid that if something doesn't change and my son is sent to prison, I'll do worse than pitch a piece of sculpture. That's my current situation, Dr. Crisp."

Sully wanted to fall back into his Southern instincts and say, *Ryan, bless your heart.* But her eyes almost dared him to try sympathy on her.

"That's a lot to deal with," he said.

"Well, I *have* to deal with it. And I have to do it without hurling art supplies. So—what have you got?"

"At the moment, another question. Bear with me."

She snapped a nod.

"Would you say you were an angry person before your son's arrest?"

She straightened her small self in the chair again, head barely coming to the top of the back, feet dangling just off the floor. "I got angry when people did stupid things, if that's what you mean. I've never been one to hold back when I think somebody's in the wrong."

Sully had no doubt about that. "Was it ever a problem before?"

"I don't see how that matters."

"Maybe it doesn't," Sully said. "But it's always a good idea to check out all the possibilities."

Her eyes moved away again, and she frowned at the picture on the wall—a painting of White Sands in a folk-art frame he'd just hung there that morning.

"When my boys—Jake, mainly, because Alex just wanted to be like his big brother—when they told the judge they wanted Dan to have custody of them, yeah, I saw red."

Sully watched her swallow, but beyond that she scarcely moved, as if the memory had frozen her.

"I stood up and yelled something at my ex-husband. I don't even remember what it was. The judge told me to either sit down or leave the courtroom. I apologized, but I know I made his decision for him. He said his reason for awarding custody to Dan was that my job took me out of town too often to be the more effective parent, even though I had all of that covered and in writing. I knew he based his call solely on my outburst."

She was obviously using every thread of willpower she had to keep from reenacting the scene right there.

"You were blindsided," he said. "I wouldn't call that an out-of-control reaction."

Ryan put up a hand and gave him the squint he was already starting to expect when he was about to be called on the carpet.

"Look, don't do that," she said.

"What did I do?"

"You're trying to make me feel okay about myself. I don't need that."

"I'll consider myself buzzed." Sully slanted toward her. "But just so we're clear, what I'm actually doing is making sure you have perspective. The kinds of things you've had to deal with are not just the normal stuff of life. I don't know anyone who could handle those situations with perfect aplomb." He put up his own hand before she could protest. "I'm not saying your actions have been okay, but I don't want you to think we're going to turn you into Mr. Spock. We wouldn't want to turn off your feelings. That's where the signals are that alert us to what we need to pay attention to."

She pressed her lips together, revealing a pair of lines on either side of her mouth, the only real sign of wear on an otherwise ageless face.

"So what did you do then?" Sully asked.

"Like I said, I had an opportunity to go to Chad, and I couldn't pass it up."

"Was it just the opportunity that compelled you to go?"

"What do you mean?"

"Did you leave the States angry?"

Back to the painting. Sully waited her out.

When she looked back at him, her eyes glittered. "Yes, I was angry. I knew my boys chose their father because it was Disneyland when they were with him. He was going to let them do whatever they wanted, and I couldn't stand to watch it."

"Anything else?"

"What else do you want?"

"Just giving you a chance to say everything you need to say. You don't have to worry about how it comes out in here."

"It was obvious that throwing a tantrum wasn't going to bring my boys back to me. There was nothing I could do, so . . ." Ryan shrugged and leveled her eyes at him.

You left because you couldn't stand the pain, Sully wanted to say to her. But it was too soon.

He leaned back. "How did it go in Chad?"

"I was only supposed to be there for a few weeks, but it turned into a six-month project."

"Sounds intense."

"I was at a center in N'Djamena run by the Christian Children's Fund. They're trying to rehabilitate child soldiers demobilized from the FUC in Darfur."

"More fuel for anger."

"Beyond. But I never felt like I was going to lose it."

"What made the difference?"

Once more she became still, as if she were trying to avoid being seen. For someone who called herself out of control, she was in almost complete charge of her body language.

"When I was taking pictures, telling the story," she said finally, "I felt like I was doing something about it. I kept thinking that if I could capture the images that were tearing at *my* heart, someone might be compelled to try to stop what was happening to the kids who are still out there fighting on *all* sides in that mess." She cupped her hands in front of her, as if she held the images she spoke of. "Some of those boys were still hard as nuts. Or they tried to be. They were as young as ten years old. I just kept shooting and shooting, hoping they would show me what was under all the hate somebody else had drilled into them."

She let her hands drop and looked at Sully as if she'd all but forgotten he was there. The soft layer she'd begun to reveal slid back toward its hiding place behind her eyes.

"And did they ever show you?" Sully asked.

"One did. He was twelve. Thin as a pole, like my boys." She balled her hand into a fist and looked at it. "He was the toughest of all of them—he would even spit on the ground when he saw me with my equipment. And then one night I found him out on the volleyball court, crying his eyes out." Ryan shook her head. "It was the moment I'd been waiting six months for, and I couldn't even raise my camera."

"What *did* you do?" Sully asked.

"I sat down with him, and he put his head in my lap and cried himself to sleep." She swallowed again as the layer disappeared once more. "The next day I packed up and came back to the States. Okay—so I have a question."

Sully wanted to back that truck up, but he said, "Ask away."

"Where is the Christian part of this counseling?"

He took his time refolding his legs. The wrong answer would send her straight for the door, after she took him out at the knees.

"You warned me that you didn't want me beating you up with Ephesians," he said.

"I meant don't just quote Scripture to me and expect me to change. If I could do that, I would have already. I read the Bible. I pray." She gave him her squinted look. "It isn't working right now."

"But you do want faith-based counseling," Sully said.

"Okay." She brought up her hands parallel to her face as if she were forming goalposts and spoke between them. "Before I went to Africa, I was the tithing, pew-sitting kind of Christian. I went to Bible study, I sang the praise songs. I was there every time the doors opened. And don't get me wrong—"

Sully was sure that wasn't going to happen. She was leaving no room for error between those goal post hands.

"All of that is important," she said, "if it leads you to a real experience with God. I think a lot of the people in my congregation in Chicago had that. I didn't."

"So what changed in Africa?"

"What didn't? I never darkened the door of a church while I was there, but I talked to God more than I ever had in my life. Maybe not talked. Yelled. Ranted."

Her eyes blazed. Sully had a moment of pity for God.

"I wanted to know how he could let those children be used to kill people."

"Did you get any answers?" Sully asked.

"No. I got—" Ryan glanced at her watch. "Look, our time's almost up, and I don't feel like we've gotten anywhere."

"Actually, I think we might have just arrived. Tell me what you got."

She gave him a doubtful look. "I got images. And not like—like woo-woo."

Yes, she'd already established that there would be no woo-woo.

"It isn't like I purposely imagined what I wanted something to look like, the same way I don't set up a shot when I'm making pictures. I just take what's there."

"Tell me some more," Sully said.

She resituated in the chair. "I would be in a situation, maybe praying, maybe shooting, and I'd get a clear picture in my mind of something that might not have anything to do with what I was thinking about. And I would know it didn't come from me." For the first time, she looked at him without a challenge in her eyes. "Does that make sense?"

"I'm getting there," Sully said. "Give me an example."

She directed her gaze to the painting again. "The night Khalid cried himself to sleep in my lap, I didn't want to move, so I sat there for hours, with mosquitoes the size of garbage trucks feasting on me, and I got a clear picture in my mind of Jake." She glanced at Sully. "My older son."

"Right."

"He was curled up in his bed at home, in a fetal position, staring at the wall and crying without tears. It was like a shot God framed for me, which is why I know it isn't just me thinking it up." Her voice went dry. "That and the fact that the images aren't what I would set up. Believe me."

"I know you want to leave here with something," Sully said. "And I don't blame you. You've struggled with this for a long time."

He slanted forward again, arms resting on his knees, shaping his words with his hands. "I want to talk more about your relationship with God next time. It's the key to all of this—that's where the Christian part comes in. But in the meantime—and I just want you to hear me out on this—I think you can start to use your ability to visualize—"

"I told you I don't set it up—it just comes to me." She, too, slid forward, so that her feet finally hit the floor. "I know where you're going with this, and I'm sorry, but when some detective tells me my son is a racist, I can't see me stopping to calm myself with a vision of"—she chopped her hand toward the painting—"White Sands. By the time I do that, I'll probably already have clawed his face."

Sully watched her wrap herself back up and pondered his options. He had to be quick, or this could be the shortest relationship in therapeutic history.

"Let's try this, then," he said. He dug into his pocket and found the miniature hourglass he'd swiped from his Would You Rather . . . ? game and set it on the trunk. Sand began its slow trickle down.

"This is just a temporary tool," Sully said.

"Let me guess. Every time I start to blow, you want me to turn this over and not do anything until it runs out, and by then I should be cooled off." She gave him the squint and shook her head. "I don't think so."

"No," Sully said. "I suggest you just keep it in your pocket as a reminder that the control *we* have lasts about that long. If we don't bring God in, we got nothin'."

She gave him a long look. "All right," she said and snatched the plastic hourglass from the trunk and curled her fingers around it. "So—next week? Same time?"

As he saw her out, Sully watched her stuff the hourglass into the pocket of her cargo pants. It wasn't going to work, and he knew it. But Ryan Alexander-Coe would have to figure that out for herself. As he pulled out the voice recorder to make his notes, that was the only thing he knew about her for sure.

CHAPTER TEN

I walked out of the Healing Choice Clinic ready to throw the hourglass into the cactus garden.

I stopped at the car, hand still in my pocket fingering the plastic thing, and breathed in the breeze. I watched a few cars lazily turn the corner of Union and University, probably on their way to New Mexico State a block down.

Where Dan had a contract for six sculptures.

According to Ginger.

I yanked my hand out of my pocket before I could crunch Sullivan Crisp's little device. That would give him way too much satisfaction. I slid into the driver's seat, tossed it onto the dashboard, and squeezed the steering wheel instead. I was more ticked off now than I was when I walked in there.

I started the engine and got the air conditioner going, but I didn't pull out of the parking lot. Maybe I should go back in and tell him to give his three o'clock Tuesday appointment to somebody who *wanted* to talk about herself for an hour. I wanted *him* to talk, to give me some answers. And since that obviously wasn't the way it worked, he could have his little temporary tool and his buzzing and his chair that swallowed me up like Alice in Wonderland. Not to mention that wretched painting of White Sands. If the clients weren't nuts when they went in there, they were sure to be when they came out.

I turned up the fan and let the cold air blow my hair into spikes that I knew made me look even more like a maniac. One thing the crazy doctor and I did agree on: "letting it all out," at least that way, was as worthless as breasts on a boar—as my New Jersey–born mother used to say. If I went back and threw his hourglass in his face, I'd want to squeal out of this parking lot and go finish off the job I'd almost started in Dan's studio.

So what *was* I going to do?

Drive to Alex's soccer practice. Put the hourglass in my purse. Turn it over before J.P. or Dan or my own thoughts about Jake had a chance to transform me into Attila the Hun. That was what I was going to do.

Because I couldn't think of anything else.

I tried over the next three days.

I wrapped my hand around the hourglass when J.P. stood in front of me and read, out loud, the nutrition information on the Goldfish crackers I brought for snacks.

I stared at it every time I listened to Uriel Cohen's voice mail tell me she wasn't available and would get back to me as soon as possible. Obviously she didn't have her ducks in a row yet. Besides, I didn't have anything more to tell her. That required more staring at the hourglass.

I actually turned it over and watched its sand trail merrily to the bottom when Dan informed me that Jake still didn't want to talk to me, that the mere mention of it only drove him further into his cave. At that point I wanted to call Dr. Crisp and tell him that the sand had run its course and God wasn't taking over. At all.

If anything, I felt further from God than I had since before Africa. No images came to me—no clear pictures of Jake's heart opening up and letting me in, no flashes of other hands reaching out to help him. I asked for them. I begged for them, until I heard the echoes of my own voice taunting me. I was more strung out than I ever dreamed of being.

But if one thing ruled me more than anger, it was flat-out

stubbornness. "You don't take after anybody strange," my mother would say to me under her breath and cast a furtive glance at my father. It was that paternally inherited trait that made me keep on with the hourglass and the prayers—at least until Tuesday, when I could storm into Sullivan Crisp's office and tell him to stop playing games and *help me.*

I just had to get through Saturday first.

Alex's team had their first game that day in Alamogordo. I didn't ask why we had to travel an hour when there must be other teams they could play right in Las Cruces. Poco invited Alex and me to ride with her and Felipe in her van, and when I saw that Victoria and J.P. were also piling in with their boys, I vowed not to even bring it up. That, or the fact that none of the boys' dads seemed to support their sons' soccer, which made it impossible to hang out with anyone *but* women. I was glad I'd decided to carry my camera. That would give me something to fool around with en route, so I wouldn't be so likely to let them get to me.

The vehicle was a nine-passenger van, which required tiny Poco's full attention to drive. I was surprised she could see over the steering wheel. J.P. sat up front with her, not surprisingly, so that she could co-pilot.

How does *Poco get anywhere without you acting as her GPS?* I wanted to ask. Only fear that I would upset Poco and have us all plunging off San Augustin Pass kept me quiet. Victoria sat beside me, gazing out at the toasted desert as if there were actually something to see, and humming to herself. J.P. saved me the trouble of telling her she was driving us nuts.

"Was I humming?" Victoria looked straight at me with her pale blue eyes.

I so wanted to say no, just to tick J.P. off. I twisted in my seat and pointed the camera at the four boys in the back two rows. Tongues immediately came out. Eyes were crossed. Alex made devil horns with his fingers at the back of Bryan's head. I took a few shots, which incited more misshapen mouths and thumbs in ears.

"Do something original," I said.

They hesitated only slightly before Alex hooked his arm around Felipe's neck and pulled him into a half nelson. I shot that.

"What are you trying to do, Ryan?" J.P. said. "Start a brawl?"

"Hey, get this!" Cade said and made a pig nose at Bryan with his fingers.

Bryan retaliated with his knuckles in his nostrils, all of which I captured as unexpected laughter gurgled up my throat.

Until J.P. snapped her fingers in front of my lens.

"Enough—all of you," she said. "We don't fool around like that in the car. Do you want Mrs. Dagosto to have an accident?"

I'd always thought that was a stupid kind of question to ask a kid. Did she expect him to say, "Sure—why not?" I was tempted to say it myself. Where was that hourglass?

"We'll be there in ten minutes," Poco said. "You guys need to get your game faces on. Isn't that what Coach Dan says?"

I heard boy-giggling behind me, a sure sign that they were making game faces worthy of Halloween.

"I don't think that's what he means," J.P. said.

When she turned back to the traffic to advise Poco that her turn was coming up in ten miles, a stubby finger poked me in the back.

"Hey, Mrs. Coe," Cade said, "are you gonna take pictures of us during the game?"

"That would be cool!"

"Mom, will ya?"

J.P. stared at me as if I were supposed to read the appropriate answer in her eyes.

"You bet I will," I said. "I'll take a whole slide show of you guys."

"But you have to focus on the game," J.P. said, wagging a finger at them. "No mugging for the camera."

"You want the real thing, right, guys?" Poco said.

Cade snorted. "Like I'm so gonna be posing while we're out there playing."

That was my thought, as well. J.P. shot him a look that could have withered a houseplant.

After we arrived at the First Street Soccer Complex and sorted out the shin guards and cleats and sent the boys off to join Dan and the others, J.P. wasted no time planting herself in front of me. Tendrils of hair had already straggled out of the ponytail protruding from the back of her ball cap and flailed frantically in the wind like they, too, wanted to get away from her.

"They have enough trouble staying focused out there without you bringing in this distraction." She pointed at my camera as if it were an AK-47.

"They're so jazzed about this game," I said. "They're going to forget all about me when they start playing."

"And you know this how? Have you ever even been to a youth soccer game before?"

"Sunscreen?" Poco said and nudged a tube into my hand.

I shook my head and handed it to the translucent Victoria without taking my eyes off of J.P.

"No, I haven't," I said. "This is a first for me, and I'm going to make pictures to share with my son."

"Just try to keep it as unobtrusive as you can, then. Don't be running down the sideline."

"Oh—thank you—gosh, I did plan to station myself out there with the goalie and get a few shots. Now I won't."

I continued to stare at her until she huffed and looked away. "I was just saying—"

"Yeah. Got it. Thanks."

Before she could just say any more, I turned and climbed up the bleachers and dug in my bag for a longer lens. By the time I was assessing the light, Poco, Victoria, and J.P. had settled in with the other mothers in another section. I felt like a piece of mold that had cleared the Petri dish, and I was fine with that.

The sun was so bright I could practically feel freckles popping out on my arms, and there wasn't a cloud anywhere in sight to subdue it. One thing I had to say for New Mexico, it could produce a sky-blue like nowhere else I'd ever been, and I had made pictures on every continent except Antarctica. Here it was a flawless bowl that met row after row of distant, dusty hills unfazed. Behind me, the Sacramento Mountains rose to it. Before me, the San Andres did the same, as if they all must pay homage. New Mexico made it clear why we look up to find God.

Which made it all the more frustrating that I wasn't finding him these days.

Photographing in that light was a challenge, but I played with it until I got some good contrast and began to shoot the minute the ball was in play. The Las Cruces Winds' bright red shirts flashed across the field, scattering and clumping and spreading out again like confetti tossed in the breeze. Even after sitting through daily practices and taking lessons from Alex each evening until dark, I still had very little idea what was going on down there. I just tried to capture the intensity on their little faces and the boy-power in their legs and the unharnessed grins that followed every Wind tackle. At least I knew what that was.

And I knew what it was when Alex drilled the ball past the other team's goalie and scored the first point of the game. I must have made fifteen shots before I saw him look up from the field and into the bleachers, straight at me.

It was such a normal thing for a ten-year-old boy to do—seek out his mom in the stands and make sure she had seen. But it wasn't normal for us. For me. It was like a gift I didn't deserve, that he was giving me anyway. A piece of me melted as I waved to him.

We won two to one, with Cade allowing a goal by the other team but scoring the point that made up for it. J.P. probably would have grounded him if he hadn't. It occurred to me even as I shot the celebration going on below that in one week Cade had gone from the kid who couldn't dribble two feet without messing something up to the hero of the moment. What was that about? Did he just figure he'd better improve if he knew what was good for him with his mother?

But as I lowered my camera and watched the boys fling themselves at Dan, I had to begrudgingly consider the possibility that it might have something to do with the coaching. I'd caught Dan in my sights several times during the game. Once he was grinning and pumping the air and shouting, "Way to be there, Felipe!" which was the little guy's fifteen seconds of glory, as far as I could tell. Another time, Dan had his hand on Bryan's back as they both stood on the sidelines, Bryan nodding, Dan coaxing a smile from him, even though at that point he had yet to get into the game. Right now the team was dumping a cup of ice on Dan's head, which he obligingly lowered so they could reach it. I got a picture. For Alex.

My throat was parched by that time, so I bought a pair of large Cokes from the concession stand and went in search of the boy. He broke away from the pack and hurled himself toward me, stopping just short of giving me a hug. I remembered from Jake at ten that it was not cool to touch your mom in front of your friends.

"Did you see me?" he said.

"Uh, hello, you were amazing."

"Yeah, well, y'know, I can't help it."

He grinned. I loved those two front teeth, big as a rabbit's in his small face.

"I got you a Coke," I said.

He took it with another grin, gulped about half of it, and then and only then said, "I'm not supposed to have something carbonated right after the game."

One more thing I didn't know and should have. I looked around to make sure J.P. wasn't watching. Alex looked around too.

"What?" I said.

"When Dad's done, can you ask him if I can hang out with you for a while instead of going right home?"

I almost dropped my cup. "Of course. You can ask him yourself if you want."

"He might get mad."

"Your dad—mad at *you*?" I said.

"No."

"At me."

He nodded and took a long drag through the straw.

"You know, Alex, even if he does get mad at me for whatever reason, it wouldn't be your fault."

Straw still in his mouth, he turned his huge brown eyes to me. He didn't believe that for a second. He just sucked noisily at the now-empty cup, making that disgusting noise boys seem to love. When he cocked his head to look at me, to see if it was bugging me, another piece of me melted away. If he did that sounds-like-a-fart armpit thing, I would dissolve completely.

Because of the win, the mood in the van was lighter than I'd feared it would be after J.P.'s and my little camera conflict. She was the one, in fact, who suggested we stop at Plateau Espresso to celebrate before we headed for Las Cruces.

The Plateau was perched on a hillside and made excellent use of the brilliant, airy light with tall tables and bright metal chairs and wind chimes singing in the windows. The boys clumped at a table in the corner, too worn out to indulge in any shenanigans, and drank lemonade. J.P. parked us several tables over, where I was the only one with coffee. The three of them were having smoothies, as if they, too, were in training. I felt deliciously wicked ordering an extra shot of espresso.

"When can we see the pictures?" Victoria asked. She had apparently missed the earlier confrontation. I'd learned that Victoria missed a lot.

"Let me weed out the bad ones," I said, "and we'll do a little slide show for the boys—whenever."

J.P. pumped her straw up and down in her cup. "When Cade first started sports, back in T-ball, Mike had the camcorder at every game. I finally said, 'Are you going to watch our son's entire childhood through the lens of a camera?'"

"He must have said no," Poco said quickly, "because I've never seen him with a video camera."

Actually, I'd never seen him at all.

J.P. just guzzled her smoothie and silently insinuated yet again that I was a caffeine-addicted unfit mother. It was time to break out the hourglass. Instead, I squeezed my cup until the plastic lid popped off. Coffee startled out and onto her khaki knee.

I didn't mean to do it, and my apology was genuine. She ignored the napkin I offered her and rushed off to the bathroom, leaving the three of us in an awkward silence I couldn't sit through.

"Look, Poco," I said. "I appreciate you trying to make me feel welcome, but it probably isn't a good idea for me to hang out with the three of you. You have a nice little friendship circle going here, and I'm messing that up."

Victoria gave me the expected long, blank look as if I were speaking in Sanskrit.

Poco put her hand on my arm. "No, Ryan," she said. "I think you're good for us."

"I don't know that much about coffee klatches, but I don't think this can be considered good."

"I didn't say comfortable. I said good."

"Whatever it is, I think you'd be better off without me. I'm fine with just doing my own thing."

Poco exchanged glances with Victoria, who actually seemed to be tuned in. "But we're not fine with J.P. doing *her* own thing, all the time, and trying to make it ours. You're the first person to come in here and stand up to her." Poco glanced around the coffee shop. "You don't see any of the other moms hanging out with her, do you?"

"So why do *you*?" I said. "Did you get assigned to her or something?"

"In a way."

I looked at Victoria in surprise. "By whom?"

"Well." She stared at me full on with her fluid eyes. "By God."

"She means it's the Christian thing to do," Poco said. "J.P. has a good heart, and she can actually be fun." Her lips twitched. "When she isn't telling us how to be mothers."

"When is that?" I said.

"The thing is, she's a great mom, but she's way too protective of—"

She sneaked a look at the boys' table and lowered her already soft voice so that I had to lean in to hear her.

"Just about the worst thing Cade has ever had to deal with is losing to a team that plays a little dirty."

"And his mother." I put up my hand. "See, I'm not as nice as you two."

"J.P. doesn't need nice," Poco said. "She needs real. But she sees you as being way too worldly for us. Especially with what you're going through, you and Dan and your boys."

Victoria leaned in, too, until I could hardly see her face for the hair.

"You make her feel frumpy," she whispered.

I laughed out loud.

"Okay, so she is a little frumpy," Poco said. "Just don't leave us yet, okay?"

"Here she comes," Victoria hissed.

They went back to their smoothies with too-obvious concentration, and I felt like I was back in middle school, which was where I'd abandoned girl drama in the first place. But I sighed and made sure there were no coffee drippings on J.P.'s chair and tried to smile at her when she sat down.

"Did you get it out?" I said.

"Oh yeah. I always carry a Tide to Go in my purse."

Of course you do.

She didn't have much to say for the first few miles of the trip back to Las Cruces. The kids bantered about boy things, and Poco kept up a running commentary on the scenery, as if I were a visitor from a foreign land.

"Have you been to White Sands, Ryan?" she said as we approached it outside of Alamogordo.

"Once," I said, "and that was one time too many." I winced. "I hope that isn't anybody's favorite place in the world."

"As a matter of fact, it is," J.P. said.

Why did I know that?

"I love it too," Victoria said, voice dreamy. "It's so easy to get lost there."

I had no doubt Victoria could get lost in her own house. I couldn't help saying, "You can get lost in the sand?"

"No," she said. "In yourself."

"Oh," I said. "That's about the last place where I want to get lost."

Poco blinked at me in the rearview mirror. "Why didn't you like it, Ryan?"

"It feels like a wasteland."

Victoria shook her head. "You have to slow down when you're there. That's the only way you see the hidden beauty of the dunes. It's the absolute stillness of it."

"No offense," I said, "but I found it eerie."

"Not comforting?"

"Uh, no."

"I don't find it comforting either." J.P. turned in her seat. "I find it scintillating."

She pronounced it *skintillating*. I wasn't about to correct her.

"We should take you there." Poco nodded, as if she hoped I'd start nodding with her. "One morning early, before it gets crowded."

"No. Overnight camping trip."

I stared at J.P. Poco went slightly off the road.

"We're going camping?" Cade said behind me.

"Not you. Us. Moms only. Full moon is the best time to go, so we'll do it Friday night. Backpacks only—it's backcountry camping." J.P. narrowed her eyes at me. "Have you ever actually roughed it?"

Until then I'd already been planning how I was going to turn her down flat. But had I ever roughed it? Oh, please.

"What's the date?" Poco said.

"September 25. We'll come back Saturday afternoon. The boys don't have a game until Sunday that weekend."

She must have her child's entire schedule committed to memory. I might make her feel frumpy, but she made me feel woefully inadequate. And that was not something I was used to feeling.

"You're on," I said.

J.P. gave a satisfied nod and turned back around. Poco beamed at me in the mirror.

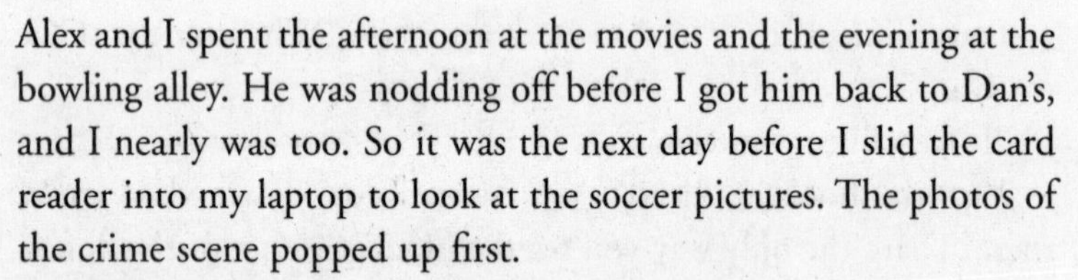

Alex and I spent the afternoon at the movies and the evening at the bowling alley. He was nodding off before I got him back to Dan's, and I nearly was too. So it was the next day before I slid the card reader into my laptop to look at the soccer pictures. The photos of the crime scene popped up first.

I hadn't submitted any of them to Frances, and I'd forgotten to delete them. A knot formed in my chest as I clicked on the first one to get rid of it. Whether it was the photographer in me or the desperate mother, I wasn't sure, but I clicked to the enlarged views instead.

The first one was of the paramedics surrounding Miguel Sanchez. Detective Baranovic's words came like an assault. Two broken legs. Serious internal injuries and a fractured skull. A coma he might never come out of.

I rushed to the next one, and then the next, of the truck bumper. I was still close in when I shot that one, before the officer shooed me behind the tape. My biggest concern had been getting a good angle for the story. Before I'd found out it was *my* story.

I put my finger to the touch pad, but a flash of bright orange caught my eye, something out of place on the faded blue and rust of the old truck.

I clicked on the orange and zoomed in on it. And felt my mouth drop open.

Next to the Land of Enchantment license plate was a bumper sticker. LCYS, it proclaimed in proud orange letters. Las Cruces Youth Soccer.

I sat back, eyes still glued to the screen. The sticker showed no wear, so it hadn't been on that rusted bumper for too long. The detective told us the truck belonged to Miguel's mother. Did somebody in the family play soccer?

Did Miguel?

Did he don a bright uniform on Saturday mornings and chase a ball around on a field and look up in the stands for his mom when he scored a goal?

I pressed my hand to my mouth. If he had, he probably never would again.

It was a thought that might have taken me over the edge, if another one hadn't pulled me back: if he played soccer in the same league, Dan might know him.

No, even Dan would have said something.

But what about Alex? Miguel was older, but it was a small organization. Was there something Alex might know about this boy and why Jake would be in his truck? It was obvious Jake wasn't going to tell me, but now, after today, Alex might.

If I wasn't going to get any more God-images, this was all I had to cling to. And I did.

CHAPTER ELEVEN

Monday morning at ten o'clock, Martha and Kyle were both seeing clients and, for the moment, were out of each other's faces. Olivia was studiously typing at the computer, something Sully had seldom seen her do before—another personal-growth tip from Kyle, he was sure. All was quiet at Healing Choice, and Sully could leave it for an hour with relative assurance that it would still be standing when he got back.

The plan had come to him over the course of the week. It was clear that he wasn't going to track Belinda Cox down using her legal name, not if she was now going by Zahira. He had to go with that for now, because it was all he had.

That and a thirteen-year-old photo, which until Thursday night he'd thought was virtually useless, especially in its current state. He'd straightened it out and left it under a pile of art books for three days, but it still looked like it had been used as a large spit wad. He was flipping channels that evening, half watching, half ruminating, when he landed on *CSI*. One look at the police sketch artist in the episode—some supermodel in a cameo role—and he had an idea.

A few calls on Friday had led him to the crisp-sounding Tess Lightfoot, who told him on the phone, in no uncertain terms, that she was a "forensic artist," working as an independent contractor, and that she'd meet with him Monday morning at ten thirty at a coffeehouse called Beans and Bytes. Sully hoped she could sketch out an updated version of Belinda Cox, especially with the details Sarah Secretary had given him at the church.

Porphyria had thought it was a good idea too. Though her voice had sounded a little thready, she had been eager to turn over all the stones with him on the phone Friday night.

"If I can't locate her by name, I might be able to track her by face," Sully said to her. "But not the face she had—what?—over a dozen years ago."

"Well, no," Porphyria said. "Time isn't kind enough to anybody to leave them looking like they did back when."

"With one exception. Time has treated you with a great deal of grace."

"Now, when did you start that?"

"Start what?"

"Shameless flattery." Porphyria gave him the throaty laugh. "You want something from me, son?"

"Just your reassurance that I'm not going after Belinda Cox for revenge."

"So that's what all this procrastination is about."

"As if you didn't already know that. The closer I get, the more worked up I get."

"And don't you think that's normal?"

"Not for me."

"Mm-hmm."

Sully stopped pacing his kitchen and straddled a chair. She was about to take him down anyway; he might as well sit.

"It's normal for everyone else on God's earth to want to chew barbed wire when they think about somebody that destroyed their family," she said, "but not Sullivan Crisp."

"But we're talking about vengeance, which last time I checked, was supposed to belong to the Lord."

"No, we are talking about your perfecution complex."

"Persecution complex?"

"I did not say that. I said per-FE-cution."

Sully grinned. "New psychological term, Dr. Ghent? You want to define that for me?"

"You think you have to be perfect, and you persecute yourself when you aren't. And just like any other complex, it keeps you so focused on it, you can't go on and do the next God-thing." She gave a soft grunt. There was obviously more to come.

"And?" Sully said.

"I used to think perfecution only occurred in women."

"I always have been in touch with my feminine side."

"And right now you're in touch with your stupid side. Come on, Sully—you know you'd like to tear Belinda Cox's arm off and beat her with the bloody stump, but you also know this isn't about what you'd like to do, it's about what you *have* to do. And what you have to do you can't do alone."

"I just said that to a client three days ago."

"I hope she's listening to you better than you are."

Sully grinned now as he turned onto Amador Avenue and grabbed his sunglasses from the visor. He didn't go far here without his shades. Or without a Porphyria fix. Both kept him moving forward.

According to the cryptic directions Ms. Lightfoot had given him, the coffee shop was in the downtown mall. When he'd mentioned it to Olivia, she'd rolled her eyes.

"It isn't really a mall, it's just a piece of the street they won't let cars go down. There's, like, nothing there unless you go on Wednesday for fruit and stuff."

She was right. The Downtown Mall was a ghost town at the end Tess had directed him to, except for a storefront that promised to save kids, a movie theater that showed art films on weekends, and the Beans and Bytes.

Which seemed to pride itself on being uninviting. The glass on the door was smeared with at least a month's worth of fingerprints, and the windows were so plastered with flyers, Sully wondered if it was even in business anymore. The door opened, though, into a cave-like darkness and the mournful sound of the Dave Matthews Band.

Sully stood just inside for a few seconds to let his eyes grow accustomed to the lack of light. He could barely make out a guy in dreadlocks at the counter.

"Welcome to Bytes," said the formless voice. "What can I get for you?"

"A woman—"

"Can't help you there, pal."

"No, I'm looking for one who—"

"Internet's in the back," he said, still straight-faced. "Try eHarmony."

Sully grinned. "Can you make a Frappuccino?"

The guy cocked an eyebrow.

"Okay, just make it a coffee with a lot of cream and a lot of sugar. Decaf."

"Dude," Dreadlocks said. "Why do you even bother?"

Sully looked around, but there were no women in the place. A circle of older Hispanic men had pulled several tables together in the back and were having a lively discussion in Spanish. From the looks of it, they were talking about either politics or their wives, jostling each other with good-natured elbow nudges. It made him feel as if he were on some shelf, looking down at life.

"One sugar and cream with a shot of coffee," Dreadlocks droned from the counter.

Sully took it with him to a table where the Sunday *Las Cruces Sun-News* was scattered across the top. He took a blistering sip from the cup and perused the front page. Above the fold, the name Ryan Alexander appeared beneath a photo of two men in white shirts and bulging bellies standing in a hallway. *City Council Budget Impasse*, the headline read. Sully chuckled to himself. She hadn't shot the council in heavy discussion. She'd caught these two politicians out in the hall, where, as Sully understood it, the real deals were made.

He found another of her photos on the front page of the Life section. She'd snapped a picture of a dark-haired woman in a black leotard, obviously a ballet teacher, surrounded by a circle of plump four-year-olds in yellow tutus. They were all looking up at the camera, creating the perfect image of a black-eyed Susan blossoming on a hillside.

Sully shook his head. It must be a huge challenge to go from Sudanese child soldiers to the local dance studio.

"Sullivan Crisp?"

Sully looked up at a woman who had somehow appeared at the table. She moved like water as she put out her hand and shook his and floated into the chair across from him, all in one fluid wave. Sully knocked the front page of the Life section to the floor.

"You want your usual, Contessa?" called Dreadlocks.

She nodded and turned back to Sully, sliding long fawn-colored hair over her shoulder.

"Is your name really Contessa?" Sully asked.

"No," she said. "He just calls me that." She wrinkled her nose in the direction of the counter. "And he's the only one who gets away with it. Just so you know."

"Duly noted."

"So what have you got for me? I have about fifteen minutes, so . . ."

"Of course." Sully pulled the picture from the inside pocket of the tweed blazer he'd worn for credibility and which was starting to itch. He tried to smooth the photo on the tabletop.

She picked it up, moved a pair of rimless glasses from the top of her head to her eyes, and studied it. Sully studied her.

Tess Lightfoot wasn't beautiful, not by magazine cover standards. But then, who was? Still, she was put together well. Her hair was thick and shiny and seemed to have come nowhere near a goat lately. The brown eyes were bright and quick and educated. She hadn't smiled yet, but even in repose her mouth curved, revealing the slightest of overbites and a row of square white teeth.

She looked up at him and returned the glasses to the top of her head. Nodding at Dreadlocks, who put her "usual" on the table, she tapped Belinda's picture with her fingernail.

"How old is this picture?" she asked.

"Fourteen years—about that."

"It's certainly seen better days. Do you know anything about her life since this was taken? Health issues? Traumas?"

"She's moved a lot," he said. "Worked as a counselor. The only recent piece of information I have is that she goes by Zahira—or works for somebody by that name . . . I'm pretty sure she's not a belly dancer."

Tess snorted—an unladylike sound, but it made Sully grin. She glanced at her coffee, still untouched. "Okay, here's what I can do. I'll try to run this through my computer program at home when I have a chance. I have several cases right now with the police department, so it'll have to wait for those to be done."

She tapped the photo again as she took a sip and winced toward the counter. "Did he make this hot enough? The problem I might run into is the quality of the photograph. If it doesn't scan effectively, I may have to do a hand-drawn rendition." She gave the picture yet another tap. "What happened to this, anyway? Did you throw it away by mistake?"

"Something like that," Sully said. She was pulling him along on a piece of silk, and he could feel himself sliding off. "I'd appreciate you just doing what you can."

"All right, well . . ." She glanced at her watch and didn't seem to like what she saw. "So you don't know anything about the way her relatives aged?"

"As far as I know, she doesn't have any family left."

"Do you know if she smoked?"

"I don't think so."

"Did she drink? Overeat? She looks pretty thin here."

Sully shook his head. It was disconcerting that after a year of intense research, he knew so little about the woman who had ruined his wife's life.

"What about her personality?" Tess said.

"I'm sorry?"

"Was she happy-go-lucky? A worrier? Mean as a snake?"

Sully stared at the picture for perhaps the thousandth time. "She thought everybody had to wrestle with the devil. As far as I know, that continues to be her mission in life."

Tess didn't say anything. Sully looked up to find her dissecting his face. Who needed a scanner with those eyes?

"All right, well, I have to go," she said. The picture went into her bag, the hair over her shoulder, the cup into her hand. "I have your number. I'll call you when I get to this. Nice to meet you. Larry, I need an ice cube for this coffee."

"You're not ruining my masterpiece with an ice cube," Dreadlocks told her. Too late. The door had already closed behind her, plunging them once more into dimness.

Sully took a sip of his own coffee, which was now lukewarm and far from a masterpiece. He had the feeling Tess Lightfoot was never going to get around to Belinda Cox's photo. Dang, he should have made a color copy and given her that and kept the original. She raced so swiftly, he hadn't even had a chance to tell her that Belinda Cox dressed like a Native American wannabe and was covered in freckles and was still a blonde.

He dropped the coffee cup surreptitiously into the trash can by the door as he left. Out in the blinding sunlight, he fumbled for his sunglasses and felt a vague disappointment. Less than he expected to feel at another dead end. More than he wanted to at the thought of not seeing that fascinating woman again. He wondered if she was married. Not that he was interested in a relationship, but—too bad. Just too bad.

I savored my time with Alex, but it was hard during our soccer tutorials in Dan's backyard not to drift mentally from learning to dribble to looking for opportunities to talk to Jake. When I came on the scene, however, everyone else disappeared like bats in the sunlight, including Ginger and Dan. I could live without them. I didn't think I could live without my son.

Finally, late Monday afternoon, when Alex and I were in Dan's kitchen having a water-chugging contest, Jake appeared in the doorway. His face flickered unwelcome surprise when he saw me, and he took a step back as if he thought he could hide behind the long string of fresh garlic cloves that hung from the ceiling. He was almost thin enough to pull it off.

"Alex," I said, not taking my eyes from Jake, "why don't you go out and set up those cones I brought so we can practice our ball control?"

He went out the back door.

"Jake, sit down," I said.

"Dad said I don't have to—"

"I'm not going to ask you questions about what happened. Just sit."

I sat next to him and pulled my chair in close. "What does *whereas* mean?"

He stopped picking at the mole on his arm. "What?"

"*Whereas.* What does it mean?"

"I don't know," he said.

"How about *inalienable*? Do you know that one?"

He squinted at his hands. "No."

"Inalienable rights?"

"I don't *know.* It's, like, in the Constitution or something."

"Or something," I said. "Can you spell it?"

Jake's miserable gaze went to the ceiling. "You know I can't. Why do you always have to rub that in?"

"I'm not rubbing it in. I'm trying to show you how I can save your butt."

The gaze came down in a glare. "You said you weren't asking me questions about that."

"I'm asking questions about you, and the answers prove that you did not write that note they found in the truck with you."

He went back to the mole. "Okay, so maybe I do know what that stuff means."

"No, you don't. Listen, I'm going to share this with your lawyer, not to embarrass you—"

"Why can't you just leave it alone?" Jake's voice cracked, and he shoved the chair back and knocked it onto its back on the plank floor. "I'm not afraid of going to prison, so just leave it alone."

There was nothing *but* fear in his eyes as he left the chair lying there and escaped from me once more. I righted it before Ginger could emerge from her lair and accuse me of busting up the furniture—or pick the thing up and swing it at me.

When I returned to the backyard, Alex was kicking at the dirt with his toe between two of the orange cones I'd picked up at a sporting goods store. As soon as he saw me, he smiled an automatic smile.

"Juggle for me," I said.

He immediately obliged, bouncing the ball off his knee.

"So are you pretty good friends with Cade and those guys?" I said.

"I am with Felipe and Bryan. Cade's kinda bossy sometimes."

Cade didn't take after anybody strange.

"Do you know any kids on the other teams in the league?" I said.

Alex grinned and popped the ball onto his shoulder where he was able to bounce it three times before it dropped. "I know everybody."

"Everybody?"

The grin grew wider. "And everybody knows me."

"Fibber," I said.

"No. Serious. Ask anybody at Burn Lake."

His eyes teased me as he smacked the ball with his instep in my direction. I trapped it, the only skill I had actually mastered.

"Do you know Miguel Sanchez?" I said.

"Yeah," he said, just before his face froze. "Well, maybe I don't know *him*."

"Alex."

I pushed the ball aside and nodded him toward a cable-spool table just beyond the porch. It had a rooster weather vane coming up through its center, but there was room to sit at it on smaller spool stools. Alex took one as if he were placing himself into a dentist's chair.

"You do know Miguel," I said.

He nodded.

"How well do you know him?"

"Not that good. He's Jake's friend, not mine."

I could barely keep my chin from dropping to my chest. "So Jake and Miguel are friends. Good friends?"

"Yeah." Alex still wasn't looking at me. All the little-boy charm had slipped way.

"Like, spend-the-night-at-each-other's-houses friends?"

"No. They just played soccer."

"Miguel's in the same soccer league as you guys."

Alex shook his head. You would think I was beating the information out of him.

"He wasn't at first. He just hung around Burn Lake, and me and Jake and Ian would mess around with the ball while we were waiting for Dad to get out of meetings and stuff. Jake asked him to play with us."

I groped for control. "So—is he pretty good at soccer?"

"Oh yeah." First light came back into Alex's eyes. "He played like those guys from South America on TV."

"That good?"

"Jake even told him to try out for the select team."

"That sounds important."

"It's like the best players in the whole league. They get to travel out of town, all the way to Albuquerque and stuff."

Alex went on for five minutes about the glory of being on the select team. I nodded and made occasional appreciative noises while my mind raced elsewhere.

If Jake was impressed by Miguel Sanchez and befriended him,

how could he possibly have tried to kill him? And why hadn't Jake volunteered any of this information himself? I felt my eyes narrow as I wondered if Dan knew—but again I dismissed the possibility. He wouldn't just let Jake go down like this.

Alex was looking at me, his eyes clouded again with misgiving.

"What's wrong, guy?" I said.

"Are you gonna tell Jake I told you?" he asked.

"Wouldn't he want you to?"

Alex shrugged.

"What does that mean?" I mimicked his lifted shoulders.

"He doesn't like me saying stuff about him to people. This one time, I told Dad that Jake stopped these guys from picking on this girl on the bus, and Jake got all mad." He widened his brown eyes. "I don't get that, but he just says he doesn't like people talking about him, so I don't."

"This is a little bit different. People are saying Jake hurt Miguel. It would help if people knew they were friends."

Alex gave a quick nod and stood up. "Can we practice some more? You gotta work on your passing, Mom."

"Just one more question. You said Jake and Miguel and Ian all played soccer together—"

"I knew it. I knew you were trying to drag Ian into this."

I looked up at the back porch in time to see Ginger slap the screen door behind her—and burst into tears. She came to the railing, leaned on the pole, and openly cried.

I had lain awake nights with the images of starving African children rattling in my brain, their ladder-ribs and rickety femurs knocking at my memory and making sleep itself a mere dream. But when Ginger started to cry, I stifled a yawn. One more tear and I would doze off. A few more sobs and I might lapse into a coma.

"I am not dragging your precious Ian into anything," I said. "I'm talking to my son about his friends."

I turned back to Alex, who was watching Ginger with just about as much concern as I was feeling.

"I guess we better talk about this later," I said to him with a wink.

"Yeah." He attempted to wink back and looked as if he had a bug in his eye.

"No! Don't you talk about my son, ever!"

I only looked at Ginger to make sure she wasn't going to throw a flowerpot at me, but she wasn't in rage mode. She was just bawling, mouth open, howling out of her throat. It was enough to bring Ian and Jake from around the side of the house, and Dan up the walkway from the studio. Was that all it took to get this group's attention? You just brought out the crocodile tears, and they all came running?

Ian went straight to his mother and put his arm around her. He looked at me, face puzzled.

"Is there a problem?" he asked.

"Nothing you need to worry about," I said.

"I kind of do." He pulled Ginger to arm's length. "Mom, go get a Kleenex or something, will ya?"

She nodded and melted into the house. I stared as Ian joined Alex and me at the table. Jake was still standing just beyond the patio.

"She flips out easy," Ian said to me. "Right, Alex?"

Alex rolled his eyes.

"But seriously, did something go down here? If I know what it is, I can calm her down."

In spite of my agitation, I had to stop and study this kid. While most teenage boys weren't as sullen with their mothers as Jake was, they weren't usually this solicitous with them either. Even now, he glanced at the door like he was totally responsible for the woman.

"Look," I said, "I was just sitting here having a conversation with Alex. It didn't have anything to do with her."

"What's up, buddy?" Dan said behind me.

"Mom's upset, and Jake's mom and I were just trying to deal with it."

"Actually, no," I said. "*I* was just trying to spend some time with my sons."

"Not this son." Jake stepped onto the patio, arms jammed into the pouch of his sweatshirt, eyes bulleted at me. "I'm over it, okay? I'm not talking to you again, about anything, I don't care what it is." He glanced at his brother. "You shouldn't either, Alex. She doesn't care about you. She's just trying to get to me—"

"Stop!" I said. "Jake—you just stop."

I stormed across the bricks at him. Ian stepped between us.

"Come on, guys," he said.

"Step aside."

"Danny, do something!" Ginger cried from the doorway.

"Ryan—"

"All of you, just *stop*!" I had both hands up, and I could feel them shaking. My breath heaved in and out of my nose as I jabbed a finger at Ian. "You do not come between me and my son. And you"—I jockeyed around him and pointed at Jake—"do not misrepresent me to your brother. And you"—I whirled on Dan, who was now mere steps behind me—"need to ask the nymphette over there to stand clear when I'm spending time with my boys."

I took a step into Dan's space. He looked down at me with the first faint stirrings of anger in his eyes. "Don't fight me on this, Dan. We have enough problems as it is."

I stopped counting the number of doors that slammed after that. Jake's bedroom. Ginger's screen door. Dan's studio. When Ian had taken off after his mother, only Alex was left, and I advised him to scoot on and get his homework done, which he did without a murmur.

By the time I got to my car, I was too drained to slam anything myself, and I didn't feel any better having opened up on my ex-husband's new family like a submachine gun. As I started the engine, I looked at the hourglass on the dashboard. *God, where were you? Why didn't you stop me?* Where *are those images?*

The sun had already dropped behind the hills when I made my way slowly down Dan's driveway, and the artsy forms I passed were mere blobs in the fading light. I had gotten child soldiers, hard as cast-iron skillets, to sob their stories into my lap. And yet I couldn't make my own son tell me what he was so obviously hiding. Either one of my sons.

I stopped at the end of the driveway and squared my shoulders in the darkness. All right, then. If they wouldn't tell me, I was going to have to find out from someplace else. And in the first God-image I'd had in days, I knew where that might be.

CHAPTER TWELVE

Sully had just finished praying before his session Tuesday afternoon when his cell phone rang, which was a good thing. He'd forgotten all about it, and all he needed was for it to go off while he was talking to Ryan.

He did answer it now, though, in case Porphyria was calling. It was Tess Lightfoot.

"I have your age progression ready," she said.

"You do?"

"Well—yeah. Isn't that why you're paying me the big bucks?"

Sully laughed. "I'm just surprised. That was quick."

"That's the other reason you're paying me the big bucks."

Her voice was as smooth as he remembered it.

"You might want to come by my office so we can look at it on the computer. I have a few questions that could mean some changes."

"So you were able to scan it with the computer."

"Still another reason why—"

"I'm paying you the big bucks." Sully felt himself grinning. "I'm starting to worry about my bill."

"You should."

She gave him an address, and he agreed to meet her at six. Then he turned off his phone and tapped it on the desk.

His conversation with Porphyria had reassured him for a few days, but now that he was about to see the face he'd been looking for, anxiety crept along his nerve endings again. Saying he could discern the difference between normal anger and bloody-stump revenge was one thing. Knowing he could do it when Belinda Cox was looking back at him was another. And if he was this worried about just seeing her picture, what was going to happen when he confronted her in person?

Sully wiped the sudden beads of sweat from his upper lip and stood up to go out and meet Ryan. *One God-thing at a time, Dr. Crisp,* he could hear Porphyria saying. *One God-thing at a time.*

Ryan was literally pacing the reception room when Sully got there. This was either going to be productive—or it was going to be a disaster.

Once again she eschewed the polite greetings and small talk and went straight for the chair. She dropped the hourglass onto the trunk between them. "Did you expect this to work?"

"I assume it didn't," Sully said.

"Not at all."

"You want to tell me about it?"

"Is that like 'How did it make you feel?'"

Sully shook his head, still watching her try to look bigger in the chair as he settled in his own. "No, it's just 'You want to tell me about it.' Although I guess journalists misuse the 'How did it make you feel' line as much as therapists."

"I think it's a cheap shot," she said. "I don't ask that many questions anyway. I just make pictures."

"Speaking of which, I saw some of your work in the paper. I was impressed."

Ryan put a hand on top of her head and closed her eyes. "Look, don't try to get me to loosen up. I need *help* here."

"That's exactly where we're going, Ryan," Sully said. "Nobody can look at this stuff wound up like a spring."

He saw her swallow, but otherwise she didn't respond.

"What *I* see in your pictures is that you share in the emotion of what's going on in front of the camera. Doesn't matter that it's kindergartners in tutus, there's heart and soul in there." He tilted his head at her. "I don't see a tough, no-nonsense person behind that camera."

"I don't try to be tough," she said. "I just do what I have to do. Only right now I don't know what *to* do, and that's what I want you to tell me."

Holy crow. They were at a crossroads already, and she was still trying to figure out how to get her feet to touch the floor. He felt like he was entering a minefield.

"I can tell you," he said, "but it will be a whole lot more effective if I help you figure out how to tell yourself." He refolded his legs. "How do you see things when you get ready to make a picture? That's how you say it, right? Make a picture?"

She gave him a doubtful look before the goalpost hands went up and she focused between them. "I see it in layers in a frame," she said. "I find all the compositional elements that are going to make the reader look at the photograph and think about it a little while longer. What's in the foreground? What's in the background? Where is the light?"

"Why do you do all that?"

"Well, because . . ." She shrugged. "The longer I can capture the viewers and make them think about what they're seeing, the better chance I have of them understanding what I'm trying to say with the photograph."

"Bingo."

She gave Sully a blank look.

"You just described what we're about here," he said. "Only I'm the photographer, and you're the reader. I have to bring out all the layers, all the elements that are going to get you to look at your life and think about it. And the longer and deeper I can get you to do that, the better chance you have of understanding it all."

Ryan studied his face as if she were looking for traces of a clandestine plot. The only thing missing was the bare lightbulb.

And yet there was something desperate in her eyes, something that tugged at Sully's heart. This was no high-strung woman trying to get the best of her road rage.

"All right," she said. "What is it you want me to look at?"

Sully took another step into the minefield. "I want you to look at the thing you want the most right now."

No pause. "I want my son to be acquitted."

"What if he weren't? What would be the next thing you would want?"

"You're not going for 'To get him out on an appeal.'"

"I'm not going for anything. Let's say he did get out, but he still wouldn't talk to you?"

"I'd be back where I was before this happened."

"And what did you want then?"

"I wanted my sons to love me again. I still do. I just want to be their mother." She brought herself up abruptly in the chair. "Where *are* we going with this?"

"To another layer," Sully said. "You're having to work pretty hard at being a mother right now, yeah?"

"Thanks to my ex-husband, yes. Look, if you're saying my anger stems from him, that is not a news flash."

"Did you get angry before you were married to Dan?"

"You mean like when I was a kid?"

"Sure."

She actually smiled—ruefully, Sully thought.

"I wasn't allowed to. You didn't pitch fits in our house."

"What happened if you did?"

"I never tested it out."

Sully found that hard to believe. He waited until she squinted.

"I never tested it out *personally*," she said. "I just saw what happened when somebody else did."

"For instance?"

Ryan pulled her knees toward her chest, then caught herself. "When I was five, my mother got me a boxer, from the pound. I wanted to call him Slobber."

"'Wanted' to . . . ?"

"He didn't stay long enough to call him anything. My father came home from work and said okay, fine, you got a dog. You have to take care of him."

"You were how old?"

"Five."

Holy crow, Sully thought, but he nodded her on.

"I was feeding him, and a couple of kibbles fell on the floor. Slobber and I went for them at the same time, and my father picked me up and screamed at my mother to get that blankity-blank dog out of our blankity-blank house and take him back where he blankity-blank came from."

"How did your mother react?"

"She said he was being unreasonable, that the dog wasn't going to bite me."

"Did she yell back at him when she said it?"

Ryan's eyebrows twisted. "My mother never said anything worse than 'good gravy' to anybody."

"So what happened?"

Ryan shrugged. "Slobber went back to the pound."

"And you?"

Once again she raised her knees and forced them down again. She wasn't going into that fetal position the little girl in her longed for.

"I don't think I did anything. What would be the point?"

"So you weren't allowed to *express* anger. But did you *feel* it?"

"You mean like I do now? I guess not, no."

Sully waited.

"Maybe when I was younger than that. I probably got so used to controlling it I didn't even feel it anymore."

"So you didn't start consciously feeling anger until after you were married," he said.

"A few years after." Ryan's voice sharpened. "Right after I got pregnant with Jake. I wanted Dan to get a real job so we'd have health insurance when I quit work to stay home with the baby. He said he would—and he didn't. That was probably when it started." She shook her head. "I wasn't violent. I just yelled, and he blamed it on hormones. It went downhill from there. What's the point?"

"That resentment could be what fuels your anger. That might be one layer, anyway."

"Like I said, that is not breaking news."

"So when Dan flaked out on the job thing, what did you do?"

She scowled. "I worked until I had Jake, took the minimum six-week maternity leave, and went back to my job. Obviously Dan wasn't going to take any responsibility. Somebody had to."

"And that continued."

"For the most part. There was a period before I got pregnant with Alex when he was teaching at the Art Institute in Chicago, and I thought he was finally growing up. That's the only reason I agreed to have another baby."

"But that didn't last."

"Of course not."

"So once again you had to be in charge."

She folded her arms across her chest. "I wasn't trying to be the Gestapo—but if somebody didn't take control of our lives, we were going to end up on the street with two kids. It's not like I tried to make him into a nine-to-fiver. I helped him start a business where he could have a venue for selling his stuff, and he just ran it into the ground while he was telling me it was doing great. When that went under and we lost all our savings, that was it."

Sully leaned forward, straight into the minefield. "I want to put something to you, and I just want you to look at it as a possible layer. If it doesn't ring true, we'll move on, okay?"

Her eyes squinted. "I can already tell I'm not going to like this."

She didn't have to like it. All he wanted her to do was consider it—before she headed for the door.

"Let's just explore the idea that you have a basic conflict going here." Sully held out one palm. "On the one hand, you want things to go a certain way, and you've learned to put yourself in a position where they go that way—because if you don't, the consequences could be pretty disastrous."

She formed the lines on either side of her mouth, but she nodded.

"But at the same time, you resent having to be in that position in the first place, where it's up to you to take all the responsibility. And it's that conflict that makes you so mad you want to throw things." Sully cocked his head. "How does that sound?"

"It sounds like psychological bilge water." Her feet hit the floor as she jerked to the edge of the chair. "I did not lose it at my ex-husband's last night because I was 'conflicted.' I blew up because his girlfriend accused me of putting down her son when I barely looked at the kid. That woman is in worse shape than I am."

"What did she do?" Sully asked.

Ryan rolled her eyes. "She cried. I have nothing against shedding a few tears when the situation calls for it, but she was sobbing like I'd tried to castrate the boy. She was hanging on to the porch pole with mascara running down her face like Tammy Faye. I mean, get a grip."

Sully had a hard time reining in a grin.

"And *that's* the reason I'm here," Ryan went on. "I don't want to turn into a version of her. I mean, I don't see myself boo-hooing like that, but for every trail of snot coming out of her nose, I could throw some kind of projectile, do you know what I'm saying?"

Once again the desperation quickened in her eyes.

Sully steepled his fingers under his chin. "I can't say for sure without seeing—what's her name?"

"Ginger." Ryan licked her lips as if she were trying to get a bad taste out of her mouth.

"I'm not making an official diagnosis here, but she could be histrionic."

"Is that an actual mental illness?"

"It's a personality disorder," Sully said. "And again, I wouldn't go to Dan and tell him his girlfriend has HPD."

He waited for her to nod, which she finally did with obvious reluctance.

"My point is, you don't fit that profile. You don't go off randomly or deliberately for the sake of drama. When histrionic people seek help, it's usually just to have an audience. They think the problem is with everyone else, and they want to tell you about it in graphic detail so you'll sympathize and enable and everything else they thrive on. That isn't you."

"Great," Ryan said. "So I'm not like the Spice Girl. How does this help me?"

There was none of the relief the average client would have felt. But then, Ryan wasn't the average client. Back to the minefield.

"It helps you rule out certain things," Sully said. "It's like going to a medical doctor with headaches. They immediately try to determine that you don't have a brain tumor. Once they do, they can move on—"

"To what?"

"In our case, to looking at another layer—*while* we're giving you come coping mechanisms to use in the meantime."

"Such as."

She seldom seemed to put anything to him as a question. It was always as a challenge. An I-bet-you-don't-know-the-answer. He wasn't sure he did.

"The usual approach would be things like trying to stay away from the situations that trigger your anger."

"When the situation is right in my face all the time? Look, I know you probably think I'm just trying to be difficult. I've been accused of that before."

"No, I don't think that at all," Sully said. "What I think is that you're smart enough to know what doesn't work for you. Most of the time."

"Most of the time. What's the exception?" She turned her head to look at him from the corner of her eye. "I'm not going to like this, am I?"

"You're probably going to hate it," Sully said. "But in therapy, often the thing you resist is the thing you need the most. Do you know anything about quicksand?"

"Quicksand. No."

"When somebody gets stuck in quicksand, what do you think is their first instinct for getting out?"

She gave her hand an impatient flick. "They probably panic and start thrashing around."

"Which is the worst thing they can do, because the more they agitate the quicksand, the more it will liquefy and the faster they'll sink. The best thing they can do is relax, take a few deep breaths, spread out their arms and legs, and just let their body's natural buoyancy bring them to the top." Sully tilted his head at her. "If anybody's in quicksand right now, Ryan, it's you. You're trying everything you know to do, and yet the more you struggle, the deeper you go. That isn't *wrong*. It's just an instinct that isn't serving you well in this situation."

"You're telling me I need to surrender and just let my son go to prison?"

"I'm not saying stop trying to prove Jake's innocence," Sully said. "I'm saying let's work on letting go of the conviction that you can control not only the outcome, but everyone else's actions along the way." He smiled at her. "The good news is, if you expect to come across quicksand, which I think you can in the weeks to come, you can carry a pole to support yourself when you start to sink. That, I think, would be God."

Ryan put up both hands, palms toward Sully as if he were trying to push her against a wall. "I don't think about God as somebody who rescues me when I and everybody else have screwed up."

"How *do* you think of God?"

"No, let's get back to you telling me that if I'm going to be healed of anger, I have to totally give up control." Her voice rose to the pitch he was certain was reserved for the ex-husband and the Spice Girl. "*What*—is the *matter* with you? If I give up control, I'm going to lose my son—maybe *both* of my sons. You can't make me do that. I'd rather stay angry."

"I'm not trying to make you do anything, Ryan," Sully said.

But she was already on her feet, fumbling to get her purse strap over her shoulder.

"This is not what I need," she said. "Matter of fact, I don't think you can give me what I need."

She charged for the door, and although Sully followed her down the hall, he didn't try to stop her.

"Bill me," she barked at Olivia. To Sully she said, "I'm sure what you do works for most people. I guess I'm just not most people."

She could say that again. Sully watched her slam out the door and break into a virtual run across the parking lot. She was arguably the most challenging client he'd ever had. And yet a sad ache wrapped itself around his gut. She was like a stray cat. He wanted to pick up her soul and hug it until she gave in to her hurt so she could heal. But he knew if he tried it, he'd be shredded to ribbons.

He hoped she'd come back, though. Because unlike "most people," Ryan Coe risked losing everything if she didn't.

He turned to Olivia and Kyle, who was sitting in a client chair at Olivia's desk. Each of them seemed to be struggling for an appropriate facial expression. Sully parked his hands in his pockets and went over to them.

"So," he said, "I know I don't have to remind you two that confidentiality applies to things that happen in the lobby."

Olivia's eyes grew to saucers. "I'm not going to tell anybody. But can I just say I'm glad she won't be coming in here anymore? She's, like, not that nice."

"Let's not write her off yet," Sully said. "We'll give her a chance to calm down."

Kyle was nodding. "I don't think she's done."

Sully moved toward the hall. "I'm headed out in a few minutes, unless you need me for anything."

"I'll walk you back," Kyle said. He leaped from the chair and followed Sully across the lobby. "Do you have dinner plans?" he said. "I found this great place where they serve Ethiopian food."

"Ethiopian food?" Sully said. "Isn't that an oxymoron?"

"No, man, it's great."

Sully shook his head, hand on his office doorknob. "Can I take a rain check? I have plans for tonight."

"I'm going to hold you to that," Kyle said.

Sully pulled the voice recorder out of his pocket and said into it with a grin, "Have dinner with Kyle. No Ethiopian."

"What is *that*?" Kyle said.

"It's a tape recorder."

"How long have you had it? Since the Clinton administration?"

"What's the deal?" Sully said. "It works."

Kyle shook his head and strolled off down the hall, arms dangling at his sides. For a moment Sully was reminded of himself, ten years younger and surer and worldlier. Funny how life itself made you so much less certain that you knew a dang thing.

Sully had barely pulled a Frappuccino out of the refrigerator on his office patio when he heard a prim tap on the door.

"Come on in, Martha," he called with more enthusiasm than he actually felt. He wasn't up for another prepared speech outlining Kyle's shortcomings. Despite the confrontations in the break room between the two of them, which Olivia reported regularly, Martha obviously wasn't satisfied. She delivered a version of the outline to him every chance she got.

Martha shook her head when Sully held up his bottled Frap and again when he nodded toward a chair in front of the desk.

She remained standing and flipped open the ubiquitous leather portfolio. "I just wanted to update you on a few things."

Sully leaned on the front of the desk and propped the bottle between his knees.

"Mr. Hillman has dropped his suit against us," she said. "Another source reported abuse at his home, and this time CPS found evidence."

"I hate to hear that," Sully said. "But that probably works for everybody concerned. Especially the kids on the receiving end of whatever he was dishing out."

"It doesn't hurt us either." Martha ran her finger neatly down the page again. "And your instincts about Bob Benitez."

"Is that Bob the Blabber?" Sully asked.

Martha almost smiled. "Just as you predicted, he's moved on to other things on his blog."

Sully grinned. "So far you're batting a thousand here, Martha. What else you got?"

The potential smile faded. "I'm still having trouble locating any of the people who complained about Carla Korman. I keep getting disconnected numbers and bounce-back e-mails. I'll continue to work on it. I assume you don't want me to send in the paperwork to have her license revoked without corroborating all of this."

"Right," Sully asked.

There was no doubt that Martha had more integrity than any three of your average people put together. He probably ought to sit down with her and Kyle and mediate.

Sully grinned inwardly. Or he could just send Martha out to have Ethiopian food in his place and see what happened.

"That's all I have for now," she said.

"You've gotten a lot done in a short period of time. I appreciate it."

He expected the usual professional nod, the modest thank-you, but she lowered her eyes to the front of the portfolio she hugged to her chest as if she were looking for her next cue there. He was going to get the outline after all.

"I know I'm not the avant-garde psychologist you and Kyle are," she said. "I am willing to learn new techniques, but I think I'll probably always be more traditional."

She looked at him expectantly. Sully was, for once, clueless.

"Well, I just wanted to put that out there," she said. "Have a nice evening."

"You too," Sully said, though by the time he got it out, she was already closing the door behind her with her usual flawless propriety.

He took a long draw from the Frappuccino. What had just happened? Did he miss something?

Whatever it was, tomorrow was going to have to be soon enough to find out—after he had his own next step behind him. He abandoned the bottle and headed for the door.

CHAPTER THIRTEEN

I couldn't go straight to Alex's soccer practice after my session. In fact, I couldn't think of a single place I *could* go where someone wouldn't call the cops to report a woman who was looking to commit assault and battery.

Hands still shaking on the wheel, I drove around, nowhere, anywhere, trying to scold my thrashing anger back into its cage. I thought the farther I got from the Healing Choice Clinic the more chance I'd have of regaining control.

But by the time I nosed into downtown Las Cruces in the middle of what they called rush-hour traffic, I was convinced Sullivan Crisp had somehow stripped me of control against my will and was holding it hostage in his yellow room while I rammed around, pounding my fist on my steering wheel and shouting at nobody.

Another surge of rage shot through me, and I had to jerk the Saab to the curb to avoid rear-ending the Harley in front of me. I turned off the ignition and threw the keys onto the floor on the passenger side.

What part of "I just want you to tell me how to control the anger I have every right to feel" didn't he understand? How much clearer could I make it?

Yet even as the ire continued to charge up my backbone, I knew it wouldn't do any good to find another therapist. It was therapy itself that wasn't for me. I'd already thought of all the stuff he said, long before he said it. Except for that psychobabble about my being conflicted between wanting control and resenting having to have it. *What?*

I was going to have to navigate this thing myself—go with the only God-image I had—the one that had come back to me more than once since it had first formed in my mind when Alex told me Jake and Miguel were friends. Maybe starting right now was the only way I was going to get myself calmed down.

I rescued the keys from the floor and started to put them back in the ignition when I realized where I was. The Downtown Mall was a block away, three blocks from the scene of the crime. It was either a God-thing or pure chance—and I didn't believe in chance.

The sun slanted late afternoon rays over the low roofs as I hurried across the largely deserted mall. The temperature was only in the low eighties, but I could tell from my shadow that my hair was in sweaty spikes from sitting in the closed car, railing at the world. I was already feeling calmer, though. Having a plan, taking some action—that was the only thing that ever helped me. Not rehashing my marriage to Dan Coe.

I pushed through the glass door that said *Bienvenida!* in gold decal letters, some of which were peeling off. I hadn't noticed that the day I'd charged through there with my camera. A short Hispanic woman led me to a table in a front corner, where I could see everything—from the entrance framed in silk hibiscus and twinkly lights to the swinging kitchen door I had passed through to get to the alley.

I remembered little else about the place. It had been empty that afternoon except for the group of people I'd joined at the back door. I studied the woman who seated me, but I couldn't tell if she was one of them, or if she recognized me.

She brought me a basket of tortilla chips, shiny with grease, and a bowl of salsa with a fiery spiciness that singed my nose hairs from two feet away. I ordered an iced tea and nibbled at a chip.

I hadn't brought my camera in with me, and I felt naked without it. Still, as I tried to look like any hungry customer eager to try out the chimichangas, I collected images automatically:

The large-breasted girl with mocha skin at the cash register who was every bit as pretty as the woman on the Spanish soap opera on the TV above her head.

The family at the next table, parents focusing on their toddlers and forgetting they once had eyes only for each other.

The waiter wearing a long oven mitt up to his armpit, carrying a precarious row of plates heaped with beans and rice and bubbling cheese—his one claim to greatness.

But it was the busboy I framed in my mental lens. Something simmered beneath the skin of his studiedly bored face as he swept abandoned dishes into a plastic tub. It could have been hostility. Anger. Bitter frustration. Whatever it was, it was the thing I had come to see. If this was the life of Miguel Sanchez, it might lead me to what had happened beyond the back doors, in the alley, between two young boys who should right now be kicking a soccer ball back and forth.

My server was back. "You are ready to order?" she said.

"What do you recommend?"

"Everything is good. You like carne asada?"

"Love it," I said, though I had no idea what it was. "I'll have that."

She took hold of the menu, but I didn't let go.

"I'm sorry," I said. "I didn't catch your name. I don't like to just say, 'Hey, you!'"

"I am Vera," she said.

Vera what? I wanted to say, but that would have been too pushy even for me. "So, Vera," I said as I let her have the menu, "is Señora Sanchez working tonight?" And please don't let her be you.

Her eyes clouded. "No. She is not working here anymore."

"Oh. Because of her son?"

"Yes," she said with a sigh she seemed to have been holding in for a long time. "Very sad."

"It is. I'd like to go see her. Does she still live in . . ." I snapped my fingers as if I were trying to remember.

"El Milagro, yes."

"Right. I can never remember that."

Her eyes may have narrowed ever so slightly, or it could have been my guilty conscience mirrored there. But when she went off to put my order in, the next part of my plan fell into place.

It was close to 6:00 p.m. by the time Sully located the address Tess had given him.

Even then he drove around the block twice before he pulled into the driveway. She'd said he'd be coming to her office, not a home in a residential neighborhood. He checked his notes once more before he unfolded himself from the Mini Cooper and moved cautiously to the front door. Tess herself appeared in the storm-door glass, eyebrows in a quizzical twist.

"I sent the snipers home for the day," she said. "It's safe."

Sully grinned sheepishly. "I wasn't expecting a house."

She opened the door and nodded him in. "I can't afford office digs, so I freelance from here. You're slumming today."

He was far from slumming. The room he stepped into was sparsely furnished, but it was obvious every piece had been carefully selected—a basket, a clay jar, a replica of a Native American drum serving as a coffee table. Rich blue pillows on cream couches and chairs gathered on a bamboo mat invited him to join the scene.

"My office is in the back," Tess said and led him through a sunny dining room.

Sully followed, eyes on the chestnut flow of hair that cascaded past her shoulders. She wore a loose pink sweater over jeans and a pair of straw flip-flops that snapped happily as she eased through the kitchen. Despite the brisk wit he remembered, she seemed softer in the light she'd invited into her home. And prettier.

Tess stopped in the dimly lit room off the kitchen and went straight to a tall desk that housed what had to be a twenty-four-inch computer monitor. A framed certificate hung above it, proclaiming that Tess Lightfoot was certified by the International Association for Identification as a Facial Identification Specialist. The one next to it added that the University of Montana had granted her a degree in forensic anthropology.

Tess patted the back of one of the high stools in front of the desk.

"Have a seat," she said, "and we'll take a look."

Sully sat after she did, but a new thought came to him that made him suddenly unwilling to move any further forward with this. Any minute that oversize screen was going to light up with an image of Belinda Cox, and true or not, it was going to throw him from distant memory into the raw reality of what he was about to do. Until now he'd always had the option of cutting his losses and moving on. Once he saw her as she might look today, that choice would be ripped away, no matter what his motive was.

"Are you okay?" Tess said.

Sully tried the default grin. "Could you have found a bigger screen?"

She gave him an appraising look and slid her glasses down from her head. "Any bigger and we'd have to back out of the room. You ready?"

Sully abandoned the grin and nodded.

Tess did some clicking as she talked. "I scanned your photo in, and the software used growth data to predict the structural changes that our subject's face would undergo between age thirty-five, you told me, and her current age, which would be forty-eight. The program re-created the photo for us according to the specifications I gave it, and—here we are."

The screen filled with a face that beckoned Sully with the same patronizing expression he'd been searching out for a year. But the look came from an older, harder Belinda Cox, whose long, flat nose had lengthened toward thinner lips, whose upper lids had dropped beneath sparser eyebrows. Small, soft pouches had puffed the skin beneath eyes that were now a paler blue, and the pair of vertical lines between them had pinched tighter.

"I've done multiple looks to account for possible weight gain and loss," Tess said, "although she couldn't have gotten too much thinner without becoming emaciated."

She clicked a series of progressively bloated Belindas into view, then reversed the process until a skeletal version appeared. They all looked the same to Sully. All condescending. All dangerous.

"Now, I can use Photoshop to paint any changes right on the image," Tess said. "I have it set up in grids so we can do specific areas at a time."

Sully shook his head. He could feel Tess watching him, but he kept his own gaze riveted to the screen, unable to look away from the proverbial train wreck.

"You told me you don't know anything about her lifestyle," she said, "but if you've come up with any details since we talked, we can put those in."

Her voice brushed against him, and Sully tried to focus.

"How about jewelry?" he said. "Someone told me she wears a lot of Native American stuff."

"Good." Tess's fingers nudged the keyboard, and within moments Belinda Cox was adorned with clay beads and turquoise baubles. They were jarring against her too-white skin.

"Freckles," Sully said.

Tess frowned. "Those usually fade with age."

"Nobody told her that. According to my source, she's still covered with them."

"She should have worn sunscreen," Tess said and sprinkled brown spots across the nose and forehead. "Anything else?"

Sully felt a small sizzle of energy. "How close do you think this is to what she actually looks like today?"

Tess pushed the glasses up and sat back in the chair, pulling her long legs up into a bow. She'd kicked off her shoes, and she curled her fingers around her toes.

"A computer can't perform exact transformations," she said. "The critical task is to maintain the look of the person." She swept her hand across the screen. "Particularly around the eyes. Most things about our appearance do change with age, but we usually maintain a certain recognizable manner of expression." Tess glanced at Sully and smiled with her lips together. "I'm not trying to skirt the question. This should make it possible for you to recognize this woman, if you don't expect every detail to match."

Sully nodded and went back to the screen. Tess was right. Belinda Cox still had the same manner of expression—the expression she'd shown his Lynn when she went to her in the agony of depression. The look Cox had when she told Lynn she needed to repent so she could be a good mother. The countenance that brought bile up his throat.

"I can give you an image with glasses, shorter hair, longer," Tess said. "We can experiment as much as you want."

She spoke with the calm of soft water, and she was watching him again, eyes exploring as if she were looking to see what her next words should be. Sully let go of a breath he hadn't been aware he was holding.

"I think we're good," he said. "To tell you the truth, I don't know how much longer I can look at her."

Tess unfolded her legs. "I didn't think she was somebody you were crazy about. Shall I print this out for you?"

Sully nodded and watched her hands flow over the computer until a gentle whir signaled that Belinda Cox was coming out of the printer.

"Sun tea?" she said.

"I'm sorry?"

"Would you like some sun tea? It's probably the last batch for the season." Tess waited, eyebrows up.

"Do you have sugar?" Sully asked.

She got up and sailed across the office to the kitchen, hair swaying across her back as she moved. "Do we have a sweet tooth, Dr. Crisp?"

Sully followed her into the kitchen, where she waved him to a well-stuffed red-checked chair that would have seemed incongruous amid anyone else's stove and refrigerator.

"How did you know I was a doctor?" he said.

Tess dropped ice cubes into two tall glasses that looked as slender as she did. "I checked you out. I wasn't going to invite you into my home without making sure you aren't a serial killer."

In spite of his darkened mood, Sully grinned. "I don't think most of them report that as their occupation."

"You forget that I work with the police department." Tess filled the glasses with a golden liquid that already had Sully's mouth watering, and she nodded toward a set of French doors. "Let's sit outside—there's a heavenly breeze."

Sully was ensconced on a sage green padded chaise lounge on a back porch drenched in sunset light before he fully realized that their business was complete and Tess had moved them seamlessly into a social conversation, complete with minty ice tea and a breeze that chattered in the cottonwoods. He was okay with that.

"What else did you uncover when you checked me out?" Sully asked.

Tess stretched out her legs on the chaise angled toward his and crossed her ankles.

"Actually, I already knew about you from your books and your radio show and all of that. I just didn't realize you were working here now. Nice office, by the way."

"We try," Sully said. "This is great tea—and I consider myself a connoisseur of sweet tea."

"Being from the bayou and all that," she said.

She had a cute way of wrinkling her nose. Sully hadn't noticed that before.

"I would think you would have to pay attention to the office environment when you're counseling people," she said. "That's why I don't see my own clients at the police station. They would let me, even if it's not case-related, but the atmosphere isn't conducive to interviewing distressed people."

"I didn't think about that," Sully said. "You're talking to people who've just witnessed a crime. I imagine they're pretty upset."

"To say the least." She leveled her eyes at him. "When I have the option, I bring them here."

Sully stopped in midsip. "Am I that transparent?"

"More like translucent." Tess nudged an ice cube with her finger. "It's obvious you aren't trying to locate this woman so you can notify her about a high school reunion. And incidentally, you don't have to tell me why you want to find her. I'm convinced you aren't stalking her. I don't think that's your MO."

Sully set his glass on the small stressed-wood table between them and resituated himself in the chair. "You do a lot of work with the police, right?"

"I actually work with fifteen different agencies, but yes, I do all the forensic art work for LCPD."

"So—if a police detective were trying to find this woman . . ."

"Miss Freckles," Tess said.

"Belinda Cox is actually her name."

Tess put up her hand. "Wait. Now that I know, are you going to have to kill me?"

Sully felt his face relax into a grin. "No. You're safe there."

"I'm sorry, go on."

"What would the next step be?"

Tess gave a short laugh. "Whatever the police would do, it isn't what *you* should do, trust me. But let's see." She brought her knees up and hung her wrists lazily over them. "You said she was going by Zahira?"

"That's what she has printed on her checks, I was told."

"Just Zahira?"

"That's it."

"Sounds like she's trying to create an image."

"Brilliant and shining."

"I'm sorry?"

"*Zahira* means 'brilliant and shining.'"

Tess laughed. "You don't think it fits?"

"How did you know?"

Her laugh was longer and lighter this time. "That being the case, I wouldn't just walk down the street flashing her picture around. But you could try the Chamber of Commerce, the Better Business Bureau . . ."

"You really think she'd be registered there?"

"If she's the kook you seem to think she is, there's more than likely been a complaint against her." Tess shrugged. "You could pretend to file one yourself, and they might tell you she's already been reported."

"I don't know if I could pull that off."

"How badly do you want to find this woman?"

She was watching him again, and Sully did feel transparent.

"I'm not sure I can get on with my life unless I do," he said.

"Then there you go." She floated up from the lounge. "I'll put that photo in a folder for you."

Sully watched *her* this time. She padded softly across the porch and slipped inside and yet left herself lingering in the air. He drained his glass and decided to ask for a refill.

CHAPTER FOURTEEN

Frances Taylor was a strange-looking woman. Her skin was deathly pale, a trait I attributed to the fact that as senior photo editor she never seemed to emerge from the cave they called the photo room. She sat in her office, peering at the computer screen and listening to the police scanner. When she looked up at one of us to make an assignment, her eyes bulged from their sockets in a way that made me wonder if her thyroid was on the fritz. The photo room lights were kept low, which made us all tend to speak in hushed tones the way Frances did, only her voice had the exact consistency of fine-grit sandpaper, and it seldom uttered anything unrelated to photos for the *Sun-Times.*

I was only vaguely aware of any of that as I sat across the desk from her at 7:00 a.m. on Wednesday.

"Don't get me wrong, Ryan," she said, supplementing her words with the constant action of thin, heavily veined hands. "I've wanted you to pursue a major feature for the online paper ever since you got here. I know you'll be amazing with an audio/slide project."

"Then I don't see the problem," I said. "There isn't much going on news-wise right now, so I can start working on it right away."

"It's the subject that concerns me. With illegal immigration such a hellacious mess, a piece about the lives of Hispanic legals in Las Cruces isn't exactly going to be titillating. They're just a fact of life here."

"But I see something teeming beneath the surface."

"Teeming. What? A plot to overthrow the city council?"

"No." I could barely control the urge to roll my eyes. "It's something more primal. I won't know exactly what it is until I get in there and start to shoot."

Frances nodded, but I wasn't seeing agreement in her face. "That's the way you've been used to working, I know that. And I have no doubt you'll find something. But is anybody going to care, that's the question."

"This is what I do—I uncover what isn't obvious to everyone and make them wonder why they didn't see it themselves."

She sighed. "All right—work on it between other assignments for a week, see what you come up with, and then we'll review. Get some audio too. The only way you're going to sell this is with a multimedia approach."

"Fine," I said.

She started to type again before I even stood up.

"Oh, do you know where El Milagro is? I couldn't find it on MapQuest."

Her hands paused. "El Milagro? That's one of the *colonias*, I think. About twenty miles north of here off I-25."

"Thanks."

"Look, Ryan, that whole thing has gotten so much press already, I don't think you're going to uncover anything new."

"We'll see," I said.

And if I didn't, I wasn't sure where else I would go.

Once I got beyond the northern outskirts of Las Cruces, there was nothing but unforgiving desert and my own thoughts.

What did Frances mean by "that whole thing"? I should have stopped to look it up, so I didn't waltz into this place looking like an idiot. But I was pushed for time, and besides, I wasn't looking for what the press had already revealed about El Milagro. Not unless they'd ever done a piece on the Sanchez family.

I hadn't been able to come up with an address for any Sanchez that wasn't right in Las Cruces proper. From the looks of what I was passing, there weren't any addresses to *have* up here. So far all I'd seen were tumbleweeds, a few ill-fated structures someone had tried to build with hay bales, and the occasional windowless junked car—most of them dating back to the fifties and sixties.

I was getting concerned about pulling this off. I had my press pass and my camera and the audio equipment, so just making random pictures wasn't going to stir up that much curiosity, I was sure. But how was I going to explain why I was looking for Señora Sanchez in particular? I could say I was doing a piece about what happened to her son, but I couldn't bring myself to do that, on a number of levels. I was just going to have to pray and wing it.

So far no highway signs were alerting me to anything about El Milagro, and I was getting close to the twenty miles Frances indicated. There appeared to be some kind of community off to the west, so I took the next exit and abruptly found myself on an unpaved road that rose up in a dust cloud around me.

I slowed down to let it settle and crept the Saab toward a cluster of buildings at the top of a small rise. The only indications of life were the sparsely spaced utility poles that spoiled the sky. It didn't seem to me that there were enough of them for the number of dwellings that came into view as I drew closer.

Or maybe there were. When I turned into the first road, oddly named Angel Wing Place, I was convinced nobody could be living in the places I saw.

A disconcerting assortment of houses lined that unpaved street and all the other ones I drove down with my chin dropped to my chest. Some were cinder-block shacks with curled-up tin roofs. Others were boxy manufactured homes, vintage 1960 or '70, whose window frames bled trails of rust down their bleached and battered facades. Most were tattered single-wide trailers, some added on to with scrap wood, all attached by orange extension cords to the power poles.

On the sagging porch of a collection of stones and brick that tried desperately to be a house, a woman sat on a kitchen chair, watching two small children splash in a mud puddle. I glossed over the fact that the desert didn't typically have puddles and tried not to stare at the gaps between the bricks and the complete absence of shingles on the roof. I tried not to stare at all. It was, after all, this woman's home.

I came upon a playground around the corner and pulled up. I didn't realize until then that my mouth had gone dry. As I scanned the yard children were supposed to play in, it felt even more like I was chewing sawdust. The ground was bare except for the clumps of weeds at the bases of the slide and the monkey bars and one of those things that went around in circles until somebody threw up. I wouldn't let a child get within a half mile of that equipment.

Feeling like I was going to suffocate, I got out of the car and leaned on the door. My usual prayer—*God, please give me the story I'm supposed to tell*—nearly screamed in my head.

A smell thick as fog hit me in the face. Raw sewage. I'd know that odor anywhere, and now I knew why the place had seemed so familiar as I drove toward it. This was as bad as any Third World country I had ever been in.

"Can I help you?"

I jumped like I'd been shot.

"Sorry. I didn't mean to scare you."

A small Hispanic man with a graying ponytail tied at the nape of his neck did a full search of me with his eyes.

"I'm Ryan Alexander, with the *Las Cruces Sun-Times*," I said.

I pulled my badge toward him, and he moved in close to examine it. Most people barely gave it a glance. When he stepped back, he nodded.

"We can't be too careful," he said in perfect yet Hispanically clipped English. "Someone without a child in the backseat stops at the playground, we have to check it out."

I nodded too.

"So—can I help you?" he said again.

Can I help you? I wanted to cry out to him. And yet he didn't have the weary, hopeless look someone had the right to wear if he lived here. Any hint of pity from me would have closed every door in my face.

"You have never seen a colonia before," he said.

I tried to smile. "Is that where I am?"

"El Milagro," he said. "The Miracle."

The irony was so clear in his voice I couldn't pretend not to hear it. I probably couldn't pretend anything in front of those sharp eyes.

"I'm sorry," I said. "I've come completely unprepared. I had no idea."

He nodded at the camera. "I'm surprised the newspaper sent you up to take more pictures. By now, I think they would have a whole gallery devoted to our cesspools and our unfit wells and our illegal propane tanks."

"I don't know. I'm new in Las Cruces." There. My worst fear had been realized. I did sound like an idiot. "But that's not what I want."

He just looked at me.

"What I'd like to do is make some pictures of the people who live here. This is a community, right? You aren't just about cesspools and propane tanks."

"Some people think so." He gave me another long look. "We'll see if we can find some people for you."

He held out his arm, gallant as a prince, and I knew I wouldn't be going solo today. When I'd grabbed my bag and fallen into step beside him, I said, "So are you the mayor here or something?"

His laugh was like a grunt. "Mayor? No, we have no mayor. We are an unincorporated settlement. No running water, no solid-waste disposal, no natural gas. So . . ." He shrugged. "No city government."

"So there's no infrastructure here at all?" I said.

"Not here. Not in any of the other thirty-seven colonias in the county."

"There's more of these?" I erased that with my hand. "I'm sorry. I don't mean to put down your home here."

"No. Feel free to put down the living conditions. We didn't create them. We hate them too. Just don't put down the people."

"That's why I'm here. To show who you are."

I didn't know it until it came out of my mouth, but I was sure of it.

He told me his name was Paolo Velasquez, but I could call him Paul. I wanted to call him *Saint* Paul after he squired me around the colonia like a visiting dignitary. Anyone who could not only survive in the squalor I saw, but live there with such compassion, was right up there with Mother Teresa.

His heart seemed to break anew as mine did when I shot the children playing merrily in the watery runoff from an upstream dairy farm. He, too, chewed at his lip when I photographed the old man picking through the ruins of his burned-out, uninsured mobile home, destroyed when dodgy wiring set it on fire.

And Paul gave a sigh identical to mine when we came across two small girls who couldn't have been more than four, curled up together like a pair of left-behind kittens asleep in the back of a car. He said their mother was at work in a nearby pecan orchard and had no child care for them. They were safer in the car than in the house.

There were smiles in some of my shots—the pregnant girl who had just come from the free clinic in Las Cruces with the news that her unborn baby had a heartbeat. Paul said many of them were not so lucky. And the teenage boy who stopped shooting a basketball at the netless hoop on the weedy court and posed like Michael Jordan. I wanted to ask him if he knew Miguel, but my heart wouldn't let me.

In fact, I said nothing about the Sanchez family as I made my pictures and gathered my audio. I felt enough like an intruder.

Paul walked me to my car when I said I thought I had enough for now. His eyes were still kind, but his voice when he said good-bye was firm.

"Don't romanticize us in the newspaper," he said. "We're not noble savages. We're just poor people who believed in *el milagro* and were given chaos by unscrupulous land developers. We don't want anyone to fix it for us. We just want them to show us how."

"May I come back?" I said.

He raised his chin. "Bring the pictures. Then we'll see."

I drove away slowly, determined not to leave him in the dust.

I was late to soccer practice and, having missed the day before completely, I wanted to make it up to Alex somehow. Not that he said anything to me about it. The child seemed to have the resilience of a Slinky. Maybe it was myself I was making it up to. Or maybe I just wanted to give him everything after what I'd seen that day.

I was watching him, alone, when J.P. came down to the bench behind me in the bleachers.

"Are you free at seven tomorrow morning?" she said.

"I start work at seven," I said.

She frowned.

"Why?" I said. "You need help with something?"

She looked a little startled. "No, we just need to have a planning meeting about our trip this weekend."

I had completely forgotten about it, although I wasn't admitting that to her.

"I can squeeze it in," I said. "Where?"

"You know where Milagro is?"

"I'm sorry—what?"

"Milagro. It's a coffee shop on University Avenue. The only one worth going to as far as I'm concerned."

Still reeling, I nodded. "I'll be there," I said.

After practice I asked Dan if I could have Alex for a while. Alex inserted himself between us, brown eyes dancing.

"I want Mexican food," he said. "You could come too, Dad."

Dan ruffled Alex's hair and inspected a speck on his cheek and basically did everything but look at me.

"I need to get home to Jake, buddy," he said. "Ginger has things to do."

Undoubtedly a manicure, a massage, a face-lift. Maybe a trip to the doctor for some Valium. How about a side of strychnine with that, Ginger? I hated it so much that she was spending more time with my sons than I was, I couldn't even think about her without images of homicide. And I was sure those weren't coming from God.

"You guys have fun," Dan was saying to Alex. "I know Mom will have you back in time to do your homework."

Alex parked his ball cap backwards on his head as Dan moved away. "So, can we?"

"Can we what?"

"Can we do Mexican? I'll take you to our fave place."

Whose fave? I wondered. What constituted *our*?

"Whatever you want, pal," I said.

Alex's fave Mexican restaurant was less authentic than the one I'd been in the night before, but the ambience made up for that, and the salsa was measurably milder. The inside of Arriba! was cool and rich with a smooth tile floor and thick furniture with parrots carved into the chair backs. Fans turned overhead, and the Hispanic woman who waited on us had a content way about her. I wondered if she knew how rich she was.

Alex and I ordered fajitas to share, and he munched happily on chips while we waited. He was so engrossed in telling me about this cool trick he and Felipe pulled on the computer teacher—no, seriously, Mom, the teacher thought it was funny too—that I was completely flabbergasted when he abruptly came out with, "So how come you and Dad got divorced?"

I feigned choking on a chip and drank half a glass of water while I tried to find an answer I could give that didn't make his father sound like a deadbeat. When I put the glass down, I was no closer, and Alex was waiting, hands jittering on the tabletop.

"We have different ways of approaching life," I said. "And those two ways just didn't fit together anymore."

"What's your way?" he asked.

"Um—I like to plan and figure out how things can work and then try to help them work that way." How could this possibly be making any sense?

"So Dad's way's the opposite."

"I guess you could say that."

Alex narrowed the big brown eyes as he poked the straw up and down in the Coke I wasn't supposed to buy him after a soccer game. I wanted to let it go if he would, but I couldn't, not and live with myself.

"What?" I said.

"Nothin'—except that's not what Jake said."

"Oh? What did Jake say?"

Alex was suddenly still, and his gaze drifted guiltily to his lap.

"You don't have to tell me if you don't want to," I said.

"Whew." He brightened his face and drew a hand dramatically across his forehead as if he were sloughing off sweat. "I'm not supposed to tell, but I forgot for a minute, so thanks, Mom."

He raised his glass to toast mine and then greeted our arriving food with more enthusiasm than it warranted. He was done with that conversation. I, of course, could think of nothing else until I drove him home.

"Are we late?" he said when we pulled up to Dan's place.

"Maybe a little. Can you still get your homework done?"

"Piece of cake." He looked at me sideways. "But will you go out to the studio and tell Dad I'm here? That way I can *definitely* get it done."

I wanted to settle the thing right there, tell him his father and I were not getting back together no matter how many times he shoved us in that direction. But his eyes were so hopeful. And he did throw his arms around my neck and tell me I was the best. I needed to ride on that for a while.

It wasn't quite dark as I picked my way through the sculpture park to Dan's studio. The metal musicians were turning to velvet silhouettes, their instruments catching the last orange glint of the sun. New Mexico quiet settled over them, so still that I wasn't sure Dan was actually out there.

But I found him standing at the base of his swirling sculpture, working at a small space on its metal finish with a square of sandpaper. As gently as he smoothed it, he could have been rubbing powder on a baby's bottom. A faint image of him changing Jake's diaper, his own face freckled with powder, passed through my mind.

"Excuse me?" I whispered.

He kept sanding. "I saw you. What's up?"

"Alex wanted me to tell you he's back. Said it would give him more time to finish his homework if I did it."

A smile twitched around Dan's eyes. "Uh-huh."

"You know he's playing Cupid with us," I said.

"All kids think their divorced parents are going to get back together. It'll pass."

"He asked me tonight why we split up."

The sanding slowed. "What did you tell him?"

"Whatever it was, it isn't what Jake told him. Do you know anything about that?"

Dan pulled the paper back, inspected the metal, blew on it. "My guess is that Jake gave him some version of what I told him."

"Which was?"

"That things change."

"That's it?"

"That's what I told him then, and he seemed satisfied with that. He hasn't asked me lately."

"Would you give him a different answer now?"

I wasn't sure why I asked it. Maybe because I wasn't ready to scream at him—or throw the discarded chunk of aluminum that was next to my foot.

Dan wasn't going to answer anyway. He went back to sanding in small, even circles, and I turned to go.

"I might," he said. "I've given myself a different answer." He stepped away from the sculpture and looked up at it. "What do you think of it?"

"What do *I* think of it?" I said.

"Do you still think I'm fooling around with artistic monstrosities in a world that needs hard work to change it?"

I was stunned by the words I'd hurled at him in the last fight we'd had before I asked for a divorce. The last fight *I* had had, while Dan stood with his arms crossed over his chest, X-ing me out.

"Why are you asking me that now?" I said. "What difference does it make?"

"I'm answering your question." He turned to me. "I took all the anger you heaped on me about my work because I wanted to keep the peace. I thought that was honoring God." His gaze traveled up the sculpture and held there. "Since you left, I've learned that God doesn't want peacekeepers. He wants peace*makers*. And sometimes you have to disturb the peace to make real peace." Dan shrugged and refolded the square of sandpaper. "That's a huge change for me. If Jake asked me now, I would say I can't be married to his mother because I won't keep the peace with her anymore. And I'm not sure she and I know how to make it."

I stared at him for a long moment, even after he returned to the twisting tower and resumed the steady, abrasive work of smoothing just one tiny corner. I don't know how long I would have remained there without anger and without answers if a shadow hadn't fallen across the doorway.

"Dad," said an adolescent voice that squeaked at the end. "I need to talk to you."

Dan's entire demeanor changed. He tossed the sandpaper aside and wiped his hands on his muslin smock and smiled at Jake as he stepped into a shaft of light.

"Sure, buddy," he said. "What's up?"

I didn't move. I couldn't have gone far anyway, with Jake between me and the doorway. He didn't seem to see me—there was no stiffening as he moved closer to Dan and stood with his back to me, arms dangling awkwardly at his sides. It struck me once again how small he was. And how uncertain.

"Ian's got a meet Saturday, and I want to go," he said.

"Where is it?"

"At the school."

I held my breath. If Dan let him do that, so help me . . .

"You know you can't, Jake." Dan's tone was apologetic. "That's against the rules the judge set. You're not allowed on school property."

"It's not during school."

"Doesn't matter."

"But I wanna see Ian compete. This is a big deal. He's been there for me, y'know?"

My heart ached. This was the most I'd heard Jake talk in weeks. He sounded like a normal teenager, making a case for something a normal teenager should be allowed to do. It was the abnormal that squeezed at my chest.

"I hate this," Jake said. "It's like you have to be some jailer. Dude, I'm not gonna do anything at that stupid school."

"I know that." Dan put his foot on a gas can and leaned on his knee with his forearms. "Look, I believe in you, Jake. But the court says I have to treat you like I can't. I hate it, too, but we just have to deal with that until this thing is over."

"So—I can't go."

"No, son. You can't."

Jake jerked around and stalked out of the studio without ever seeing me. Dan watched him go, his mouth drawn into a concerned line, his eyes resolute.

It was a Dan I'd never seen.

"I think I'd better go after him," he said. "Can you see yourself out?"

I nodded, but I couldn't leave. The sunset was casting its last pink light through the studio windows and turning the detritus on the floor to fairy dust. It was as magical as what I'd just witnessed—Dan defusing what could have been a volatile disaster, and would have been in *my* hands. Just as any piece of metal in the room would be if I tried to make art with it.

I stepped to the winding sculpture and rested my hand on its coolness. I'd stopped going into Dan's studio the last six months of our marriage. Back when I thought Dan needed a real job and a cause if he was going to make a difference in the world the way I did. Back when I thought I couldn't love him anymore.

I let my hand fall from the metal. Too much mystical New Mexico light. Too much clean air that hid nothing. Too much exposure to things that broke my heart.

Pushing back an unfamiliar wall of sadness, I hurried out of the studio and across the park to my car. I was just pulling out of the driveway when my cell phone rang. I didn't recognize the number, but I answered it anyway, just to get away from the despair pressing on me.

"This is Ryan Coe," I said.

"I know it is," said a shrill voice. "We have to talk."

"Who is this?"

"It's Ginger Tassert," she said, as if I should have recognized her at the first syllable.

"I don't know what we have to say to each other," I said, though I did pull off to the side of Dan's dirt road in case she came up with something.

"No, *I* have things to say to *you.* Meet me tomorrow on the patio at the Milagro Coffee House at one thirty."

"Uh, some of us work for a living."

She'd already hung up. I stared at the phone and recalled the image of Dan watching our son with wisdom in his eyes. It didn't match the memory of Ginger pitching a rubber hose into the sculpture garden. I couldn't get them to mesh.

But it didn't matter. It was too late for any other image.

Way too late.

CHAPTER FIFTEEN

The air had a fallish nip the next morning at seven thirty when I pulled up to the Milagro Coffee House—the only place in Las Cruces anybody wanted to go to, apparently. I'd always loved Midwestern autumns, but New Mexico was different, with only the gold of the occasional aspen and the burnt red of the ubiquitous chile peppers to break up the monotonous brown. I hugged my tweedy jacket around me as I hurried across the parking lot.

Victoria and J.P. were already at a heavy wooden table in the middle of the café, Victoria looking sleepy-eyed but otherwise no more dazed than usual. J.P. appeared to be on her second sixteen-ounce cup of caffeine. Either that or she was the ultimate morning person. For once her hair was scooped tidily into its ponytail, and she wore fresh lipstick that hadn't even bled onto the rim of her cup. It probably wouldn't dare.

I waved to them and joined Poco at the counter, where she almost had to stand on her tiptoes to be seen over it.

"I'll have a café mocha vodka Valium latte, please," she said to the bespectacled twentysomething male at the register.

He didn't even blink. "Rough morning?"

"I think I have too many children, Ben," she said.

"You only have two, Poco. That'll be $3.99."

Poco smiled her enigmatic smile at me as she pulled out a five and slid it across the counter.

"And for you?" the guy named Ben said to me.

"I'll have what she's having," I said.

"It's a decaf, sugar-free, nonfat café mocha."

I looked at Poco. "That's dessert, for Pete's sake. No—I need a black coffee, extra hot."

"There's your trouble, Poco," Ben said. "You start drinking it like she does, and you'll have those kids whipped into shape in no time."

Poco took her change and shook her head, as always setting her bangs into a small frenzy.

"$2.95 for you," Ben said to me.

I handed him my debit card and studied Poco, who simply stood smiling beside me. It struck me that I knew little about her. About any of them. Far less than they knew about me, unfortunately.

Poco and I took our cups to the table, where J.P. was waiting with legal pad and pen. She'd already made four columns on it, with one of our names at the top of each. I could already feel my neck hairs bristling. Was I about to get an *assignment* from her?

"I assume everybody is still in for tomorrow night," she said before my buns even touched the seat.

Poco and Victoria nodded. I sipped. My jury was still out until I heard the whole plan.

"We need to leave my place no later than five. Sunset is at six thirty, so that should give us plenty of time."

"Everybody go potty before we leave," Poco said. "J.P. doesn't make bathroom stops."

"It's only a one-hour trip," J.P. said.

She looked at each of us as if to make sure nobody was going to dispute that. I just kept sipping. They did make good coffee there at Milagro. At least that part wouldn't be a bust.

"We'll do the sunset/moonrise thing in the park," she went on briskly. "You'll enjoy it."

Or else.

"Then we'll sign in at the camping check-in."

"Did you reserve a campsite?" Poco asked.

J.P. shook her head. Tendrils were already making their escape from her ponytail and hanging fretfully on either side of her face.

"It's first come, first serve," she said. "But this isn't their busy time of year."

I wondered if they *had* a busy time of year. It still mystified me that people traveled for miles to see that endless expanse of nothing but white sand. It actually still somewhat mystified me that I'd agreed to this trip myself.

I looked up from draining my coffee cup to see J.P. surveying me over the top of her glasses.

"You know we have to backpack in, right?" she said.

"You mentioned that," I said.

"We have to carry everything we're going to need."

"You mentioned that too."

"Including water."

I scratched a nonexistent itch on the side of my face. "When are we going to get to the part I don't know? I have to be somewhere at nine."

"I just wanted to make sure you understood that this is not a glamour gig, in case you want to change your mind."

Now I remembered why I'd agreed to this. No way was I walking away from the dare in her eyes.

J.P. broke the stare first and wrote something in Victoria's column. "I'm putting you down for that picnic set you have with the plastic plates and mugs."

"If there's no water, why don't we use paper?" I said.

"Because we care about the environment." She tossed me a glance that excluded me from the *we.* "We'll wash our dishes with sand."

"You're going to show us how to do that, right?" Poco gave her signature nervous laugh.

J.P. jotted in Poco's column. "You can bring hand sanitizer and toilet paper."

Victoria pulled her nose up from her coffee mug. "They have toilets?"

"No," J.P. said.

Victoria blinked behind her round glasses and went back to the cup.

J.P. continued to dole out the duties—including food preparation —until she came to me. She poised the pen over my column.

"Well?" I said.

"I don't know what you can do." Her shrug clearly indicated that she didn't think I could do much of anything that mattered. She put down the pen and bobbed a tea bag up and down in her cup. All this edge, and she was drinking Earl Grey?

A silence fell, awkward as an adolescent. "Ryan could be our official photographer for the trip," Poco said into it, voice straining toward chipper.

"We have yet to see the ones she took of the Alamogordo game," J.P. said.

"*She* doesn't appreciate being talked about in the third person when *she* is sitting right in the room," I said. "But *I* have your pictures right here if you want to see them."

I pulled out my laptop, turned it on, and pulled up the photos. The screen filled with the El Milagro woman sitting on her sagging front porch with her splashing children in the foreground.

Victoria shook her hair away from her face and craned her neck to see. "Whose mother is that?"

"Sorry," I said. "I took these yesterday for an assignment. Let me find—"

"What's the assignment?" Poco said.

It was another valiant attempt to make me look good for J.P., which I had no desire to do. Still, Poco was the most decent one in the group, and I didn't want to be snitty with her. "It's on the lives of the people up at El Milagro," I said, still clicking forward and coming up with nothing but the faces that had smiled so bravely for me.

"I don't get it," J.P. said.

Now, *her* I could be snitty to all day and it wouldn't bother me a bit.

"Doesn't matter," I said. "Let me just find those soccer shots."

"Wait." Poco put her hand on my arm and pointed to the picture on the screen, of a woman who had come by to check on the little girls sleeping in the back of a car. "I know her. That's—" She stopped. Her top teeth clamped on her lower lip.

"She looks familiar to me too," J.P. said.

As she slanted forward for a better look, Poco gave a starched laugh. "You know what they say. All us Hispanics look alike." She squeezed my arm again, in much the same way she was squeezing out her words. "You need to watch your time—we should let you get to the soccer pictures."

I did a double take. She shook her head at me so slightly her bangs didn't move.

"Okay," I said.

I set up a quick slide show and sat back while the three of them bent their heads over my laptop. There is something about viewing photos of people you adore that evens out the playing field. Even J.P. made motherly noises and nudged Victoria over the midkick shot of Bryan with his blond hair flying about his face. The nut never falls far from the tree.

Poco insisted that I give them a second showing, slower this time, and J.P. wrote the numbers on a clean sheet of the pad so they could place orders with me.

"How much will you charge per print?" she asked. She produced a calculator from her purse.

"I won't charge anything," I said. "Just tell me what you want and what size and I'll print them at home."

"Yes, but we'll want them on photo paper. That's expensive."

"I have plenty." I patted the pad with my hand and gave her my best squint. "It's what I do."

I left right after they all placed their orders and J.P. wrote out another copy, for her records. I got the feeling if I didn't come through, she wanted evidence for a civil suit.

Halfway to my car, Poco caught up with me and tugged at the strap on my computer bag.

"I hope you didn't think I was being rude in there," she said.

I laughed out loud. "You would have to take some serious lessons to come close to rude."

"I know a lot of those people in the pictures you were showing us from the colonia."

I stopped at the driver's door to my Saab and leaned against it. She was talking fast and glancing back toward the café.

"I don't talk about my volunteer work in front of J.P.," she said. "She's always asking me to help out at the church, and I tell her I don't have time, which I don't because I'm doing other things, but she thinks stuffing envelopes for the capital funds campaign should take priority, and I think I'm more useful elsewhere. I'm not going to win that argument with her, you know what I mean?"

Before I could even formulate an answer, she shook her head, and this time the bangs did fly. "No, you don't know what I mean because you aren't afraid of what anybody thinks. I wish I could be more like that."

I shifted my bag to my other shoulder. Hopefully there was a point to all this.

"Anyway—two days a week I volunteer at the CDC."

"Which is?"

"The Colonias Development Council. It's a nonprofit. They do, well, everything to try to get environmental justice, farmworker rights—it's huge. But what I wanted to tell you is that I know the woman in that one picture—the last one you showed us."

"By the car?" I said. "With the two little girls?"

"Yeah." Poco took a step closer to me. "That's Elena Sanchez."

I formed the name soundlessly with my lips.

Poco nodded. "Miguel's mother. I've known her for a long time."

I felt the strap to my bag slide down my arm, and I almost let it dump to the ground. Poco and I grabbed for it at the same time, and in the process our foreheads nearly touched.

She didn't move away when she said, "She's upset and confused. She doesn't know why someone would do this to her boy. But—"

"Not just someone," I said. "She thinks it was my son—just like everyone else does." I pressed my thumbs against my temples. "And there I was taking her picture."

"Isn't that why you're up there?" Poco said.

"Excuse me?"

"I don't know how these things work, but why did you pick that story unless you wanted to know about Miguel's family?"

I could only stare at her, mouth hanging open, so that I not only sounded like a lunatic, I probably looked like one as well.

She gave a tiny shrug. "If I were in your situation, I would want to know who they were, what they were like." She squeezed my arm a final time. "If I can do anything to help, say the word. But just so you know, I won't say anything to anyone else about it."

I mouthed a thank-you and watched her start to walk away. But I couldn't let her go. "Poco," I said.

She turned without missing a beat, as if she'd known I'd call her back.

"Elena Sanchez," I said. "How is she holding up?"

"She's strong."

"What about Miguel?"

Poco came back toward me. "He's still in a coma. The longer that goes on, the less likely it is he'll make a full recovery. But they're praying for a miracle. They haven't lost hope." She pressed her palms together as if she herself were praying. "You shouldn't lose hope either, Ryan."

I nodded. Not because I had any hope. Because I didn't trust myself to speak.

Poco took a few steps backward. Just as she swung around to go, she added, "She works in the coffee shop at the Ocotillo Bookstore on the mall at lunchtime. It's in the back."

Sully set the phone down and put a check mark next to the last item on his list: Call Better Business Bureau and lodge a complaint against Zahira.

"What is the nature of the complaint?" the woman had said in brisk formalese.

"Bad psychology," Sully told her.

"Pardon me?"

"She's a bad psychologist," Sully said. He'd already had his finger on the End Call button by that time. He was pretty sure she did too.

"I think you want the PCMFT board for that. Let me give you their number . . ."

"She doesn't have a license with them."

"They can handle that for you too."

She'd rattled off the number and hung up, leaving Sully licking a bad taste out of his mouth. He reached for his cell phone and dialed Porphyria's number. It was the only way he could think of at the moment to get rid of it.

The voice that answered was faint, almost fragile. Sully hesitated and was about to apologize for a wrong number.

"Are you waiting for me to start this conversation, Dr. Crisp?" the voice said.

It was stronger now, and Sully grinned into the phone.

"It didn't sound like you, Dr. Ghent," he said.

"Who did it sound like?"

Actually, it still sounded like a weaker version of the voice he depended on to shoot sense into his craziness. The verve was still at the center, but the edges were frayed.

"It sounded like somebody who isn't feeling up to par," Sully said. "What's going on?"

There was no queenly comeback. Sully felt his grin fade. "Porphyria?" he said.

"I'm here. I'm just trying to decide how to put this so you won't think you have to get on the next plane and come on back here."

"Don't decide," Sully said. "Just say it."

"We're discussing the possibility of replacing the old pacemaker with a new one."

"What's to discuss? If it needs to be done, let's do it." Sully clicked back onto the Internet. "I can get a flight out tonight."

"And you would do that for what reason, Sully? This is not major surgery."

He heard the rich chuckle.

"And I am not a delicate patient. I'll come through it just fine. You are not the only doctor who knows anything."

Sully wasn't buying the jocularity. Porphyria never forced anything, but there was something lurking behind the laughter, and she wasn't about to tell him what it was. He got up and paced behind the desk. "You're going to keep me posted every step of the way, right? And if you can't, then Winnie will."

"Mm-hmm. Just like you're telling me everything."

Even without her old-soul eyes looking into him, Sully felt himself color up. "Do you have my phone tapped?" he said.

"No, just your mind. Where are you with Belinda Cox?"

It was a clear ploy to change the subject, but Sully followed her anyway. To do anything else was futile. And it was, after all, why he'd called.

"I'm at a dead end at the moment. Maybe I'll give it a rest for a while."

"Don't you use me as an excuse to walk away from what you know you've got to do, Sully. I'll be here when you're done. Don't you worry about that."

There was no point in arguing with her. If he showed up at her hospital room tonight, she'd order him out before he got in the door. Besides, she was right. As always.

"I'll tell you what I do want from you," she said.

"Anything," Sully said.

"I want you to find that woman, and I want you to have a come-to-Jesus with her until she is on her knees, and then I want you to call me and give me every delicious detail. That's what I want you to do."

"Done," Sully said.

Only he knew as he hung up that the account he gave Porphyria wasn't going to happen over the phone. He was going to deliver it in person, the minute he was finished with Belinda Cox. If he ever found her.

He knew it was finality that lurked behind Porphyria's laughter, and it frightened him to the core.

CHAPTER SIXTEEN

The Ocotillo Coffee Shop was definitely not the upscale Milagro. It was a mishmash of local art on alternating red and purple cinder-block walls, and boxes of teas on top of a Pepsi cooler, and a female customer yelling at her eight-year-old daughter that she was not going to let her read vampire books so she might as well put them back. I saw it all with my photographer eyes, but my mother eyes were on the woman behind the counter.

Elena Sanchez looked different to me than she had the day before when I'd shot her picture. The harsh fluorescent light from the fixture overhead showed the skin beneath her eyes to be dark and sunken, and exposed a finely sharpened vertical line just above and between her eyebrows. She wasn't smiling for the world today or exchanging trills off her tongue with Paul.

Today she wiped the counter as if she were polishing a Chippendale table, hands moving in an almost hypnotic rhythm. Unless I missed my guess, she was merely trying to keep going, pretending if she did all the right things everything would work out. But the image in my head was of her lying awake at night, unable to sleep until she knew how her son's story would end. Just like me.

I set the equipment bag on a table close to the counter. She looked up and gave me a smile, on cue, yet not without warmth. Her face had perfect, square symmetry, and her skin was a flawless caramel.

"What I can get for you?" she said. Her English was blocky and accented and sounded correct even though it wasn't.

"Black coffee," I said.

"You will like something to eat?"

I looked down through the glass countertop at a display of oversized muffins juxtaposed with seeping breakfast burritos and sugary sopaipillas. It all blurred into the background when I saw the can on the counter above them.

It may have once contained pineapple juice. Now it had a slot in its top and a photocopied photo wrapped around it. A handsome, wide-faced Hispanic teenager in a soccer uniform smiled his mother's smile. *Miguel Sanchez is in a coma,* said the sign taped to the counter. *Your donations for his medical bills are appreciated.*

"Anything look good for you?"

My head jerked up, and I found myself meeting Elena's eyes. The hospitable glow faded from them, and for an awful moment I was sure she knew who I was. But she only nodded at the can.

"Do you think maybe that make the people too sad when they come for the coffee?" she said.

I had no idea how to answer.

"It has make *you* sad." She reached over as if she was going to remove it, but I put my hand on top of it.

"It's all right," I said. "I'll just have the French roast."

She gave the can one more doubtful look and turned to the pyramid of mismatched mugs on a tray behind her.

"Personally, I think people *should* be sad about it."

I looked up at another Hispanic woman with a long braid, wearing black sweats with a flowered scarf thrown around her shoulders like an afterthought. She pushed two dollar bills and her mug across the glass. "I'll have a refill, Elena, when you have a chance."

Elena nodded with her back still to us.

"That's her boy," the woman said to me. "Sweetest thing you've ever met. Some bully ran him down like an animal in an alley."

"I know," I said.

My voice was sharp, but she didn't recoil.

"Are you doing a story on it?" she said.

I followed her gaze to my chest and saw she was staring at the press pass dangling on its lanyard.

"I might be." I glanced warily at Elena, who was coming our way with two steaming mugs and a quiet smile. Uneasiness niggled at the edges of my plan.

"I'd certainly be willing to talk to you," the woman said, "and I won't be as modest as Elena." She took her mug with one hand and squeezed Elena's arm with the other. "You doing okay?"

"Much better today. I think Miguel is better too." The smile grew real. "When I kiss him good night last night, I see the moving under his eyelids. He never did that before."

I turned to the table and unzipped my bag and fumbled around in it, anything to keep from looking at the fragile hope that shone like tears in Elena Sanchez's eyes.

"Let's talk over here," said the woman with the scarf.

I hadn't offered to interview her, but I followed her to the corner with my bag and set up the recorder while she retrieved her glasses from the turquoise beaded chain that tethered them around her neck. She nodded at the microphone I'd propped on the table.

"Are we ready?" she said.

In spite of the aging quiver in her voice, she had a purposeful way about her, like her sole mission was to inform me about Miguel Sanchez. This was what I'd come for, but the coffee in my stomach felt like it was being stirred with a stick.

"I'm glad there's going to be some press about this," the woman said. "Just to set the record straight."

"Is there a record?"

She sniffed. "People assume because the boy's Hispanic he must be an illegal immigrant. Or at least he's dealing drugs or is involved in some other kind of trouble that got him exactly what he deserved."

"You're saying he wasn't."

Two wiry hands sliced the air. "Miguel was a straight-A student. He was about to be inducted into the National Honor Society, one of only two Hispanics this semester, and the only one ever from his colonia. He was a debater, and you see that he played soccer."

She pointed toward the can on the counter.

"He was just selected to play on a prestigious team. They don't let gang members do that. Nor do they let them compete in forensics, which takes self-control and intellect and a sense of justice."

She raised what little chin she had, and I was once again compelled to show my agreement, but she was not painting the picture of Miguel Sanchez I wanted to see.

"So why do you think this happened to him?" I asked.

"I have absolutely no idea. I will tell you this, though." She leaned toward me, pressing her fallen bosom against the edge of the table. "If the white boy who did this does not do hard time for it, those precious people up there in El Milagro won't riot in the streets. But I personally will not let it go. This won't die until justice is done—we'll see to that."

"And who is *we*?" I was surprised I could speak around the mass in my throat.

She adjusted the scarf, leaving it in no better position than it had been in to start with. "My husband and I have something of a following in this town. He is a major blogger, among other things. We'll make the necessary noise." She looked again at the recorder. "I'm not looking for free publicity by talking to you—we don't need it."

"I won't use your name," I said. "But I do need to know what it is."

"Cecilia Benitez. My husband is Bob Benitez."

I was evidently supposed to know who that was.

"We're major supporters of the CDC," she said. "ACLU, HRI . . . Bob is a leading immigration and naturalization attorney in Las Cruces. And, as I said, he writes a widely read blog."

When I still didn't give her the response she seemed to expect, she studied my press pass as if to determine whether I was only impersonating a reporter.

"You'll have to excuse me," I said. "I'm relatively new in town."

"Oh, then there you are." She cleared the air with her hands.

"We work closely with both illegal immigrants seeking a better life and legals and U.S. citizens whose rights are being tromped on. We're trying to help Elena through this. She's working two jobs to pay Miguel's medical bills because she doesn't have insurance. She used to work three, but she had to give up her job at the restaurant to spend time with Miguel."

She glanced toward the counter, where Elena was helping a large-bellied man choose a muffin.

"I don't think Miguel knows whether she's there or not," she said, voice lowered. "They say it's important to talk to coma patients, just in case they do have some awareness, so we always have someone in his room talking to him during visiting hours. Quite frankly, I think that's more for her than for him."

Her voice faded, and I turned off the recorder. She was an enigma, this Cecilia Benitez. Ready to storm the courthouse one minute, unwilling to deprive Elena Sanchez of her hope the next.

"If you want to take some pictures of her now," Cecilia said, "you'll catch the real thing. This is the way she is all the time." She gave Elena one more long, admiring look before she picked up a drawstring bag.

There was one thing I needed to know before she left. "Is she angry?" I whispered.

"You'd think she would be. I'd be screaming for justice to anyone who would listen if that had happened to my son. Wouldn't you?"

I couldn't give her an answer. Fortunately, she didn't seem to need one.

I put out a hand to shake hers in a thank-you, but she was already headed away from me, toward the counter.

"This lady wants to talk to you about Miguel, Elena," Cecilia said. "She's a reporter, but I think you can trust her."

The same fear I felt in my eyes glimmered in Elena's.

"It's all right." Cecilia patted Elena's brown hand. "This is a chance for justice for your son."

Elena came out from behind the counter and inched onto the

chair Cecilia had just vacated at my table. She blinked at the recorder. I turned it off.

"You don't have to talk to me if you don't want to," I said. I could hear Frances in my head, demanding to know if I'd lost my mind. No—I just knew I might not be able to handle what this lady had to say.

While she continued to look warily at the recorder, I thanked myself silently for using my maiden name on my press pass, just in case she'd been told who Jake was. I felt like an extortionist again, lying to get information out of a woman who had already had enough removed from her.

"What you want to know about Miguel?" she said.

That he's a violent, drug-running gang member who provoked—somebody—into backing over him with a truck. That was what I wanted her to tell me. But if I asked her about her boy, I was going to hear again what a model junior citizen he was, and I was going to feel like my own son was the coldhearted gangbanger.

"I'd like to know about you, actually," I blurted out.

She smiled fleetingly and looked down at her lap. "There is nothing to know about me."

"I understand you're working hard . . . being brave . . ." Ugh. Could this sound any more like a low-budget talk show?

The smile was gone, and her face firmed. "I have faith God will take care of Miguel."

"Is that what holds you together, God and hard work?"

The vertical line between her brows deepened. "I don't understand 'holds you together.'"

"Why aren't you angry? Something horrible has happened, and you just go on."

Her eyes widened within the soft folds of her eyelids. I put my hand to my mouth and pretended to merely wipe my lips. I'd spoken more vehemently than I'd intended. The big-bellied man looked up from his muffin two tables over.

"You need more coffee, Laurence?" Elena said to him.

He waved her off, but I felt his eyes continue to keep surveillance after Elena turned back to me. They certainly watched over Señora Sanchez in this part of town.

"This is a bad thing that has happen," she said. "But why will I be angry when it is already done? What is the good from that?"

"Can you *choose* not to be angry?"

"I just do not feel it here." She passed her hand across her chest and left it there to rest. "But *you* are angry, yes? For my Miguel?"

Before I could answer, she curled her fingers around my wrist. Her touch was warm, and it surprised me with its strength.

"It has happen to you," she said.

"Excuse me?"

"Some pain for your child. It has happen to you. Yes?"

I was forced to nod.

"You want to know these things for *you*. So ask your question."

I couldn't, not with those eyes coming close to what I was about. And yet, what *was* I about? I was a mother, desperate to believe her son wasn't capable of a travesty. I didn't think I could do desperate until I found out who Elena Sanchez's son was. Now I could do nothing else.

"Why, señora?" I said. "Why do you think someone would do this to a boy who is so good, who everyone seems to love?"

"Hate."

She said it without a thought, and without rancor. Only the sharp line between her brows signaled something deeper than resignation.

"The hate is all around," she said. "When I was young, my cousin was kill in Los Angeles because it was Tuesday."

"I'm sorry?"

"Or because he wore the wrong hat. We don't know. But I learn about hate then."

"But you aren't hateful."

"No, no. My family, we came here to come away from the hate—and still we find it—but we will not live *in* hate. You see that?"

I nodded.

"That boy who run the truck over Miguel—he hate him for something we can never know, perhaps."

"You don't want to find out?"

"Will that wake Miguel from his sleep? I do not need to know. But you do, yes?"

I tapped the press pass. "I'm a journalist."

Slowly Elena shook her head and circled a finger toward the recorder. "Then why do you not use your machine?"

"Elena–*que pasa*!"

I didn't look to see who had breezed into the shop. As Elena turned to him, I gathered the recorder and stuffed it into the bag with the camera. When she bustled behind the counter, I waved to her from the entryway.

"Thank you," I managed to say.

"Vaya con Dios, Grafa," she said. "You will come back."

It wasn't a question. But I knew the answer.

By the grace of God and the authority of Frances, I got two assignments back-to-back after I left the Ocotillo Coffee Shop. They kept me from torturing myself with what I'd learned there. But neither grace nor authority got me out of my meeting with Ginger. By one thirty I had the photos for both stories e-mailed in, and I didn't have a meeting with Frances until three.

I was still tempted to skip the Ginger thing, tell her I had to take emergency pictures somewhere. But I'd done enough lying for one day, albeit by omission, and like Jake, I'd never been good even at that kind. I considered having Alex tell her, and then punished myself for even thinking of that by showing up at the Milagro—again—at one thirty sharp.

Ginger's red Mustang wasn't in the parking lot, and as I crossed to the shop, I didn't see her on the patio where she'd said to meet her, so I went inside and ordered a panini, though I bypassed the coffee. I had enough caffeine in me to push a semi. When I came out, Ginger was at a table, sending a text message. She snapped the phone shut when she saw me and looked pointedly at her watch. I didn't dignify that with a response.

"I'm going to get straight to the point," she said, and then didn't. She pushed her sunglasses to the top of her head and tucked the cell phone back into her Coach bag and adjusted a gold hoop earring that could have doubled as a bracelet, all the while flashing so much bling on her fingers I was surprised she could operate them at all.

She finally seemed about to tell me what the point *was* when my lunch arrived, carried by the sizzling-blue-eyed barista who'd just taken my order. He didn't have morning barista Ben's dry wit, but he made up for it with well-cut biceps his T-shirt couldn't hide. They evidently weren't lost on Ginger, because she beamed up at him and said, "I'd love a cappuccino."

So far I hadn't seen anyone at Milagro order from the table, but Blue Eyes said, "I'll get that started for you," and hurried off. He never once took those blues from her generous cleavage.

The moment he was inside, Ginger drew a bead on me. "There's no other way to say this. I know what you're doing."

"There'd better be another way to say it, Ginger," I said, "because I don't know what you're talking about."

"I'm talking about Danny. Evidently you didn't take the hint from me the other night."

"You gave me a hint? All I saw you do was throw a garden hose."

She crossed her legs and yanked her pencil skirt toward her knees. It didn't move much, but I took it as some kind of end punctuation.

"Sorry," I said. "I'm still clueless. What is it I'm supposedly doing that involves Dan, besides discussing our sons with him?"

"That's just it. What is it you have to discuss for an hour every time you come over, which is every day? I know you're not trying to get child support out of him—hello!—*he* has the kids."

I could taste the first of the anger, bitter in my mouth. I took a sip from the water Blue Eyes had brought me with my still-untouched sandwich and forced myself not to spit it at her.

"Well?" she said.

"Look, whatever my children's father and I have to talk about has nothing to do with you."

"It does when you're doing it to try to get him back. Before, I thought you were just trying to upset him, but now I know what you're up to."

I stared at her.

"Don't play dumb with me." She shook her head, spilling the curls into her face so that she had to toss them back. The sunglasses remained intact. "He's a different man now, isn't he, since you left him?"

She had me there, but I didn't answer.

"I've watched you, and I know you've seen it. Well, let me tell you something. There are two reasons for the change in Danny." She held up two crimson talons. "One is me, and the other is you."

"Me."

"He started to change the minute you did him a favor and left him. And *I* finished the transformation. Not only have I helped him create a beautiful home and been there for his boys, but I've brought my son into the mix, and he has been like a big brother to Jake. His grades have improved—" She put up her hand, as if I'd tried to stop the rant. "Beyond all of that, I have shown Danny that he is an attractive, sexy, desirable man, every minute of every day."

She sat back, eyes smoldering. My own anger was giving way to sour amusement. I had never seen such an act.

And she wasn't done.

"*Our* relationship has passion, Ryan," she said. "Passion and romance, two things I know you never gave him, because he eats them up like he's been starving for years."

"Cappuccino." Blue Eyes had appeared soundlessly and put

Ginger's frothy mug and the check on the table. "You can just pay when you leave."

Between the come-hither smile she gave him and the passion-and-romance speech he probably overheard, I was surprised he didn't give it to her on the house. She didn't even wait for him to be out of earshot this time.

"What Danny and I have is deep and real," she told me savagely. "So don't even think you're going to come in and destroy it."

So much for amusement. I had the insane urge to stick my finger in her cup and flip foam across her plunging neckline. "If it's so deep and real," I said, "why this little scene? You obviously have nothing to fear from me."

"Fear?" Her voice squealed in a way I knew she hadn't planned on. "I'm not afraid, Ryan. I'm just trying to keep you from making a complete fool of yourself."

"Because you care so much about me." I shook my head. "Try again."

"All right, fine. I just don't want our household upset by you trying to take away—"

"'Our' household? Are you living there now?"

"No. Not yet."

This was crazy. Why was I even giving her the satisfaction of ticking me off? I moved to the edge of the chair.

"Look, whatever you and 'Danny' want to do is none of my business."

"That is a true statement."

"I'm not there to try to break up your romance. I'm there to be with my sons. Period."

She scooped up her purse and replanted the sunglasses on her nose. "I'm glad we're clear, then. But if I see any evidence to the contrary, we will have this conversation again. And I will not be so nice next time."

"Oh, were you nice this time?" I said. "I must have missed that."

She flounced off, giving me the last word. But as I breathed slowly into the perfumed space she left behind, I didn't feel triumphant. I felt strangely sad. For Dan. Because he was mixed up with a woman who thrived on drama and staged romance and would get it from the nearest barista if she couldn't get it from him. For all his faults, I didn't think he deserved that. I felt no deep satisfaction.

Besides—she'd left me with her check.

CHAPTER SEVENTEEN

I glanced at my watch while Frances was looking at the photos on my laptop. She'd arrived late for our meeting. It was now almost four thirty, and I was supposed to meet the soccer moms at five.

Not that I wouldn't enjoy getting J.P.'s hackles up, but that would break Poco out in hives, and I couldn't do that to her. I'd felt smaller and meaner and dirtier as the last two days had gone on, and I needed to see myself as something besides a lying, calculating woman who had failed at motherhood and left her husband to be preyed on by a psychiatric case in stilettos.

"All right," Frances said. "Talk to me."

I blinked at her.

"About your story, Ryan."

Make that a lying, calculating failure with an attention deficit disorder.

I shook myself back to the array on the screen. "I'm just getting started. I was only up there yesterday, and then again today."

"Let's see." Light flickered on her pale face as she clicked each one into view.

"This man has hepatitis A from the total lack of sanitation," I said, "but if he doesn't go to work, he misses a payment on his land and the lender will seize the property and the fifteen years of payments will be totally nullified—that's the scam they all fell for. This is the cemetery—it's hard to tell which looks more dead, that or the streets where people are still alive."

"As I said before, you're going to need audio to sell this. Do you have any for me to listen to?"

I shook my head, probably too sharply. "I got some, but I haven't edited it yet."

"I'd like to hear the raw material," Frances said. "That's what these meetings are for. Not that you don't know what you're doing. You're a lot more experienced than—"

"It isn't that. I just need to get more, that's all."

Frances frowned as she pulled up the whole array again. "You're going to have to start with some audio to set the tone before the pictures come up so the readers are a little bit in the dark about what they're about to see. We don't want them thinking this is just going to be another bleeding-heart liberal put-down of all of us who have the gall to live above the poverty line." She looked at me, eyes popping in the near darkness. "It isn't, is it?"

"No!"

"Then what are you going for, exactly?"

"The truth," I said.

She nodded without seeming to agree with me and turned back to the screen. "Of course, the quality is excellent, no problems there—oh, wait."

"What?" I sounded testy, and I didn't care.

"I love this."

She was looking at Elena Sanchez, face pressed to the car window.

"Now, I can see something in *her,*" Frances said. "It goes deeper than just 'I'm poor and I want somebody to pay my bills.' What's her story, do you know?"

My mouth went dry. "I've only just started talking to her."

"Well, talk to her some more. I think this is what you need, right here." She pushed back from the desk with her palms and sat straight-armed. "Right now you're only at about second base with this story. She can get you a home run. Otherwise I think you might strike out." Frances gave herself a wry look. "I'll be glad when the play-offs are over. I'm starting to talk like a sports commentator."

She dismissed me by turning back to the police scanner. "Have a nice weekend," she said. "I can't believe I'm letting you out of shooting the Whole Enchilada Festival."

I gave Elena Sanchez one more long look before I turned off my laptop.

By the time we reached the White Sands National Monument, I was over J.P. Winslow. Done. Ready to turn around and head back to Las Cruces barefoot, with all four of our packs on my back.

All the way there, while she was driving, she went through a memorized checklist of everything we were supposed to have brought. She chewed Victoria out for spacing out on the matches, and proclaimed what a good thing it was that she herself had brought extras. That went for the hand sanitizer Poco had left behind and the trash bags I didn't even know I was supposed to have packed.

I wondered silently why she'd even bothered to give assignments if she was going to bring everything anyway. I only kept that to myself because Poco was looking a little like, as my mother would have said, a sheep-killin' dog. Once she was royally reamed for the hand sanitizer faux pas, she stopped trying to make happy conversation. That left J.P. to carry on for the remaining twenty minutes of the ride with a tirade about Cade's teacher.

So, yes, upon arrival, I would cheerfully have hiked over San Augustin Pass and traversed the Organ Mountains with the coyotes to get away from J.P. Winslow. The only thing that held me back was the challenge in her eyes when I caught her looking at me. There were too many other tests in my life just then that I couldn't seem to pass. Hers I could ace with both hands tied behind my back. And I had to, for the sake of my eroding self-esteem.

J.P. left the engine on in the Suburban as she opened the door in the parking lot.

"I'll go in and sign us up for the sunset tour," she said. "There's no point in all of us going in."

I opened my door and climbed out. "I'm going to have a look around."

"Don't go far. I'm only going to be about five minutes."

"Thanks, Mom," I said.

I wasn't all that interested in the assortment of bizarre cacti planted in front of the building, but I wandered among them anyway. The plaques informed me that once I got into the dunes themselves, I would see little vegetation, because they moved too fast for plants to grow.

The dunes moved? In spite of myself I found that sort of intriguing. An image came to mind of ghostly mounds of sand marching across the desert—but to what destination? And why? That was the part that nettled me, I realized. The sense of drift, the lack of purpose. It occurred to me that Dan must love it out here.

I smacked myself internally and forced my focus onto the next sign. My eyes immediately glazed over the whole business about the crystallized form of gypsum from the evaporation of Lake Lucero that broke down into grains of sand and was blown across the Tularosa Basin, where it piled into dunes.

"That people pay to walk around on it," I muttered, "and then buy a T-shirt that says they've been there."

"We need to get going."

I looked up at J.P., who was standing on the gravel walkway, tapping a brochure against her leg.

"Poco and Victoria went in to use the restroom," she said. Her pointed look indicated that I might want to do the same.

"I'm good," I said.

"There aren't any toilets out there."

"I'm *fine.*"

"Then you probably aren't drinking enough water. I'm not interested in carrying you out if you get dehydrated, and it can happen like that out there." She snapped her fingers.

Poco and Victoria joined us in the car, and we passed through the gate, where J.P. collected a buck fifty from each of us to cover the entrance fee. As we continued down the paved but sand-dusted road and passed the last of the yuccas and the creosotes and the bear grass, I had the suffocating sense of being at a point of no return. Especially when the only living thing left to see was the occasional burst of orange at the top of a stark-white dune.

"I thought nothing could grow out here," I said, as much to make sure I still existed as to get information.

"That's the top of a Rio Grande cottonwood tree," Victoria said.

I turned to stare at her. She sounded like an excited little girl.

"No way," I said.

"Oh yes. It's been buried by the dune over time, but it can survive as long as some leaves are exposed." She almost pressed her nose to the glass. "Isn't it stunning? Oh, and see, that's the tip of a yucca. You only see about two feet of it, but there could be thirty feet under the sand."

Obviously mistaking my disbelief for burgeoning interest in desert foliage, she got up on one knee and pointed. "You see that pedestal of sand there?"

"Uh-huh."

"That's the trunk of a tree that has held on to the gypsum when the dune moved on. That's good, because it provides food and shelter for the animals."

"Animals?" I said. "What could live in this?"

"Little kangaroo rats and Apache pocket mice. I've even seen a kit fox and a couple of weasels. Only one snake."

I watched, amused, as Victoria clapped her hands.

"They're all nocturnal, so we may see some tonight."

"Hopefully not the snake." Poco's nervous giggle was back.

"But the best, the *best,* is the bleached lizard. It totally matches the sand. We might see one, or we might just see its footprints in the morning. I like that even better—it's like seeing that fairies have been here."

Victoria hugged her knees happily to her chest. I found myself envious of the filter she was seeing through. To me this was a wasteland where small animals had to forage through the night to survive. Had I always been like this?

"There's our guide," J.P. said as she pulled into a small parking lot connected to the dune field by a low wooden boardwalk.

"Who needs a guide when we have Victoria?" Poco said.

J.P. grunted. "You don't want to get lost out there, trust me."

"Is that the voice of experience?" I said—with a sort of evil hope in my voice.

She glared at me in the rearview mirror. "You're kidding, right?"

"J.P. doesn't *get* lost," Poco said.

So we'd returned to our roles. I reeled in my next barb and busied myself getting the camera ready. Frances had said it was easier to make pictures in the evening here.

Camera on its strap around my neck, I followed the trio down the walk and got ready for another commentary on gypsum and alkali flats and buried trees. But our guide was remarkably quiet as we followed him down the boardwalk, which, I saw, extended far from the road and into the dunes.

"See the lizard tracks?" Victoria whispered to me.

I looked where she was pointing. Tiny feet had left their imprint on ripples in the sand that must have looked like foothills to their owners. As we walked, the miniature footprints disappeared under a soft blowing of sand that began to take on a reddish-pink hue as the daylight faded. The shadows lengthened, and the surface patterns pronounced themselves more clearly.

Frances was right. While in the stark sunlight, the white dunes came out gray if I didn't overexpose the photo by one or two stops, but now I could use the internal meter and capture their true colors—apricot and salmon and the skin of a peach.

I stopped and shot a slice of dunes and the silhouette of a yucca's tassels against a suddenly fiery sky. Camera raised, I shot the sun dipping below the distant San Andres Mountains. When it finally disappeared, I could almost hear it hiss in the stillness that fell with it, leaving the desert bathed in a light full of mystery as the sands glowed against the dark horizon. This I couldn't photograph.

"Ryan," Poco whispered. "Turn around."

I did, and gasped. As the sun had made its flashy descent in the west, the moon had risen silently and without fanfare in the east. Round and full as a ripe, silver fruit, it hung in the darkened sky. A whole minute passed before I could raise the camera again. It almost seemed a sacrilege to make a picture.

But once I got started, I couldn't stop. I took shot after shot, experimenting with a filter, focusing on the silhouettes of the women with the moon as their backlight, capturing the lone star that winked shyly near the lunar splendor. I might have stayed half the night if Poco hadn't tugged gently at my sleeve.

"We're leaving," she whispered.

"Okay," I whispered back.

Everyone spoke in hushed tones. The stillness demanded it. There was not a sound beyond the muted padding of our feet on the boards. Nothing arose to stop the thoughts or steer them away from themselves. J.P. was at least right about that. It was easy to get lost in them.

I found it terrifying.

By the time we reached the car, my palms were so sweaty I could barely hold the camera. I was actually grateful when J.P. unlocked the car and set off the alarm that made the horn blast repeatedly, splintering the silence. I was so grateful, in fact, that I didn't even gloat when other parties shot killing looks at her until she managed to turn it off.

"That definitely ruined the moment, didn't it?" she said.

I stared at the back of her head. Was that self-deprecation I heard?

"Okay, onward," she said. "We go around two curves and there's the entrance to the walk into the campsite." She turned to back the car up and looked sternly at Victoria and me. "You did bring your flashlights, didn't you?"

"The moonlight should be enough," I said.

"You did forget."

"Didn't you bring extras?" I said sweetly.

She scowled.

"Just checking," I said. "I brought mine."

When we got to the check-in point, two guys with everything they owned in fanny packs were just finishing up at the registration book. They threw laughing glances over their shoulders as they hurried off down the path. I guess I'd have laughed, too, if I'd run into four suburban housewives loaded up like beasts of burden. I'd seen pack mules in Bolivia with less stuff on their backs than we had.

"You are not serious," J.P. said at the sign-in book.

Poco edged over to her. "What's wrong?"

"They took the last campsite!"

"Didn't you make a reservation?" I said.

"I told you, they don't take reservations. But nobody ever camps out here at this time of year."

Victoria blinked at the path. "*They* do."

"Yes, those guys and four other parties. Probably all together for some kind of beer fest."

Her efforts at blaming somebody else for what was no one's fault were failing her. I watched her shoulders slump.

"I'm sorry, guys," she said.

"You couldn't have known," Poco said.

J.P. stared at her, as if not knowing was a notion she'd never entertained. I looked at the four of us, all roughed-out with no place to go, and incorrigible laughter burst from my gut.

"I don't see what's funny," J.P. said.

"Well, look at us. Hillary didn't take this much when he climbed Mt. Everest. We could live in the wilderness for weeks, but there's no room in it for us."

Poco covered her mouth, but I knew there was a giggle lurking there. I couldn't tell what was going on with Victoria. Her hair was hanging in front of her face.

"So now what?" I said, looking at J.P.

"We go home. I don't see what else we can do."

She stomped off, swaying slightly under the pack, and I felt a little bad.

"She was looking forward to this, wasn't she?" I said.

"It's okay," Poco told me.

Though it obviously wasn't. J.P. drove all the way out to Highway 70 in a brutal silence that put White Sands to shame, ignoring Poco's suggestion that we at least go to dinner—or coffee and dessert maybe? Chocolate was known to make anything better, she said. J.P. didn't even grunt.

Until we stopped to turn onto the highway, and saw the roadblock. Then she exploded.

"*Now* what?"

"It looks like the road's closed," Poco said.

"I can *see* that. What's the deal?"

"I bet it's a missile range test," Victoria said.

"In the middle of the night? That's ridiculous, if you ask me!"

"Maybe that's why they didn't," I said.

"Didn't what?"

"Ask you."

J.P. twisted halfway around, but Poco put her hand on her shou[illegible]der. "You know what, let's just go toward Alamogordo and see if [illegible] can find something to eat. I'm starving."

"We didn't have dinner," Victoria said.

"Of course we didn't have dinner! We were going to cook w[illegible]ers over a campfire and eat under the stars."

I was startled by the disappointment that showed through the thin place in J.P.'s anger. I felt small and mean again.

"Just turn left, okay?" Poco said. "We'll find something."

We found nothing, because in two miles the highway was blocked in that direction as well. At least on this end there was a marked car with its light flashing and someone military-looking at the wheel. When J.P. pulled over behind him, he got out and came to the driver's side window.

"Can I help you?" he said.

J.P. filled him in on our plight in a voice meant to change the entire schedule of the White Sands Missile Range. The man was unmoved.

"It's going to be two, three o'clock in the morning before the road opens again in either direction. You can go on past me, but you won't be able to come back through until then."

"I see," J.P. said. "It would be nice if you would inform the public about these things."

"We do, ma'am. Watch the news. Check it online. Read the papers."

"Thank you," J.P said, increasing the starch in her voice. "We'll move on now."

I wanted to sit back, arms folded, and enjoy her misery, but she was already stewing in her own embarrassed juices.

"I guess we have no choice," she said as we pulled back onto the road.

We rode in silence again for a few miles, until Victoria said, "There's a motel."

"Where?"

"On the right."

J.P. swung across the road and stopped with a spray of gravel in front of a strip of doors with a room labeled *Office* on the end.

My laughter bubbled up again. "This is where you come for a two-hour tryst."

J.P. looked at me in the rearview. "Is that the voice of experience?"

"J.P.!" Poco said.

She shoved the gearshift into reverse. "Okay, so I guess we'll go into Alamogordo. I think they have, like, one hotel—it's a Holiday Inn."

Poco pulled out her phone. "I'll call first."

We waited while she got the number and chatted sweetly with someone—who told her they had no rooms available and to try the Motel 6. That, too, was full for the night.

"What is going on that we don't know about?" J.P. looked at me in the rearview again. "Was there something in the paper about some big event?"

"The Whole Enchilada Festival," I said, "but that's in Las Cruces."

"There are never enough rooms in Las Cruces for those things. The overflow comes out here."

"And I would know that how? I just moved here."

Poco put up her hand. "Okay, listen. This place doesn't look that bad. Why don't we see if they have a couple of rooms?"

"It looks like you could get a disease in there," Victoria whimpered.

"A disease?" I said. "We were going to sleep on the ground in the desert with the snakes and the kangaroo rats. How could this be worse?"

The whimper turned to a squeal.

"Oh, for Pete's sake, Victoria," J.P. said. "You're not doing to die. Let's just go in and make the best of it."

"We'll order room service," Poco said and giggled.

We all went in, walking as if we were attached with Velcro, and learned from a semi-toothless individual of undetermined gender that there was only one room left, with a double bed. We took it.

"I bet there'll be another room available at about ten," J.P. said as we lugged all our stuff from the car to the door.

I was surprised by her sudden willingness to adapt. Victoria, on the other hand, was winding up like a manic toy soldier.

"I don't think I can sleep in there," she said before we even unlocked the door.

J.P. went in first and turned to us with a mock-cheerful face. "Well, it ain't the Ritz-Carlton."

I slipped in behind her and surveyed the dark-green walls, which matched the bedspread and the flattened carpet and the Formica on the dresser. The only thing that wasn't the color of cooked spinach was the overhead fixture, because there wasn't one. A bare bulb illuminated the room in light that made us all look like we were headed for our coffins.

"Ritz-Carlton?" I said. "This isn't even the Motel 6."

"Motel One and a Half." Even as small as Poco was, she had to squeeze between us to get into the room. She wrinkled her nose. "Somebody has smoked in here."

"Ya think?" J.P. said. "We could get cancer just breathing."

Victoria gasped from the doorway. "Seriously?"

Somehow we all managed to cram ourselves into the room, backpacks and all. J.P. arranged the food on the dresser, Poco stacked the packs in the corner, and Victoria set about unfolding her tent.

"Where do you think you're going to put that?" J.P. said.

"On the bed."

"You're going to pitch your tent on the bed?" I said.

Victoria tossed her hair back and looked at me with actual gumption. "I'm sure not sleeping on that floor," she said and continued to spread the tent across the mattress.

Where she intended to drive the stakes in I had no idea.

As Poco handed J.P. a can of Lysol, they exchanged a look that held a hundred previous shared conversations. I felt as if I were outside a scene looking in, and I wished, just for that moment, I could be part of the picture.

Victoria finally got the tent up with the stakes tied to the headboard, in time to share the motley feast J.P. and Poco put together while I shot photos.

"I don't know who you plan to show those to," J.P. said as we downed Cheetos and uncooked hot dogs and the Hershey bars and marshmallows meant for s'mores. "But if I see one in the paper . . ."

"I have a question," I said. "How come we get to eat all this junk and our kids don't?"

"Because we're the mothers," J.P. said simply. "What did you want, filet mignon?"

"I'm not complaining," I said, mouth full. "I've eaten a whole lot worse on assignment."

I winced. I hadn't meant to say that. But Poco pounced on it like a kitten.

"Like where?" she said.

"Oh, just around."

"Alex told Cade you've been to Africa." J.P. looked at a Cheeto and then at me. "Is that true?"

"That was my last assignment, yeah."

"What did you eat?" Poco asked.

"Meat of questionable origin."

"Oh my gosh," Victoria said.

I couldn't tell if she was grossed out or impressed. I was starting to squirm, especially when J.P. licked the orangey gunk off of her fingers and looked at me dead-on. Here we go with why-did-you-leave-your-children-and-go-to-Africa.

"Okay, so we talk about ourselves all the time," she said. "And we don't know a thing about you."

"Not that much to know," I said.

"Well, now, that's a lie." J.P. counted on her still-cheesy fingers. "You've traveled all over the world. You have your work in the paper. And you haven't told us what happened between you and Dan."

"And I'm not going to."

"And you don't have to," Poco said, minus the arm pat because she had a marshmallow poked onto the end of each finger.

"Yes, she does," J.P. said. "We're stuck in a green hole for the night and none of us has anything interesting to say about ourselves, so it's up to her."

"Forget about it," I said, but I didn't feel like decking her. She had a twinkle in her eye I hadn't seen before.

"All right, then," she said. "I'll tell you what I'm seeing."

Poco giggled. "This ought to be good."

"Give it your best shot," I said. "I'll tell you if you're right."

J.P. pushed the usual tendrils of hair away from her face. "I'm looking at you and Dan—and at first I'm wondering, *What did he ever see in her? She's a snob.*"

"J.P.!" Poco looked at me nervously, but I waved J.P. on.

"And then I started to spend time with you, and I knew I was right. You are a snob."

For some unknown reason, another laugh burst out of me. Poco and Victoria looked at each other as if they were making an unspoken plan to procure a straitjacket.

"But then I notice him looking at you when you don't *know* he's looking at you, and I see something."

"How about, 'I'm sure glad I'm not married to her anymore,'" I said.

"You'd think that, but no."

"J.P., you are just rude!" Poco said.

She was, but it was growing on me.

"Go ahead," I said.

"It's like he's seeing something he didn't expect. And then there's the respect, which I totally don't get, but see, we don't know you."

I abandoned the rest of my Hershey bar and propped a foot up on the dresser. "I think you're totally wrong about Dan. But what do you want to know about me? I'm warning you, it isn't that fascinating."

J.P. looked at Victoria and Poco. "Girls?"

"Go for it." Poco had obviously given up on reining J.P. in. She pulled open a bag of Peanut M&M's and offered it to Victoria, who selected a yellow one.

"I want to know where you stand on God," J.P. said.

"Excuse me?"

"We're all Christians, which is part of why we hang out together. I'm assuming you are?"

"I am," I said. "I haven't found a church here yet."

"I'm not talking about whether you go to church—although I don't see how you can practice Christianity without the body of Christ." She shrugged. "That's a whole other conversation. What I mean is, do you have a relationship with the Lord?"

I bristled.

"What's wrong?" she said.

"I hate it when people talk churchese."

"Then how would you put it?"

I hesitated. This could be the end of what was taking the shape of a genuine conversation among women. An hour before, I'd longed for it. But it if meant skirting the issue that was central to my being, it was going to be over before it started, and I'd be back where I'd always been: outside looking in.

"All right," I said. "I don't just *believe* in Christ and all that he stands for. I *know* it's the truth. But that looks different for me than it does for a lot of people."

"What does it look like?" J.P. asked.

"It looks like I pray and study the Bible, and then I get out in the world and it all falls apart. I get ticked off and I act like a snob and I do stupid things like leave my husband."

Eyes widened. I rushed on before anyone could hook onto any of that.

"But what saves me are these images that God gives me, like pictures I might take, only they don't come from me. I know that sounds kind of woo-woo . . ."

"No," Victoria said. "It sounds wonderful to me."

"It would," J.P said drily, but she leaned toward me. "So go on. What happens when you get these images?"

"Sometimes nothing, because I don't know what they mean right then. Sometimes they tell me that I'm being an idiot. It's different every time."

"That is beautiful." Victoria shook her head at me, pale eyes wide and shining.

"That's not too different from what I experience with God," Poco said. "Only I don't see, I hear. Sort of. It's my thought, only it's not, if that makes any sense."

J.P. nodded, but there were still questions in her eyes. "I have to read it and then do it. That's my relationship with the Lord or however it is you want to say it. That works for me."

"So you do it and Poco hears it and I see it."

We all turned to Victoria. Her eyes were closed, long lashes resting in the hollows beneath them.

"She's asleep," J.P said.

"No, I'm not. I'm feeling it."

J.P. nudged my foot with hers. "Now that's woo-woo," she whispered.

And then she smiled, and I almost grabbed the camera. A smile made J.P. Winslow a handsome woman.

CHAPTER EIGHTEEN

I woke up before the sun the next morning. That will happen when you sleep in a chair that's uncomfortable just to sit on, let alone spend the night in. I pulled the forest green drape open enough so I could see my watch by the crack of light from the outside fixture. Victoria stirred on the bed and resettled.

Her hand had fallen out of the confines of the tent and rested like a lady's white glove on the sheet she'd sworn was crawling with cooties. Poco was curled into her sleeping bag on the sliver of floor between the bed and the swollen bathroom door that didn't close all the way, and both of them snored, responsively, as if they were chanting a psalm.

I couldn't find J.P. until I picked my way into the bathroom and discovered her ensconced, fully clothed, in the empty tub, face pink and mushy with sleep like a three-year-old's. I sat on the toilet seat lid and watched her, half expecting her to sting me with a zinger from the depths of slumber.

She opened her eyes and closed them again.

"Breathe a word of this to anyone and I'll cut your heart out," she said. "Forget it. You're heartless anyway."

No, I thought as I tucked a towel around her bare shoulder, I had a heart. And right now, it ached with a longing that was foreign to me.

"What time is it?" J.P. said.

"Six o'clock."

"We were supposed to be watching the sunrise on the sands right now."

"So why can't we?"

J.P., who had conducted the entire conversation from behind her eyelids, opened them and squinted at me. "You hate it out there."

"I did. Until last night."

She came up on one elbow. "So you do admit when you're wrong."

"On the rare occasion when I am."

"Doggone it."

I watched her climb stiffly from the tub, hair in the worst disarray yet.

"What?" I said.

"That means now I'm going to have to admit I was wrong too."

"To bring us on this trip?"

She winced at herself in the mirror. "No. That I was wrong about you."

I squirmed. Just when I'd started to feel a little comfortable, I was going to be expected to "open up." I'd already done more of that the night before—and on into the wee hours—than I ever had in my life.

"You're not as much of a snob as I thought you were," J.P. said.

"Is that supposed to be a compliment?"

"Yeah, and thanks for throwing it back in my face."

She left the bathroom. I sat there, still on the toilet seat, confronted with a faint image of myself shrinking down to nothing, shouting insults until I disappeared completely. When J.P. came back in, carrying a hairbrush, a toothbrush, and a tube of toothpaste, I was surprised she could still see me.

She pulled the pointless scrunchie out of her hair and went after the tangled mess with the hairbrush like she was raking the lawn. "I only know one person who's harder to get along with than you are," she said.

The scrunchie went back on the ponytail, and she squeezed an inch of paste onto the toothbrush with the precision of a scientist.

I wasn't sure why I was still sitting atop the toilet, watching her attend to her hygiene. But I said, "Who would that be?"

"Me," she said and started in savagely on her enamel.

I waited until she spit and rinsed before I said, "Well, for once you'll get no argument from me."

"I'm better than I used to be." She stopped soaping up her hands and gave me a look. "Don't say it."

I put up my hands, feigning innocence. She went back to lathering.

"I was a real witch when I was going through my divorce," she said.

I felt my chin drop.

"We have more in common than we want to have. My ex left me for a younger woman. And I use the term *woman* loosely. She was all of twenty-five. Mike's enjoying raising her."

J.P. ducked her head to the sink and scrubbed at her face, while I got my mouth closed and organized the thoughts chattering in my own head like a group of gossiping women.

So—J.P. was angry. She needed control of everything she did have left or it might get away from her. She was fighting to be in charge of her life, because she hadn't succeeded in being in charge of someone else's.

J.P. was me.

She finished rinsing and, eyes still screwed shut, felt around for a towel. I handed her one, but when she tried to pull it away, I held on.

"I'm sorry," I said.

She didn't ask for what. I didn't explain. She just stopped pulling on the towel, and I let go. When I got up to leave the bathroom, she straightened and looked at me in the mirror.

"I've seen Dan's little chippy," she said.

"Chippy?" I said. "Now there's a new one."

"Just so you know, she can't hold a candle to you."

I nodded in the mirror.

"Now, do you mind if I pee in private?" she said. "You're as bad as my kid."

We reached the gate at White Sands just as a sleepy-eyed park ranger was opening it.

"Next to sunset," he said before he waved us through, "this is the best time of day to be here."

Evidently not many people knew that, because as J.P. drove the Suburban beyond the last yucca stem and clump of Indian rice grass, we remained the only vehicle on the road. As far as I could tell, we might be the only people left on earth—it was that still. Even we four women kept silent as we climbed out of the car and by unspoken agreement made our separate ways up the dunes.

I climbed at once to the top of one with my camera, padding through sand that was both soft and firm, treading carefully so I wouldn't disturb a world that was allowing me to share its secrets. From there I could see the Sacramento Mountains to the east, smooth and pink, and the San Andres still hiding in the shadows to the west. When I looked up, I was tented by a blue-topaz sky. Gazing down, I saw my own shadow, distinct on the pristine sand. I found myself surrounded by a majesty I didn't even try to photograph, that I could hardly look at without a startling sense of my own insignificance. It occurred to me that the shadow of an ancient Native American in this place may have been his only mirror, the only way he could see who he was.

I wished I could see that myself.

That startled me, too, that thought. It wasn't a wish, or even a scrap of thinking that came from me. It was a prayer—to have a vision of myself that I didn't have to create. Because the one I'd constructed was quickly falling apart.

I raised the camera, more to drive myself away from that path than to capture anything on disk. But I lowered it again. It was clearly a God-path. If I stepped off of it, it would be at my peril.

I closed my eyes—and there was the image I'd been waiting days for. My own footprints in the sand on the slope below. *You know where you've been,* the silence whispered to me. *Now—will that lead you someplace you need to go? Or will you let time blow over your tracks before you find your way?*

I squatted and pulled the camera before my face. That couldn't be God. It was too maudlin. Too iffy. I gave a J.P. grunt. Too woo-woo.

Beside my foot was a set of tiny pronged prints that crossed the dune and disappeared over the other side. I shot some close-ups. I started to stand and realized there were other prints I hadn't seen before. Small soft human ones, left by playing children perhaps. Another larger set, probably made by boots. Maybe a lone hiker seeking solitude. Still more from tiny animals skittering through the night, looking for food.

I shot them all, why, I didn't know, except that they told a story, and I was trained to make pictures of stories. Even if I didn't know what they meant.

Before I stood up, I trailed my fingers through the sand. It was tender, and it sparkled even without much sunlight. What had the guide said about that last night? That the scratching together of the grains as they were blown across the basin gave the sand its brilliant, sparkling white. The wind seemed to have created all of this—marching the dunes across the desert one avalanche at a time, blowing it smooth and round with no sharp edges, whispering it into delicate ripples, rubbing each individual grain until it dazzled.

I tried to capture that now with my camera—the amazing things the wind could do, what it could create, without ever being seen . . . And then I turned away from the lens.

"All right," I said out loud to God. "I get it."

When I made my way down the dune, Victoria lay against the bottom, arms and legs spread as if she were about to make a sand angel.

"It's like being in on a secret, isn't it?" she whispered.

I sat beside her. "I was thinking something like that, yeah."

She nodded, indenting the sand with her hooded head. "I knew you'd like it. I'm not a morning person, but this is one of the few things I'll get up for." She closed her eyes, and I thought she was finished. But in a whisper she added, "You have to get up early if you want to hear God."

I didn't close my own eyes this time. Maybe I didn't always have to. God had given me an image right here that I could see with my eyes wide open.

When J.P. and Poco joined us, both as quieted by the dunes as Victoria and I, we decided to seek out breakfast. The easy silence only lasted until we were at a table in a truck stop on the eastern outskirts of Las Cruces, warming our hands around mugs of coffee, or in J.P.'s case, tea. Victoria dipped her napkin in her water glass and scrubbed the rim of hers before she'd take a sip.

The moment the server went off with our order, J.P. looked at me.

"Poco has something to tell you."

I looked at Poco in surprise, but I had nothing on her. She appeared to be stunned.

J.P. rolled her eyes. "What we were talking about when Ryan was packing the car. I thought we agreed we were going to bring it up."

"*We*," Poco said. "Not me." The nervous giggle was conspicuous by its absence. "If you want to talk about it, go ahead."

J.P. gave her a long, silent chance to reconsider and then turned to me. "We were discussing this thing with your Jake and Miguel Sanchez."

I gripped my coffee mug. Once again, the moment I started to feel comfortable, J.P. had to poke me in the eye.

"You don't think he did it, do you?" she said.

The only reason I shook my head was because she didn't make it sound as if I were completely out of my mind. Still, irritation crept up my backbone.

"Nobody wants to think their kid is capable of that," J.P. said, "so I guess I don't blame you."

"J.P., this is not at all how I remember our conversation," Poco said, voice stiff.

J.P. sat back in the booth. "I wanted you to tell it in the first place."

"Tell *what*?" I said.

"Jake and Miguel were friends, Ryan," Poco said. "Did you know that?"

"I know they played soccer together—and Jake talked him into trying out for some special team."

"The select team," J.P. said. "It's hugely competitive. Jake made it."

"I know," I said.

"And so did Miguel Sanchez," Poco said.

"I know that too."

J.P. brushed the ever-present tendrils impatiently off of her forehead. "Which is why it makes no sense that Jake would want to hurt him. They're friends. He's not a threat. Neither one of them was named captain—Poco's Diego got that."

I felt my eyes widen at Poco. "Your son is on that team too?"

Poco nodded. "I was at the tryouts. Jake and Miguel were hugging when the announcement was made, and punching each other the way boys do. Then the other boy Jake hangs around with, who also—"

"He's your ex-husband's girlfriend's kid," J.P. said, nudging me.

"Ian Tassert?"

"Huh?" Victoria said.

Poco shook her head. "No, his last name's Iverton. He hiked Jake up on his shoulders and was parading all around with him."

"Anyway," J.P. said, "we just didn't know if you were aware that Jake and Miguel were friends."

"I was. But Dan—was he at the tryouts?"

"No," Poco said. "He had tryouts of his own going on. I guess that's why he sent Ginger to watch Jake and Ian."

J.P. grunted. "It's like, not only can you not believe Jake did it, you don't know why he would have done it if he did do it."

"Huh?" Victoria said.

J.P. started to explain, but Victoria shook her head. "Ginger Tassert?"

J.P. bobbed her tea bag up and down. "Yeah, what about her?"

"She lives in one of the apartment complexes we own." She gave me a half smile. "I have some good news for you there. She's about to be evicted because she hasn't paid her rent in three months."

I didn't tell her that was not good news at all. I could still hear Ginger saying she didn't live at Dan's—yet. And why hadn't Alex told me Ian had also tried out for the team?

"Ryan, are you okay?" Poco said.

I was saved from answering by the ringing of my cell phone. Dan's name came up on the screen, and only because I wanted to get away from the table did I excuse myself to take it. I could always hang up when I got outside.

"Ryan?" Dan said.

I froze, hand on the doorknob. "What's wrong? Dan—what is it?"

"It's Jake. He wasn't in his bed when I went to his room this morning."

"What?"

"They found him."

"Who is *they?"*

"The police."

"The *police? What* is going on?"

"I'm trying to tell you. He sneaked out and went to the high school for Ian's meet. A teacher knew he wasn't supposed to be there, so she called the cops."

I made my way out the door and sagged against the front wall of the café.

"So he's back home with you, then," I said. "And he's okay?"

"He's okay."

"What aren't you telling me?"

"He's not with me. They're holding him at the police station."

"Why?"

"The judge says he either goes with you, or he goes to the county jail until the trial."

I stood straight up again and started for the door. "I'm on my way. Meet me there with some of his clothes. I'll get the rest later."

"Ryan."

I stopped and shoved my hand through my hair. "Look, the judge is saying what I told you from the start: Jake needs to be with me. You can't fight me on this now, Dan, so don't even start."

"I'm not the one who's fighting you." Dan's voice was brittle and frightened. "It's Jake."

"What do you mean?"

"He won't go with you. He's choosing jail."

I sat down hard on a bench on the porch.

"Ryan?" Dan said.

"Jake is *not* going to jail."

"He's made a choice."

"Are you *kidding* me, Dan?"

"Look, I'm not going to argue with you about this. I'll go in and talk to him again."

"Do *not* let them put him in jail until I get there, do you hear?"

"I hear," Dan said. He hung up.

I flung myself back into the café, nearly knocking over a waitress with a tray as I plowed my way to the table. "I have to get to my car—right now," I said.

"Ryan, what's wrong?" Poco said.

But J.P. was already on her feet, grabbing our server by the sleeve. "We need some to-go boxes and the check," she told her. To me she said, "You can tell us on the way."

She and Poco scrambled for their purses and mine. Victoria sat silently moving her lips as if she were praying.

I hoped she was—because at the moment, God and I were not speaking.

CHAPTER NINETEEN

Dan was waiting for me in the lobby at the precinct when I got there. I knew before he spoke that he hadn't been able to talk Jake into going home with me.

"Did you even try?" I said.

He looked away from me. "What do *you* think, Ryan?" he said. "You think I want him to go to jail?"

"No—but I don't think you're doing much to keep him out. How did he leave the house without you knowing?" I hit my forehead with the heel of my hand. "Oh, wait, you were out in your studio. Or Ginger was showing you what a desirable man you are."

"Stop." Dan's voice broke. "I'm not going to have this conversation with you. If you want to go in there and talk to Jake, nobody's standing in your way."

I turned toward the front desk.

"Except Jake himself," Dan said to my back.

I whirled around. "Thanks to you. 'Dad said I didn't have to talk to you.' Heaven knows what else you've said."

"You don't get it, do you? He won't talk to you because you do all the talking—at the top of your lungs. He's sick of it, Ryan. We both are."

He shoved his hands into his pockets and walked away from me. It took every ounce of what little self-control I had left to go to the desk and ask to see Jake.

The female officer gave me a steely look before she picked up the phone and called for someone to escort me in. When she hung up, she said, "I'd calm down before I went back there if I were you."

There was no calming down. There was only maintaining enough control not to shove the tank-shaped police escort aside and push every door open until I found my son. When he showed me into the room where Jake sat at a table alone, I held on until he shut the door behind him. And then I held on some more.

"Jake," I said, "I'm not going to yell at you. I just want you to come to my house. You don't have to think of it as home. You don't have to think of it as anything except that it isn't a jail cell."

Jake was slumped so far down in the chair his shoulders barely cleared the tabletop. His forearms lay listlessly in front of him as he picked at the mole on his wrist. It was bleeding, as were several of his cuticles.

I took a step toward him. "Son, you don't want to go to jail."

"Don't tell me what I don't want to do!" He shoved himself back until the chair tilted out from under him. He staggered forward to get his balance and stood curved over the table, chest heaving under his baggy shirt. "Why don't you get it?" he screamed at me. "I'm doing this my way, and I want you to leave me alone!"

"Your way? Your way is not to tell things that could save you—like the fact that you and Miguel Sanchez are friends."

He flung himself from the table and stumbled to the door and banged on it with his fist. It was opened immediately by the officer who'd shown me in.

"Problem?" he said.

"Take me to jail." Jake's voice teetered on the edge of panic. "Take me now."

I grabbed at the back of his shirt and caught a fistful of cloth.

"Ma'am, let go."

"He's my son! You can't put him in jail for something he didn't do."

"What he did do was break the rules of his custody. He had a choice, and it looks like he made it." He removed his handcuffs from his belt.

"What is it with you people and choices? I'm his mother—*I'll* make the choice!"

The officer didn't even look at me. He turned weary eyes on Jake, who was trying to yank his shirt out of my hand.

"What are you going to do if I release you to your mom?"

"Run away."

"Then there you go. Ma'am, I have to ask you to let go."

I didn't have to. Jake clenched his hand around mine and ripped it away. Before I could reach for him again, he pressed his wrists together and presented them to the officer, who hesitated, cuffs in hand.

"You sure you want to do this, son?" he said.

Jake looked back at me and nodded. I came completely apart.

One piece of me screamed. Another slapped its hand on the table. Still another hurled itself at the door that closed behind my son and the officer who was taking him off to a cell.

The jagged pieces still hadn't come together when I somehow made it out of the room and down the hall and across the lobby to the front door. That was why, when I squealed the Saab out of the parking lot, I took the corner too sharp and too fast and fishtailed off the road on the other side. I stomped down on the brake and rocked viciously to a stop, my rear bumper inches from a utility pole.

Everything shook as I pulled the car forward, kicking up divots and lurching back onto the road. I drove a block to an empty insurance office parking lot and parked sideways across three spaces. The engine died, and I let it. All I could do was lean back in the seat, feet pressed to the floorboard, and beat the steering wheel until my hands could no longer take it.

Then I pulled my fists to my mouth and choked out one aching sob after another. For the first time in my life, I wished I knew how to cry.

Sully put his cell phone on the desk and twirled it with his finger. He'd done the laundry, replenished his supply of Frappuccinos, changed the oil in the Mini Cooper, and answered every e-mail. And it wasn't even noon yet.

He stopped the phone's twirl before it could sail off the edge of the desk. It had all been an attempt at three things, and it had failed at all of them.

One was to keep him from thinking about Porphyria. She was supposed to have the pacemaker replacement this morning, but Winnie hadn't phoned him yet.

Two was to give him the sense that he was accomplishing something, because he had still come up empty-handed in his search for Belinda or Zahira or whoever she was at the moment. He'd even tried a realtor Friday afternoon, asking in what part of town he might find a place to open an alternative counseling center.

"We could try the university area," the broker had told him. "I know there's already one there—Healing Choice, I think it's called . . ."

If he hadn't been depressed before that, he definitely was now.

The third was to steer him away from obsessing about Tess. She'd asked him to let her know how things went with the Better Business Bureau, et cetera. But had she meant that, or was she just saying what it would have seemed impolite not to say when he was leaving Tuesday night? Sun tea had turned into chips and salsa, which had led to shrimp quesadillas she'd whipped up while they asked each other impersonal questions and secretly looked for deeper meanings. At least, that's what he'd been doing. He was pretty sure she'd done the same thing, with a lot more finesse. So maybe she did mean for him to call her. He would know in the first thirty seconds if she didn't. If, for instance, she said, "Sullivan who?"

Holy crow, Crisp. Just do it. What are you, twelve?

He flipped open the cell, but the office phone rang. Somebody who didn't know the clinic was closed on Saturday—but he answered it anyway, to avoid having to deal with any more adolescent angst.

"Healing Choice," he said.

A slight pause was followed by a vaguely familiar cheery voice. "I'd like to speak with Sullivan Crisp, please."

"Speaking."

He was greeted with a huge sigh. "Oh, thank goodness. This is Sarah Quinn. Pachico Hills Community Church?"

"Sarah—oh, Sarah!" Sully rubbed the back of his head and groped for a way to keep this short.

"I'm so glad you left me your card," she said. "It took me awhile to find it, or I would have called you soon—"

"What can I do for you, Sarah?"

"Are you still looking for Belinda Cox?"

Sully stopped twirling his cell phone and planted his hand on it. "I am," he said.

"Well, it just so happens—and this has to be the Lord, because there is just no other reason why it would have come up when I was just passing through the room."

"What came up?" Sully asked.

"Somebody who came in to see Pastor mentioned Zahira. Now, I wouldn't even have paid any attention to that if you and I hadn't just been discussing it the other day." Sarah lowered her voice conspiratorially. "All I heard was him saying he thought she was long gone from around here, but that she had shown up with some kind of storefront business in Mesilla."

"Mesilla," Sully said, heart pounding. "Is that close by?"

"You're practically in its front yard."

There was a polite knock on the door.

"Listen, Sarah," Sully said. "I've got somebody here, but I can't thank you enough for this information."

"You are more than welcome—now, you call me if you find her."

Sully managed to extricate himself and get to the door, just as Martha was tapping again.

"Dr. Fitzgerald," he said. "Do you *live* here?"

Martha's blonde head preceded her in. "Do you?"

"I didn't see your car out there."

"I just got here." Her face colored. "Actually, I was driving by and I saw *your* car, so I thought I'd try to catch you." She nodded at his desk. "Am I interrupting something?"

"Nah," he said. He forced himself to tuck the Sarah conversation away. "Sit down. Can I get you anything?"

She looked at his empty Frap bottle and shook her head. "I won't keep you long."

Sully motioned again to one of the client chairs as he sank into the other one.

"I just need to talk to you about Kyle," she said.

Dang. "You still haven't settled your differences?" Sully winced at the way that sounded. "I could sit down with the two of you."

"No, we've come to terms. I handle my clients my way, and he handles his as he sees fit." She rushed on. "And I'm almost entirely certain we are both within the parameters of the Healing Choice approach."

Sully tilted his head. "You're almost certain."

"That's what I wanted to talk to you about."

Martha folded her hands in her lap. Even in Saturday jeans and an oversize orange sweater, she managed to look proper. "Kyle has five clients now," she said.

"Are you concerned that he's taken on too much too soon?"

The current version of her smile tightened.

"I'm sorry," Sully said. "I'm second-guessing you. Go on." There was nothing else he could do now but hear her out.

"He's diagnosed three of them as being possibly suicidal. From my experience here, that seems like a high percentage."

"Did he discuss that with you?"

"I wouldn't call it discussing," she said. "He actually thanked me for giving him some cases he could get his teeth into."

"He didn't talk about them by name?"

"No. But I reviewed all those files before I gave him the clients, and I didn't see any red flags."

"Not everybody checks the I've-had-suicidal-thoughts box who should," Sully said. Her smile changed again, and he unfolded his legs and slanted toward her. "I'm not trying to negate your concern, Martha. I'm assuming you've brought this to me because you want me to suggest some possibilities you might not have thought of."

"That isn't all."

The office phone rang again, and her eyes shifted to it. "The answering service picks that up after hours," she said.

"Let me check," Sully said. If it was Sarah with more details, he wasn't missing it.

"Sullivan Crisp," he said.

"Okay, I lost it." It was an obviously distraught female voice.

"I'm sorry?" Sully said.

"I screamed at my son in front of a cop. I tried to break a table at the police station. And I almost ran my car into a telephone pole. My son is in jail, and I can't get him out because he won't come home with me and I'm afraid I'm going to hurt somebody if I don't get a handle on this." Her voice finally snapped. "And I can't. I can't calm down. I can't stop wanting to break things."

"All right, Ryan," Sully said. "Where are you right now?"

"Home."

"Good. You probably ought to stay there."

"You *think*?"

"Are you alone?"

"Yes. I told you, I'm afraid I'm going to hurt somebody."

He wasn't sure how much of an exaggeration that was. He could hear things being picked up and slammed down.

"I'm not going to tell you to sit," Sully said, "but I do suggest you get to a room where it's soft. Pillows, stuffed animals."

For an instant, he had a life-sized picture of Ryan Coe with a teddy bear.

"You're getting the idea." Her voice had already come down several decibels, but it was still shrill and serrated. It could have cut a loaf of bread.

"Okay, now, talk to me. What set you off?"

He could hear her draw in a ragged breath, and he took the

opportunity to look up at Martha. She was already halfway out of the chair, pointing to the door.

"We'll talk later," she mouthed to him and slipped out.

"I don't know if I can even tell you this without flipping out again," Ryan said.

"If you feel yourself heading into dangerous territory, we'll stop," Sully said. "Fair enough?"

"Yeah, whatever." She hauled in another jagged lungful of air and launched into her story. She ended with, "My son picked jail over me."

Sully smeared his hand across his chest. The hurt wasn't buried far beneath her anger. He could feel it in his own soul.

"I'm sorry, Ryan," he said.

"There is nothing I can do, and I can't stand it. I want to go down there and shake that sanctimonious broad at the front desk and work my way in from there—but I know it isn't going to do any good."

Sully didn't point out that she'd be locked up, too, either there or in the psych ward.

"I also want to go scream at my ex-husband," she said. "But that would only make him think he's right."

"About what?"

"He says my anger is what made Jake commit this crime, and it's my anger that made him choose to go to a stinking jail cell instead of with me." Her pause was full. "Is he right? *Is* it me?"

Sully rubbed the back of his head with his free hand. "We haven't sorted all of that out yet. But I do know this: even if your rage is a factor, it isn't the whole reason. I don't think Jake's actions are just a way to get back at you for being angry. There's probably something else going on."

"Then I'm *not* nuts. Before this part went down, I learned some things that make me even more sure Jake didn't hurt that boy."

"Really. Tell me your theory."

She didn't seem to catch on that getting her to talk some more was an attempt to calm her down.

"Jake and Miguel Sanchez, the boy who was hurt, were soccer buddies. Jake even talked Miguel into trying out for a select team even though he wasn't in the league, and he made it. They both did. But Ginger—do you remember me talking about her?"

"The Spice Girl," Sully said. "Your ex-husband's—"

"His whatever. She has a son—Ian. Nice kid, considering she gave birth to him. He's like a big brother to Jake, who worships the ground he walks on. Jake even broke the rules of his bail to go to some meet the kid was in. Anyway, Ian tried out, too, and didn't make it. That could have put Jake between a rock and a hard place."

"How so?"

"What if Ian wanted to mess Miguel up for beating him out, and Jake was sucked in enough by whatever power Ian has over him to take care of that for him?"

Sully didn't say anything.

"That's pretty thin, isn't it?" she said. "I don't have any reason to think Ian would even be upset. I'm told soccer isn't his thing."

"You're just looking at possibilities," Sully said. "Have you mentioned this to anybody?"

"I was just putting it together when Dan called me. I didn't have a chance to tell him—not that he would believe me. He'd say I'm just trying to slime Ginger and her kid."

Sully heard something fall—or be flung.

"He probably wouldn't believe anything bad about Ian—but he's perfectly willing to let Jake go down for it without batting an eye. I do not under*stand* that!"

"No, you don't," Sully said quickly, before anything else could be thrown. "Because it doesn't make sense. No wonder you want to throw things. *I* would want to throw things if it were my kid."

"Great. You want to come over here, and we'll throw things together?"

He could imagine her shoving her hand through her hair.

"Okay, not funny. Are you going to give me some suggestions or what?"

"I can. There are things you can do to get through the weekend—and you can call me anytime. I'll give you my cell phone number. And then, Ryan, I think you need to pursue this with a therapist, because you're in it for the long haul. It doesn't have to be me—"

"Who else am I going to go to? I don't want to start all over and tell this whole thing to somebody else. Besides—" There was another rush of air. "At least you're not telling me I'm nuts."

"The people who are 'nuts' don't call me. They just blow up the police station."

"I hadn't thought of that," she said.

"Then you're definitely not nuts. Can you come in Monday?"

"I can wait until Tuesday, unless you gave my appointment away."

"Not yet. You sure?"

"Yeah." Her voice had wound down.

He didn't hear any more objects crashing. "You wanted some suggestions for the interim?" he said.

"Yeah, or I know I'll do something I'll regret."

Sully mentally ran through the options. She wouldn't like any of them; he hoped she was desperate enough to try one.

"How about this? Start with one set of muscles, tighten them up, and then consciously release them—"

"Have we met? Can you actually see me doing that?"

"Maybe not at the moment," Sully said. "But it might help you before you go to bed."

"What else have you got?"

"Anything you do is going to mean getting quiet and making an intentional effort to slow yourself down and stop beating up on things you can't lick right now." Sully shook his head. "So sit down."

"How do you know I'm not?"

"Just a hunch. Are you sitting?"

"Now I am," she said.

"Now think of the last place you went to that gave you a sense of calm." He hoped she even knew what that was.

"This is getting freaky," Ryan said. "I was just at White Sands this morning, and I think it was the first time I felt calm in my life."

"Great. So it's fresh in your mind. Now close your eyes—and yes, it's going to be woo-woo. Can you deal with that?"

"I guess I'm going to have to. All right, they're closed."

"Go to the place. And try to not only see it, but experience it with all your senses. Listen for whatever sounds you remember."

"That was the beauty of it. There were none."

"Then savor the silence. Feel the air on your skin or the sand between your toes—whatever you experienced tactilely."

"Okay. Go on."

Sully frowned slightly. She was obviously doing a checklist, but at least the edge in her voice was rounding off.

"Do the same with taste and smell. Just be there in every physical way you can."

She was quiet for all of ten seconds before she said, "Okay, then what?"

"Do you still want to tear up the police station?"

"Actually . . . no."

"Then it's working."

"Yeah, but for how long?"

"Until the next time you get that feeling, and then you do it again."

"I'm going to be spending a lot of mental time at White Sands."

"Good."

Ryan let another long pause form, and Sully waited her out.

"Okay," she said. "I'll take that cell phone number you offered. As long as you're sure you don't mind having your ear chewed off at two in the morning."

Sully grinned. "It's what I do."

When she hung up, Sully went out to the patio and gazed over the top of the adobe wall where the sun was turning the aspen leaves to copper coins. It was barely noon, and both he and Ryan had already found themselves at their respective crossroads. He was sure she would go to White Sands in her mind.

He just wasn't sure where to go in his.

CHAPTER TWENTY

I woke up Sunday with my pillow over my face and my cell phone ringing in my hand. Too groggy to check the ID, I fumbled the cell to my ear and mumbled a hello before my eyes were even open. I was instantly awake when I heard Dan's voice.

"Ryan, can you get over to county?"

I came off the bed, already scrambling for my jeans. "What's going on? Did something happen to Jake?"

"He's okay physically . . ."

"Dan—*what*?" I clamped my hand to my forehead and closed my eyes. "I'm sorry. Tell me."

"Evidently he had a rough night. I don't know any of the details, but they called and said he wants you to come get him."

I froze with one leg in my jeans and one bent at the knee.

"Can you go?" he said.

"I'll be there in ten minutes. Are you coming?"

"No. I'll drop by your place later and leave his clothes. We'll have to decide what to do about his school."

Right. Ginger was not coming to my home to tutor my son.

"We'll work that out." I shoved one arm into the sleeve of my leather jacket, still wearing the T-shirt I'd spent the night in. "Do you know what happened? Did someone hurt him?"

"No." Dan was clearly on the edge of tears. "They just said he told the guard this morning he changed his mind and he'd go with his mother. The guy who called me said he was pretty shaken up."

I could hear him barely holding on.

"Listen, you go, and please—"

"I'm not going to yell at him," I said.

"I wasn't going to say that. Just tell him I love him."

"You can tell him yourself when you come to bring his stuff."

"I can't see him, Ryan. I can't see him and not bring him home."

"I know the feeling," I said.

I wasn't prepared for what I saw when they released Jake to me. He'd looked thin and vulnerable the day before, but that couldn't compare to the almost transparent boy who seemed to have lost all muscle mass in the night and shook like a wet Chihuahua. The fear in his eyes was so deep I wasn't sure he would ever emerge from it.

He said nothing all the way home, and I didn't press him. I was afraid one word, even a kind one, would shatter him. When we got into the house, he glanced around briefly and said, "Where's the bathroom? I want to take a shower." It hit me like a kick in the stomach that he hadn't been there before.

While he stood under the water until I was sure it had long since turned cold, I built a fire in the kiva and heated a bowl of canned soup and set a cup of hot chocolate with whipped cream on the table next to the couch. Despite my lack of domesticity, I did everything short of producing a cat curled up on the hearth to make it homey.

Still, when he emerged from the bathroom, face scrubbed until his skin was raw, dressed in the black shirt and jeans he'd worn the day before, he sat on the edge of the sofa with his knees together and his shoulders curved inward until they nearly met at his sternum.

"I have a T-shirt you can change into if you want," I said. "I bought it for you at one of the festivals I was shooting, but I never got to give it to you."

"I'm okay in this," he said.

"It doesn't smell like jail?"

"They made me wear those orange things."

He retreated back into himself. I retreated to the kitchen so I wouldn't howl in horror. I poured the soup into a bowl and turned to take it back to the living room and nearly ran into him, right behind me.

"Do you want to eat in here?" I said.

"I'm not hungry," Jake said, but he sat on the edge of one of the metal Harley-Davidson stools at the snack bar.

I'd bought the set because it looked very boy. That was what I had in mind when I picked out everything for the house. The indestructible leather couch and chairs in the living room. The Chicago Bears towels in the bathroom. The Xbox and plasma screen in the den. None of it suited the airy Southwestern feel of the house, but I wanted it to be home for my sons.

But to Jake it was probably just another interrogation room, only this one had curtains and a closer who shared the same gene pool. I bit back all the questions I wanted to ask. He took two spoonfuls of the soup, but I could see he was forcing it down.

"Don't worry about it," I said. "You might be hungry later. Did you get any sleep last night?"

He shook his head.

"Was it too noisy?"

"They left the lights on all night."

"Oh, and you hate that. You couldn't even stand a night-light when you were a kid. Alex had to practically have a hundred-watt bulb in his face, but you wanted it totally dark."

I was rambling to fill up the silence.

But maybe silence was what he needed after all. I didn't know.

And neither, it seemed, did he.

When I suggested he take a nap, he said he wasn't tired. When I offered to turn on football, he shrugged, and I took that as a yes. He finally dozed on the couch under a Bears blanket, and I muted the TV and watched him.

He looked even younger and smaller when he was asleep, without the stoic, I-can-handle-this mask he'd worked so hard to wear. With his hair back from his face, I could see how chiseled and fine-tuned his bone structure was, how he was growing into a sensitive young man who, if he were true to himself, wouldn't be able to hide what stirred inside.

I wasn't aware that I was trying to cry again until I heard my own hard sobs. An image came to me unbidden, unwelcome . . . my son withering under a brutal light that never went out. I knew in that moment that he wouldn't survive in prison. And even if he never loved me as his mother again, I had to keep him out.

That conviction grew stronger as the day wore into the night. Jake didn't eat. He slept only fitfully and spent most of his time staring at his hands as if he didn't know what to do with them. Most telling was the way he shadowed me every time I left the room he was in. He tried to make it look like it was merely a coincidence that we wound up in the kitchen at the same time, when moments before he seemed to be conked out on the couch. After three or four times, I knew he was afraid to be alone. Before, that was all he had wanted.

When it was time to call it a night, I suggested he sleep on the couch, and I curled up in the recliner and pretended to drift off. I was awake for every leather-crackling toss and turn he made, every trip to the bathroom, every sigh that came from some sad place in his soul.

"Can I get you anything?" I said around three.

"A new life," he said.

"A new life?"

He didn't answer. His breathing became shallow and even, and I wasn't sure he hadn't been half-asleep already when he said it.

But it still made my decision for me about the next day. In the morning, after I'd brought in the paper—and discovered a bag of Jake's clothes on the front porch—and made the coffee and taken a shower, I sat on the edge of the coffee table and put my hand on his arm. He came awake with terror in his eyes.

"It's okay," I said. "It's time to get up."

"Why?" he said. "I'm not going back, am I?"

"No. But you do have a job."

He licked at dry lips and squinted at me.

"Get up," I said. "You're working for me now."

He didn't argue, and I was glad. I didn't want to tell him I wasn't leaving him alone, not for a minute, for a number of reasons. Not the least of which was that if he wanted a "new life," what did he intend to do with the old one?

We spent the morning at a ribbon cutting for a new preschool and a post-robbery scene at a liquor store. Jake carried equipment I usually lugged myself and held lights I didn't need and gave me directions I could have gotten from Perdita. He did it all without complaint. He was quiet, though not sullen, and it took every scrap of self-restraint—and a few mental visits to White Sands—not to try to coax him out. At least he'd stopped trembling, and when I asked him where he wanted to go for lunch, he chose Arby's.

I called Frances while he took a bite of roast beef and chewed it endlessly, as if he couldn't quite make himself swallow it. I'd already told her he'd be with me today.

"What else do you have for me?" I said to her.

"Nothing at the moment. I'm going to free you up to work on your colonias piece."

"Oh."

"I'm thinking you should go to that area off the mall and get the food, the crafts, the smiles for the tourists—you know, the stuff that lets us believe they're happy being poor and oppressed. That'll be jarring next to the rest of it."

My heart took a dive. She was sending me with Jake right into the neighborhood where his life had fallen apart.

"Keep your cell phone on, of course," Frances said. "How's your son doing?"

"Uh, fine."

"Is this some kind of take-your-kid-to-work thing?"

I could hear her typing, so I didn't have to answer.

"I'll call you if I need you for anything," she said. "Go for the home run."

I closed the phone and tossed it onto the table. Jake winced.

"I'm sorry," I said. "Did I startle you?"

"I just get freaked out," he said.

I took a bite and waited to see if there would be more, but he continued to tear up the sandwich he wasn't eating.

"Look, I don't want to freak you out more," I said, "but I have to go over by, like, Second and Third Streets and shoot some stuff for a piece I'm doing. On Mexican legals."

I waited again. He stopped ripping at the bread.

"Are you okay with that?" I asked.

"Why wouldn't I be?" His old defensiveness crept back into his voice.

"Look, Jake, I'm not trying to bring something up here. I just need to know if you can handle going down there right now."

He shrugged. Frustration needled at me, but I took a deep breath.

"All right, I'm going to ask you some questions, and all you have to do is nod or shake your head. I think we can pull that off without getting into a shouting match, don't you?"

He sat back in the chair and nodded.

"Did you spend much time down there by where Miguel got hurt before that day?"

"That's the only time I ever went."

"Did you ever meet any of Miguel's family?"

"No."

"Did you see his mother at the select team tryouts?"

His face jerked up. "How did you know about that?"

"Diego's mother," I said. "She was just telling me how good you were to Miguel," I said. "Did you see Miguel's mom?"

"Why do you want to know that?"

"I just need to know if you think she or anybody else in their family would recognize you if we saw them this afternoon."

"Only his mom came to the tryouts," he said in a voice I could barely hear. "I didn't even meet her."

I tried to envision the afternoon ahead. I could do all long shots and avoid the Ocotillo and the other restaurant where Elena Sanchez had worked. If Jake wore his ball cap and I kept him busy, it might work. With one exception.

I swallowed. "I need to ask you one more question, and it's only to protect you from somebody wanting to attack you or something."

He squinted at me, the way I knew I did at people when they were making no sense. But he shrugged.

"The day Miguel was hit by the truck," I said. "Did anybody see you sitting there in it before the police came?"

"There wasn't anybody else around."

"Nobody? Then who called 911?"

"I did."

I stared at him. "*You* did? Jake, I don't understand. Did you have a cell phone?"

"You said just one more question."

My head spun like a bicycle wheel, and I stuck the first stick I could find into its spokes. "Okay. That's all I need to know. I think we'll be all right down there. But if you see anybody you recognize, who might know who you are, just—tug on your earlobe."

"Do what?"

"Like a signal. I'll see that, and we'll split. Deal?"

A long breath came out of his nose, the relief I knew he was trying to disguise.

I was glad that afternoon that he didn't talk much. I needed the mind space to mull over what he'd told me. He'd been in the alley alone, in a truck he didn't know how to drive. And after he ran over his friend with it, he magically pulled a cell phone from somewhere and called 911. It was a good thing I did have work to do, because otherwise I couldn't have kept from shaking Jake until he gave me answers.

There was a little activity in front of a dark-looking coffee shop at one end of the mall, so we stopped there first. A group of older Hispanic men were having a good-natured argument, and they mugged enthusiastically for me before I could even raise the camera. I wasn't happy with the busyness of the scene—it would look cluttered online—so I switched to a 400 lens to get a long view of the empty mall.

All the while, I tried not to let Jake see me glancing at him to make sure he wasn't about to go into posttraumatic shock. We were nowhere close to the alley, but I had come to think of it all as Miguel's stomping ground.

I was shooting the last series for the day when Jake gave a stifled cry. When I looked up, he was fumbling for his earlobe.

"What?" I whispered. "Who did you see?"

I looked where he was looking. Detective Levi Baranovic approached us from no more than five feet away. How long he'd been standing there, I didn't know.

"Mrs. Coe," he said. "Jacob."

I didn't correct him, though I did want to throw Jake behind me and shield him with my body.

"Is there a problem?" I said. "Jake was released into my custody. I was told I could bring him out in public if I kept him with me."

He cast his green-eyed gaze over Jake. "Would you just step over there while I talk to your mother?"

Jake's eyes went wild.

"Why don't you pack up my camera," I said, handing it to him. And with a hard look at Baranovic I added, "I won't be long."

The detective lowered his voice to a growl. "You're taking pictures of these people for the paper?"

"Yes."

"What are you trying to do?"

"I'm trying to tell their story."

"What story? Don't you think Elena Sanchez and her family have been through enough without you trying to make them look like what happened to Miguel was his fault? Their fault?"

I had to talk with my teeth clamped together to keep from screaming. "You have no idea what I'm trying to do. They're suffering from injustices most people don't know about. That's what this story is—"

His gaze sharpened. "So you're going to tell their pitiful tale and make it look like you're on their side, so your son couldn't possibly have—"

"Are you going to charge me with something, or can I take Jake home? Because I don't think you have the authority to insult me." I started off, but I turned back. "No, wait. How about if I ask you a question, Detective? Have you people traced the 911 call? From the day of the shooting?"

He parked his hands on his hips. "It was a disposable cell phone. There's no way to trace who made the call."

"I'll tell you who made it—Jake himself."

"And you know this how?"

"Because he told me."

"Did he tell you anything else?"

"No."

"Look, I'm going to tell *you* something, Mrs. Coe: leave this to us. Meanwhile, if you raise sympathy for the Sanchez family, which I agree they deserve, you're going to make things worse for Jacob when he goes to trial."

"I don't see that."

"You should. You're part of the media—you've seen it happen. You've probably *made* it happen."

"What?"

"Do you want your son tried in the newspaper? Because that's what will happen if you do this." He jerked his thumb toward Jake. "Why don't you put your camera away and prepare your son for what's about to happen to *him*?"

I didn't watch him go. Jake did, and I knew he'd heard every word.

CHAPTER TWENTY-ONE

All right, I hate to admit it," Ryan said the moment she climbed into the chair. "You win."

Although Sully could see the telltale puffs of sleeplessness under her eyes and the tension in the muscles of her neck, she wasn't as tightly wound as he'd seen her before. She was, he guessed, too exhausted for a fight.

"I didn't know we were in a competition," he said, grinning. "You wanted no part of my Game Show Theology. I couldn't get you past the buzzes. We didn't even make it to the ding-ding-dings."

He could have predicted the squint.

"I'm too tired to tell you that you're a freak."

"So how did I win?"

"I tried what you gave me, and it worked."

"Then it sounds like *you* won."

Her smile was wan. "Does that mean I'm cured?"

"What do you think?"

"I think it got me through the weekend and yesterday without destroying any more property. That and the fact that I have my son with me now."

Sully felt his eyes widen.

Ryan filled him in on all that had transpired since their conversation Saturday, complete with her success at not grilling her son until he broke, which, she said, she might have done if she hadn't had White Sands to escape to.

"That's taken everything I've got," she said. "I'm grateful for the advice you gave me, but seriously, I don't know how much longer I can keep from blowing." She put her hands to her throat. "I can feel it right here, just waiting to explode."

"You're free to explode in here if you need to."

"But I don't want to. Isn't that the point of therapy?"

"The point is for you to identify what you feel and express it in a way that's true to you but doesn't ultimately make things worse than they are, for you or anybody else."

She squinted again, and new lines fanned out from the corners of her eyes. "I know what I feel."

"And that is?"

"Anger."

Sully resituated himself in his chair. Time to go in. "My guess is that anger is the way you're *expressing* how you feel. But *what* you feel is something else."

"And you know what I feel how?" Before Sully could answer, she put her hand up, eyes closed. "Forget I said that. I come to you for help, and then I keep throwing it back in your face. It's my default reaction when I'm frustrated."

"That may be one of the most astute things I've ever had a client tell me."

Ryan grunted. "I bet you say that to all the girls."

"Do you think that?"

"No." She did her signature hand-through-the-hair thing. "That's my other default reaction. Sarcasm."

"And I have to tell you, it's pretty funny sometimes."

"I'm glad you're amused."

Sully leaned forward. "Listen, Ryan, we're not trying to change your defaults. Sometimes they serve you well. What we're trying to do is give you other options."

"Then bring them on."

"I want to try something." He grinned at her again. "You're going to think this is woo-woo, but I want you to trust me."

"Trust is *not* one of my default reactions," she said drily.

"I don't know. You walked out of here angry last week, but when you were in trouble, you called me." He tilted his head at her. "So—you want to try trusting me again?"

She cocked an eyebrow. "Depends what it is."

Sully went to the table in the corner where he'd set the two-by-two wooden sandbox he'd made Sunday, complete with the finest-grade sand he could find at Home Depot. When he carried it to her, Ryan's mouth went up on one side.

"You're right," she said. "This *is* woo-woo."

"You haven't seen anything yet." Sully held it on one palm like a waiter's tray. "Where shall I put this so you can play in it while we talk?"

"Excuse me?"

"Just with your hands—unless you'd like some toy trucks or a bucket."

She was shaking her head, but she made a lap for the sandbox. It was a perfect fit.

"You're going to explain this to me, right?" she said.

Sully crouched beside the chair and put a hand in the sand. He lifted up a palmful, let it slide between his fingers, made an S in the pile and smoothed it over.

"Is this supposed to be calming?" Ryan said.

"It can be. Or it can keep you busy physically while we pursue things that might make you want to go into your default."

She looked doubtful.

"How often do you 'flip out' when you're on an assignment?" Sully asked.

"Never."

"Besides the fact that you have a tremendous amount of integrity, I think a lot of that is that you're physically busy." He shrugged. "That's why some people work out, punch a bag, that kind of thing."

Ryan tapped a finger on top of the sand. "You aren't afraid I'm going to throw this at you?"

"Are *you* afraid of that?"

She put a whole hand in and let the sand cover her fingers. "Weirdly, I'm not. I just want to help my son so bad I'll do whatever it takes."

"Then here's what I think it's going to take." Sully nodded at the sandbox. "You're doing fine, by the way."

"Uh-huh."

Sully sat down. "I think what we need to do is go back to when you first learned that anger could cover up hurt."

Her fingers stopped. "Did I learn that?"

"Let's find out. You told me your father would blow up over trivial things."

"He had to have control. When he didn't, he basically pitched a fit until he got it back." Ryan poked a hard finger into the sand. "Are you going to say that's where I got it?"

"He modeled behavior for you, but I don't think you 'got it' like a disease."

"I think I inherited a lot of his personality traits—most of which are not my favorite things about myself." The lines beside her mouth deepened as she poked more holes in the sand. "I tried to be a nice person for years, but I always felt like a fake because all this stuff was just seething under my skin. When I was married to Dan, I couldn't do it anymore. I wasn't a fake then, but I wasn't a nice person."

"Which is why you're here." Sully shrugged. "Ultimately, who we are can't be hidden. But here's the deal: when we face the worst that's in us, somehow we become better than we are—better than we ever thought we could be."

"So I face the fact that basically I'm not a nice person."

"Was your father a nice person?"

She considered that with a sift of sand through her fingers. "Sometimes. He wasn't *always* popping his cork about something. In fact, he was usually decent to me. It was my mother he took things out on."

"We'll get to her later. Tell me about your relationship with your father."

Ryan paused in the sifting. "This is going to take us someplace, right? I mean, at the moment, I feel like I'm in a Woody Allen movie."

Sully was liking this woman. "This isn't analysis. There is a point."

"My mother stayed out of my father's way, for obvious reasons, which left me alone with him a lot of the time."

Sully saw a red flag, but he let her go on.

"Once the dinner dishes were done, she'd go up to her craft room to make whatever new thing there was to make—decoupage, macramé, teddy bears. My father spent the evening supervising my homework, and then we would discuss, I don't know, current events or religion."

"How old were you?" Sully asked.

Ryan looked up from the sandbox where she had begun a pyramid. "I could tell you all of Jimmy Carter's screw-ups at age eight. When I was ten, Father was taking me to a different religious ceremony every weekend so I could decide for myself whether I was going to become Greek Orthodox or Unitarian or whatever."

"You're not exaggerating."

"Not at all. By then my parents were living completely separate lives—she was teaching Sunday school, and he was on the lecture circuit for the ACLU. It's a wonder I'm not schizophrenic." She looked sideways at Sully. "Am I?"

He shook his head. "What was your relationship with your mother like while your father was on the road?"

"I was on the road with him. He tutored me in hotels during the day, and I sat through his lectures at night. I saw most of the United States before I was fifteen and asked if I could please go to high school and be a normal kid."

"What was his reaction to that?"

Sully watched her hands in the sand as she continued to stack the structure she was building.

"It was one of the few times he did yell at me. Told me I was giving up a real education to become a cheerleader." She gave Sully a wry look. "Can you see me with a pair of pom-poms? I mean, seriously."

"Definitely not your style. But he didn't refuse to let you go to public school?"

"No. He couldn't raise me to make my own decisions and then not let me make one. I had to do all the research and present him with a dossier on every school in the county, mind you, but I got to choose." She pushed the pyramid over with the side of her hand. "He gave up the lecture tour, though, and worked from home, which was the end of my parents' marriage. My mother was way too independent by then to put up with his domination."

"And you stayed with your father?"

"Only for as long as I had to. He bought a house and started entertaining all these big-name liberals and expecting me to play hostess. That's why I got on the school newspaper staff and joined the photography club—so I'd have an excuse not to be there for every soiree." She dusted her hands off and frowned at Sully. "Is this taking us where we're supposed to go?"

"I think so." Sully rubbed his mouth. Asking what he had to ask could land that sandbox right in his lap. "Let me ask you a question," he said. "I'm not trying to put ideas in your head."

"You want to know if he sexually abused me."

Sully blinked.

"My roommate in college asked me that." Ryan rolled her eyes. "She was an overenthusiastic psych major. She said my relationship with my father sounded incestuous to her."

"And?"

"I told her she was a fruitcake. I mean, I admit it was a weird set-up and my father was way too—something—with me, but as for anything sexual, no. Quite frankly, I think the old man might have been gay."

Sully was having a hard time keeping his chin from dropping.

"He never looked at another woman the whole time we were

traveling. He barely looked at my mother. And after they were divorced, he didn't date—even though he wasn't a bad-looking man. He was actually kind of charismatic from behind the podium."

"You're saying *was.*"

"He died a year after I got out of college. Sudden heart attack at one of his own dinner parties." Ryan started on another pyramid. "One of the reasons I know I'm not a nice person is that I've thought more than once how glad I am he died that way instead of suffering from a long illness. He would have expected me to take care of him." She pulled her hands from the sand and looked at Sully. "So what does all this tell you?"

He didn't even know where to begin. She'd given him more information in twenty minutes than most clients did in four sessions. And he was certain there was more.

"I have to agree with your roommate about one thing," he said. "Your relationship with your father *was* incestuous—but maybe only emotionally so. He depended on you to fill his life the way a wife usually does. It looked like love, but it was an egotistical using of you. That's what incest is."

"So you're saying that's why I'm angry." She was motionless, watching him.

"It could be part of it. Your father's love seemed to depend on what you could do for him. Didn't you start getting tired of the whole set-up when you were in high school?"

"I wouldn't use the word *tired,*" she said. "*Ticked off* works. But everybody was ticked off at their parents for something."

"This whole thing with your father is interesting." Sully pulled one leg up into the chair and folded it under him. "He was angry and controlling, but he didn't take it out on you in ways that are typically seen as harmful."

"No," Ryan said. "He just smothered me." She sat back stiffly from the sandbox.

"Can you talk about that?" Sully said.

"I don't think it means anything. It happened long before I came along."

"What did?"

"They had another baby before me, but he died. SIDS. They called it 'crib death' then. I didn't even know about it until I was twelve. Father and I were sitting in a restaurant in Boston, and he just spun out this tale about how I would have had a brother, but he only lived to be six months old. The baby died in his sleep. Father said if they'd had a baby monitor, they would have heard him struggling for air and they could have saved him."

"That must have been hard to hear."

"I don't know. I spent a lot of time after that wondering what it would have been like to have a big brother. That stopped when I brought it up another time and asked what his name was."

"What was it?"

"Ryan."

Sully tried not to wince openly.

"Yeah, it didn't take a rocket scientist to figure that one out. Even at twelve I knew I was the replacement child." She shrugged and went back to the sand, though she didn't seem to know what to do with it now.

"That may explain a few things, though," Sully said, before she could dive any further behind the sarcasm.

"Such as?"

"Your father's pain. His guilt. His fury with your mother. I'd be willing to bet it all came out as anger—but he couldn't direct it at you. He had to protect you the way he didn't protect the baby."

"Which was why he never wanted me out of his sight." Ryan studied her quiet hands. "So you're saying that's what *I* do?"

"It's a possibility. It would be worth uncovering the hurts to find out if it is."

"I don't want to do that." Ryan picked up the sandbox and set it on the trunk. She ran a hand through her hair, leaving several grains of sand on her forehead, which she smacked away.

"Are you afraid to?" Sully asked.

"No!" She scowled at him. "Yes—and I deal worse with fear than I do with anger, so let's not go there."

"Really. What do you do when you're afraid?"

"I lash out at people, cabinet doors, mirrors. You name it."

"So it all gets expressed as anger." Sully unfolded his leg and tilted toward her again. "Ryan, that's what we're here to deal with. My job is to help you navigate the fear and the hurt and whatever else comes up, so you'll know how to do it on your own. Isn't that what you want?"

"I want you to tell me how to do it, and I'll do it. I don't want to experience the past again." She put both hands to her temples. "That's absurd, I know. I am a complete mess!"

"It's good when it gets messy," Sully said. "Hard, but good, because that's when the stuff we need to see comes to the surface. That's where God is." He gave her a slow smile. "We've started to see what hurts, Ryan. And that is a very good mess to be in."

CHAPTER TWENTY-TWO

By Wednesday, I suspected Jake's memory of his night in jail had paled enough that he was ready to reconsider his decision to stay with me.

I wasn't pushing him to talk, though I had to practically bury myself in mental sand not to. I didn't even hover over his schoolwork or nag him about his lack of food intake or mention that he might consider combing his hair more than once a day.

But the kind of togetherness we were forced into didn't fit either of our personalities. He went to work with me all day. Did his homework in another therapy room while I was with Dr. Crisp. Sat on the top row of bleachers with me while we watched Alex's soccer practices. And spent the evenings in my home office doing the schoolwork I picked up from the district while I worked on the colonias story on my computer. I was a prime candidate for Mother of the Year—but he still had to be sick of me.

I couldn't deny the whole thing put a crimp in my routine too. Though I made sure I took snacks to soccer practice when I was supposed to and told Alex every day that he was awesome, I didn't go to Dan's to "work on my dribbling" with him, and not spending time with Alex was ripping me apart.

To my surprise I missed the soccer moms too. I wasn't even sure I wanted to talk to them about what was happening. I just wanted to be with them. We waved to each other at practice, and Poco folded her hands to her chest to show me they were praying for us, but according to his restrictions, Jake wasn't supposed to be involved in any school or community activities with other kids, and

I wasn't taking the slightest chance. Ever since my run-in with Detective Baranovic, I felt like I was under surveillance.

Jake's and my only time of separation was during the night. After Sunday he slept in the room I'd fixed up for him, though I woke up several times in the wee hours to see him standing in my doorway. I sensed he just wanted to make sure I was still there—or that he was.

I would then lie awake for an hour or two, though I didn't mind that so much. It was then that I started to get the God-images again.

They were faint and out of focus, but there nevertheless. An image of sand motionless in an hourglass. And of Jake alone in the alley, picking up a cell phone, checking Miguel for a pulse. They were comforting on the one hand, though I couldn't have said why.

Yet they tormented me too. Time was not standing still. I had to do something with the new information I had—that maybe Ian had a motive for wanting Miguel hurt, however far-fetched—and that Jake was the one who called 911 on an unexplained cell phone. But the scene with Detective Baranovic had done more than just make me paranoid. It convinced me he'd be more interested in an investigative report from a crazy psychic than from me. I'd have to put this together myself.

When I told Uriel Cohen about Jake's call to 911, she was more impressed with my detective skills.

"So what do we do with this information?" I said. Although I wanted to, I didn't add, *Why aren't* you *doing some investigative work? What* are *you doing, anyway?*

"It might help show that Jake tried to help Miguel Sanchez after he hit him," she said. "A jury likes remorse."

I didn't tell her anything else.

In the crazy small hours of wakefulness Wednesday morning, I began to process what I'd talked to Sullivan Crisp about. I expected to be mad at myself for opening a vein like that. I even tried to be annoyed with Crisp for handing me the scalpel. But I didn't have the energy. I knew it wouldn't have felt good anyway, not the way anger usually did when I first let it go. All I could do was lie there and ache and think of those dunes on the desert.

And pray. I realized I hadn't prayed in weeks. I had only expected God to give me visual answers to questions I didn't ask.

As a result of all that nighttime activity, even two cups of coffee didn't fully wake me up when the day dawned. Jake and I went to the downtown mall to shoot the Farmers and Crafts Market, with me still trying to get the dust bunnies out of my head.

I did have enough wherewithal to steer clear of the Ocotillo Coffee Shop, but I had absolutely no edge as Jake and I wandered up the mall, shooting a box full of scrawny kittens and a woman holding two runny-nosed toddlers on her lap while she sold sandwich bags full of chili powder.

"Mom."

It had been so long since I'd heard Jake say that, I didn't realize it was him until he said it again. He was so close I could feel his breath on my cheek. When I looked at him, he was yanking on his earlobe, eyes frantic.

I let the camera fall against my chest and looked where he darted his gaze. Elena Sanchez was no more than three feet from us, deep in Spanish conversation with a half-blind woman crocheting booties.

"We should get out of here," Jake whispered. But adolescent boys can't whisper, and the upward shot of his voice drew the attention of more than one person.

I shook my head, still groping wildly for a sane thought.

"Mom?" he said again.

"Okay—here." I pulled the strap over my head and pressed the camera into his hands. With my lips near his ear, I said, "Stay close, and just take pictures. Keep the camera in front of your face. I'll make sure she doesn't see you, and we'll just move away. Okay?"

He stared at the camera.

"Okay, son?"

"Yeah," he said. "Okay."

He turned from me and did as I said. I glanced over my shoulder just as Elena looked up from the blind woman. Her face broke into a smile.

"Grafa!" She came to me, hands outstretched, and clasped mine between them.

"Are you well?" I said.

My voice was shrill and unnatural, but she didn't seem to notice. Behind me I could hear the camera clicking.

"I am well," she said. "Miguel, he left the hospital."

"Really?" I said. I wasn't sure how that could be, but I nodded with her as she beamed.

"He is now in—what is called? Long-term care."

She pronounced each word with pride, as if Miguel had graduated to a higher level. My heart sank.

"Is he still . . . the same?" I said.

"In a coma still, yes." Elena blinked rapidly. "But he is no in intense care, and this is good."

"Of course," I said.

Then we locked gazes, and I saw the same truth in hers that I tried to keep out of mine. Long-term care was not graduation.

She gave my hands a squeeze and let go. "You will pray?"

"Every day," I said.

"Then God, he will take care of Miguel."

With a sad smile, she melted back into the crowd. I turned to find Jake, who was only a step behind me, the camera swaying on its strap around his neck.

"Can we go?" he asked.

"Absolutely," I said.

He said nothing as we wove through the shoppers and crafters, and he was still quiet in the car until we pulled into the drive-through at Starbucks.

"Do you want a hot chocolate?" I said.

He shook his head. His face was gray.

"Son—please, talk to me."

"What does it mean that Miguel's in long-term care?"

"May I take your order, please?" the box squawked at me.

"No," I said and pulled out of the line and into a parking space. I turned to Jake.

I selected my tone carefully. "It means they can't do anything else for him in the hospital. But it also means he's stable."

"What's stable?"

"He's not in danger of dying." I didn't add that he wasn't in danger of living, either.

I waited. He curved over until his hair covered his face.

"Jake."

"Let's just go back to work," he said.

I looked at my watch. I didn't have another assignment at the moment. It was ten, which meant the morning crowd would have thinned out at Milagro Coffee.

"We need food," I said.

I took El Paseo Road, stealing glances at Jake as I drove and wishing he would just cry. I had just turned left onto University Avenue when he sat up straight and pointed.

"It's up," he said.

"What?"

"His piece."

I made a fast turn into the New Mexico State campus.

"There?" Jake pointed. "See it?"

I pulled into the parking lot of a large adobe building. Before us on the lawn was an enormous stand of slender poles, cantilevered to hold themselves together like a molecule. The impression was that if you took one away, it would all fall apart.

"It's part of his gravitational series," Jake said, awe in his voice.

"Your dad's?"

He nodded. "That is sick."

"I don't know," I said. "I actually think it's kind of amazing."

"Mom," he said. "That's what *sick* means."

"Oh."

"Thanks for stopping. I just wanted to see it."

He seemed to be calmed by it, which made my own unsettled feeling worth it.

Milagro Coffee was nearly deserted when we got there. Jake and I took a table near the back, and I told him to put the reader card from the camera into the laptop while I ordered us some drinks.

"Hot chocolate?" I offered again.

"Mocha," he said.

When I came back to the table, he was already looking at the laptop screen. I sat beside him and put his mocha in his hand and sipped at my coffee as he clicked through the shots I'd taken of kittens and old women. I stopped him when a close shot of a pair of large, soulful black-brown eyes came up.

"Wait," I said. "When did I take that?"

"You didn't," Jake said. "I did. You don't want to see these."

"Yes, I do. Let me look."

I put my cup down and peered more closely. The light wasn't quite right, but the composition was compelling. And there was something else.

"Jake, do you see that?" I pointed to the reflection in the child's eyes. "Is that a ball—what is that?"

"It's a balloon she was looking at. I was just trying something. It didn't work."

"It almost did. Let me see what else you got."

He clicked again and brought into view a tiny Hispanic girl, the owner of the dreaming eyes, with a kitten curled into the curve of her neck. This time he'd gotten good contrast, no shadows. He'd captured the softness and the innocence, but he hadn't lost the too-old sadness of a scene in which both the child and the kitten would have to grow up too fast.

"This is good, Jake," I said.

"It's okay."

"I'm serious. I wouldn't say it if it weren't true."

His face flushed, a blotch of pink here, a splash of red there. "That's why I do bad in school."

"You're going to have to explain that one to me."

Jake shrugged. "They always make you write everything, and I can't write—not like I can show things in pictures. Dad says he had the same problem in school."

"Until he went to college. The professors at Northwestern said he was the most gifted student they'd had in twenty years."

Jake flipped his hair back to look at me. "You knew Dad in college?"

"That's how we met."

He nodded at me, as if he wanted me to go on. It wasn't a subject *I* wanted to pursue, but it at least had Jake out from behind his hair.

"There was a rash of student suicides on campus that semester," I said. "People were having a hard time dealing with it, so the art department put out a table in the commons with clay on it and offered 'art catharsis.'"

I'd found it sort of lame at the time, but Jake seemed to be digging it now, so I continued.

"I was taking an art class that semester, so I went, and I was sort of poking some holes in a wad of clay when this guy comes up with hair down to here." I pointed to my shoulder. "And he grabbed a hunk and stuck it on a Coke bottle and made this English bobby. You know what that is?"

"Yeah—cop in London."

"Right. He made it like a cartoon in three dimensions. Big belly and clown shoes and suspenders. I just stood there watching him—I mean, not just because I thought he was hot—"

"Was it Dad?"

"Uh-huh."

"Then I don't want to hear about him being hot, okay?"

"Right. Anyway, after he gave it a billy club behind its back and this huge moustache, like a walrus, he gave it to them to fire it. I said, 'So you must be an art major,' and he said no. And he just walked away." I pondered the memory for a second. "He obviously did not find me hot."

"Dude."

"Sorry. So about two weeks later, I'm in class and he comes marching in and goes up to the professor, wanting to know where his sculpture is—you know, like the art department had stolen it or something. I tuned in to the conversation because I still thought—"

Jake put his hand up.

"Anyway, the art professor said he wouldn't give it back to him until he promised to sign up for sculpting the next semester." I couldn't hold back a smile. "So I signed up for it too. I was horrible at it, but your father was obviously so gifted. And then after the first week he stopped coming to class, and the prof asked if anybody knew what was going on with him because he was going to fail the course if he didn't start showing up. I volunteered to find out."

"You were, like, stalking him," Jake said.

The correct response to that was that I always went after what I wanted. But I couldn't say it. I could barely go on with the story, actually. Only the light in Jake's eyes, the light I hadn't seen in him for so long, made me willing to tell anything to keep it there.

"I went to his dorm, and there was all this *stuff* he'd made. I didn't get most of it, but I knew the art people would go nuts over it. I helped him take all of it to the department and, like I thought, they were gaga over it. After that, I just stayed on him to keep doing it, keep taking classes, and he finally changed his major."

I took a long drink of my now-cold coffee, which did nothing for the lump growing in my throat. How long had it been since I'd thought of my supporting Dan in the beginning, when he was a reluctant artist?

I cleared my throat and pointed to the laptop. "So show me the rest."

Jake licked at his lips and turned to the screen. He had taken several more shots, all of which showed a feel for his subjects that made up for the lack of technical skill. Most of that could be fixed. The more I studied them, the bigger the lump grew, until I couldn't swallow.

Jake sat back and actually took a long gulp from his cup.

"You say you never spent any time with Miguel except for soccer," I said, voice thick. "But, Jake, you know these people." I pressed my hand to my chest. "In here. It shows in these pictures. And I know, I *know* if you did hurt Miguel, you didn't do it on purpose."

He stiffened, and I stopped. He was done. So, in fact, was I. We were moving into a forest of emotion neither one of us would know how to find our way out of.

"Okay, no more." I fished out my cell. "Let's see what Frances has for us."

What Frances had was a summons to her office, delivered the instant she picked up the phone, in a taut voice I hadn't heard her use before.

"What's wrong?" I said.

"I'll see you in twenty minutes—alone," she said and hung up.

I closed the phone slowly against my cheek. Several different scenarios flipped through my head, none of them good.

"Are you busted?" Jake said.

I looked down to see that he already had the laptop packed up and was handing me the reader card. I started to say it was just a routine check-in, but he was studying me. He'd watched me that way even as a baby, sitting in his high chair, eyes intent as a scientist's, as if he were gathering data from the way I heated his strained carrots and dug in the dishwasher for the little spoon. The moment I caught him deep in observation that way, his face had always softened into a shy smile, complete with sweet baby drool. He'd trusted me implicitly then. I wanted that trust again.

"Yeah, it does sound like we're busted," I said. "We have to go over to the paper."

I reached for the laptop bag, but Jake got to it first and slung it over his shoulder. He was quiet again until we got in the car.

"Is it because of me?" he said as I headed toward the *Sun-News* building.

"I honestly don't know," I said. "But don't worry about it."

He gave me a teenage-boy grunt.

"What?" I said.

"I've screwed everything up, and I'm not supposed to worry about it?"

"Jake, you haven't—"

"Yes, I have!"

"What's happened with you has created its own set of problems, there's no denying that. But this one isn't yours to solve. The only thing you have to do is help yourself."

I sneaked a glance at him in the guise of looking back to change lanes. He'd crossed his chest with his arms, hands in the opposite pits. I had about ten seconds before he'd shut down again.

"If you want to unscrew something for me, son, start talking to me about exactly what happened."

Jake didn't answer, and for the first time since he'd come to stay with me, I felt the kind of frustration with him that was going to have me turning up the volume and getting in his face if I didn't back down now.

What was that expression Crisp used? Dang? Jake came so close, and then he ran away—like his three-year-old self on the beach, wanting so badly to put his toe into the water, but scampering away just as it raced up to his little-boy foot. I used to coax him, "It won't hurt you, Jake! It's fun, watch!" And Dan always scooped him into his arms and said, "When you're ready, right, buddy?"

A pain shot through my hands, and I realized I was squeezing the steering wheel. Jake was turned from me, forehead on the side window.

"When you're ready, son," I said. "Just let me know."

I got him settled in my cubicle with homework and a Dr Pepper, promised myself I would stop plying him with junk beverages, and headed for Frances's office with my laptop. I hadn't had time to get into a snit about being summoned, but I worked myself into one by the time I stuck my head in her door.

"Is there a problem?" I said.

"Good morning to you too," she said. The pop-eyes were more watery than usual.

"I got summarily called to the principal's office. I didn't think you wanted to make small talk."

She motioned to the only chair not piled with assorted files. When I didn't sit, she said, "I don't appreciate your using the paper for your own personal vendetta."

"Excuse me?"

"Don't pretend you don't know what I'm talking about, or I will lose all respect for you—and I'm already heading there."

"If you're talking about the colonias story—"

"What else would I be talking about?"

"It isn't a vendetta. It's a bona fide—"

"Don't insult my intelligence, Ryan! You've already slapped me in the face by not telling me it was your son who ran over that Mexican kid. I had to find it out from some detective who called the main office to complain that the perpetrator's mother was using her journalistic status to influence the victim's family." Frances's eyes bulged farther than I'd thought possible. "I've given you a lot of rope because you're supposedly the ultimate professional. I didn't expect you to hang me with it."

I didn't say anything. I just opened the laptop and turned it on.

"Aren't you going to tell me I'm wrong?" she said. "That Detective Baranovic, who until now has been a friend of the *News*, is lying?"

"No." I turned the laptop toward her. "I'm going to show you."

I clicked to the picture of the old men at the coffee shop and juxtaposed it to the man with his burned trailer. Then I set the children asleep in the car next to the one Jake had taken of the balloons in the child's sad eyes. I went through them all, and I watched Frances's face as she looked at the screen, begrudgingly at first, and then with distaste, and finally with the mixture of horror and compassion I had felt from the other side of the camera.

When the series started over and she continued to study the photos, I sat on the edge of the chair.

"Yes, I went up to El Milagro to find out what I could about the Sanchez family, thinking I might discover some piece that could be used in Jake's defense. What I found was this story." I tapped the top of the screen. "If anything, what I've learned makes things worse for my son. Elena Sanchez doesn't even know who I am, and I'd like to keep it that way."

Frances looked at me over the lid of the computer. "You haven't been wearing your press pass?"

"Yeah, but they only know me as Ryan Alexander. I don't even know if they know Jake's name. And Elena Sanchez just calls me *Grafa*."

"Short for *fotografa*." Frances sat back and folded her veined hands under her chin. Everything on her face pulled to a point. "I don't like you not being totally up front with these people."

"Oh, come on, Frances—don't be a hypocrite. Some of the stuff that goes on in this department is one step shy of the tabloids, and you know it."

She ignored that and once again tapped the computer. "But this I like. It's over the fence, Ryan. Even without audio."

"I have audio. But . . . over the fence?"

"It's a home run."

"Oh," I said.

"I think you have enough here, especially if you have sound. Put it together and run it by me."

"I could still use a few more shots of—"

She turned the laptop toward me and motioned with her hands to get it off her desk. "Wrap it up, Ryan. For my sake—for yours. Do we understand each other?"

No. But I was walking out of there with my job intact and the Sanchez story still alive. At the moment, I couldn't expect more than that.

"Oh, and Ryan . . ."

I turned in the doorway. Frances was squeezing the bridge of her nose with two fingers, eyes closed under bulbous lids. "If you need anything, you know, for your boy, let me know. A good lawyer . . . time off . . .”

The starch went completely out of me.

“My daughter got picked up on a DUI on her twenty-first birthday,” she said, “and I discovered then that as a parent, you’re the only real advocate your kid has.”

“Yeah,” I said. “I hear you.”

CHAPTER TWENTY-THREE

Sully's session with Ryan the day before had gone well. She hadn't stormed out or threatened to hurl projectiles. She had, in fact, seemed ready to face her pain.

So why was he pacing around his office like a kid with ADHD? Sully stopped, his hand in the mini-sandbox, and sifted its contents through his fingers. Porphyria would say he needed to settle down and do some self-therapy. If she could talk to him right now.

Winnie had called Sunday to report that the pacemaker replacement was a success, but the doctor wanted to keep Porphyria in the hospital until he was sure it was working properly. It was just routine. Porphyria had already been hospitalized for sixteen days. Insurance companies didn't let you do that for "routine." Nor was it routine for his energetic mentor to be sleeping every time he called.

Sully forced himself to flop into a chair and stack his ankles on the desk. He was out of Frappuccinos. That wasn't routine either. And he couldn't blame it on Ryan Coe or his beloved Porphyria. It was this Belinda Cox thing.

Knowing her alias was Zahira and that she was "ministering" somewhere in Mesilla left him not much further than he'd been before Sarah's call. He'd prayed for clear guidance. He knew better than to proceed before he got it. How many times had he told a client: "If you don't know what to do, don't do anything yet." Holy crow. He hated his own advice sometimes.

In an effort to think about something else, Sully reached for Carla Korman's file on his desk. He had to agree with the sticky note Martha had put on it: there was nothing in her background at

Healing Choice or elsewhere to indicate that she would do the kinds of things people had complained of. Even the complainants couldn't indicate it, because not one of them was reachable. He'd talked to Rusty Huff about it, but he couldn't give Sully any more information than they already had.

Sully picked up his recorder. "Now I know why I didn't become a private detective instead of a therapist," he said into it. "I stink at it."

Kyle stuck his head in Sully's open doorway. "You still playing with that dinosaur?"

"I'm pretty much hopeless."

"Do you have dinner plans?"

Sully let a grin slide across his face as he dropped the recorder into his pocket. "Ethiopian food?"

"Nah. I've got someplace else in mind."

"Then you're on."

When Sully met him in his office, Kyle was simultaneously turning off his computer and sliding his arms into the sleeves of his jacket. Sully hadn't been in there since Kyle had moved in, and he liked its inviting look—rugs and lamps and sepia photos. In one a striking young woman looked out from the frame, hair blown back from a face that was all smile and bright eyes and personality.

"Pretty lady," Sully said. "Girlfriend?"

Kyle looked at the photo as if the young woman could see him loving her with his eyes, and shook his head. "That's Hayley. My wife. You all set?"

"Depends what you're going to subject me to," Sully said. He decided to postpone the questions that crowded in.

They both folded themselves into Kyle's Mini Cooper, which, Sully pointed out as they headed down Union, had a loose fan belt.

"I know. I haven't had a chance to have it fixed. I understand you're pretty handy under the hood."

"I hung up my wrenches about a year and a half ago," Sully said.

"Okay, the suspense is killing me. What thing I can't pronounce am I going to have to eat?"

"Man, the surprise is the best part."

Sully *was* surprised when they sat down in a new steakhouse whose menu boasted nothing more exotic than a fried olive appetizer.

"What, no sushi?" Sully said. "No Asian duck quesadilla or some dang thing?"

"I already gave up on you," Kyle said.

When they'd ordered rib eyes and an order of the olives, Sully was ready to get to his questions, but Kyle dove in first.

"You know I've listened to your podcasts, read all your books."

"You mentioned that." More than once, to the point of overkill.

"It makes me feel like I know more about you than I do—you're that transparent with your work. But I realized I don't know anything about, say, your family."

"I could say the same thing about you." Sully cocked an eyebrow at him. "For instance, you're married?"

Kyle kept his eyes on the martini glass full of olives that their trim, raven-haired server set on the table. When she was gone, he smiled the same smile he'd given the photograph on his desk.

"I *was* married. It's still hard to think of myself any other way."

Ouch. "Divorce?" Sully said.

"No. Hayley died in an accident eighteen months ago."

"Oh, man, I am so sorry."

"Yeah, thanks. It was a pretty tough shot."

Sully wiped his hands on his napkin. "You're doing great for being only a year and a half out."

"I have my moments. Thank God for himself, right?"

"Yeah."

"I don't know what I'd do without the Lord." Kyle toyed with a breaded olive. "I'm closer to him now than I ever was before—since the night I sat on the edge of the bathtub with a kitchen knife pressed against my wrist." He left the olive in the glass and leaned back. "I told myself I just wanted to see if I could feel anything, but all I *knew* was pain. You might never have been that far down, but I just couldn't take it anymore."

Sully nodded.

"And then it was like something stopped my hand. Well, not some*thing*—I knew it was God saying, 'I'll take you when *I* want you.'" Kyle gave Sully a sheepish smile. "Sorry. I didn't mean to put a damper on the evening."

"No, no, it's okay. So you got help after that."

"From your books. Your radio show. The podcasts on suffering last year did more for me than anything."

"That's not meant to take the place of therapy."

"I know. That disclaimer is all over your stuff." Kyle's eyes went to the server approaching with their dinners and lowered his voice. "But it worked for me, Sully. If it weren't for you, I probably wouldn't be here."

Rib eyes, baked potatoes, half-ears of corn, and enough bread for a family reunion appeared. The waitress took her time getting it all on the table, slowed down by the need to chat with Kyle, smile at Kyle, all but curl up in Kyle's lap. Sully himself was more or less invisible. He waited until after the final, hopeful, "Can I get you anything else?" before he leaned into the table.

"Look, Kyle, if you do need to talk—"

"I didn't take this job to get free therapy. I just wanted to work with the person who taught me so much about helping people in pain."

Kyle looked openly at Sully, eyes wet but unashamed. Sully looked back and wished Martha Fitzgerald could have heard that. Therapists could become as educated and well trained and professional as it was possible to be, and their own personal pain and recovery would still find its way into their practice. He'd tell Martha that wasn't always a bad thing.

"You haven't tried your steak." Kyle cut into his and observed it critically before he said, "Now that's what I'm talkin' about."

Sully sawed off a piece and chewed while he watched Kyle dig in. He was definitely young. People over forty didn't attack a steak the way Kyle did. In spite of his loss, and his self-conscious gourmet status, he hadn't yet learned to savor life's flavors. But this new revelation had peeled off a layer that was older than his years.

"So what about you?" Kyle said. "Where did all your gutsy wisdom come from?" He grinned as he chewed. "If you don't mind me asking."

Sully grinned back and inhaled the steak and the selection of starches like he hadn't eaten in weeks, and gave a more detailed version of his schooling in psychology at Vanderbilt under Porphyria Ghent than he shared with most people. Kyle devoured his meal, never taking his eyes from Sully while he talked, not shifting his gaze to the flirty server who came by every three minutes to check on him or letting it wander to the tray of decadent desserts she was hefting. He listened in that way only somebody who'd been there could do.

Kyle finished eating before Sully and ordered coffee and flan. Sully passed. He still had a quarter of a steak to finish.

"You're going to get extra caramel sauce—you know that, don't you?" Sully said when the waitress had run off happily with Kyle's dessert order.

"Huh?"

"Don't tell me you haven't noticed her trying to crawl into your pocket. You could probably get a neck massage. To go."

"Not interested. I've come a long way, but not that far. But speaking of pictures on desks . . ." Kyle stopped and took the coffee from the server, who now identified herself as Zoe and gave him every option for his coffee, from full-out cream to skim milk.

Sully shifted in his seat and tried to mark out a direction. It had been awhile since he'd been with a colleague who wasn't a mentor or didn't need one.

"I think you're spot on," Kyle said when Zoe was gone. "She's making another whole trip to get the flan."

"Don't be surprised if she puts her phone number on the check—which, by the way, I'm picking up."

"No way. I invited you." Kyle sat back with his coffee and sipped in spite of the steam pouring from it.

Sully watched him and felt something give within, a thawing of ground long hardened. "The picture on my desk," he said. "That's my wife and baby. Was them. I still have a hard time putting them in the past tense."

Kyle grimaced. "How long has it been?"

"Fourteen and a half years," Sully said. "And there are times when I don't think I'm as far along as you are."

The flan arrived, flooded with sauce, but Kyle didn't touch it.

"In your podcasts, the series on suffering, you never said exactly what it was you had to deal with, but I had no idea it was something that devastating. Do you mind me asking what happened?"

By now Sully was unsurprised that he didn't, in fact, mind. As Kyle listened, Sully described his thirteen years of burying his guilt and pain and anger under a career designed to heal the hurts in people's lives when he couldn't face the gaping wound in his own.

"You said I probably haven't been where you were, ready to slit my wrists," Sully said, "but I almost ran myself off a bridge. It took that for me to get the kind of help I was offering everyone else."

"Which now makes you an even more incredible minister than you were before," Kyle said.

"I don't know. I took a three-month leave of absence, and when I did test the waters again, I was scared spitless. That's when I did the podcasts."

"But since then you've been incredibly productive. I mean, the speaking tour." Kyle folded his hands behind his head. "I caught your act in Little Rock, which was where I was living at the time, and I bought the DVD Healing Choice produced when you spoke in Oklahoma City."

Sully rearranged his silverware on the plate Zoe had yet to remove. Should he tell Kyle the underlying motive for doing those particular cities, and Amarillo? That he'd chosen them because they were places Belinda Cox had lighted before she wound up in Las Cruces?

"So are you ever going to go public with this?" Kyle asked. "Not that you necessarily should, but if people knew, I mean, think of the impact it could have."

"The story's not over yet." Sully gave Kyle one more search for mere curiosity. He saw only his own former self, grasping for understanding wherever he could get it. That, and the pain he knew Kyle would never be rid of.

"I'm looking for Belinda Cox, Lynn's so-called therapist," he said. "She's apparently somewhere in Mesilla, still practicing—something. I'm struggling with whether I should find her and stop her. If I even can. I'm questioning my motivation."

Kyle pushed his untouched plate of flan aside and leaned forward, hands flat on the table. "You have to do this," he said. "Not just for your own grief work, but for the people this woman could be keeping from getting real help. You owe them that. And Lynn and Hannah."

"That's what I'm thinking." Sully put his fist to his chest. "It's what I'm feeling, what I keep hearing from God. But I get frustrated, and I wonder if I'm getting it wrong—if I'm not just supposed to let it go."

"I don't think so. You probably feel that way because you're going it alone. I'd help you, man. I'll go to Mesilla with you and knock on doors or whatever it takes. It's not that big a place." Kyle sank back against the booth. "I guess I'm coming on pretty strong, but I know what you're feeling. If there was anything I could do to make Hayley's death mean something, I'd do it in a heartbeat. You have that chance."

"Who wants this?" Zoe was once again at tableside, biting her lower lip at Kyle and holding up the check.

"Me," Sully said.

She looked startled when Sully took it from her hand, as if she truly had never noticed he was there.

"Um, you can take it up front," she said.

Sully pushed his plate away and extricated himself from the booth where, it seemed, he'd just spent several years. In spite of the ancient pain thudding dully in his chest, he had to grin to himself when he looked at the check. Zoe had written a phone number across the bottom.

Kyle had that effect on people. He made you want to trust him. Sully could see where she was coming from.

CHAPTER TWENTY-FOUR

Alex had a game on Saturday, which I wouldn't have missed if I'd been having a heart transplant. I felt so estranged from him again, as if all the ground we'd gained in September was lost when October blew in. I had to be there to cheer him on and smuggle him a Coke and somehow reconnect.

Jake, however, was not enthused. I had dragged him out every morning at dawn for the week he'd been with me, after he hadn't slept well to begin with. When I sat on the edge of his bed to wake him up Saturday morning, he groaned like a bear being rousted from hibernation.

"I wish I could just leave you here to sleep in," I said.

"Why can't you?"

I pulled the pillow from over his face. "You know why."

Jake grabbed it back and clamped it to his chest. "No, I don't. I'm not gonna go anywhere. I don't want to go back to jail."

It was the first time he'd mentioned it, but I hadn't forgotten the condition he'd been in after just one night in that place. He peeked at me now through the slits he made with his eyelids.

"Would you just stay in bed the whole time?" I said.

"No doubt."

"Don't answer the door if anybody comes. I'll take my phone with me so you don't have to worry about that. Nobody ever calls on the land line."

"Nail the door shut from the outside, I don't care . . . No, don't do that."

"Wasn't planning on it. Okay, I'm trusting you because I know I can."

As I pulled the covers up around his shoulders, I felt them soften and give.

"Speaking of phones," I said, "what happened to your cell?"

"Never had one," Jake mumbled as he churned to his side. "We're the only kids in the United States that don't have them."

I stood up so I wouldn't ask the question that tore at my lips. At the door, I stopped and turned to look at his back again, already rising and falling in even breaths. I couldn't let it pass altogether.

"You weren't in that alley alone, Jake," I said. "Whenever you're ready to tell me who was with you, we can start to beat this thing."

He didn't answer.

The soccer game was another winner, on almost every level. Without Jake, I could sit with the soccer moms, who picked up right where we'd left off a week before. Poco basically didn't let go of my hand the entire time. J.P. wanted to know every detail of what was happening with Jake. Victoria smiled one long smile at me, though she did toss her hair out of her face long enough to inform me that Ginger was being evicted from her apartment that day. I tried not to let that distract me from watching every move Alex made on the field. I didn't want to think about where Ginger was going to live now; I hadn't gotten full-blown angry for several days, and I wanted to keep it that way.

Alex scored a goal. So did Cade. Bryan blocked several of the other team's attempts. And little Felipe ran around like an eager terrier, missing the ball half the time and still getting hoorahs from his teammates and his coach.

I watched Dan too. He seemed gaunt and tired, but he put the same energy into high-fiving and cheering and coaxing that he always did. I wondered if that was holding him together the way my picture making and bizarre therapy sessions and tangled nights of God-talks were keeping me from flying apart.

I left the bleachers in time to buy Alex the customary contraband soft drink and met him at the end of the game. As he gulped, eyes dancing, I said, "What do you say you come to my house and we practice in my yard today? I think I've forgotten everything I've learned."

"Mom," Alex said, "you haven't even learned that much yet."

"Hey, cut me some slack!" I nudged the bottom of his cup. "So what about it?"

He pushed the straw up and down.

"What's wrong?" I said.

"I kind of already told Felipe I'd go over to his house."

"Oh."

"I didn't know if, you know, because of Jake . . ."

"It's okay, Alex. Don't ditch Felipe. I'll catch you next time."

"You sure it's okay?"

"Absolutely. And look, this thing with Jake is going to be over soon, and things will get back to normal—whatever that is."

Alex sucked down some more carbonation and looked at me. His brown eyes were no longer dancing. "Is it really gonna be over soon?"

"When I find out what happened, Jake will be cleared, and we can look for our normal."

He stared at his straw. "What if you can't?"

"If the court says he's guilty, he'll get some kind of punishment. It might just be like what he's doing now."

"Which is nothing. Is he going nuts?"

I laughed. "No. He's doing pretty well, actually."

"I'd be going nuts."

"I know you would."

He sucked the cup dry, complete with the obnoxious boy-noise, without looking at me. "If they say he has to go to jail, will you tell me?"

"Uh, I think you'll know, Alex."

"I just want to know right away."

"Then you'll be the first."

"Hey, Alex!" another boy-voice yelled.

"Go," I said.

I hitched my bag up on my shoulder and watched him tear toward Felipe and grab him in a headlock.

"Where's Jake?"

I turned to find Dan at my side, shaking out his hair and repositioning his ball cap on top of it.

"Asleep," I said. "I'm on my way back to him right now."

"Do you have time for breakfast?"

I tried not to let my chin drop.

"I just need to talk to you," he said. "And we both look like we could use a decent meal."

"Okay," I said.

After ten minutes of preparing myself in the car as I followed Dan, we pulled up to an adobe dive that proclaimed it had the best *huevos rancheros* north of the border, and I was no closer to knowing what I was supposed to do with this. Pre-Crisp, I would have gone in armed to the teeth with invective. But my last talk with Sullivan made me doubt that was the way to go. We just hadn't gotten far enough for me to know which *was* the right direction.

Dan looked even more drawn and worn close up. He had what resembled carry-on luggage under his eyes, and their golden brown was shot with road maps of red. But it was his mouth that exposed him completely. There had always been something peaceful about Dan's lips—even in repose they formed a small smile, as if he knew of the joy that lay beneath almost anything.

That expression had driven me to slam cabinet doors when he'd continued to wear it despite near bankruptcy. I'd have given anything to see it there now.

With the waitress off to shout out our order in Spanish, Dan turned his worn-out face to me.

"How is Jake? You probably think I'm being a coward not seeing him. What was it you used to say . . . I'm avoidant?"

I rubbed uncomfortably at my chin.

"I'm falling apart over this," Dan said, "and Jake doesn't need to see me losing it. He needs to be with somebody who can tough this out with him. And that's you."

It's about time you saw that, something in me wanted to say. Smugly. With a smirk and a side of *If you'd figured that out a long time ago, maybe . . .*

Maybe what? a different something in me said. Maybe we'd still be right where we are?

"I actually don't think you're being a coward or avoidant or passive-aggressive." I almost smiled. "Remember that one?"

He almost smiled back.

"It's killing me not to be able to say that I yelled and screamed and shook Jake, and he finally told me everything." I put up my palm. "I didn't—I couldn't—not the way he was when he came out of jail."

Dan's eyes filled.

"He's doing better now," I said quickly. "I did find out he has a gift for photography." I told Dan about Jake's pictures, and he seemed to bask in it.

"It doesn't surprise me," he said. "He fools around with some stuff when he's out in the studio with me, but it's hard for him to admit it's good. I guess I was like that." He gave a small shrug. "Until you came along."

The food came along, too, and I only half listened as the señora and Dan exchanged a concoction of Spanish and English while the huevos and hot sauce were distributed. My mind flipped back to my conversation with Jake and further to what I'd told Sullivan Crisp. Now God was dangling it in front of me with a vague image of me pushing and pulling at a wad of clay.

Dan motioned his fork toward my plate. "Is your breakfast okay?"

"It's fine." I took a breath. "I was just thinking how ironic it is."

"What is?"

"That I was the one who pushed you to pursue your art, and I was the one who made you miserable when you did."

Dan stared down into his plate. "We don't need to get into that."

"*We* don't. *I* do. Just call it part of my therapy work."

He looked up at me, eyes startled.

"Jake and I drove past your work on the campus, and I saw what it was you were always trying to do. Only, I think you couldn't do it because you couldn't be all that you were with me."

"Look, Ryan . . ."

"Just hear me out—I'm on a roll."

He put his fork down.

"I'm not trying to pass the buck," I said, "but I think when I tried to get you to be who I thought I wanted you to be, I was taking out on you what my father did to me. And I just want to say—I'm sorry."

I pushed a hunk of egg around in a puddle of salsa and wished Dan would say something and hoped he would say nothing. Whichever he did, I couldn't respond with anger anymore, but I didn't know what else to do.

"It wasn't all you, Ryan." Dan's voice was husky. "I let you and the boys down. I can't make it up to you, but I'm trying to make it up to them."

I nodded at my breakfast. He breathed a sigh so long and so full, it was as if he hadn't breathed in a long time. I'd set him free. I was left wrapped up in sadness.

"They're no good cold." He tapped his fork on my plate.

"So—is Ginger moving in today?" I said.

"I'm sorry—what?"

"Ginger," I said. "I assumed she'd be moving into your place now."

Dan looked genuinely offended. "In the first place, I'm not going to have any woman I'm not married to live in my house with me. Especially not with two boys under my roof."

"She just said some things to me that led me to believe . . ." I trailed off and wished I hadn't said it.

Dan frowned. "What she led you to believe is what she wants to believe," he said. "Let's just say she's more liberal in her interpretation of the term *extramarital*."

"That's way too much information," I said.

"I want you to know I'm not setting a bad example for Jake and Alex. Ginger never spends the night at my place, and I don't sleep over at hers. We haven't even—"

"Okay, Dan, got it." I was seeing images I *knew* weren't coming from God. I took a bite of egg.

Dan's phone rang. When he looked at it, his face colored at the tops of both cheeks. That was Dan for *I'm in an awkward position right now, and I wish somebody would get me out of it.*

As he put his hand over the mouthpiece, I pushed my chair back and held up the check. "You want me to take care of this?" I whispered.

Dan shook his head, looking absolutely adolescent. The warm fuzzies I'd started to feel bristled like porcupine quills at the back of my neck. Ginger might not be able to get the man into bed, but she still had him in every other place.

I was halfway home and still chastising myself for whatever it was I'd started to feel when my own cell phone rang. A garbled voice said, "Mom?"

I swerved involuntarily. "Jake? Are you okay?"

"No."

At least, that was what I thought he said. It was less a word than a sob, which turned into two and three, raspy and young and terrified.

"Son—what's wrong?" I was already speeding up and jerking my head over my shoulder to get into the fast lane.

"Miguel's dead!" he said. "Mom, he's dead!"

I jammed my foot on the accelerator and cut in front of an SUV. "Jake—did you have a bad dream?"

"It's real! That lawyer called. She said Miguel's dead!"

After that I understood nothing else that he said. He sobbed into the phone while I took every turn on two squealing wheels and left the door hanging open as I jumped out in my driveway and tore into the house.

Jake was on the couch in a fetal position, rocking himself and still clutching the phone. I peeled it out of his hand, threw both it and mine to the floor, and took him in my arms.

"He's dead!" he wailed over and over. "He's dead!"

"I have to call the lawyer, Jake," I said. "I have to find out what's going on. Can you hold on just for a minute?"

I pulled my cell phone to me with my foot, and with angry, twitching fingers I fumbled for Uriel Cohen's number. She picked up on the first ring.

"Ryan," she said. "I am so sorry. When Jake answered I thought he was you, and I just started talking."

"Then you did call."

"I thought it was your cell phone."

"What did you tell him?" I was gritting my teeth, but I could hear my rage slipping between them.

"It's not good," she said.

"Did you tell him Miguel Sanchez is dead?"

"Like I said, Jake didn't say hello, so I just started talking."

"I don't care about that! Tell me!"

Uriel sighed heavily. "Miguel died a few hours ago. Detective Baranovic called me."

"Why you?"

"He has to re-arrest Jake, and he wanted to give you the opportunity to bring him in. It's customary to do that through the attorney."

I slipped out from under Jake and somehow got myself into the kitchen before I exploded into the phone with a violent whisper. "Re-arrest him?"

"They have to book him for murder. And, just so you can be

prepared, the judge isn't going to release him to you or his father this time. He may set bail."

"You didn't tell Jake *that,* did you?"

"No, I didn't tell him that. I wouldn't have told him anything if I'd known it was him and not you."

I sucked in air and couldn't seem to get enough. I grabbed onto the sink to keep myself from hurling the phone through the window. "All right," I said. "What do I do?"

"I'll meet you both at the precinct. Tell Jake not to say a word to them until I get there—he might want to start talking now, and he shouldn't. Speak to your ex about what kind of money you can pull together." She hesitated. "And, Ryan, get yourself calmed down. I know it's hard, but if you go down there raving—"

"Mom!"

I hung up and ran for the living room. Jake was at the front window, his face in a spasm of horror.

I followed his terror through the glass to the white car at the curb whose door had just opened. Detective Baranovic climbed out and nodded to two uniformed officers in a patrol car behind him.

Jake threw himself at me, hands groping at my sleeves, my collar, my hair. "Don't let them take me back to jail! I can't go there!"

"Okay, listen—Jake, listen." I clamped my hands to the sides of his face. "Just be quiet one minute."

My voice was harder than I wanted it to be, but it was the only way I could keep from becoming hysterical myself. His screams subsided into sobs.

"I'm going too. The lawyer'll meet us there, and I'll call your dad and we'll get you back here as soon as we can. We'll pay whatever bail we have to."

"I can't go in there alone, Mom!"

His arms went over his head, and I watched panic seize his face. I grabbed his wrists in my hands and pulled him to me.

"You're not going to be alone, Jake," I said. "God's going to be there."

He gave his head a wild shake.

"Listen to me! I've been in some scary places, and God was always there. If he doesn't make a picture in your head, then you make one." I shook his wrists. "Just like you did in the mall, okay? Just frame it in your head like I showed you and focus on it. Swear to me that you'll do that."

I took his face in my hands once more and shook his head up and down until he was nodding on his own. The sobs dissolved into ragged breaths I knew he was barely controlling. At the knock on the door, I kissed his forehead and let go of his face.

When I peered out the window again, Detective Baranovic was standing on the porch, just to one side of the door as if he expected me to open up on him with an assault rifle. Or my mouth. His body looked steeled for what Uriel Cohen had warned me was coming. What she couldn't have prepared me for were his eyes. They had the same fighting-it-back look I could feel in my own. This wasn't about Jake for him.

I'm the only chance for closure Miguel has, he had told me.

And I knew with terror in my heart that he had come here to have it.

CHAPTER TWENTY-FIVE

Things began to pass in a series of images that were all too real.

Uniformed officers with guns on their belts handcuffing Jake and reading him his rights while he silently wept.

Me sitting on a bench in court, chilled to a place in me that couldn't be warmed by the jacket Uriel Cohen wrapped around my shoulders.

Hearing a judge with a voice like barbed wire arraign Jacob Daniel Coe on murder in the second degree. Listening as he announced that there would be no bail, that he was remanded to the Dona Ana County Jail—announced it in the same tone he used for the jaded drug dealers who came before him, as if Jake, too, were a criminal beyond hope of rehabilitation.

In another image I watched my son let himself be led away without saying a word. He didn't have to. The curve in his back spoke of a shame that wasn't his to feel.

In still another I sat with Uriel Cohen in a corridor of the courthouse while she talked to me about options. Until I told her to shut up and leave me alone because I hated her options and I wasn't so crazy about her, either. Before she heaved her body down the hall, she patted my shoulder. I hated that too.

All of those images were punctuated with me trying to find Dan. I called his cell and his house phone. I even crunched my teeth and found Ginger's number on my call history and dialed it. No one answered anywhere. When Uriel left me in the courthouse, I was pulled so tightly between panic and wrath I knew I was going to snap—and that wasn't one of the options. Not for me, not for Jake, not for—

Alex.

If they say he has to go to jail, will you tell me? he'd said. *I just want to know right away.*

I didn't know whether I was going to tell him or not. But I snapped the phone open once more.

"Poco," I said when she answered. "Do you still have Alex?"

"He left before lunch. Dan picked him up."

"Where did they go? I can't find anybody!"

My voice echoed in the empty hall, taunting me with its helplessness.

"I don't know," Poco said. "Ginger was in the car. Alex told Felipe he didn't want to go."

"Go where? Did he say?"

"No. Ryan, what's going on? You're scaring me."

I strode down the hall, one hand with a death grip on the phone, the other one shoving its way through my hair. "Keep talking to me, Poco," I said, "or I am going to blow—so help me, I'm going to blow."

"Okay, where are you?"

"I'm at the courthouse."

"Tell me what's happened."

I knew she was forcing her voice into calm, counselor mode, and I clung to it as I went through it all for her. The more I talked, the less like an image everything became. By the time I got to my car, I was almost blinded by its stark reality, and I began to shake. Head to toe, in spasms I couldn't control.

"Ryan," Poco said, "do not drive. Do you hear me? Just sit in your car, and I'll come get you."

"You don't have to do that."

"If I hear the motor start, I'm calling the police. Stay there."

Her firmness surprised me, but I folded into it.

"Okay," I said and crawled into the front seat of the Saab, where

I sat, phone still clutched to my chest, until she pulled up beside me ten minutes later. Victoria got out of the passenger side, pulled me out, and wrapped me in a blanket that smelled like the inside of a Catholic church I'd once photographed—a strange detail from the past flashing into the present darkness. I was pretty sure I was losing my mind.

"J.P.'s going to meet us at your house," Poco said when they had me tucked into the backseat with a covered mug of tea.

"What about your kids?" I said.

"They're all at my house. You just worry about you, Ryan."

"I can't worry about me. I have to worry about Jake."

I saw them exchange glances.

"Drink that," Victoria said.

"I don't drink tea," I said. And then I took a sip and it tasted like arms around you and the promise of cookies. By the time we got to my place, I had finished it.

J.P. was waiting on the front porch, the insulated bag she used for soccer snacks over her shoulder. I told her I wasn't hungry and then proceeded to drink the cup of tomato soup she put in my hands after Poco pointed me to the couch. My insides slowly warmed and stopped shaking, and my mind gathered itself away from flashes and images and back into the clear, steely situation I was faced with.

"I hate this," I said.

J.P. grunted.

"I hate that there is absolutely nothing I can do. I can *always* do something."

She took the cup from me and refilled it from her Thermos. "There has to be something."

"Maybe not, J.P.," Poco said. "Maybe all we can do is surrender—"

"To what?" I said. "I just surrendered my son to the police. If I could go in his place, I would."

"I'm talking about God."

The angry flickers bit at me. "I don't think I can go there right now. It's hard for me to believe that I should just give up and let God handle Jake from here." I glanced upward. "No offense, but I haven't seen him doing much up to this point, you know what I'm saying?"

"I know what you're saying." J.P. tucked the cup between my hands. "Polish that off."

Poco sat facing me on the leather ottoman. "I *don't* know what you're saying." Her voice surprised me again. "God hasn't been doing much? You had Jake for a whole week. He didn't act like he hated you, at least not when I saw him. You're getting to be a mother again. You don't think God had something to do with that?"

"But I can't be a mother right now! One kid is in jail, and the other one is who knows where with his father and some bimbo!"

I held out the cup, and J.P. took it. I wanted to get up and run from them, but Victoria suddenly climbed onto the back of the couch, dangled her legs on either side of me, and sank her hands into my shoulders. She kneaded them like dough, and I felt the lump rise in my throat.

"How am I supposed to be a mother when I can't even be with my sons?"

"William's looking for Dan," J.P. said.

"Who's William?"

"Victoria's husband."

"He's also leaving a note at Dan's place for him to call you. And if nothing else, they'll be at the soccer game tomorrow."

"You can go see Jake tomorrow too," Poco said. "They have visiting hours on Sunday afternoons."

"How do you know that?" J.P. said.

I remembered something—something about Poco not wanting J.P. to know she was volunteering at the CDC center instead of doing church work. But Poco told her, straight out, daring J.P. with her eyes to say a word. For a few seconds I was distracted enough from my own mess to be impressed.

When it sank down on me again, I said, "I just want to do something right *now.*"

"Okay, we *are* doing something," Poco said. "Victoria's massaging and J.P.'s feeding and I'm . . ."

"Being the optimist." J.P. put up her hand. "Not necessarily a bad thing."

"And you," Poco said to me without a glance at J.P., "are letting us take care of you so you'll be ready for tomorrow, whatever it brings."

"You all have families to get back to," I said.

"Those helpless men can take care of themselves and the kids for a change," J.P. said. "Besides, we have a sleepover coming to us."

Victoria stopped rubbing my shoulder blade long enough to say, "Oh yeah, huh?"

"I'm going in search of blankets and pillows." J.P.'s palm was already facing me in *stay* position. "Poco, get a fire going." She paused and added, "Uh, please."

I let them stoke a fire in the kiva and make pallets on my living room floor and rub my shoulders and my feet until I drifted off on the couch still wrapped in the incense-soaked blanket. When I woke up, somewhere in the crazy small hours, Poco whispered from the floor below me. "Surrender."

I wished I could.

They left soon after the sun came up, but only after I had another cup of tea in one hand and a slice of cinnamon toast in the other.

"We'll see you at the game at noon," J.P. said. "I'm going to have a ham sandwich there for you."

I didn't tell her I didn't eat ham. I probably would now. I was doing a lot of things I never thought I'd do.

One of those things was calling Dan yet again and hoping he'd answer the phone. He didn't. It was going to be hard not to light into him when I got to Burn Lake. How could he suddenly render himself incommunicado when we had a son in trouble?

I did promise myself I wouldn't do it in front of Alex. On the way to the soccer field, I was rehearsing how to tell my younger son when it hit me that not only was Jake terrified at being back in jail, but he had just lost a close friend. No one in his life had ever died before, and I wasn't sure he even knew how to grieve. Or if he would let himself in front of the kinds of people I'd seen last night, going to the same place he was.

The image of him shuddering alone in a corner of a cot, holding back his anguish so no one would jeer at him, had me gritting my teeth again.

I didn't see Dan's 4-Runner when I pulled into the parking lot, which was strange. He was always there at least a half hour before a game.

J.P. greeted me not with a ham sandwich but with the same indignant expression she'd worn the first day I met her. "You obviously didn't know anything about this."

"About what?"

"Dan calling off the game."

"The coach for the Mesilla Mountains got a message last night." Poco pointed across the field to a flat-faced man in red shorts who appeared to be giving some bad news to a group of soccer boys.

I started toward him, but I hadn't taken two steps when the air exploded behind me. Screams erupted before I could even turn around. When I did, my own screams joined them.

Smoke billowed out of the boys' restroom building. Even as mothers grabbed their children and fled, the smoke began to dissipate as if to say, *Just kidding.*

"Was there anybody in there?" a voice bellowed. The other coach tore past me, cell phone in hand. I could see mothers already punching frantically at their own phones, while others pulled their boys to them and counted heads, over and over. I could only stand and stare—until the coach emerged from the restroom, red-faced and coughing, but shaking his head.

Within moments sirens pierced the air, and the boys wriggled from their mothers to get a better view of the engine that roared into the park. Guiltily, I thanked God that Alex wasn't there and hurried over to my soccer moms.

"Everybody okay?" I said.

I got a series of white-faced nods. Even J.P. was momentarily speechless.

"What *was* that?" Poco said.

I didn't say anything, but I'd seen enough small bombs go off to be sure that was what we were dealing with: kids messing around with stuff from their garage just to see what would happen. I looked around to see if any of the boys from the other team were snickering behind their hands. One of them was running from the parking lot, yelling in that high-pitched way that came out of sheer panic.

"Somebody threw a rock at somebody's windshield!" the kid screamed.

Everyone with an automobile started for the lot, but the police officer who had arrived only minutes before put out both arms and ordered everyone to stay back.

"Hey, Mrs. Coe!"

I turned to see Cade Winslow high up on the bleachers with Bryan and Felipe. He was waving his pudgy arms as if he were trying to take flight.

"It's your car!" he shouted to me.

I shoved my way through the small crowd and plowed into a policewoman acting as a barrier.

"Stay back, ma'am," she said.

"I have to see!" I said. "I think it's my car."

"Red Saab?" said a tall man at my right with a better view.

"Yes!"

"Looks like you're going to need a new windshield."

Heart in my throat, I tried again to get around the officer, but she was deceptively strong and held me back easily with one arm. Another officer approached with his fingers curled around something wrapped in paper.

The first officer let go of my arm. "You say that's your car?"

"I've been telling you that for five minutes!"

She nodded as if I were being the soul of cooperation. "You'll want to go see that gentleman right over there. Gomez!" she called to the officer who was unwrapping the object. "She's the owner."

Gomez's face was grim when I got to him. He wore plastic gloves and held the paper out of my reach as he handed a rock to someone else and said, "You better bag that."

"*What* is going on?" I said.

"That your car?" he said, gazing at the paper.

"*Yes*, for the fifteenth time."

"It could be a random act, or you could've been the target." He looked up from the paper. "You know anybody who would want to send you a message?"

"What message?" I said.

"We should wait until a detective gets here."

"That message?" I jabbed at the paper and saw my finger shaking.

He glanced around and then lowered the paper for me to see. A chill went up my spine.

MIGUEL SANCHEZ IS DED, someone had written. *NOW SUMBUDY MUST PAY. WATCH YORE CHILDS.*

The note's broken English had been printed in pencil, some of the letters formed backwards, as if the writer were not only illiterate but juvenile. Below it was a picture of something exploding, torn, I could see, from *Proceso* magazine, because the title and *page 32* at the bottom had survived the ripping from the magazine. It reeked of grease, as if it had been wrapped around a Taco Bell burrito instead of a rock, and it pulled the nausea right up my throat.

"Ring any bells?" Officer Gomez said.

"Excuse me," I said. "I'm going to be sick."

The bomb squad wouldn't let me into the women's restroom. I had to throw up on the ground beside a pear cactus and then stagger to the stone water fountain, where I soaked my face to wash away the smell that wouldn't leave. Poco, Victoria, and J.P. surrounded me, but I held out my hands to keep them from touching me.

"I'm poison," I said.

"What are you talking about?" J.P. said. "Here's a Handi Wipe."

I shrank away. "Just get your kids and stay as far away from me and my family as you can."

"You aren't making sense."

"Somebody made a threat because Miguel died. You have to keep your kids safe, and the only way to do that is to keep them away from us."

"Ms. Coe?"

It was Officer Gomez, standing several yards away with a younger man in a sport coat whom I'd seen at the precinct, one of the detectives I'd passed in a hallway.

"I have to go," I said to my friends.

They stepped back and let me pass, faces pale and shattered. J.P. was already looking beyond me toward the little-boy sounds, eyes fearful.

As much as I wanted them to insist on staying with me, I got why they didn't. I got it because I finally got what it meant to be a mother. It meant fierce protection of your children at any cost. It meant giving up your allies if you had to. Even if you might never find allies like this again.

Detective Nelson only questioned me for ten minutes. He already knew who I was, knew the whole story behind Miguel Sanchez. He didn't say it, because he didn't have to: the note was intended for me, and the threat was real.

"This is not a professional job," he told me as I sat shivering in one of the pavilions. "But I think we have to take it seriously."

I nodded toward the object in his hand—what looked like the lid to a jar, somewhat battered but still intact.

"What's that?" I said.

"Piece of the bomb," he said. "If you see anything the least bit suspicious, even if you aren't sure it's anything, you call."

As he gave me his card, I asked to see the paper again.

"We'll check it for prints, all of that," he said.

I almost gagged again as I took a whiff. It had none of the aroma of the real Mexican cooking I'd come to know. Nor did the attempt at broken English ring true somehow.

"I'll have an officer drive you home," he said. "We're having your car towed in."

A cold fear gripped me. Could I be any more out of control of things?

I had Officer Gomez drop me at the nearest Hertz and rented a Ford Taurus for the week. It was like driving a piece of tin, but it had a trunk for my camera equipment—although I couldn't see myself going to work the next day.

As I drove aimlessly around, I actually couldn't see anything except the note. The note that didn't smell right, didn't sound right, that tried too hard to look like something it might not be. It certainly didn't line up with what I knew of the people in El Milagro.

But if not them, who? And who was it that they wanted to "pay"? Jake was already paying.

By then it was late afternoon, and I headed for Dan's place. He didn't know about any of this yet, and he had to. As hard as I tried to keep from believing it, Alex might need extra protection.

As I drove the last dusty stretch toward the house, I tried Dan's cell phone again, but he didn't pick up. Yet when I pulled into the driveway, the 4-Runner and Ginger's red Mustang were parked cozily side by side. There was absolutely no way I was talking to her right now.

I bypassed the house and headed for the studio, through the sculpture park where the metal musicians mocked me with their merriment. I'd only taken a few steps beyond the patio when I heard the back door open. I smelled her perfume before she said a word.

"Dan's not out there, Ryan," Ginger said—pleasantly.

She clicked her way across the patio in black kitten heels, her cleavage exposed as always by a red V-neck sheath that clung to her like a second skin. The makeup was in a heightened state, even for her, and a pair of sparkling earrings dripped nearly to her shoulders.

"Where is he?" I said. "I've been trying to get in touch with him since yesterday."

"I took the family on a little trip. We all needed to get completely away from everything. The stress was getting to us."

"Yeah, well, the stress just got worse. Could you tell him I'm here?"

Ginger shook her head, setting curls and earrings into a dance. "He's in the shower."

I was close to vomiting again. "Then could you get him out? It's important."

"I'm sure it's nothing that can't wait. We have some important things of our own going on here."

"No, it can't wait while you give Dan a Swedish massage."

"We're celebrating our engagement. Is that important enough for you?"

I forced myself to register nothing. Even my words came out like wooden blocks.

"Then why don't you just give him a message for me?" I said. "Miguel Sanchez has died. Jake has been charged with murder and is being held without bail until the trial. Someone wanting revenge set off a bomb at the soccer field and threw a threatening note attached to a rock at my car. We're all in danger right now." I narrowed my eyes until I could hardly see her. "Is that important enough for you?"

Ginger stood there—just stood there—as if nothing I'd said computed. I held my shoulders up in a shrug, until she said, "I'll tell him." And then she twirled on a kitten heel and disappeared inside the house.

It was then my turn to stand there, and I did, waiting for the anger to fire up and save me. But there was no anger. There was only a deep despair I didn't know what to do with.

CHAPTER TWENTY-SIX

In spite of Kyle's pep talk, Monday morning arrived and Sully still hadn't called Tess to get the ball rolling on Belinda Cox.

He couldn't blame concern over Porphyria. When he finally got to talk to her on Friday, she sounded tired but alert, and pleased that he had confided in Kyle.

"It's about time you did some male bonding," she said. "Now all you need is a good woman in your life."

Sully had nearly swallowed the phone, although he shouldn't have been surprised that Porphyria could read his life even from thirteen hundred miles away.

"I don't know if I'm ready for that," he said to her.

"You're always the last one to know, Dr. Crisp," she said.

So, no, the real reason for putting off the call to Tess was out-and-out fear. The kind experienced by middle school boys with crushes on girls, who know they'll stutter like Porky Pig if they actually speak to the object of their affection, and who are convinced the same thing will happen if they don't.

Sully sat now with his phone in his hand as he had at least ten times over the weekend. This time he was in his office, but he'd gone through the same process in his kitchen at home, in the driver's seat of the Mini Cooper, even that morning at the new coffee shop he'd discovered.

Yes, he could do this without Tess. Kyle had offered to help. Or he could go it alone. But what other excuse did he have to call her? And wouldn't her trained eye for faces make her able to corroborate that anyone they saw in Mesilla was or wasn't "Zahira"?

He looked at the picture of Lynn and Hannah.

"What do you think, girls?" he said.

Holy crow. They were still so real to him he could smell the strawberry scent of Lynn's shampoo, feel Hannah's soft face as she nuzzled his neck. Thinking of Tess's hair and Tess's face felt like infidelity.

Sully put his finger to Lynn's photographed cheek. "I know what Porphyria would say about that," he said to her. "I just haven't thought of any woman but you two for so long. But, hey, it's just a phone call, right?"

Lynn stayed as she was, gazing into their baby's eyes. Sully dialed the number and held his breath until she answered.

"Hey, Tess. This is Sully. Sully—"

"Crisp," she said.

Her voice sounded bright. Not like he'd interrupted her. Not like she put him on a par with a telemarketer.

"Hey, I could use a little advice," he said.

"You sure could." He heard her silky laugh. "We need to talk about that shirt you're wearing."

Sully looked down at his Hawaiian print and blinked.

"I saw you going into Milagro Coffee this morning when I was coming out of the drive-through. I was going to holler at you, but you got away too fast."

She'd noticed. She'd wanted to holler.

Okay, he was pathetic.

"What did you want to holler?" Too cutesy? Too coy?

"I was going to holler, 'Crisp, for heaven's sake get a new wardrobe.'" There was a smile in her voice. "No, seriously. I was wondering how the search is going. Has the picture helped?"

"Funny you should ask," Sully said. "That's kind of why I'm calling."

"Good. Listen, I'm finishing something up. You free this afternoon for coffee?"

Sully grinned at the phone. The way things were done on the male-female front had obviously changed in twenty years. He liked it.

"You read my mind," he said. "Can you do Milagro twice in one day?"

"What—you didn't like Beans and Bytes?"

"If you'd rather go there . . ."

"I've seen you pretend to drink coffee, Crisp. They don't have enough sugar for you at that place. See you at Milagro at one thirty."

"Can't wait," Sully said.

Then he hung up and felt like the nerd at the junior high dance again. He'd sounded too anxious. Maybe even desperate.

Holy crow. Mr. Authenticity was having an identity crisis.

The phone rang again. It was Ryan Coe, and she started in before he could even get out, "Sullivan Crisp."

"Do you have any openings today?" Her voice was brittle and small.

Sully sat straight up. "You sound urgent."

"I could physically go to White Sands, and I'd still be coming apart."

"Then let's see if we can hold you together." Sully looked at his watch. It was only ten fifteen. "Does eleven work for you?"

"I'm working," she said. "Can I just come in at three today instead of tomorrow?"

"If you want to wait that long, it works for me." Sully held the phone tighter, as if he could keep her from slipping away. "What do you need right now?"

"You mean this minute?"

"Or sooner."

"I need you to tell me I can handle this. And you have no idea how hard that was to say."

"I think I do," Sully said. "What are we handling?"

She let a small silence fall. When she spoke again, the tears broke through. "Thank you," she said.

"For . . . ?"

"For not just saying I could handle it when you haven't heard what's going on."

"I'll never do that," Sully said. "We're for real here."

He heard nose-blowing. It didn't get any more real than that.

Ryan broke into an explanation that brought Sully to his feet and had him pacing the patio. The more she talked, the calmer she sounded and the more agitated Sully became. He hoped that didn't bleed through the phone.

She concluded with the Spice Girl's announcement of her betrothal to the man Sully was convinced Ryan still loved.

"I've tried everything you told me to do. I don't even have the energy to throw anything. I don't know what to do."

"Of course you don't," Sully said. "Nobody does in a situation like this." He chose his words breath by breath. "I think it's what you're not doing that's working."

"Something's working?"

"You're talking to me, making perfect sense. You've admitted you don't know what to do. That's a long way from coming apart."

"You're not inside my skin right now."

"No," he said. "But I've had times when I felt like a handful of confetti. I was sure that one more puff was all it would take, and I'd never be able to come back together as a whole."

"And then you did."

The statement was so firm, Sully knew she wanted to believe it.

"I did. And there *was* one more puff, and another, and I was still in that little pile in a hand."

"Whose hand?" she said.

"God's," Sully said. "No doubt about it. But that's hindsight. I didn't know it at the time."

Ryan let out a long, frayed breath, and Sully waited for the threads that hung at the end of it.

"I'm not a handful of confetti. I'm Humpty Dumpty's shell—after the fall."

Sully listened for her sarcastic edge, but he didn't hear it.

"Okay, so I'm supposed to let God hold on to the pieces until I get to you."

"There it is," Sully said.

"We already know all the king's horses and all the king's men couldn't do the job. I hope you've got something better."

"*We* do," Sully said. "We've got the King himself."

He got her to promise she'd call him if she felt herself crumbling again between then and three o'clock. When she hung up, he held on to the phone and prayed for the strength of the almighty hand. The fall from the wall was good. But it could hurt so much.

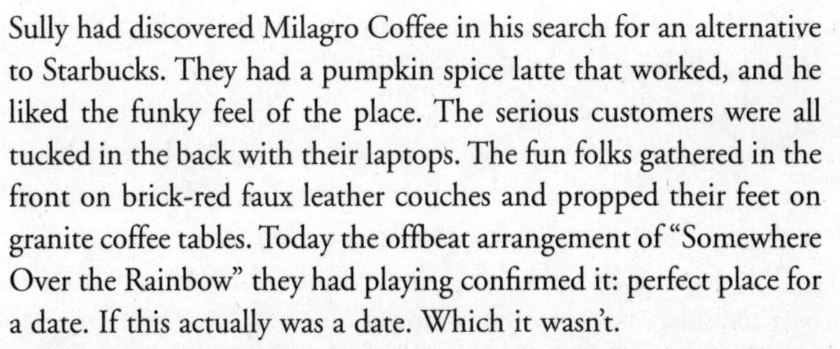

Sully had discovered Milagro Coffee in his search for an alternative to Starbucks. They had a pumpkin spice latte that worked, and he liked the funky feel of the place. The serious customers were all tucked in the back with their laptops. The fun folks gathered in the front on brick-red faux leather couches and propped their feet on granite coffee tables. Today the offbeat arrangement of "Somewhere Over the Rainbow" they had playing confirmed it: perfect place for a date. If this actually was a date. Which it wasn't.

Ben the barista greeted him at the counter. "What kind of bagel do you want today, Doc? You haven't tried the green chile."

"Just that great latte you make," Sully said.

He turned around to give the place a nervous look for Tess and found himself gazing straight into her eyes.

"Crisp, I am going to have to teach you how to drink coffee."

"So what's he having?" Ben said.

She glanced a smile over Sully and ordered something for him. "Have you had their paninis?" she said. "They're the size of a UFO."

"You want to split one?" Sully said.

"Are you buying?"

"Absolutely."

"Throw in a turkey and provolone," she told Ben. She looked at Sully, another smile teasing at her lips. "If you eat like you drink coffee, there's no way I'm letting you pick the entrée."

Sully felt himself melt. Holy crow, he liked this woman.

When they were seated across from each other at a corner table, steaming cups between them, Tess looked at him expectantly, and Sully told her about his dead ends and the phone call from Sarah. Tess gave him the undiverted attention he remembered, and the more she nodded and coaxed him with her magic eyes, the more he drew out the story. He didn't want it to end. She might stop looking at him.

"So," she said when he was out of details, "have you been to Mesilla to look for her?"

Sully shook his head. "I'm not sure how to approach it."

She looked at him, coffee cup poised under her chin. Sully gave her what he knew was a sheepish grin.

"Okay, so I'm procrastinating."

Tess returned his grin and took a sip, eyes still on him. "I know Mesilla pretty well—not that there's that much to know. I can go with you if you want. Unless you need to do this on your own."

"No, no." Sully set his cup down before the foam could jitter over the side. "I'd enjoy the company."

"Good. Because I'm not finished teaching you how to order coffee."

Over the largest panini on the planet, they agreed to visit Mesilla at three the next day. They talked easily. Sully found out she loved jazz and had been kicked out of her high school art class for sketching a realistic version of Adam and Eve in the Garden, pre-Fall. He confessed that he flunked sixth-grade Spanish and thought jazz sounded like they were making it up as they went along. Every difference made them seem more alike. When Tess left with a coffee to go, Sully started the countdown until three o'clock tomorrow.

I managed to keep Humpty Dumpty's pieces together—or, as Dr. Crisp had pointed out, *God* did—until I was leaving the *Sun-News* building for the Healing Choice Clinic around two forty. And then the phone rang.

I tucked the Bluetooth around my ear and continued pulling out of the parking lot in the rental car. When Dan said hello, I jammed down too hard on brakes I wasn't used to and threw myself into the steering wheel. I pulled around the corner and parked at the curb.

"Are you okay?" he said.

"No. Just when I think you've changed, you pull something like this."

"Look, I'm sorry. I didn't even know my phone had been turned off until this morning. What's going on? Is it Jake?"

For a minute I was stunned. His son was in jail for murder, and Ginger hadn't given him one word of my message.

"Ryan!"

I reeled myself back in and told him everything. There was only a paralyzed silence on the other end until I got to the part about the bomb at Burn Lake.

"With two teams of kids there," I said, "it's a miracle nobody was in the bathroom when it went off."

"Two teams?" Dan said. "Coach Rosa didn't tell his kids the game was called off?"

"You didn't tell yours either."

"I didn't get the call until Sunday morning."

"What call?" I said, but then I shook my head. "Forget that. Our son is in jail for murder. Alex could be in danger, too, if that note was for real. And I'm not sure it is—something about it seemed wrong to me."

"Can we see him?"

I stopped ranting at the sound of Dan's voice. He was still in shock, and I wasn't sure he'd heard most of what I'd just said.

"I tried yesterday, but you have to have an appointment," I said. "The next one I could get was for tomorrow."

"I want to go with you."

"They'll only let one person in at a time."

"I don't care. I'll just be there. You can tell him I'm there."

"If you want—"

"You shouldn't go alone."

That was what tore the pieces right out of God's hand and scattered them all over the front seat of my car. I wasn't sure how we ended the conversation. I drove to Sullivan Crisp surrounded by shards of myself.

It was 2:45 when Sully got back to the clinic, and he headed straight toward the therapy room to prepare for Ryan.

"Dr. Crisp," Olivia said from her desk as he crossed the reception area.

"How's it going, Liv?" he said, still moving.

"Dr. Martha wants to see you."

"I have a client coming in."

"Lucky for you." Olivia immediately clapped her hand to her mouth.

Sully sighed inwardly and abandoned the door to go over to her.

"Sorry," she said between her fingers. She lowered her hand. "It's just—she's all grouchy today, and I know she wants to talk to you about Kyle, and I wish she'd leave him alone." She flounced her arms into a fold across her chest. "There. I said it."

"What does that mean, Liv?"

Olivia squeezed her arms in tighter. "I know stuff is confidential, but she had her door open when she was talking."

Sully waited.

"She was checking his background with somebody on the phone," she whispered. "It's like she thinks he lied on his résumé or something."

Sully gave her a closer look. Tears sparkled on her lower lashes.

"I think she's looking for a reason to fire him. Only you can do that, right?"

"Nobody's firing anybody," Sully said. "And you're right, stuff is confidential. You haven't mentioned this to Kyle?"

She shook her head, sending her dream catcher earrings into a frenzy.

"Good job," Sully said. He strode back across the reception area to the door. He now had eight minutes to get himself ready for Ryan.

But he was no sooner through the door than he saw Kyle strolling toward him, one hand in his pocket, the other swinging as if all the two of them had to do was make plans to spend a Sunday watching football. Sully felt a pang of guilt. He'd just made a date with Tess for what Kyle had suggested the two of *them* do. That suddenly mattered.

"Hey," Sully said. "You have a minute?"

"Sure, what's up?"

Sully glanced at Martha's door, which was opening even then, and nodded Kyle into his office. He'd have to talk fast.

"Look, I just wanted to thank you for offering to go to Mesilla with me," he said with the door closed.

"No problem. When do you want to go?"

"Well, here's the thing—a woman I've been working with on this has offered to help me out."

"Got it," Kyle said. "I can't compete with a beautiful woman."

"Who said she was beautiful?"

"Isn't she?"

"Drop-dead gorgeous."

"Then there you go." Kyle grinned. "Now who's going to get extra caramel sauce on his flan?"

Kyle left, and the door opened again before it even shut behind him. It was starting to look like a turnstile.

"Five minutes, Sullivan," Martha said. "That's all I need."

"If I *had* five, they'd be all yours."

"Then I'll take *one*." She backed the door closed. "I have to talk to you about Kyle."

Her arms folded. Her jaw set. She wasn't going anywhere.

Which left Sully no choice but to glance at his watch. "I have one client, Martha, and wouldn't you know she'd be coming in right now?"

"Yes," Martha said, "wouldn't you know?"

It was the first time Sully had seen anger in Martha Fitzgerald's eyes. It matched the subtle tremor in the skin around her mouth, as if she were barely holding back. "So when *can* we have a conversation about this?"

"Mrs. Coe is here, Dr. Crisp," Olivia said too loudly outside the door.

Martha jerked it open, and Olivia stumbled into the room. Martha seared her with a look that Olivia openly returned before she whirled with a jangle of jewelry and left.

"I know you don't want to hear what I have to say, Dr. Crisp." Martha's voice shook. "But if you don't, I'm afraid you are going to be sorry."

Sully listened to her march down the hall. Maybe tomorrow he would have his confrontation with Belinda Cox and get that behind him. Then he could focus on Olivia and this thing Martha had against Kyle. Right now he had a client who was barely holding it together, and he was about to go in there with his hackles up. He ran his hand down the back of his neck. *One God-thing at a time, Dr. Crisp.*

CHAPTER TWENTY-SEVEN

It's seventy-five degrees outside," Ryan said. She perched on the edge of the chair-and-a-half like a small de-nested bird. "But I can't get warm."

Sully opened the trunk and pulled out a Navajo blanket he'd picked up at the Farmers and Crafts Market.

"Will this help?" he said.

She nodded and took it from him. He watched her drape it, crooked, around her shoulders and resisted the urge to help.

"Good?" he said.

"Yeah," she said—and burst into tears.

For the next fifteen minutes she sobbed like someone who was unfamiliar with weeping, and brought herself under control, and called herself a wimp, only to start all over. Sully put a Kleenex box in her lap and waited. When she'd blown her nose with finality, she shivered back into the blanket and shook her head.

"How much of my fifty-minute hour did I just waste?"

"Not a second."

She spread her fingers and dragged them through her hair, leaving the top standing up in dark, weary canes. "I've heard people say a good cry makes them feel better. That must have been a bad cry, because I don't."

"Actually, therapy isn't just about feeling better—it's about getting better, which usually involves feeling worse for a while."

She gave him a look.

"Speaking of which, Ryan, are you eating?"

"I forget to."

"Sleeping?"

"When I get exhausted enough."

"How's your concentration?"

She entwined her fingers around the blanket fringe. "When I'm working, I'm fine. It's when I don't have something else to focus on that I start obsessing."

"How about Humpty Dumpty's shell?"

"I brought it with me. In pieces. At least I still have all of them. I think."

Sully studied her for a moment. She might think the cry had done no good, but despite the red swelling around her eyes, her face once again had that alert look that always made her seem bigger than she was.

"By the way," she said. "If you tell anybody about me going off the deep end like that, I'm going to have to hurt you."

Sully grinned. "You're protected by doctor/client confidentiality. Or I am." He tilted his head at her. "Do you really think you 'went off the deep end'?"

"Don't you?"

"Didn't look like it to me. I thought it was a very real response to what you're dealing with. And like you said, all Humpty's pieces are still here."

She focused straight ahead, and Sully wondered if this was the way to go. Sometimes a bunny trail was a God-thing. Sometimes it was just a bunny trail.

"I just remembered what I've been trying to figure out all day," she said.

"Oh?"

"When I was in college, I took a literary criticism class, and we spent one whole session talking about whether there's anything in the Humpty Dumpty poem that indicates he's actually an egg."

Sully recited it in his head. "There isn't."

"But we think of him as this giant ovum because that's what's always in the picture. I think that's one of the things that sealed my decision to become a photographer. Pictures have an even more powerful influence than words."

"And you wanted to have a powerful influence," Sully said.

She shrugged. "Doesn't everybody? But I wanted it to be real. I found out early on, when I took a job with a magazine that I won't name, that some people aren't above manipulating images."

"How do you mean?"

"This particular publication routinely altered pictures or even created them from parts of several pictures. That's why I went with AP. Newspapers usually try to hold the line on manipulation."

Sully saw the purpose of the bunny trail. Besides, this was pulling her together. "Do they do that because they have an agenda?"

"That—or they just want this perfect picture. True photojournalists care more about accuracy and integrity than they do about 'mood.'"

"What's it about for you?"

"It's about living with what's there. You can't blur the edges of what's real and what isn't. I consider myself to be an artist, but I think art can be straight and honest and to the point. Dan and I had some heated discussions about that."

Sully nodded for her to go on, though she hesitated.

"He'd say that as a sculptor he just felt *led* to make whatever it was he was working on. Instead of seeing something and then shaping it, he just let it unfold to him. I said art required structure and he said art was fluid, that there was only an implied sense of structure beneath it that he went with."

She sat up straight and glared at him. "How did we get off on this?"

"I think it's a good place to be," Sully said. "You've just uncovered something important about you and Dan."

"A lot of difference that makes now. He's obviously 'been led' far away from me."

"It could make a difference in how you deal with Jake together

—maybe eliminate some conflict that you don't need in the midst of everything else."

"You're going to explain that to me, right?"

"I think you already did. You and Dan have different approaches, but you're both looking for what's real, and you're both reporting that honestly."

"We're talking about our art, though."

"Not something more?"

"You think this is like some metaphor about my life?" Her swollen eyes flashed. "I don't see how understanding what I should have seen when we were married makes any difference now. Dan and I don't have a life together anymore, and we never will. End of story."

"Is it?"

"I was the one who wanted the divorce. And yes, I see now that it wasn't his lack of responsibility alone that broke us up. He said it himself—he couldn't deal with my anger with him for not being something he never claimed to be in the first place. I was so busy being angry over what he didn't do, I never appreciated what he did offer." She flung out her hands. "He and I just had this conversation two days ago, and I told him I was sorry, but it was obviously too late because he's engaged to somebody else. There—are you happy now?"

"Are *you* happy—that's the question."

"It is what it is," she said, but she was crying again, with the blanket bunched up and wrapped around her neck, and her knees drawn into her chest. "I hate you for making me do this."

"I'm not making you—"

"I know, okay? But I have to blame *some*body."

She cut herself off and stared at him. Sully waited, holding his breath.

"That's what I do, isn't it?" she said. "I have to blame someone else, when it's all my fault."

"It's not all your fault—"

"No, let me finish." She threw off the blanket and made the goalposts with her hands. "I screwed up with Dan, but I couldn't stand to take the blame, so I made it his fault and left him. And I'm still making it his fault, this whole thing with Jake, when if I had stayed and fought for my kids instead of running away to Africa, Jake wouldn't have gotten into trouble—or he would fight for himself, instead of just letting this happen to him. I'm running around being outraged at everybody else when it's *me* I should be screaming at!"

"Okay," Sully said, "before you start doing that, let's just back that truck up for a minute."

She turned her head toward him, hands still in position, as if she couldn't let those conclusions get away. "Are you going to tell me I'm wrong?"

"No, because I don't think you are, totally. But if we're going to put Humpty back together again, we need to do it piece by piece."

Ryan gave him another long look before she sank against the back of the chair and wadded the blanket into a ball in her lap.

"You've made some decisions that you regret," he said. "Choices you made when you were angry. But we've already talked about the fact that anger is your default response for anything dark you might be feeling. You were hurt by Dan's withdrawal and Jake's decision not to live with you. And you were frustrated—you had no control—so again you fell back on your automatic response, which is to get mad. Making sense so far?"

"It sounds like you're trying to let me off the hook."

"What hook? I'm doing what you do when you come on a scene you have to photograph. I'm seeing what's there and I'm reporting it back. Can you bear with me?"

She squinted.

"You could have gotten angry with yourself," he said, "but that's not what was modeled for you by your father."

"Uh, no."

"You tend to point the anger outward, because that's what you know how to do. You didn't know how to play in the sand or use your gift for visualization. Until today, you didn't even know how to cry." Sully leaned onto his thighs with his forearms and shaped his words with his hands. "Usually it's the mother who teaches the child those skills. Yours wasn't around to do that, or she wasn't allowed to by your father."

Ryan opened her mouth, but Sully moved on.

"I'm not trying to set you up to blame your parents. This isn't about blame. It's about understanding what's gone on, what's still going on, and finding a different way."

"A different way than blaming and screaming."

"Right."

"But where does that leave me?" She was shivering again, and her voice was thick from the holding back.

"In a good place," Sully said. "Because you have no control. You can't fall back on your old shtick. You can only surrender to what God is giving you—and that's answers."

"I'm not hearing them."

"Then see them." He sat back. "What would you do differently now if you were still married to Dan?"

She looked as if she were about to protest, but she closed her eyes. "I'd support his art. I'd let him be who he was."

"And what about Jake? What would you do if you were in that courtroom and he'd just told the judge he wanted to live with his father?"

Ryan swallowed so hard Sully could hear it. "I would put my arms around him, even though he would hate it, and I would tell him how much I loved him, and that I would still be there for him." She let go of a sob. "But I don't know if it would have changed anything."

"But it would have changed *you,*" Sully said. "And it still can."

Ryan put both hands behind her neck and pulled her head into the blanket still bunched in her knees-up lap. "Why did I ever think anything else mattered but love?"

"Now's the time to stop asking 'why didn't I,'" Sully said, "and start asking 'why don't I?'"

She nodded and sobbed, far past her fifty-minute hour.

CHAPTER TWENTY-EIGHT

I went to Miguel Sanchez's funeral on Tuesday afternoon. The Catholic church was packed with Hispanic people, and it would have been hard for me to blend if they hadn't all been focused on the funeral mass, said in Spanish, and on their mourning.

The only person who didn't appear to be stricken almost to paralysis by grief was Elena Sanchez. She was sober and regal as she passed up the aisle, a black lace scarf draped from her head to her shoulders. Perhaps the loss hadn't hit her yet, but I doubted that was it. She'd known that day at the market that Miguel was already gone. I just wanted to know what was holding her up now and moving her forward.

One thing I did know: it was not revenge. Not from her or anyone else in that church. The sense of deep resignation I felt there was not behind the bomb and the note. The family and friends of Miguel Sanchez were devastated, maybe even confused. But they weren't angry.

Except Cecilia Benitez, who, with the well-dressed man beside her I assumed was Bob Benitez the blogger, looked ready to organize a demonstration.

I left before the service was over, specifically to avoid her. But I was only halfway down the steps when she called to me. I didn't stop moving as I glanced over my shoulder at her.

"I have someplace to be," I said. Which was true. Dan was meeting me at the jail to see Jake before soccer practice.

"You know you're the reason for all that, don't you?"

I stopped on the bottom step and dragged my hand through my hair. *Dear God, please, not today.*

Cecilia caught up to me, tossing the ubiquitous scarf over her shoulder. "They had to put the overflow crowd in the parish hall and show the service on closed-circuit TV," she said. "And we have you to thank for that."

I didn't even try to pretend I knew what she was talking about.

"Your online article about the colonia," she said. "It was spot-on, Ms. Alexander. Bob thought so too—he blogged about it—everyone read it." She stretched her arm up toward the church. "And that's the kind of crowd we're going to see at the courthouse when this goes to trial."

I put my hand to my mouth. She nodded at my tears.

"You don't have to say anything. I just wanted to thank you—for the whole community. We'll see justice done."

She returned to the church before I had to answer.

When I arrived at the jail, Dan was already standing at the check-in counter talking to the officer behind the glass window.

"I can't get an appointment," he said.

"You gotta call ahead," said the officer, whose face hung over his collar like a muffin top. He punched the button of his ballpoint pen several times. "You want the one I have for Thursday or not?"

"Take mine for today, Dan," I said.

He stared at me. If I could have, I would have stared at myself. I had counted every minute that had stood between me and my son so I could see for myself that he hadn't been devoured by the monsters behind these walls, and now I was giving away the chance to see him.

The officer clicked his pen again. "Y'can't do that. It's—" He glanced at a sheet on his side of the counter. "It's Ryan Coe or nobody. Who's it gonna be?"

"Go," Dan said. "You're what he needs." He pointed to the tears starting to flow from his eyes. "He doesn't need this."

The officer stood up and jerked his head toward a steel door. As the door buzzed and clanked open, I looked back to say, "Don't leave. Please," but Dan was already nodding.

I was handed a visitor's badge, which I dropped as I tried to walk and clip it on at the same time. The floor was gray and smelled like sour Clorox, and we had to pass through two sliding steel doors before I was finally told to sit on a long bench that ran the length of a fluorescent-lit room. Another bench faced it, and between them was a narrow table with a foot-high divider.

"Read the sign," said Officer Number Two and sauntered off.

NO TOUCHING, KISSING, REACHING ACROSS THE DIVIDER, it said. At the other end, a skinny man with missing teeth and an infested-looking goatee was following those rules with a man in a suit who was taking notes. It made me wonder if Uriel Cohen had been to see Jake. She'd said she would when I talked to her the day before and begrudgingly apologized for sending her packing. She told me it happened all the time. It was all routine for her.

For me it was all surreal. I flattened my palms against the spasms in my thighs as the door before me slid open and Jake stood there, blinking, as if he'd just stepped out of a dark closet. The deputy had to point him to the bench. I stood up but was frowned back to my seat. Jake sank into his place and stared at the divider between us.

"Jake?" I said. "Son, are you all right?"

He clearly wasn't. All the progress he'd made in our week together had been erased in less than seventy-two hours, leaving him unwashed, pulled in, and bleeding from his cuticles. The one thing that hadn't disappeared was the shame and it yanked me from my own paralysis.

"Look at me," I said.

"I can't."

"Then just listen. I love you, Jake, no matter what you did or didn't do. Miguel's death doesn't change that. Nothing changes that. Do you understand?"

Jake did look at me then. I was crying—and he had never seen me cry.

"They won't let me hug you in here," I said, "but I would if I could. I should have done it a long time ago. I should have been there for you no matter how hard you tried to push me away. But I'm here now. Your dad and I aren't going anywhere—no matter what you tell us about what happened—and you have to start talking now, Jake."

He planted the heels of his hands against his forehead and rocked back and forth. "She said there was a bomb."

"Who said?"

"That lawyer."

I clenched the edge of the table. "Uriel Cohen told you about the bomb?"

"It's real, Mom," he said, still rocking. "That's why I can't talk. Because it's real."

I sat still. "You know who planted it? You know who wrote the note?"

"I can't tell you. I was gonna tell you everything before she told me that. Now I can't."

"Jake."

"Just let it go, Mom. Please. Or somebody else'll get hurt."

"It was the same person who made you run over Miguel, wasn't it?"

"I can't—"

"Jake." I leaned as close to the divider as I dared, and even then the deputy took a step forward. "Was it Ian?" I whispered. "Did you do it for him?"

Jake pulled his hands from his forehead and searched my face. "No, Mom," he said finally. "I didn't do it for Ian."

I stopped breathing. Jake couldn't lie, and he was telling me a truth I didn't want to hear. I was still staring at him when the deputy tapped him on the shoulder.

"Time's up," he said. "Let's go."

Jake stood up, but he didn't take his eyes from mine. They were waiting for something. Something I'd promised him only moments before.

"I still love you, no matter what," I said. "I love you, and I'm not giving up on you. Do you believe me?"

The deputy took him by the arm, pulled him toward the barred door. Still Jake watched me. As the door slid open, he nodded.

Sully had already pulled into the plaza in the center of Old Mesilla when he realized he'd left his cell phone on his desk at the clinic. He glanced at Tess, who was tucking her hair up into a ponytail. The only person he wanted to talk to anyway was right here with him. Unless Porphyria called, of course. But Porphyria knew he was on what was hopefully the final leg of his journey and wasn't expecting a call from him until tomorrow.

"You're turning green, Crisp," Tess said.

"Maybe I'm hungry," he said.

She surveyed him with those eyes. "On the off chance that you're not lying right now, let's go to the Café don Felix. That'll be a good place to start asking around anyway."

She turned to open the passenger door, but Sully touched her arm. "Listen, thanks."

"For what?"

"For coming with me. I'm a little nervous about this."

"Crisp, you are not a little nervous. You are scared to death. I don't need to know the details, but it's quite obvious that if you do find this woman, it isn't going to be pretty. Maybe you should tell me what my role's going to be when this goes down."

At least he'd thought that much through. "All I want to do today is locate her," he said. "Then I'll come back alone and—talk to her."

Tess nodded, never moving her eyes from his. "I don't know what she did to you, but I wouldn't want to be her."

"You could never be her," Sully said.

Tess nodded as if she didn't see him turning red from the collar up.

"I'm glad," she said.

The Café don Felix was on the southeast corner of the plaza and oozed as much natural charm as the authentic old Mexican square itself. It had a good feel, which Sully needed. He was sweating profusely, and not just from the promise of jalapeños that arose from the salsa a little girl of about nine placed on the table between Tess and him.

"What can I get you?" she said. She had enormous blue eyes and wore a miniature apron with straws and an order pad in the pocket.

"Tell us what's good," Tess said. There was no wink to Sully, no isn't-she-cute in her voice.

"All our tortillas are homemade and served hot, and our burritos and chimichangas are the best in Dona Ana County." The girl pointed to the list of Mexican entrées on a white board. "I personally like the gorditas. They're small, but very tasty."

"Fix me up with an order of those, would you?" Sully said.

She lowered her chin at him. "You're going to want two—unless you have rice and beans on the side."

Sully knew he couldn't eat any of it, but he couldn't disappoint that face, either.

"How about if you make it two, and we'll share," Tess said. "With some french fries."

"Oh, those are good too," Mini-server said. "And what can I get you to drink?"

Tess shot a glance at Sully and said, "What do you have that's disgustingly sweet?"

"That would be our fruit punch. I know because my mom won't let me drink it."

When she had skipped off, Sully let go of the grin he'd been holding back. "She was about half-cute."

"She's amazing. That girl is going places."

"You're good with kids."

"You've seen me with one kid, Crisp."

"I can tell, though."

"And you want to know why I've never had any of my own."

Sully paused, a chip midway between the basket and the salsa.

"We've already established that you're translucent," Tess said, but she laughed. "I've never had any kids because I never found anyone I wanted to have them with."

Sully liked that answer. A lot. It made him able to eat the gordita Mini-server brought, as well as half the french fries. The only thing the child couldn't do was handle the bill, for which they had to go to the woman at the register, presumably her mother.

Tess widened her eyes at Sully and nodded toward the woman.

Sully was immediately nauseated again. It was time to do what he'd come here to do.

The woman counted out his change and smiled. "Anything else I can help you with?"

"Well, yeah. We're actually looking for someone, and we heard she works around here."

"She's probably been in, then."

"Her name is—she's known as Zahira."

"Doesn't ring a bell. I don't know everyone's name—I'm better at faces."

Sully hesitated. He suddenly felt like someone posing as an FBI agent. "Belinda Cox?" he said.

She shook her head, and her eyes drifted to the woman coming in the front door. "Sorry. But I bet Angelina knows her. Ange—" She motioned to a robust woman with gray hair twirled to the top of her head and held in place with chopsticks. "These folks are looking for somebody named Zahira."

Angelina's eyes hardened. "She a friend of yours?"

"No," Sully said.

"She's not a friend of mine, either, just so we're clear. She has a—well, I don't know what to call it—a place down on Guadalupe

Street. I don't know what it was she was doing in there. She called herself a healer."

"Oh, was that The Dark Mind?" the owner said. "I thought she was a psychic."

Angelina grunted. "Psychics try to pump you up with this great future you're going to have. All she talked about was how Satan was out to take everybody down."

"You actually went in there?" Café Lady shuddered. "I thought it was kind of creepy."

The front door opened again, and she picked up a stack of menus and left Sully and Tess with Angelina, who just seemed to be getting warmed up.

"So you say her place is on Guadalupe?" Tess looked at Sully. "I know where that is."

"It *was* there," Angelina said. "Landlord closed her down. She poured wet cement into the toilet to stop evil spirits from coming in through the plumbing." She crossed her chest with a weathered hand. "I'm serious. He's a friend of mine. Now, he could tell you stories."

"So she's left town?" Sully said, heart sinking.

"Not yet. She's still in her house, which unfortunately is right across the street from mine, on Calle de Santo. Looks like she's trying to sell it, although who knows what she's done to *that* place. It's got an eight-foot concrete wall all the way across the front yard."

"Listen, thanks," Sully said and edged toward the door.

"If you've come to get her out of town, more power to you," Angelina said heartily. "This is a sweet little place. We don't like her kind here, if you know what I mean."

Unfortunately, Sully did.

As they crossed the patio, Sully could feel Tess looking at him curiously. He'd have been beyond curious if he'd been her. But at the moment, everything he ought to tell her was caught in his throat with the gorditas and the anxiety.

When they climbed into the Mini Cooper, she simply said, "If you turn right here and then right again, we'll be on de Santo. You can do a drive-by."

Could this woman get any more perfect?

He did what she said, slowing down after he made the second right.

"The way she was pointing, I think she meant it was beyond the plaza," Tess said. "A house with an eight-foot wall in front of it shouldn't be hard to miss."

The neighborhood was quaint and clean, its pastel adobes warm and inviting in the afternoon sun. Some of them had hay bales stacked with pumpkins and gourds on their porches. Others beckoned with padded wood benches and windows reflecting fireplace flames from within. Belinda Cox didn't belong here, just as Angelina said.

"There," Tess said.

She pointed to a long, high wall on the right, which had been sloppily stuccoed and was interrupted only by a burnt-orange door sporting carved sunbursts. It might have been striking at one time, but the sun and the brutally dry air had blistered it beyond repair. A few feet of straggly weeds separated the wall from the road, so that if Sully had wanted to pull over and stop, even the Mini Cooper would have stuck out in the road.

"Looks like Angelina's going to get her wish," Tess said.

Sully nodded at the *For Sale* sign planted next to the door. A slat that read *Pending* hung from it, and it gave Sully a renewed sense of urgency.

"I'll wait here if you want to try to see her now," Tess said.

Sully shook his head and took his foot off the brake. "I'll come back tomorrow. How about some dinner?"

"Crisp, we just ate."

"I know. I just want to sit at a table with you and talk."

"Then that's what we'll do. I can always eat."

No, she couldn't, and he knew it. She was just being progressively more perfect. And he wanted to tell her everything.

CHAPTER TWENTY-NINE

I'd promised I would call Sullivan Crisp at nine Wednesday morning to check in. It was more like 8:45, but I was between assignments and I needed to hear his voice sooner rather than later so I would know I wasn't crazy. I felt like a different person than I was before Saturday, and I had to make sure that was real before I went on with the plan that had begun to take shape in my mind during the night.

Dr. Crisp was breathless when he answered the phone, as if I'd caught him on the run.

"I'm sorry," I said. "I called too early. If this isn't a good time . . ."

"No, no—this is perfect."

I could hear him moving around, but he settled in quickly. I warmed my hands around the cup of coffee I'd just picked up at the Milagro drive-through. Even though I'd parked in the sun in the parking lot and the temperature was in the upper fifties, I was still shivering. That seemed to be my new natural state.

"I thought I was done crying," I said. "Then I saw Jake yesterday, and I started all over again."

"How did it go?"

"That depends." I spilled it all, succumbing to tears again when I related Jake's statement: *I didn't do it for Ian.* "For so long I believed that he didn't do it. And then I had myself convinced that Ian somehow made him get behind the wheel and run over Miguel. Jake took out all of that at the knees."

"Did he?"

"Yes." I shoved the tears off my cheeks with my jacket sleeve. "Jake's telling the truth."

"But there's still the possibility that he didn't do it at all."

"Then why didn't he say that? I know—he's scared. He thinks somebody else will get hurt—like it's all on him."

He let that one sit. I'd figured out that he did that when he knew I already had the answer.

"I know," I said. "He doesn't take after anybody strange."

"I'm sorry?"

"My mother used to say that. It's like 'the apple doesn't fall far from the tree.'"

"Now that one I know."

I could hear him grinning.

"Jake might have learned from you to take responsibility for everything and everybody—or that might just be his nature. In either case, Ryan, it's like anger. Sometimes it serves you—and other people, and God—well, and sometimes it doesn't."

"Remind me again when anger has served me well."

"Whenever you've stood up against something that wasn't right. Jesus never said getting angry was inherently bad. He showed anger himself on a number of occasions."

I had to admit those were some of my favorite Gospel passages.

"But," he said, "it never works as a way of being. And neither does a misplaced sense of responsibility, which Jake seems to have."

I closed my eyes. This was the point where I always hit a wall—where I couldn't completely buy into what he was selling.

"Talk to me," he said.

"I've come a long way."

"Absolutely you have."

"I don't want to rip up the upholstery in my car right now. I told my son everything he needed to hear. I made it all about love instead of about anger."

"Yes, you did."

I knew he could hear me crying, and I didn't care. "But if you're saying I have to let this go, I can't. If he did do it, I have to find out why and how. Otherwise, Jake's lost—and I can't lose him again."

"You don't have to let it go. I don't usually do this, but I'm going to give you a direct piece of advice."

"Please," I said.

"The only thing that seems to be holding Jake back from telling you what happened is his fear that if he does, he'll jeopardize someone else's safety."

"Right."

"So if you can get him to let go of that responsibility, he'll probably let the rest of it go too."

"How am I supposed to do that?" I said.

"Two things. One, you take the responsibility for him. I suspect he hasn't been able to be a kid for a while now, just like you at his age. And it sounds like you've already made a start in getting him to trust you to be his mom."

"I hope so." I wanted it to *be* so, because Sullivan had just given me permission to go ahead with what I'd planned. Almost. "What's number two?" I said.

"You show him how to surrender—I'm talking about surrendering to God. That's what you're starting to do, isn't it?"

"I'm working on it." I wiped my nose. "I guess that's sort of an oxymoron, isn't it? Working on surrendering?"

"It's a start. Why don't you explain it to me the way you would to your son?"

"You mean pretend you're Jake?"

"You did great with the sandbox."

"You are a strange man," I said. But I clung to the kindness in his voice and closed my eyes. "Just talk to him?"

"Yeah."

I drew in a breath and tried to see my son, bowed over himself in pain. "Jake," I said, "I'm doing everything I can to sort this out and help you. I understand why you feel like you can't talk about it, and I'm trying to respect that." I stopped. "How am I doing so far?"

"If I'm Jake, I'm already talking."

I swallowed hard. That was the easy part. I wasn't sure I knew where to go from here.

Until an image came to me, no longer gauzy and distant, but so sharp it cut through everything. In it, my hands were in fists that slowly uncurled until they lay flat and free. I didn't see the Humpty Dumpty pieces I'd thought were there. There was nothing. I'd been holding on to nothing.

"Jake . . ." I said. "I can't promise you I can get you out of this, whether you talk to me or not. But I know God can set us both free somehow, if we just stop trying to do his job for him."

I didn't know where it had come from. I just let it be there—for so long I almost forgot that Dr. Crisp was on the other end of the line until he said, "If you say that to him, you won't lose him. No matter what else happens."

I felt a peace that lasted until we hung up and a finger of anxiety crooked at me. It was one thing to say it to a man who seemed to be able to turn anything into healing. It was another to even think I could do it.

I don't know how far I would have gone with that if someone hadn't tapped on my passenger-side window. I twisted around to see J.P. peering in at me. She pointed to the lock.

"I didn't think you'd ever get off the phone," she said as she slid into the seat next to me.

"I was talking to my therapist."

"And now you're going to talk to me. No—make that, I'm going to talk to you."

"Okay," I said.

"You look terrible, by the way."

"Thanks."

"You're obviously not eating. We'll take care of that in a minute."

I didn't argue. I could only think about how much I'd missed her. How much I cared about her, about all three of them.

"Look, J.P.," I said. "I hope you understand why I can't let you all keep helping me. It looks like that threat didn't come from the

Hispanic community. I never actually thought it did. But that doesn't mean there isn't still a danger."

"You know, that's the only thing I still don't like about you." J.P. shook the ever-present tendrils out of her face, exposing the moisture in her wonderful blue apostrophe eyes. "You think you're the only one who knows how to be tough. And you're wrong, okay?"

"Okay," I said.

"Besides, this isn't about the bomb or the threat. It's about Alex."

"Alex?" My heart was too tired to pound, but I could feel the sudden fear in my teeth, my hair, my fingernails. "Did something happen?"

I grabbed for my phone, but she put her hand on top of mine.

"No, nothing happened. But I was watching him at soccer practice yesterday."

"I couldn't go. I had just been to see Jake in jail, and I couldn't—"

"Ryan, shut up. I know. Dan told me. And all I could think about was how this is affecting Alex. He was dying of loneliness, and I couldn't stand it." She blinked several times, but the tears stayed. "I want to take him home with me until this thing is over. If you and Dan will let me."

"We can't put you in that position."

"I'm putting myself there." She stuck her hand up. "You would do it for me. I know you would, and that's all I'm going to say about it."

It was all she *had* to say. I said yes.

Sully was on his office patio, gazing at the Organs and marveling at the same magnificence that existed in mountains and in tiny, feisty women like Ryan Coe, when his phone rang. It was a 615 area code, but it took him a moment to realize it was Porphyria's niece's number.

"Winnie," he said. He was already standing up, the mountains forgotten. "What's happening?"

"You're not going to like it," she said.

"Doesn't matter. Tell me."

She sighed, long and hard, and Sully was suddenly sorry for her. She'd been at the hospital with Porphyria for weeks, shouldering everything. He swallowed back his guilt.

"Aunt Porphyria has an infection. I can't even pronounce it. It's something she picked up in the hospital."

"And it's serious."

"Yeah. It is. She's not dying, okay?" she added quickly. "But at her age, it's hard for her body to fight bacteria."

"I'm coming back there," he said.

"She said absolutely not."

"She can say anything she wants, but I—"

"Please, Sully, it will only upset her, and that wouldn't be good for her right now."

He sank into one of the patio chairs and smothered his face with his hand. "Can I talk to her?"

"Absolutely. She wants you to call her later, when the antibiotics have had a chance to kick in."

"That's our Porphyria."

"Yeah. So listen, later, okay? I need to go."

Winnie hung up, but not before he heard her start to cry.

Sully glanced at his watch. It was almost four. His plan was to head to Mesilla before darkness set in. He stood up and went to his laptop on the desk to check his appointment calendar, see if there was anything he needed to clear so he could head for Nashville tomorrow. He could hear Ryan Coe saying it: why did anything else matter but love? Whether he saw Belinda Cox tonight or not, he was going to Porphyria tomorrow.

The calendar came to life on the screen, and Sully glanced over it, already certain there wouldn't be a problem. He snagged on what appeared to be a four o'clock appointment. Who was M. Shannon?

He picked up the desk phone to call Olivia, just as he heard Martha's efficient tap on the door. At least this time he had an excuse.

"I have a four o'clock," Sully said when she heeded his call to come in.

"I know," she said. "I'm it."

Sully glanced at the screen. "I'm seeing an M. Shannon."

"Martha Shannon Fitzgerald." Martha pulled up one of the client chairs and sat firmly on it. "It was the only way I could get ten minutes with you."

He stifled a sigh and came out from behind his desk to take the chair across from her. Maybe he should get this thing out of the way so it wouldn't be hanging over his head all the way to Tennessee.

"You want to talk about Kyle," he said.

"I know you don't, but we have to."

"All right. Tell me what you want to tell me."

Sully knew he sounded patronizing—he saw it register in her eyes, flickering in the anger he'd seen there only once before.

"You don't notice Kyle's faults because he's young Sullivan Crisp," she said. "He looks like you. He models his therapy after you. He drives the same model car you do."

Sully felt some anger in his own eyes. "Martha, that has nothing to do with my dealings with Kyle. What faults are you seeing that I apparently don't?"

"I checked into the clinic where he last worked, in Little Rock."

"Why did you do that?"

"Because unlike you, I am still concerned about the number of clients he diagnoses as suicidal. There was another one this week." She drew herself up in the chair. "In Little Rock, nine of his clients were hospitalized in two months. That raises a red flag for me."

"I'll grant you that seems like a high rate." He didn't point out it was better than missing suicidality and losing a patient. "What exactly do you want me to do with this?"

"I just want you to talk to him. See if there is something going on with *him* that makes him so quick to suspect clients want to kill themselves."

Sully caught his lip in his teeth. Maybe it was simple: because Kyle himself had almost taken his own life. But he couldn't tell her that.

"I certainly can't do it," Martha said. "He treats me like a has-been."

"I'm sorry to hear that."

Martha stood up. "I'm not asking for sympathy, Sullivan, but I'll tell you this: if you are going to put him in charge of this clinic when you leave, I won't be staying."

Before Sully could respond, she marched out and gave his door an uncharacteristic slam. He breathed in the anger she left behind.

All right. Tomorrow, before he left for Nashville, he would talk to Kyle. But right now, he had to go have it out with Belinda Cox and then meet Tess at her place as they'd planned. Especially now that he was leaving town. After last night, he couldn't see himself taking off for even a few days without telling Tess.

For three hours they'd sat at a table at Meson de Mesilla, where Sully didn't care that he couldn't identify what he was eating. All he saw, all he tasted, were Tess's eyes as she listened to him pour out the story of Lynn and Hannah and his journey since then. With no trace of pity, she took it in as if she'd known them. As if she knew him. By the time the coffee arrived, he was sure she did.

When the waiter had brushed off their tablecloth with a whisk broom three times, they migrated to the plaza, where Sully noticed the temperature's dip into the forties about as much as he had the garnish on the dessert. He coaxed out Tess's story then. How she'd struggled in her twenties to have her art taken seriously, only to become involved with a guy who blocked her creativity at every turn under the guise of not wanting her to be hurt or disappointed. That relationship had segued into another with a man who was an artist himself, romantic and supportive and, it turned out, married. For a while she retreated into a New Age group, where the anything-goes philosophy left her feeling rudderless.

"I went back to my Christian roots after that," she told Sully as they leaned against the creamy-white wall of San Albino Church and watched the moon rise over the plaza. "Funny how the thing you've been looking for was there all along."

Sully turned sideways to face her, his shoulder pressed to the wall. "Have you found everything you were looking for?"

"Who has? Spiritually, it's a continuing journey."

"Absolutely."

"Careerwise, I love what I do."

"Do I hear a *but* in there?"

"Isn't there always one?" She tilted her head and smiled at him. "Are you doing your psychologist thing with me?"

He put up both hands. "I'm totally innocent."

"No, you just can't help yourself. It's okay—I can't see a face without wanting to draw it, or wondering what it's going to look like ten years from now."

Sully feigned horror, and she laughed. It was a lovely thing, and he wanted to make her do it again.

"Yeah, there is a *but*," she said. "Every time I get involved with a man, my art seems to suffer. It doesn't matter whether he's artsy or not, even the Christian ones—and I don't date anyone who isn't—they just don't get it, get *me.*" She shook her head. "It's probably just me. I may be expecting too much."

"Or the men in your life have expected too much of you."

"Okay, now you are being the therapist, Crisp."

She put her hand up, and Sully folded his fingers around it.

"Hey," he said.

"Hey what?"

"Thank you again for coming here with me."

He waited for the verbal poke, or the eyebrow before she said, *You needed somebody to keep you from bursting into Mesilla like a bull in a china shop.*

It didn't come. She let her fingers curl over his. "It was my pleasure."

"Really?"

"Do I look like I'm lying?"

"I hope you're not. I hope you want to do this again. Just for pleasure next time. Can we do that?"

"Shall I pencil you in?"

Sully shook his head. "No. I'd rather you put me in ink."

She gave his hand a squeeze and tugged away, but she was still holding him with her eyes. "I want to ask you one question," she said.

"Anything."

"Do you have a picture of Lynn and Hannah?"

Sully nodded.

"Of course you do. That's a ridiculous question. And it isn't the one I was going to ask—do I get another one?"

Sully resisted the urge to stare. He'd never seen her act nervous before. Dang. She was probably gearing up to say, *Let's just keep this professional, shall we?*

"What I want to know is—would you like for me to do an age progression on them, so you'll know what they might look like if they were still with you?"

Her voice had taken on a husky sound. Sully felt his own throat thicken.

"You don't have to answer now," she'd said. "Just something to think about. It would be an honor to do that for you."

Sully looked now at the framed photograph of Lynn and Hannah. He'd caught them in a rare moment of serenity, Lynn gazing down at Hannah, whose tiny hand was reaching up to touch her mother's face. Lynn had coaxed out one of the baby's first smiles, lopsided and tentative. Even in her despair, Lynn couldn't help the look of delight on her own face.

Sully hadn't given Tess an answer. He'd been too overcome by the offer, too caught off guard to be able to say whether he would want to know exactly what he was missing. But now as he ran his finger over their faces, it was clear. *This* was the moment he wanted to remember. To know what more of those moments might have looked like was too much to bear.

He brought the picture to his lips and kissed them both.

"I'm sorry, girls," he whispered. "I'm going to make sure this doesn't happen to someone else. I promise you."

But as he set the frame back on his desk, the uncertainty rose in him again. Was that the only reason he was doing this? Or did he want to shout into Belinda Cox's face until she hurt the way they had? Was he out to stop her, or to ruin her? Now that he was so close, he couldn't see where he was going.

He shook his head. More procrastinating. *Just do the next God-thing.*

It was almost dusk. He knew it would be completely dark by the time he got to Mesilla, and he didn't trust himself to find Belinda Cox's house without the address. He had emptied the contents of his pockets on the desk before he remembered that Tess was the one who'd written it down and probably still had it in her purse. He had to grin to himself as he dialed her number. It wouldn't hurt to hear her voice before he took off to do this thing.

"Crisp," she said. "So—how did it go?"

"It didn't yet. I need the address, and I think I left it with you."

"You are hopeless. Just a sec."

He heard her put the phone down just as Kyle appeared in the doorway. Sully motioned him in and furrowed his brow at the duffel bag he had slung over his shoulder.

"You going somewhere?"

"Out of town for a couple of days," Kyle said. "I've cleared my calendar."

"You ready, Crisp?"

Sully put up a finger to Kyle and tucked the phone into his neck while he located a pencil.

"Okay—go."

"Nineteen twenty-five . . ."

"Nineteen twenty-five . . ."

"Calle de Santo."

"Calle de Santo."

"You on your way now?" Tess asked.

"Yeah."

"You sound . . ."

Sully glanced at Kyle, who had wandered discreetly to the patio door. "I sound what?"

"Like anybody would sound when they're about to do something like this. I'll be praying for you."

Sully closed the phone against his cheek.

"So this is it, huh?" Kyle said.

"Yeah. I found the woman I was telling you about. I'm finally going to get this done."

"You sure?"

Sully's neck jerked as he looked up.

"Never mind. You know what you're doing," Kyle said.

"You want to say something."

"Naw, I should keep my mouth shut."

"Hey. Come on."

Kyle nodded. "Look, this is huge, man. You just look like you need to be sure you're ready before you go wherever it is you're going."

"Mesilla."

"It's just a feeling."

Sully nodded. "You're right. I need to make a call before I go."

"Then I'll get out of your hair."

He was almost out the door before Sully said, "So you're going out of town?"

"I just need to go back and settle a couple of things in Little Rock. My house just sold. I've notified all my clients."

"Have a good trip."

Kyle tapped the doorjamb, then hesitated. "I wish I could be here for you."

"You already have been," Sully said. "Go. We'll celebrate when you come back."

Kyle gave him a thumbs-up and left. Anxiety pulsing, Sully picked up the phone again. Those antibiotics had to be kicking in by now.

Porphyria answered on the first ring.

"Dr. Crisp," she said, "can you explain to me why if you are not sick when you check into a hospital, you will be before you get out?"

Sully knew his smile was watery. "They have to stay afloat somehow, Dr. Ghent. I want to know what's going on with you."

"It's simple. I'm going to watch all this medicine go into my veins, and then I am going home."

He wanted to believe her. He might have if she hadn't coughed long enough to have to put down the phone and catch her breath. When she picked it up again, he'd changed course.

"Winnie told me. I just wanted to hear it from you."

"Mm-hmm."

"What?"

"You never could lie to save your soul, Sullivan Crisp. You've got something on your mind."

"You."

She answered him with a velvet silence. He could imagine her closing her eyes, pressing her magnificent lips together.

"I want to run something by you," he said.

"I know, and I don't know why you're shilly-shallying around about it."

"I know where Belinda Cox is."

"Ah."

"I haven't seen her yet. I'm on my way there. But dang it, Porphyria, I think I've lost sight of why I even need to do this. I keep telling myself I just want her to know the danger she's putting people in, but it sounds like everybody she's been associated with has already told her that, and she doesn't get it."

"Everybody isn't Sullivan Crisp."

"You're saying I could have some kind of influence nobody else has." Sully rubbed the back of his head. "I don't see that. She could be too far gone."

"I think you knew that ever since you went to the church, but you kept looking."

"Yeah, but why? Every time I think about confronting her face-to-face, I don't like what I see."

"In her?"

"In myself."

He could hear her breathing, as if it were an effort. Guilt lapped at him, but Porphyria wasn't going to let him stop now.

"What 'self' do you want to be when you talk to her?" she said.

"I don't even know."

"Then don't you think you better find out before you go do this thing? Personally, I only know one Sully-self when it comes to dealing with twisted human beings."

"And that would be . . . ?"

Porphyria gave a soft grunt.

"You're not going to tell me, are you?"

"No. You just need to wrap you up in some God, now, and sweat out an answer." She coughed again, longer and with more wheezing than before.

Sully gripped the phone. "I'm coming there," he said. "I'm going to get this behind me, and then I'm coming to Nashville."

"All right, son," she said. "I'll wait for you."

When they hung up, Sully looked through the light-shimmering patio door. The sun was already hissing out behind the hills, but Porphyria was right. Before he went to Mesilla, he had to see the Sully-self who could walk into Belinda Cox's house and be what she needed . . .

He stopped, hand on the door.

What *she* needed. What Dr. Sullivan Crisp would do for her if she came into his office.

Sully turned and stared at one of the red-padded client chairs. It wasn't hard to figure out why he'd never thought of Belinda Cox the way he did any other messed-up person he came in contact with—someone who'd fallen prey to bad theology or suffered a traumatic experience or hauled a load of guilt that wasn't hers to carry. It was always about Lynn and Hannah. About his need to make it right somehow.

But what about now? What about who he'd become through all of this?

You just need to wrap you up in some God, now, and sweat out an answer.

Sully pushed through the patio door and let the New Mexico air cocoon him.

CHAPTER THIRTY

Belinda Cox's house looked even more vacant in the dark than in the daytime. It struck Sully as he pulled the Mini Cooper as far off the road as he could that the place didn't have a sense of evil about it—just a sense of nothing.

He rapped his knuckles on the orange door in the wall and got no response. The door was no more than a gate, so he gave it a push, and it swung open. He forced a grin. Holy crow—it wasn't like he was doing a SWAT team bust.

The house was only about ten feet from the wall, so although no outside bulb illumined the weed-clogged stone path, he could see his way by a light that shone from inside somewhere. He stopped at the door, whose torn screen folded over itself as if it were ashamed not to have been ripped off and replaced before now. The confused panic he'd felt before he talked to Porphyria had been sweated down to a tight ball in his stomach. He could do this.

He raised his hand to ring the doorbell and realized the wooden door behind the screen was open. Odd, since the temperature had already dropped into the forties.

"Hello?" he said. "Anybody home?" He could hear music playing from the back of the house, so he shouted this time: "Hello? Miss Cox?"

Still no answer, and yet he knew the music wasn't loud enough to cover his voice. An involuntary shudder went through him. He opened the screen door and called to her again. Nothing. He pushed the inner door and heard himself gasp.

Someone lay in a heap not five feet away, in the arch between the living room and the dining room beyond. The light Sully had seen from outside shone down the hallway, onto a mass of blonde hair, a ghost-white face, a freckled arm soaking in a pool of blood.

Sully tried to cross the room, but he couldn't move. He knew it wouldn't do any good anyway. It was clear that all of the life had ebbed out of her and onto the floor.

From someplace far away a siren wailed, and still Sully stood there, feeling as lifeless as the body he'd just discovered. If he had a pulse at all, it had thinned to a thread. He was still frozen when the siren screamed itself out beyond the wall, and urgent footsteps pounded across the stones and stopped outside the screen door.

"Sir, we got a 911 call. Is everything all right here?"

"Belinda Cox is dead," Sully said.

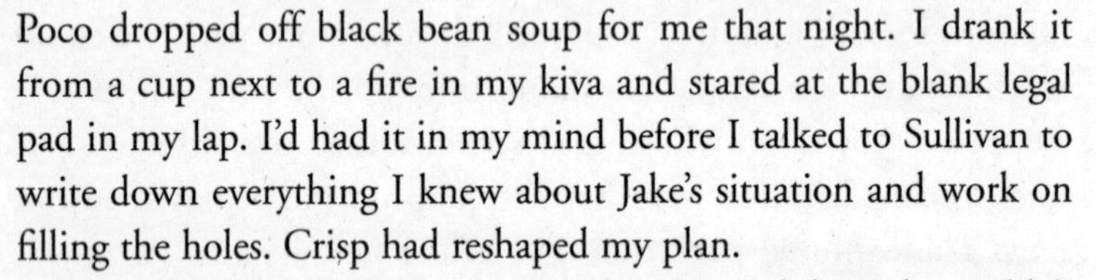

Poco dropped off black bean soup for me that night. I drank it from a cup next to a fire in my kiva and stared at the blank legal pad in my lap. I'd had it in my mind before I talked to Sullivan to write down everything I knew about Jake's situation and work on filling the holes. Crisp had reshaped my plan.

If, as he said, I was going to take the responsibility Jake couldn't take, I was going to have to get into his head. And since he was too afraid to talk, the only way to do that was to become—him.

How hard could it be? I was used to seeing what was there, putting myself into it, framing it. And there was also God—who didn't usually give me images on request, but I'd asked for that anyway.

I set the cup on the table and closed my eyes and tried to enter my son's world. Then I picked up my pen and wrote.

- Me and Ian played league soccer at Burn Lake. I also know Ian because his mom and my dad are going out. He's a cool guy. I look up to him.

- Miguel Sanchez showed up at Burn Lake even though he wasn't in the league, and we'd mess around with him while I was waiting for Dad and Alex.
- He was good. Really good.
- I told him he should try out for the select team.
- He did, and we both made it. Ian didn't.
- On September 10, somebody called Miguel's house from my house. Everybody thinks it was me. I'm not saying one way or the other because ______________
- Like an hour later, I ended up in the alley behind the restaurant where Miguel's mother works. I'm not saying how I got there or how I also ended up behind the wheel of Miguel's mother's truck with a threat letter on the seat beside me with my fingerprints on it. I'm also not saying how Miguel got run over. That's because ______________

That left a hole so big I thought I'd fall into it. I forced myself to go to the next thought.

- Miguel was hurt bad. There was nobody else around, so I called 911. I'm not saying where I got the phone or what happened to it. I don't have a cell phone myself.

So when did Miguel receive the note? Or did he?

- I wouldn't get out of the truck until they made me because ______________
- When they took me to the police station, I wouldn't talk to that detective who grilled me for an hour. I wouldn't talk to my parents either. I didn't say I did it. I didn't say I didn't. I was scared, but not scared enough to tell anybody anything—except

that I wasn't going home with my mom, and that was because ______________

- My mother kept bugging me every time she saw me. I asked my dad if I had to talk to her about it and he said no, which ticked her off. My dad didn't ask me stuff like she did.

I paused again. Dan basically told me he thought Jake could have done it since, like me, he had a lot of anger stored up, most of it toward me. Had he ever told Jake that? How did Jake feel about Dan assuming he could do something like that?

I swallowed hard. Evidently Jake didn't feel as lousy about that as he did about my assuming he *couldn't* have. I was starting to get a headache—and it was Jake's head I was in. I couldn't start thinking about what else he was feeling at this moment.

- I wanted to go to Ian's meet *really* bad, but Dad said I couldn't because it was against the rules the cops gave me.

- I snuck out and went anyway because ________________

You would do anything for Ian?

- They caught me and took me to the police station again, and this time they wouldn't let me go home with Dad. They said it was Mom or jail. I picked jail because ____________________

- It was bad in there. I didn't tell anybody how bad, but I asked if I could go to my mom's the next day.

- Mom didn't ask me a bunch of questions anymore. I couldn't eat or sleep. I went to work with her and got to take pictures. It freaked me out when I saw that detective, and when Miguel's mother said he was going into like a nursing home. I knew he wasn't ever gonna be the same again.

- The only time Mom asked me something was when she talked about the select team and Miguel. I let her know I didn't want to discuss that—because ____________
- Miguel died. I lost it.
- That detective came for me and they took me back to jail and they wouldn't let Mom and Dad pay bail. I freaked out about going back there.
- I was gonna tell Mom everything then, but that lawyer came to see me and told me about the explosion at the soccer field and the threat that got thrown at my mom's windshield. That's when I knew I couldn't tell anybody anything because I know somebody else is gonna get hurt.
- My mom came to see me in jail. It's the first time I ever saw her cry. She said she'd stand by me whether I ran over Miguel or not. She asked me if I did it for Ian. I told her I didn't do it for Ian.
- I believe it when she says she's gonna be there for me.

I almost crossed that last one out. It was, after all, only what I hoped he meant when he nodded to me as I left him at the jail. But I let it stay, because I needed for it to be true.

The list was achingly short, but it was all I knew about what my son was going through. I couldn't ask any of the other players in this thing. I ran my finger down the pad. Dan said he didn't know any more than I did. Who else . . .

I actually smacked the heel of my hand into my forehead. J.P. had even voiced it: *All I could think about was how this is affecting Alex. He was dying of loneliness . . .*

I unearthed a red pen and ran down the list again. Alex was the key to this somehow. I had thought that, back in the beginning, but all the trauma had pushed him into the background.

In red I wove in the Alex actions I knew about:

- Dad left me with Ginger when Jake first got arrested. When she went to the police station to see Dad, she left me with Ian.
- I told Mom I kinda didn't want to help her help Jake because I didn't want her and Dad fighting about it. I said I didn't know whose side I was supposed to be on.
- I didn't tell Mom that Jake and Miguel were friends in soccer until she sort of asked me.
- When I did tell her, I also said I didn't want Jake to know I told her because he doesn't like people talking about him.
- I almost told her something else once, but then I didn't.
- I asked Mom to tell me if Jake had to go to jail. She never did because of that bomb thing.
- I acted pretty cool up till then. But I guess Ms. J.P. caught me not looking cool, because I'm at her house now.

The list blurred in front of me. What had happened to our family? How had we become four lonely people who couldn't trust anybody with our feelings? How was it that Dan and Jake could put their faith in Ian, and Ginger, who had enough issues to keep Sullivan Crisp in business for the rest of his life?

I blinked hard and touched the red places on the list. My precious Alex, with all his brown-eyed charm and little-boy resilience, was probably the most alone of all of us—alone with information I was now sure he had. Information I was going to get out of him, for his sake as well as Jake's.

I was already reaching for the phone when it rang. Frances.

"Hey," I said. "I'm not on call."

"I know, but I want you on this one. Don't say anything until you hear it."

I glanced at my watch. Seven o'clock. Alex probably didn't go to bed until nine.

"It's a murder in Mesilla. A woman was killed in her home."

"Frances, I think I've had about as much—"

"I wouldn't ask you except this is going to require your kind of sensitivity."

"Why? Who is it?"

"It sounds like it's some controversial religious person. I'd just like you to go down there and see what you can shoot. It'll take your mind off . . . things."

"Right." I sighed and went for my camera bag. "What's the address?"

"Nineteen twenty-five Calle de Santo."

Sully sat in the backseat of the patrol car with the door open, drinking the bottle of water one of the officers had given him when he told him to wait for the detective who would want to ask him some questions. After that they'd ignored him—the two original uniforms, the four others who joined them, the three people who emerged from a van with *CSU* printed on the side. He watched crime tape go up, saw the neighbors gather across the street, witnessed Angelina passing out paper coffee cups, which she filled from a Thermos.

It would all have been a fascinating study in human behavior if Sully hadn't felt like someone had turned off all his nerves.

"Mr. . . . Crisp, is it?"

Sully nodded as he looked up into eyes he could see were green even in the dimness of the patrol car's interior light. Their owner ran one hand over his receding crop of thick hair and put out the other for Sully to shake.

"Detective Levi Baranovic. You doing okay, sir?"

"No," Sully said. "Not at all. I just discovered a dead person."

The detective held out an arm. "How about if we talk in there," he said, nodding toward the orange door.

It was the last place Sully wanted to go, but he followed him through it and over to a chipped wrought iron bench in the front yard. The detective stood, one foot up on the seat. "You knew the victim, Mr. Crisp?" he said.

"I knew of her. I never actually met her."

"But you knew it was her."

"Belinda Cox, yeah."

The detective thrust his neck forward, eyebrows up.

"I've seen her picture. I knew this was her house. I assumed . . ." Sully felt a glimmer of hope. "*Is* it her?"

"She hasn't been officially identified. When did you arrive?"

"Around seven."

"Did you see anyone when you got here?"

Sully shook his head.

"Hear anything?"

"No—yes."

"Which is it?"

"When I got up to the door, I heard music playing somewhere in the house. That was it."

"How did you get in?"

"The door was open."

"Which door?"

"All of them."

"The one in the wall?"

"Right."

"The screen door?"

"Yes, and the screen was torn. And the inner door was ajar."

"Why did you go in?"

"I just felt like something was wrong."

"Did you touch anything when you went in?"

Sully rubbed the back of his head. "No. I didn't even move until the police officers came in. Then I—yeah, I touched the doorframe. I guess I needed something to hold me up. You don't experience something like that every day."

"So how long would you say you were here from the time you pulled up in your car until the police arrived?"

"Not more than five minutes altogether."

The detective rubbed the stubble on his chin. "Would you be willing to come down to the precinct and give us an official voluntary statement?"

Sully was surprised, but he nodded. "Sure. Anything you need."

Baranovic pulled his foot from the bench and looked at the house as if he were trying to make a decision. "Let's go in my car," he said. "I'll have somebody bring you back for your vehicle when we're done."

"Can't I just follow you?"

His green eyes swept over Sully. "You're still pretty shook up. Let's do it this way—for your own safety."

Safety, Sully thought as Baranovic led him back through the orange doorway. Was there really any such thing?

A sizable crowd had gathered by the time I reached Calle de Santo. Nobody seemed too distraught—nothing there to shoot. Curious neighbors titillated by homicide didn't make for good photographs.

What I wanted was somebody concerned. Somebody with a story. I squirmed under my camera strap. Or did I want that—now that I had been that somebody?

A high wall fronted the house, and there was going to be no getting past that from the looks of things—although when I got about ten feet from it, the orange door that hung in its center swung open. Even as I raised the camera, Ken Perkins from the *Sun-News* bolted from the crowd. I focused just outside the door so I could get whoever stepped out. I could hear Perkins calling out, "Detective Baranovic, can you tell us what's happening?"

I kept the camera up. Didn't matter if I couldn't stand Baranovic. This was professional.

Or it was, until I saw who he had with him. The man Detective Baranovic was leading to his unmarked white car was Sullivan Crisp.

"Is this a suspect, sir?" Perkins yelled.

Baranovic just tucked Dr. Crisp into the car. I couldn't take a single shot as I watched the car weave its way among the parked vehicles and down the street.

Perkins turned back to the crowd and called out, "Does anyone know that man?"

A large woman waved a Thermos at him, and Perkins went to her, pad in hand. Another man had also waved at him to offer information, and I was about to turn away in disgust—and find somebody who *really* knew what was going on—when I realized I recognized him. Slim, youngish, sharp dresser. I'd seen him at Crisp's clinic, hadn't I? Hanging out with that child at the reception desk?

Letting the camera fall against my chest, I went for him. He saw me before I reached the curb and pulled away from the crowd, who all seemed mesmerized by the story Thermos Lady was telling. As he got closer, I could see the sheen of shock in his eyes.

"Hi," I said. "Look, forget the camera. I'm—"

"You're a client of Dr. Crisp's, I know."

"Do you have any idea what's going on?" I could hear my voice shaking.

"I just know Sully could be in trouble," he said. "Looks like they're taking him in for questioning."

"About the murder? I don't understand."

"I don't either." He tilted his head at me, just the way Dr. Crisp himself did. I could see my own fear matched on his face. "I don't know what you can do about giving him a fair shake in the paper."

"What are you saying? They think he *killed* this person?"

"I don't know, but they're scaring me, taking him off like that. I just don't want bad press for him—I mean, there's no way he was involved in this."

"Look," I said, "if you talk to the reporter, tell him only what you know—don't embellish. And say just what you told me, that Dr. Crisp couldn't—"

"Okay, yeah. Good."

He seemed so shaken, I wasn't sure he could even do that much. We were both basket cases.

"Listen, thanks," he said and started to move away.

"Wait," I said. "Mr.—"

"Neering. Kyle Neering."

"Can I take your picture—as a concerned friend? It could help."

He shook his head. "I'd rather not do that. I'll just go talk to the reporter."

"Well . . . please, if there's anything I can do for Dr. Crisp—help with bail—anything, please call me."

"I will."

"My name's Ryan Coe. He has my number."

Neering came back and squeezed my hand with his damp one. "I'll tell Sully," he said. "That'll mean a lot to him."

I watched him go, my camera still motionless around my neck. All the pictures were in my head—the interview room at the police station—metal tables, fluorescent lights, Detective Baranovic slapping the table. I didn't know how much anything I said or did could mean to Sullivan Crisp right now.

CHAPTER THIRTY-ONE

When Detective Baranovic offered a cup of coffee in the interview room, Sully thought of Tess, telling him he didn't know how to drink the stuff. That seemed like a long time ago now. He'd just lived another lifetime in this place.

When he'd arrived, they'd taken his fingerprints—elimination prints, they told him, since he did touch the doorframe and the doors themselves, and they wanted to be able to eliminate his when they took prints from the murder weapon. If they found it. Sully still didn't even know what the murder weapon was.

Another detective had asked for his cell phone, which he promised to return before Sully left the building. At this rate, Sully wasn't sure that was ever going to happen. It was eleven o'clock, and his numbness had given way to sickening horror. He wanted to get away and sort this out. Talk to Porphyria. Tess. Anybody but these people who had asked him the same set of questions no less than three times.

Detective Baranovic sat across from him now and pushed a cup of water toward him.

"I'm sorry for all this," he said. "I know you've had a rough evening."

"You could say that."

"I just want to go over a few more things with you, and then we'll see that you get home."

Sully just nodded. He was finding it harder to be congenial. He hadn't smiled for hours.

The detective turned the tape recorder on again. "Mr.—I'm

sorry. I understand it's *Dr.* Crisp. Why did you go to Belinda Cox's residence tonight?"

"I knew her from years ago. I had some unfinished business with her that I wanted to clear up."

"And what would that be?"

Sully bristled. "It was personal."

"Okay. And who knew you were going there?"

"One of my associates, Kyle Neering. And my mentor—who is back in Nashville—we talked on the phone earlier. And a friend of mine."

"And that would be?"

"A friend." Sully suddenly felt stubborn. Why did he have to bring Tess into this?

"Does this friend have a name?"

No, idiot. She goes by number. Sully smeared his hand over his mouth and hoped he wiped off any of the surliness that might have seeped out of his thoughts.

"Tess Lightfoot," he said.

Baranovic's brows lifted. Of course he would know her. Sully wasn't sure if that was good or bad. Holy crow—why should it be either one?

"How can we get in touch with Mr. Neering?"

"You can't," Sully said. "He went out of town—Little Rock. He left earlier tonight."

"No cell phone?"

"The number's in my cell phone—which you still have."

Baranovic nodded and pulled it out of his pocket. "If you'll bring it up for me, I'll write that down and you can be on your way."

Sully flipped open the phone and read off Kyle's number. Why did he feel like he was betraying Kyle somehow? Why did he feel any of the things that were tying his stomach into knots?

"I'll have an officer take you back to your car," Baranovic said.

"I'll call a cab," Sully said.

And the sooner the better.

Sleep was out of the question. I sent Frances a couple of shots of the outside of the crime scene. With that done, I wrapped up in Jake's Chicago Bears blanket and spent the night in the chair by the kiva, moving in images from Jake to Alex to Sullivan Crisp and back again until the sun crept in among rare early-morning clouds. There were a few in my head, too, but I was clear enough on two things I had to do.

At seven I was in Frances's office. Fifteen minutes later I came out with a new lawyer. We were set up for a meeting at four, at the jail so Jake could be there. I was already liking this William Yarborough—and he had to be better than the pointless Uriel Cohen.

My morning assignment wasn't until nine, which gave me time to get to J.P.'s to do the second thing before Alex left for school.

J.P. lived not far from Dan in a double-wide no one would have dared call anything but a bona fide house. It was neatly fenced, and the yard was alive with pots of fiery chrysanthemums and a pair of young cottonwoods.

J.P. and Poco and the three boys were all outside, backpacks stacked like carry-on luggage for boarding. Alex spotted me and ran to the car, and then stopped as if he were having second thoughts about giving me a hug. I grabbed him anyway and held on until I could get control of threatening tears.

When I held him in front of me at arm's length, he grinned, but it didn't quite reach his eyes.

"Did you come to get me out of school for the day?" he said.

"In your dreams. But I did come to talk to you."

"Aw, man."

I waved to Poco and J.P., who were sipping at their mugs and visibly dying to know what was going on.

"How much longer till they have to leave?" I said across the yard.

"Until Victoria gets here to pick them up," J.P. said with a grunt. "Which could be anywhere from two minutes to half an hour."

I turned to Alex. "Let's hang out by the fence for a minute." I leaned. He swung his foot along the line of rocks that bordered J.P.'s flower bed and pretended he wasn't watching my every nuance.

"I'm not sure what anybody has told you about Jake," I said. "But I promised you that *I* would tell you if he had to go to jail."

"I know. He's in juvie."

"No, he's in real jail."

"How come?"

"Because Miguel died, Alex. That means the police think Jake killed him."

He did what I hoped he would do, what I'd wrestled with half the night because I had to make him do it. His face drained of color, except for two red panic spots on his cheekbones. The foot stopped swinging, and his eyes were now two stormy pools of fear. He was clearly beyond just being sorry for Jake.

A horn blew and jerked us from the stare we were locked into. Alex turned away from me, but I caught his sleeve.

"Is there something you need to tell me, son?" I said.

"I gotta go."

"I *will* take you out of school if you want to talk about something."

"I got a test," he said and bolted for his backpack.

I waited until he was on his way in Victoria's van before I joined J.P. and Poco on the porch. Poco gave me a cup of coffee. J.P. gave me the old disapproving stare.

"What?" I said.

"I don't know what you just dumped on your kid," J.P. said. "But he hasn't looked like that the whole time I've had him. I've been making sure he doesn't watch the news or anything that would freak him out."

"I appreciate that," I said. "And if he's too much for you when he comes home, let me know."

"For Pete's sake, what did you say to him?"

My hackles were too tired to stand up, even under the what-kind-of-mother-are-you voice I'd thought J.P. had stopped using with me. So I told them.

J.P. looked at me, to use another of my mother's similes, like an old mule staring at a new fence. "I just don't think I would have done that to the kid right before he left to go to school."

"I need for him to tell me what he knows—not just for Jake's sake, but for his. He doesn't need to be burdened with the kind of information I think he has, and that's the only way I know to get it out of him."

J.P. swatted back her straying hair. "I still don't think I'd handle it that way."

"J.P. Leave it."

Our heads turned to Poco in unison, like prairie dogs attending to an unfamiliar sound.

"You don't know how you'd handle a thing like this," she said. "I sure don't."

J.P.'s pause told me she was as taken aback as I was.

"This could be the only way for Ryan to handle it," Poco said. "So just leave her alone."

I prayed she was right. Because if this wasn't what God was telling me last night, then I *really* didn't know what else to do.

"I don't know anything about kitchens," Sully said.

"No kidding?" Tess wrinkled her nose at the bottle of A-1 sauce he was about to pour on a pair of raw rib eyes. "That goes on after they're cooked, Crisp. Go sit down and have a Frappuccino."

Sully grinned for the first time in almost twenty-four hours. "You have a Frappuccino in this house?"

She opened the refrigerator and produced one. "It gave me great pain to buy it, but I thought you'd need comfort food."

Sully took it gratefully and leaned on the wood counter across from her. She chopped tomatoes with the same grace with which she cruised across a room or told him he had the taste of a ten-year-old boy.

"What were you going to say about kitchens?" she said.

"I was going to say this one is . . . it's you."

"Yeah, it is." She kept chopping, keeping up a rhythm that soothed him. "I had the cabinets made from old New Mexican furniture I collected. And I love having the pots all hanging out in the open like that." She pointed the knife above her head without looking up. "I like to see everything at once so I know what I have."

Sully took a long draw from the bottle. When he set it down, she was watching him.

"What?" he said.

"You don't want to talk about my kitchen."

"I don't?"

"You want to talk about what happened last night. That's why I asked you over for lunch."

Sully set the bottle aside and felt his grin fade. "Did the police question you?"

"Baranovic did."

"I'm sorry. I didn't want to get you involved."

"If you hadn't told them the truth, they would have found out, and it would look bad for you."

Sully felt the pang he'd been fighting off ever since he left the police station the night before. No one had accused him of anything. The detective had been more than cordial. But he couldn't stave off the uneasy feeling that an invisible finger was pointing at him.

Tess scooped up the pile of diced tomatoes and slid them onto the salad. "I'm going to ask you a question, and if you don't want to answer it, just tell me to back off."

Sully nodded.

She reached for an avocado. "How do you feel, now that the woman responsible for your wife's death is dead?"

"Funny you should ask."

"Is it?"

"I've been trying to sort that out. Part of me is shocked, of course, that anybody would do something like that—no matter how miserable she made them."

"So, no relief?"

"Not that I want to admit to."

"Isn't that just human, though? I mean, now you don't have to make sure she isn't going to hurt anyone else."

"I didn't want her dead!"

"But now that she is . . ." Tess paused, knife still at the skin of the avocado. "I'm sorry. I'm putting words in your mouth."

"Words I probably ought to own up to. But you know, I think I'm more angry than I am relieved. I wanted to have my say. It's like I'm still as frustrated as I was before."

She put down the knife and leaned on the heels of her hands. "I'm going to ask you another question, and you really, *really* don't have to answer this one."

Sully smiled at her. She hadn't asked him anything yet that he didn't want to pour out an answer to, right into her magic eyes.

"I know you'll never stop loving Lynn. She'll always be part of you. But do you think you'll ever really get over what happened to her?"

She went back to the avocado. Sully watched her cut it cleanly down to the pit and pull the halves apart like obedient twins.

"This was all about letting Lynn go," he said. "Maybe now I can."

Tess smiled and let the skin fall from the avocado. Sully hoped the easing he saw in her face was a sign that he'd said exactly what she wanted to hear.

"Are you going to broil those or what?" she said, nodding at the steaks.

Sully moved to her side of the counter and leaned over them. "You sure you want *me* to do it?"

She looked at the meat and then at Sully and smiled.

"I like mine well done," she said.

"Seriously?" Sully frowned toward the broiler. "That could take awhile."

"I know, Crisp." Tess put her hand on his arm. "If you're not going to do this, I am."

She came up on her toes and brought her lips close to him—and his dang cell rang.

"Hold that thought," Sully said. He was still grinning when he opened the phone. "Sullivan Crisp."

"This is Detective Levi Baranovic, Dr. Crisp. I have a few more questions for you. Would you be willing to come in for another interview?"

"When?" Sully said.

"Right now would be good."

Baranovic's tone left no room for negotiation. The pang Sully had been avoiding went through his soul.

CHAPTER THIRTY-TWO

Although the gray floor and the metal table were just as they'd been the night before, Sully knew the space had changed from interview room to interrogation room. Baranovic dropped a file folder onto the table between them and sat with the finality of someone who wasn't getting up until he got what he wanted.

Sully drew in a long breath. The guy was going to get the truth, because that was all Sullivan Crisp had to give.

Without the offer of coffee or water or apology, Baranovic bored into him. "Dr. Crisp, I need to advise you of your rights."

Sully stared at him. "My rights? Am I being charged with something?"

"No. It's just a formality at this point."

At this point? Was it going to be for real at some other point?

The detective was already reading from a card in his hand. Sully barely heard the familiar words he could have recited from late-night reruns of *Law & Order*, hardly saw himself signing the paper that was pushed toward him.

Baranovic slid it into the file and folded his hands on the table-top. "Dr. Crisp, you told us you did not arrive at Belinda Cox's residence until 7 p.m. Do you want to reconsider that?"

"No," Sully said. "That's when I got there."

"That's interesting, because a neighbor said it was six, which, according to the medical examiner, is much closer to the time of Ms. Cox's murder."

"I don't even know any of her neighbors," Sully said. "So I don't see how—"

"You don't know Angelina DeCristo?"

Even as Sully shaped the words on his lips, he remembered. "She could be the woman I met the day before in a café. I don't *know* her."

"She apparently knows you. She says she saw you get out of your car and go into the entrance to Ms. Cox's property. At 6 p.m."

Sully could only shake his head. "I was still at my office then."

"Anybody see you there?"

"No."

"That's your story and you're sticking to it."

"It's the truth," Sully said.

"There may be room for error there, but how are we going to get around the fact that your fingerprints are on the knife used to slit Belinda Cox's throat?"

Sully felt like his own had been cut. "I don't understand."

"We found it in the trash can at the back of her property, with blood still on the blade." His eyes narrowed at Sully, as if he were contemptuous of the sloppiness of the cover-up. "Your prints were on the handle. Can you explain that?"

"No."

"You've never eaten in her home?"

"I'd never been there before last night."

"Where are the clothes you wore last night?"

Sully licked his lips, which had turned to sandpaper. It was time to get this under control. "They're probably on my bathroom floor where I left them. Look, I don't even own a knife."

"You don't have a set of steak knives? Everybody has steak—"

"No!"

Baranovic put up his hand and lowered his voice. "Forget the murder weapon. Let's talk about your motive. You've been stalking Belinda Cox."

"*Stalking* her?"

"Didn't you look her up in Oklahoma City?"

"Yes—"

"Little Rock? Amarillo? You've left quite the trail, Dr. Crisp."

Sully ground his teeth. If the guy used his name one more time, he was going to—to what? There *was* no getting control over this. He was racing in front of a runaway train and losing ground.

"Why?" Baranovic said. "Why did you spend . . ." He flipped the folder open again. "A year looking for this woman?"

"You know what?" Sully said. "I want a lawyer."

"You sure?" Baranovic spread his hands. "A confession might be the best thing for you—make the DA go easier on you. You're an upstanding citizen. No record. We couldn't even find a parking ticket. This was obviously a crime of passion, committed by a famous Christian—a 'professional' Christian."

"I said I want a lawyer."

Baranovic looked almost sadly at the folder before he brought his gaze back up to Sully. His eyes held the first glint of last night's compassion. "There's no way you murdered that woman in cold blood, and yet the evidence doesn't lie. You had motive, means, opportunity. We have a witness who puts you at the scene. We have others who report you've been on the victim's trail for twelve months. You were just in Mesilla the day before the murder asking about her. The neighbor feels pretty bad that she all but gave you the address."

He waited, like a therapist, Sully thought crazily. This whole thing was insane.

"You seem like a heck of a nice guy, Dr. Crisp. If I could pin this on anybody else, I'd do it in a heartbeat." He shook his head. "I like it a lot better when the bad guys are gangbangers and crack addicts."

Again he waited.

Sully shook his head. "I want an attorney."

"That's your right." Baranovic stood up, picked up the folder, smacked the table with it. "I hate it. I really hate it."

When he walked out, something pounded the silence he left behind. Moments passed before Sully realized it was his own heartbeat, trying to drive him mad.

He leaned back in the chair and searched the ceiling. He didn't even have a lawyer here—he was going to have to contact Rusty Huff. Healing Choice Ministries had an attorney, but he wasn't in criminal law. What ordinary citizen retained a defense attorney?

Sully fell forward and dropped his face into his hands. It was absurd. There must be something he could say to wipe the suspicion from the detective's face, a different way to explain his fingerprints on a knife he'd never seen. Couldn't he just call Baranovic back in and go over his alibi once more, until he no longer saw it as a thin veil to cover lies? Sully couldn't leave them believing he had slit a woman's throat.

He pulled his hands away and found tears in them. They would only look like tears of remorse if he said another word. For right now, there was nothing he could do but pray.

I was packing up to leave work when Frances came out of her office, eyes bulging.

"I want to give you the first shot at what just came in."

I resisted the urge to look at my watch. I needed to get to Alex.

"They've gotten a grand jury indictment on that guy they picked up for last night's murder," Frances said. "They're taking him over for booking."

"What's his name?" I said.

She glanced at the sheet in her hand. "Sullivan Crisp. Look, I know you've got a lot going on—"

"I'm there," I said.

By the time I arrived at the downtown precinct, Levi Baranovic was already standing at the sally port, wearing sunglasses that did little to disguise his contempt for the television cameras and barking reporters clustered around him. I avoided him like a plague of locusts, as did the rest of them when a police cruiser pulled in. While they all surrounded the car, only to be herded back by an officer, I took the steps leading to the door they'd be moving their arrestee through. I'd been there before.

"You're here for the booking, detective?" Ken Perkins called out. "Isn't that unusual?"

You know it is, moron. I focused the camera on the back door of the patrol car. I could barely see Dr. Crisp's profile, but the look was there—the baffled sense that this could not possibly be happening.

"Is it because this is a first-degree murder charge?" Perkins said. "Is that why you're here—to make sure it sticks?"

I had to hand it to Baranovic. Perkins could have been speaking Dutch for as much attention as the detective was giving him. He turned to the cruiser and nodded to the uniform standing at the door. Sullivan Crisp's head rose above the bevy.

The questions shot from all directions and wound up in a snarl in the air. They wanted the facts, they said.

They wanted blood, that was what they wanted, and it sickened me. They couldn't have cared less that Sullivan Crisp was innocent. That my Jake was innocent. That anybody was. They just wanted a story—something grisly and titillating that would give people a jolt stronger than their coffee tomorrow morning when they opened the paper.

I could scream at them all the way I wanted to. Or I could make pictures of the truth. *God, give me the story I'm supposed to tell.*

The media were being moved back so Sullivan could be brought up the steps. I raised the camera as he straightened his shoulders and met Baranovic eye to eye. I shot the lack of anger in his gaze. The quiet set of his jaw. I shot until the tears blurred my view and an officer approached, waving me away.

I moved before he had to say a word. I didn't want Dr. Crisp to see me. He had enough humiliation ahead of him.

Sully now knew why arrested suspects kept their heads down when they passed through the gauntlet of reporters. It was the impossibility of keeping shame from their faces whether they were guilty or not. The handcuffs alone made Sully feel as if he'd committed a crime, but he kept his face up.

He felt something close over his arm and looked down to see Baranovic's hand.

"Vultures," he muttered near Sully's ear. "Ignore them."

He wanted to. But all he could think was that Tess would be seeing this on a screen or a front page. At least she wouldn't see what went down beyond the metal door. A sheriff's deputy searched him for weapons and left him in a holding area with men who were drunk or drugged out or used to being there. The court commissioner set bail at $500,000, high even for murder, because Sully wasn't a New Mexico resident. Another deputy took more prints, electronically this time, a ten-print and palms. A mug shot was made, his clothes taken from him and replaced with an orange jumpsuit. When he was left with nothing but a property receipt, he was finally allowed to make a phone call. When he did, Rusty didn't answer. Sully had never felt emptier.

CHAPTER THIRTY-THREE

I barely made it to the jail for the four o'clock meeting with the attorney, and I was still shivering inside and out when the guard showed me into an abbreviated version of the room I'd visited Jake in before. There was a small divided table in this one, with Jake on one side and Dan and an African-American man on the other. I was still so addled I didn't realize the guy was our new lawyer until he put out his hand to me and introduced himself as Will Yarborough. He dispensed with any other pleasantries, and I appreciated that. All I wanted to do at the moment was look at my son.

Jake looked cleaner today, and calmer by a degree. He wasn't picking at his mole or jiggling his knees back and forth, and I thought I knew why. Will Yarborough was a big man, and soft-spoken, and he didn't bother smiling at what was a decidedly unhappy situation. I was feeling calmer myself just being in his presence.

But after I searched Jake's face and made sure he showed no evidence of internal injuries or shell shock or pinkeye or any of the other things I'd visualized happening to him in there, I surveyed Yarborough with caution. So far no one in the legal system had listened, and I didn't want to expect too much.

"We have a lot to talk about before Monday," he said.

"What's Monday?" Dan said.

"The first day of the trial. You weren't notified?"

Dan and I looked at each other. The skin around his lips was blue.

"No," we said in unison.

"It doesn't give me much time to prepare," the lawyer said, "so I'd like to start by asking Jake some questions." He looked over the divider. "Are you up for that?"

Jake's eyes sprang open, and for a hopeful instant I thought he was going to let it all out. But he looked down at his hands and muttered, "No."

"Jake, please," I said.

But Yarborough shook his head at me and folded his hands closer to the divider.

"We'll get back to you, then." He looked at Dan and me. "I've read the file. Is there anything either of you can tell me that might help with Jake's defense?"

It was Dan's eyes that startled open this time. "You're actually building a case?"

A strong eyebrow shot up into Yarborough's deep-brown forehead. "Why wouldn't I? There were no witnesses. No one seems to be able to explain exactly how this all happened. My job is to create reasonable doubt."

I thought I might cry. I turned to Jake, ready to renew my plea, and stopped. His lips were moving soundlessly.

"Did you want to say something, Jake?" Yarborough said, with a warning glance at me.

"There *was* a witness," he said.

"Who was it?"

"Miguel," Jake said.

I couldn't have deflated any further if I'd been a leftover party balloon.

"Unfortunately, he can't help us," Yarborough said quietly.

"I thought he was going to wake up and tell everything. Then I wouldn't have to."

Jake looked up and moved his sad gaze to each of us in turn, like he was willing us to understand what he meant. I knew by now he wasn't going to elaborate, and the frustration pumped again. Until I thought of something.

I dug through my purse and pulled out the list I'd made on the legal pad.

"I don't know if this will help," I said to Yarborough. "It's just some thoughts. I tried to put things in chronological order."

He took it out of my hand, and I immediately wanted to snatch it back. This was ridiculous. The man was a professional defense attorney. He wasn't going to use the desperate scribblings of a hysterical mother.

As I sagged back in the chair, I could feel Dan watching me, probably waiting for me to turn the table over.

"This is very helpful," Yarborough said. "May I keep it for now?"

I nodded.

"One question—the parts in red?"

"Oh, those refer to our younger son, Alex."

"Leave Alex out of this!"

Our heads all whipped toward Jake, who scraped his chair back and stood up. The guard was already on his way from the door.

"He doesn't know anything!" Jake said. "You're just gonna get him hurt. Leave him alone!"

"Either sit down or you're done," the guard said behind him.

"I'm done." But Jake didn't turn away. He looked at me with the same pleading I'd directed at him so many times. "Mom—no Alex, okay?"

"I can't promise that, Jake," I said.

He shook his head at me, slowly. He was still begging me with his eyes as the guard ushered him through the door.

"Do you know what that's about?" Yarborough said when they were gone.

"Alex knows something," I said.

"He would have said so by now, wouldn't he?" Dan rubbed his hands across the tops of his thighs. "Maybe he wouldn't. I don't think I know either one of them like I thought I did."

"Do you want me to talk to Alex?" Yarborough said. "Impress on him how important it is for him to tell the truth?"

"Let me try first." I looked at Dan again, waiting for him to disagree. He didn't say anything.

"Let's talk outside," Yarborough said.

Dan and I followed him to the checkout counter. The female officer glanced up at me when I slid my badge to her.

"One thing he's got going for him," she said.

"My son?" I said.

"He gets a lot of visitors. Keeps him from feeling isolated. Once they feel like everybody's forgotten them, they start—"

"A lot of visitors?" I looked at Dan, but he appeared to be as baffled as I was.

"He had one right before you came."

"Who?" I said.

"Can't tell you that." She looked, in fact, as if she shouldn't have told me that much.

As we moved away from the counter, I grabbed Yarborough's arm. "Can we find out—"

"I'll work on it," he said. "Listen, I have an obligation to bring this up, so let me get it out of the way."

He pulled at his tie, the first uneasy gesture I'd ever seen him make.

"You're going to talk about a plea, aren't you?" I said.

"The DA's office has made an offer, and I have to discuss it with you."

I opened my mouth, but it was Dan who said, "No."

"You might want to hear it. It does involve some jail time, but definitely less than what he'll probably get if he's convicted."

I was still gaping at Dan when he turned streaming eyes to me. "What do you think?"

Something in me let me say, "Tell me what *you* think."

He smeared his hand across his eyebrows. "I feel like I've failed him all this time. I thought he just wanted to take the consequences for a mistake, and I thought I could help him do that with dignity." His voice caught. "But I think I was wrong. You never believed he was guilty, and now—I just want to give him a chance, even if he won't give himself one."

Dan's shoulders collapsed, and he moved away from us. I shook my head at Will Yarborough.

"No deal," I said.

"Good," he said. "Just had to ask." He tapped his portfolio. "Let me work on this and I'll be in touch, probably tomorrow morning."

"I'll be available," I said.

He shook my hand again, and before he turned away, he softened his dark eyes at me. "Jake's lucky to have parents like you two."

Sully found out some things during his night in the Dona Ana County Jail. One, no one was swayed by his doctorate in psychology or his standing in the Christian community. He was surrounded by bangers, as Baranovic called them, who would have been more impressed if he had a tattoo and a scar or two. He also discovered that even without that, everybody who passed through thought he was one of them.

And apparently if you were one of them, you were required to participate. Sully's plan was to keep to himself and pretend to sleep, but nobody was having it. The savage next to him screamed obscenities at him. The one across the corridor spat green wads into Sully's cell at regular intervals.

The guard who came to investigate that cursed Sully doubly by referring to him as Dr. Crisp. "Can I get you anything, *Dr.* Crisp? How about a nice porterhouse? I hear you're pretty good with a steak knife."

Another guard told that one to shut his mouth, but the damage was already done. For the next hour Sully was harangued with lewd questions and lurid requests for medical advice from the "doctor," until he was on the brink of hurling back a few expletives of his own.

When they finally wore themselves out, Sully was left with the glaring lights that were evidently never turned off and the relentless stench of everything heinous about humanity. Somewhere near dawn, it occurred to him that Ryan's son must be in here somewhere and had been for days. He wondered how long it took for a kid living in this black hole to actually become "one of them."

Something they were passing off as breakfast was being delivered when the less mouthy guard unlocked Sully's cell, put handcuffs on him, and led him down the corridor.

"Your lawyer's on the phone," he said when they were beyond the cells. "We have to let you talk to him."

Sully didn't mention that he didn't have a lawyer. It didn't matter, as long as this got him out of the fifth circle of hell.

The guard took him into a small room with a chilly metal table and one chair that appeared to be bolted to the concrete floor. The guard shackled Sully's ankle to it before he unlocked the handcuffs and took a portable phone from another guard.

"Hello?" he barked into it. "Yeah, I got Sullivan Crips for you."

"It's Crisp," Sully said as he put the phone to his ear. But he wasn't even sure of that anymore.

"Sully?"

"Rusty." Sully covered his eyes with one hand and hunched over the table with the phone in the other.

"I am so sorry," Rusty said. "I didn't get your message until last night, and then I couldn't get through to you. Are you all right?"

"No," Sully said.

"I got you a lawyer." Rusty lowered his voice. "I told the guy I just talked to that I was your attorney."

"Yeah," Sully said. "Thanks. Listen, I'm worried about the clinic."

"I called over there and got Kyle Neering."

"You did? I thought he was out of town."

"He said he just got in. He's blown away by all this, of course. He recommended the defense attorney that'll be calling you. Harlan

Snow is his name—Kyle says he has a great reputation in Las Cruces." Rusty gave a dry laugh. "That Kyle's a go-getter, isn't he?"

"Yeah," Sully said. "Look, you can count on him for whatever you need."

"He was all over me because I haven't gotten you bailed out yet. I'm on my way, Sully. You know the full power of Healing Choice will be brought to bear on this. We'll get you out."

"I appreciate it."

"I should be in by this afternoon. Kyle's going to try to get in to see you."

"Tell him to stay there and keep things going at the clinic. And tell him to just leave Martha alone and let her do her thing. Olivia can—"

"Sully," Rusty said. "Don't worry about all that. You've got to focus on getting through this."

Sully thanked him again and hung up. How were you supposed to get through something when your every move was locked down or cursed at or mandated by people who thought you were a cold-blooded killer?

He watched the guard unshackle his ankle, and he put his hands out to be cuffed again. It chilled him that the routine was already becoming automatic, and yet the conditioned responses he'd been using for over a decade were failing him. He didn't know what he would tell a client to do, except to pray. If God would even come into this place.

CHAPTER THIRTY-FOUR

I'd been in the Third Judicial District Courthouse three times, but when I walked in at ten o'clock Monday morning, it was the first time I didn't want to tear off the stucco with my fingernails. I gave Will Yarborough credit for that.

I'd spent most of Saturday with him, going over every detail we could scrape up. He wrote each one on a card, including what I had already given him, and spread them out in a timeline on a table in his office conference room. Holes still gaped at us, gaps we couldn't fill, but Will seemed to view each one as a challenge.

"I'm going to work with Dan tomorrow," he said when we were wrapping up, "and take one more shot at talking to Jake. I want to interview Ian, too, but Dan says he's out of town at a meet this weekend."

My face tightened. "I really feel like he knows something, Will."

"If he does, I'll find out," he'd said. "Don't worry."

I did, of course, but not as much as I would have without him at the helm.

Sunday was Dan's turn with him, while I spent the day with Alex. As always, the kid charmed me—through the service at the soccer moms' church and lunch at his "fave" Mexican restaurant and a catch-up soccer lesson in J.P.'s backyard, during which he informed me that I'd forgotten everything he'd taught me and we were going to have to start all over.

But a different little boy peeked out from behind the impish smiles. Every time I thought the moment was right to ask him what he knew that would help Jake, something stopped me. A furtive glance from under the bill of his too-big ball cap. An anxious gleam in his eyes if I was quiet for too long. A sigh that escaped when he didn't know I could hear.

So when I tucked him in at J.P.'s Sunday night, I just kissed his forehead and laughed when he wiped it off with his fingers. Maybe J.P. was right. Maybe he didn't need an interrogator. He needed a mom.

Even without getting anything new from Alex, I had a strong sense of hope as I slid into the row behind the defendant's table. Will was already there, and so was Dan. As was Ginger, dressed in a scoop-necked gray jumper that should have had a blouse under it, hair up in a tumble of curls I suspected was an attempt to look serious and maternal. Just before I decided not to waste any energy on her, I sneaked a glance at her left hand, but it was hard to tell if she was wearing an engagement ring. There was at least one piece of jewelry on every finger.

"How's Alex?" Dan whispered to me.

"Adorable," I whispered back.

"Nothing?"

I shook my head.

Ginger tucked her hand through Dan's arm and hugged it.

At the table in front of us, Will stood up and turned toward the side door, where a guard was ushering Jake in. He was dressed in black jeans and a white pullover sweater I recognized as one of Dan's. He looked young and vulnerable and nothing like a killer, and I wanted to fold my arms around him.

A rustle from the other side of the aisle drew my attention, and my heart lurched in my chest. With the same grace and dignity she'd shown at the funeral, Elena Sanchez made her way to a seat behind the prosecutor's table. Nina Hernandez stood up, as imperious and commanding as I remembered her from the preliminary hearing, and took both of Elena's hands into hers. That was what I wanted to do—look into those warm eyes, see how she was surviving, assure her I would be there for her.

Instead, I had to slant my body away and hope she didn't realize that the mother of the boy accused of murdering her son was her trusted *Grafa*.

Once the trial got under way, however, my mind attached itself in agony to the proceedings.

Will Yarborough had already told us the prosecution would present its case first, and that Nina Hernandez would paint the worst possible picture of our son and his alleged crime.

With her guidance, a solemn uniformed officer described a vicious crime scene, and the emergency room doctor listed Miguel's injuries in excruciating detail. Levi Baranovic grimly reported facts about fingerprints and phone records, and made Jake's refusal to answer questions sound like the boy was the next Son of Sam. Most damaging of all, as far as I was concerned, were Miguel's teachers and his debate coach, who all portrayed him as the boy I knew he was, a boy who had never done anything to warrant the kind of brutal retaliation he suffered.

I refused to look at the jury, to see what they were believing. Will had warned us that the prosecutor's case would appear to be airtight and that he wouldn't be able to punch many holes in it with his cross-examinations. Without that preparation I might have stood up and grilled all of those people myself.

And yet I knew I would have maintained even sans Will's coaching. As frustrated and frightened as I was, my focus kept flooding back to Jake, who sat straight-backed beside Will, scarcely moving except to rub the Band-Aid someone had put over his tattered mole. He was pale and terrified, but as much as I wanted to shake the truth out of him, I could see something brave in him, too—a stubborn refusal to give in to whatever would save him at the expense of someone else. I hated it, but I had to admire it.

We were getting close to noon, and I couldn't imagine who else Nina Hernandez could put on the stand to disparage my son. Will had predicted that the prosecution would rest before the lunch recess, and when we came back he would give the opening statement he'd deferred earlier. He looked as surprised as I was when Hernandez asked permission to approach the bench, and both lawyers went forward. Jake was left alone at the table. I sat on my hands to keep from reaching for him.

"I know," Dan whispered to me.

I looked up to see tears in his eyes. He did know.

When I turned back to Jake, he was writing on Will's pad, and I wondered if that was against the rules. I also wondered what was taking so long with the judge, a big-shouldered man who looked more like a football coach than a jurist. He directed fierce eyes at Hernandez as she expounded on something with her usual high drama. I thought his hooded scowl might be a good sign, until he nodded at her, and Will's shoulders ever so slightly sagged.

"This case will be continued until Friday, October 16, at 10:00 a.m.," His Honor said to the courtroom. "Court is adjourned."

Will put his arm around Jake and murmured into his ear. The guard waited until Will gave him a final pat before he led Jake away.

I was on Will before the door closed. "What just happened?"

He beckoned us to lean in. Although the invitation didn't include her, Ginger leaned too.

"Hernandez has one more witness, but she hasn't had time to prep him—her—whoever. She asked for two days—it looks like stalling to me, although I don't know why she'd do that. Maybe just to throw off my timing."

"Two days is Thursday," I said.

"The judge had a conflict."

"So Jake has to spend four more days in that place because she couldn't get her act together and he has something else to do?" My voice was spiraling. "That's not right!"

"I'm sorry," Will said. "But it does give us a little more time."

"For what?" Ginger said.

Will looked at her as if he hadn't noticed her before, which, unlike most men, he probably hadn't.

"I'm sorry," he said. "You are—?"

"Ginger Tassert," she said, offering one bejeweled hand.

"You know, maybe we shouldn't talk here," I said. I widened my eyes at Will, and he nodded.

"The prosecution has to disclose the name of the witness," he said, "so as soon as I know who it is, we'll put our heads together again."

He shook hands with Dan and waited while he steered an obviously reluctant Ginger up the aisle by the elbow.

"Who is she?" Will said.

"She's nobody," I said and then shook my head. "She's Dan's fiancée. And Ian's mother."

Will gave me a long look.

"What?" I said.

"I was going to tell you this morning, but I got sidetracked. I got a look at the visitor's log from lockup. The person who visited Jake just before us Friday signed in as Ginger Tassert. I didn't know she was Ian's mother."

"That doesn't make sense," I said. "Dan would have known if she went to see Jake. He was as surprised as we were that Jake had any visitors besides us."

Will folded his arms. "You think it means anything?"

"It means she's a conniving little wench."

His mouth twitched.

"Actually, she wants to insinuate herself into my son's life, make Dan think she cares about his family."

"Then why wouldn't she tell Dan she was going?"

I was already nodding. "You're right—if that's what she was up to, she'd have come back to him sobbing about how terrible it all was in the jail and how sorry she is and how she's going to—" I put up my hands to stop myself. "I don't even want to go there."

"Then it *could* mean something," Will said.

"Something about Ian?"

"I don't know. I'm going to try to see him after he gets out of school today. So far I haven't gotten any answers to my phone calls to his mother. I had her down as Virginia Iverton, though—I think. Let me check."

He picked up his legal pad and did a double take at the top page, which was folded up from the middle.

"Jake was writing on it while you were talking to the judge," I said.

"Then I think this is for you."

Will tore it off and handed it to me. The word *Mom* was printed on the front in shaky block letters.

Don't worry, Jake had written inside. *I think what I knew all along wuold happen is going to atfer all. Hang in til Friday and it will be ok. I'm sorry to put you thru this, but I had to portect you and Alex. Loev, Jake*

I read it three times and pressed it to my lips before I said, "Will, I think you should look at this." I held out the paper and let him read it over my shoulder.

"When did you say he wrote this?" he said.

"When you and the DA were at the bench."

"Could you hear what we were saying up there?"

"Snatches. Nothing I could put together."

"But Jake could have."

"Where are you going with this?" I said.

"Probably nowhere, but if he got the gist that there's going to be a new witness Friday, that could be why he thinks it's going to be okay."

"But how does he know who the new witness is when you don't even know?"

Will tucked the pad into his portfolio and snapped it shut. "Like I said, there's probably no connection. Just trying to explore every option." He patted my shoulder and left me to pore over the small piece of my son I held in my hand.

We could be grasping at straws, but I didn't think so. What I did think dropped in like one of my images.

Jake was trying to tell me something else. When I told him

before that he couldn't have written the note they found at the scene because he was dyslexic and couldn't spell, he wouldn't prove me wrong. I pressed the note to my chest. And now he had.

Harlan Snow had marched his short, tough-faced self into the prisoner/attorney meeting room Saturday morning wearing a black pinstriped double-breasted suit and a starched white shirt whose collar cut into his ruddy jowls. He'd listened closely enough to Sully's story, nodding a head of thick, wavy black hair in all the right places, but he hadn't asked many questions, and his conclusions had seemed somewhat cavalier.

"The DA doesn't have squat," he said. "Around here they can get a ham sandwich an indictment."

"Excuse me?" Sully said.

"Their solve rate is down on murders, so they're looking for a slam dunk. Baranovic's also up for a promotion. You go down, and that puts it in the bag for him. Don't worry, they're just dreaming." He lifted his chins at Sully. "You want to know about your bail."

Sully did. He'd also like to know that his lawyer thought he was innocent.

Snow was consulting his BlackBerry. "So this Healing Choice Ministries is putting up the bail in their name, rather than going to a bondsman." He shrugged. "That's a show of faith on their part, but you're going to have to wait in jail for a source hearing—so the court knows the money's really there. Could take a week."

"A week?"

"The DA's office will try to drag it out," Snow said. "They figure you won't be able to tolerate being in there, and you'll break down and give them a confession."

"There's nothing to confess!"

"So you've told me everything."

"I've told you. I've told the police."

"Good. Then hang in there, and we'll see what they have to say in our discussion Tuesday."

But it was only Monday afternoon when the guard pulled Sully out of the cell for "a meeting with the lawyers."

And there, Sully's second impression of Harlan Snow was of somebody from the diplomatic corps.

It was "Ms. Hernandez" this and "ma'am" that, in a subdued voice that tiptoed around the power of the prosecutor. She, on the other hand, was brusque and dismissive. She had clearly not come for a discussion.

"Thank you for seeing us today instead of waiting until tomorrow," Snow said. "My client has already been in jail for three days."

"I had a cancellation," she said. "And I wanted to get this done." She took a survey of Sully with small, dark eyes and consulted her notes.

"You're both aware that we have enough physical evidence to convict. What you may not be aware of is that one of your associates has reported that you have been distracted for several weeks. Not attending to critical issues, obviously focused on something outside the office."

Sully searched his mind. It didn't take long to come up with Martha Fitzgerald.

"Do you deny that you were actively looking for Belinda Cox?"

"No."

"Or that you were concerned about what you might do when you found her?"

Sully stared. Where had that come from? He'd thought it, but who had he shared that with?

Before he could come up with an answer, she stunned him again.

"We know about your wife's suicide, Dr. Crisp. We also know that the deceased was her counselor, and that you hold her responsible for your wife's death." Hernandez gave him a look that he guessed was supposed to be empathetic. "I can actually understand that motive. Doesn't make it right, but it could work in your favor if you're willing to take a plea."

"What are we talking?" Snow said.

"I could get it down to—"

"Wait a minute," Sully said. "Belinda Cox had enemies. Her own neighbor wanted her gone because she was stirring up trouble in Mesilla."

"Maybe so," Hernandez said. The empathy faded. "But none of them left pieces of themselves at the scene. Without a confession, you're looking at first-degree murder."

Sully felt like a tuning fork, struck and still vibrating, painfully, down to his teeth.

First-degree murder.

Premeditated. Planned with malice and forethought.

A crime he could be hanged for. A crime he didn't commit.

But someone else did. Someone who planted traces of him at the scene. Someone who wanted him to go down for this.

The pain went beyond his teeth and his bones. Betrayal was a pain of the soul.

CHAPTER THIRTY-FIVE

I stopped at my house Tuesday after work to drop off my equipment before I went to soccer practice at four—an effort to distract myself from the fact that I couldn't have my usual session with Dr. Crisp.

He was still in jail, and I had no idea what was going on. I even tried to wheedle something out of the poor addled girl at the Healing Choice front desk, but she wasn't talking.

I missed Sullivan's grins and his sandbox and his ability to make me talk about things I thought were completely ridiculous and turned out to be parts of myself I never knew. And yet even as I longed to be sitting in the Alice in Wonderland chair, I knew that without what he'd already taught me, I'd be tearing the light fixtures from the ceiling.

I turned to the coffeepot instead and had some espresso brewing when the doorbell rang. J.P., Poco, and Victoria were all standing on my front porch. With Alex. His face was drawn into a knot of ten-year-old misery.

Heart halfway up my throat, I wrenched the door open.

"Alex needs to talk to you, Mom," Poco said.

Victoria put her hand on his back and all but moved him bodily into the room. J.P. followed like backup in case he decided to bolt. It didn't take the CIA to see there was coercion going on.

Victoria deposited Alex on the couch and sniffed the air.

"Do I smell coffee?" Poco said.

"I don't even drink the nasty stuff and it smells delicious to me." J.P. leaned over Alex. "We're going into the kitchen so you can talk to your mom. Do we still have a deal?"

He nodded, miserable gaze fixed on his sneakers.

I fired questions at J.P. with my eyes, but she just motioned me toward the sofa and disappeared into the kitchen with Poco and Victoria. For once, I was getting nothing out of her.

I pulled the ottoman up and sat down, my knees almost touching Alex's. "You have something you want to tell me?"

"Not want to. Have to."

"You can tell me anything, and I promise I won't yell at you."

He pulled in his chin. "You never yell at me."

"Okay, then," I said. "I'm not going to start now. What is it, Alex?"

His eyes went to the wall above my head. "Well, y'know that day Miguel got hurt and stuff?"

My heart stopped. "Yeah."

"I was supposed to be doing chores, you know, like dumping garbage in the compost pile, only I really wasn't."

"Where were you?"

"I was in my room messing with this cell phone I found."

I felt my eyebrows rise. "You found a cell phone?"

"Yeah. It was on the floor in the hall and I thought it was a toy, only when I got in my room, I saw it was for real, except it didn't belong to anybody."

"It had to belong to *some*body."

He rolled his eyes. "No, Mom. It didn't have any numbers in the contacts or anything."

"So . . . you were playing with this cell phone and . . ."

"I heard Jake's door, like, bang open, and then they were in the hall right outside my room."

"They?"

"Ian and Jake. Ian was yelling at Jake."

He looked at me as if to let the enormity of that sink in.

"Yelling?" I said. "I thought they were best friends."

"Yeah, me too, and it freaked me out, so I just stayed in my room."

I tried a smile. "With your ear to the door, I bet."

"No—Ian was yelling really loud."

"About what?"

"Soccer. About how if Jake hadn't of told that bean-eater kid—that's how he said it—if Jake hadn't of told him to try out for the select team, then Ian would of made it." He rolled his eyes. "Which is totally bogus, because everybody said Miguel was way better than him."

"So he was blaming Jake for his not getting picked for the team."

"Yeah. He said a bunch of other stuff too." Alex scrunched his face. "If I say it like he did, I have to cuss."

"Got it," I said. "Go on."

"Ian said he was tired of the Mexican kid getting what *he* was supposed to have. He said that kid already beat him once and he couldn't do anything about that, but he could do something about this. Y'know, the soccer team."

"Right." Some of this was making sense, some of it wasn't. "So then what happened?"

"Ian said—" Alex deepened his voice to teenager level. "'You owe me, man. You're gonna go with me, and we're gonna make him drop out and let a real American play.' Jake said, 'What are we gonna do?' and then they went in the study where we do homework on the computer and stuff. Next to Jake's room."

"Could you still hear them talking?"

"No. I heard the printer going, though. And when they came back out in the hall, Ian was yelling again."

"About . . ."

"About the cell phone. He was all screaming about how he knew he brought it in and what the—blank—did Jake do with it."

"You had it," I said.

"I *was* just gonna hide it, because I hate Ian. Everybody thinks he's all good and cool and all that, but if you don't do everything his way, he's way mean. Grown-ups don't know that."

"Like he was being with Jake."

"Yeah, only I don't think that ever happened before. It sounded like Jake was gonna cry." Alex made a fist. "I woulda just punched him in the face."

"I'm sure," I said. "So, what did you do about the phone?"

"Ian said he was gonna have to call on our house phone, so when they went down to the kitchen, I opened my door to put it back out in the hall. I didn't want Ian yelling at Jake anymore."

"How did that work out?"

"It didn't," he said simply. "I was closing my door again, and Ian came down the hall and about busted it down. I *shoulda* punched him in the face right then, except—"

"Except what?"

"He's a big dude."

"I know. What did he do?"

All the spunk that had begun to rise seeped away. "He threw me on the bed. Told me if I didn't keep my mouth shut he was gonna tell Dad I stole his phone. I tried to kick him, but Jake told me to stop, so I did."

I closed my eyes and pulled my anger in. I'd deal with it in some sandbox later.

"So is that why you never told anybody this before?" I said. "Because you didn't want Dad to know you took Ian's phone?"

He shook his head. The misery returned to his face.

"There's something else, isn't there?" I said.

"I watched out the window when they left."

"In what?"

"Taxicab."

"Seriously?"

"I guess that's who Ian was calling. It kind of weirded me out. Kids don't take taxicabs."

Not unless they're trying to cover their tracks.

"I waited for them to come back because I was gonna tell Jake that he shouldn't hang around with Ian anymore, only that's kind of hard because him and Ginger are around all the time—but I was gonna tell him that anyway, and then only Ian came home."

"In a cab?"

"I don't know. I just saw him walking up the driveway."

"How long was he gone?"

Alex twisted his mouth in thought. "I watched two shows, so it was like an hour."

Then there was no way Ian walked all the way back from downtown. Someone must have dropped him off out on the main road.

"What did you do?" I asked.

"I wasn't gonna do anything, but Ian came in my room and acted like we were best friends or something." He gave me a blank look. "Like I really believed that. He must think I'm stupid or something."

"What did he say?"

"He was being all nice and saying he was sorry he got mad at me before. He said we had to forget about that because Jake got in trouble. He said he was gonna get him out of it, but he couldn't do it if I told anything about what I heard before they left." The brown eyes filled with sudden tears. "He said if I told anybody, Jake was gonna go to jail and it would be my fault. He said I had to pretend I didn't know anything about it, and he would fix everything for Jake. But he hasn't fixed it, Mom!"

His face crumpled, and I reached out and pulled him against my chest. He cried as if he'd been holding back a flood—because he had, for four torturous weeks.

I rubbed his back until the sobs subsided and he pulled away to drag his sleeve across his eyes. I stuffed a Kleenex in his hand before he could go after his nose.

"It's okay, Alex," I said. "You did the right thing telling me."

"Yeah, but . . ."

"What? We're not going to let Ian hurt you, if that's what you're worried about."

"But now you're gonna be mad at Dad because he's the one

who brought Ian to our house and you guys'll never get married again."

He honked noisily into the Kleenex while I fumbled for a reply. I had no idea what to do with that . . . but he'd already been through enough for one afternoon.

"I'm not mad at Dad for this," I said. "I'm just glad you told me."

He looked expectant. I groped for another subject. "Cade's mom is tough, isn't she?"

"I guess so."

"What did she do to get you to tell me all this?"

Alex blinked. "She didn't. It was Bryan's mom."

"Victoria? Mrs. West?"

"She said she felt like God was saying she should get me to tell. It kinda freaked me out, but I figured if that was true, I might get struck down dead or something if I didn't." He wadded the Kleenex and went for a layup into the magazine basket. "Do you think it's true? Or was she just *trying* to freak me out?"

"I think it's the real thing," I said.

Then I grabbed his squirmy self and rocked it for as long as he would let me.

Will, Dan, and I met in a sandwich shop around the corner from the jail at five thirty, right after soccer practice. Will had ordered an assortment of tortas for all of us, but he was the only one who ate any. He chewed and listened while I related all Alex had told me, just as I had to Dan the minute I'd arrived at Burn Lake. He'd been eerily quiet since then, even for him.

"That tells us a lot," Will said.

"Why do I hear a *but* in your voice?" I said.

"Because the only way to use it is to put Alex on the stand. Which means Nina Hernandez will have a chance to cross-examine him. She'll have a field day with that."

"But he's telling the truth!"

"She'll cast doubt by badgering him about why he waited so long to tell. 'Aren't you making it up now to try to keep your brother out of jail?' That kind of thing."

"He's not! This has been killing him."

"We know that. But she'll be able to confuse him enough to get him to stumble over it somehow."

Dan stirred. "It's still Alex's word against the evidence."

"Right." Will put down the end of his sandwich and dusted the creamy palms of his hands together. "This establishes that Ian had a motive, but it was still Jake they found behind the wheel."

"So you're saying you can't use any of this," I said stiffly.

"Not saying that at all. I can use it when Ian takes the stand."

"You're calling Ian?" Dan said.

"No. Hernandez is. Ian is her surprise witness."

"What?"

Will shook his head at me. "I don't know why—she doesn't have to tell me that—but with the information you just gave me, which she does not have, I can probably corner him on cross."

"That's perfect!"

"It would be even more perfect if when I lay all of this out to Jake, he'll tell me the rest of the story."

"Why wouldn't he now?" Dan said.

"One thing hasn't changed: he thinks if he tells, somebody's going to get hurt." Will picked up the check and got to his feet. "I'm going to go see if I can convince him otherwise."

We sat in silence, Dan and I. He dropped his face into his hands, elbows on the table, and it occurred to me for the first time what this meant for him. Mixed with the hope that his son didn't commit a murder was the threat that his future stepson did, a kid he cared about. It didn't stop me from what I was about to say, but it made me say it with more sensitivity than I thought I was capable of.

"You know I've been seeing a therapist," I said.

He pulled his hands from his face and nodded absently.

"He's helped me figure out I can't control all of this in my usual control-freak fashion. But as a mother I can take responsibility for the part Jake thinks *he* is responsible for but isn't."

"Ryan, what are you talking about?" Dan's voice was weary.

"Jake's afraid of the threat. If we take that away, he has no reason to hold back anymore."

"How are we supposed to do that?"

I folded my hands on the table, close to his. I could almost feel the tension pulsing through his fingers.

"Please don't think I'm trying to come between you and Ginger," I said. "This is not about me wanting to hurt her or split you two up or anything like that. And I know you like Ian. You treat him just like you do Jake and Alex."

He was alert now, and watching me.

"But if what Alex says is true, and I believe it is, then Ian is the one threatening Jake. The bomb thing happened after Miguel died, and whatever Ian was going to do to 'fix it' wasn't going to work anymore. He had to do something more to keep Jake quiet."

I watched Dan swallow hard, but he nodded.

"If we can prove it was Ian who set the bomb," he said, "or that he at least had something to do with it—Ian goes to jail, and the threat is over."

"And Jake talks. I'm sorry, Dan, but this is our son—"

"How do we prove it?"

I sat back and let him get his face under control.

"I don't know," I said. "When I picked up my car from the police, they said the bomb was made from Ivory soap shavings and gasoline in a jar. That evidently creates a chemical reaction that makes an explosion. The only piece they found was the jar lid from some kind of powdered dye, like maybe a crafter would use. The rest of those ingredients, though, you can find in just about anybody's bathroom and garage." I blew out air. "Ian doesn't even have a garage."

"He's staying at my place."

I stopped with an *oh* on my lips.

"Ginger lost her apartment," Dan said, "and she's been living in one of those residence inns, but I couldn't see Ian being cooped up like that. I said he could stay with me."

"This could be a good thing. Was he staying with you when the bomb went off?"

"Yeah." His voice split in half.

"What's wrong?"

"He was there alone the whole weekend. Ginger and Alex and I were away." His face worked. "That clears up something else that's been bugging me."

"Yeah?"

"You said the Mountains' coach told everyone I canceled the game that day?"

"Right."

"I didn't. He called *me.* Or at least I thought it was him. The message on the phone was garbled." His voice trailed off. "I'll look around at my place," he said finally. "But what do we do if I find something?"

Even before the words *We'll drag Ian's sorry little butt straight to the cops* completely took shape in my mind, I stopped myself. "Why don't we do whatever's going to help Jake first, and then we'll deal with Ian?"

Dan looked at me as if I'd just taken off a disguise. Maybe I had.

"I'm going to go ahead and get started on that," he said.

He scraped back the chair and stood with his hands on the back of it, opening and closing his fingers. The detritus of his art had gathered in the folds of his knuckles, the only sign of the artist who lived in a dream world. He was now a man very much in touch with the real, and it was taking him apart.

"You're a good man, Dan," I said.

His eyes misted, and with a final squeeze on the back of the chair, he left.

CHAPTER THIRTY-SIX

If they would only turn off the lights. Just a five-minute break from their accusing fluorescence. What was there to see anyway?

Sully churned on the flattened mattress that barely covered the concrete slab. Not that darkness would hide where he was. There was no stopping the putrid smells and sounds pressing in from the men he had to share the misery with.

I'm not a criminal, Sully chanted to himself. *I shouldn't be here.*

He reminded himself of that at measured intervals during the day. Just as he told himself today was Wednesday. And that Harlan Snow was pushing for a rush on the source hearing. And that once he was out of here, they would find a way to keep him out.

That was his litany. That and the prayers that sputtered and jerked from *I feel your presence, I know your light* to *Where are you? Where are you?*

Why am I here? he asked now. Was it a crime to try to get some closure?

Sully grew still on the mattress, felt the concrete slab all the way to his spine. He was never going to have that anyway. With Belinda dead, he would never be able to say what he'd been convinced would set him free. All he might ever have was a six-by-six cell in which to regret that he'd believed it would.

He pulled himself off the mattress and went to the front of the cell, a journey of three steps. How did anybody sleep in this place? It wasn't a clear conscience that did it. Sully hadn't dozed for more than fifteen minutes at a time since he'd been in here. Maybe it was revenge achieved, no matter what the cost. Or a twisted sense of justice. Or maybe just nothing left to lose.

Sully returned to the bed and sat with his back to the corridor. He tried the chant again, but it took off on its own. Was he any different? Didn't he want to see Belinda Cox squirm under his accusations? Wasn't it his goal to get justice for Lynn and Hannah—and didn't he want the consequences to be harsh? Hadn't he gone at it as if he had nothing to lose?

Yes to all of that—until the very evening he left the clinic to go to her house in Mesilla. That day it had all come together for him—that if he didn't find her to offer help, he shouldn't find her at all. The irony sucked his breath away.

"Hey. Doc."

Sully twisted toward the front of the cell. The least surly of the guards stood in the opening and nodded for Sully to come closer.

"Looks like you're gettin' a break, Doc," he said, voice low.

"Yeah?"

"Your source hearing's tomorrow morning. You got one more night in this hellhole."

Sully let his head fall forward and closed his eyes. The guard gave his bars a tap.

"Thanks," Sully said.

"I hope it all works out for you."

By Wednesday night exhaustion got the better of stress, and I fell asleep in the chair by the fire at seven o'clock. When my phone woke me up an hour later, I could barely focus.

"This murder case is your baby," Frances said, "so I'm putting you on—what's his name?—Sullivan Crisp's release from jail tomorrow."

"They found the real killer?" I said.

"No—he's just getting bailed out." I heard the computer keys stop clicking. "What do you mean, the real killer? Do you have a lead on this that I don't know about?"

I sank back into the chair.

"Come on, Ryan. If you know something about this guy . . ."

"I do," I said. "You know what—yeah, I'll go tomorrow, but on one condition."

"Which is?"

"Whatever I shoot goes on the front page."

"I can't promise that, and you know it."

"Fine. Get somebody else."

Frances sighed. "Okay—I'll do my best."

"That works," I said.

"You are difficult, you know that?"

Only when it serves somebody well, I thought as I hung up.

The phone rang again in my hand.

"Front page," I said into it. "I'm not compromising."

"You seldom do."

"Dan? I'm sorry—I thought you were my editor." Suddenly chilled, I pulled the Bears blanket around me. "You don't sound good. What's going on?"

"I found a bar of Ivory soap in the guest bathroom, but it was still in the wrapper."

I could hear the mixture of disappointment and relief stirring.

"I keep gasoline out by the studio for my generator."

"That doesn't really prove anything, does it?" I said.

"No." His pause was full.

"Dan?" I said.

"You said the lid on the jar was from powered dye. I use that. And I have a jar missing."

"Are you sure?" I didn't point out that he had a lot of stuff out there, and keeping close tabs on the inventory wasn't his MO.

"Yeah, but not sure enough to confront Ian with it. I did search his room, though, and I found something—I don't know if it means anything." His voice dropped. "I don't know if I *want* it to mean anything."

"I hear you, but—"

"It's a magazine." I heard pages rustle. "*Proceso.* The whole thing's in Spanish, and Ian doesn't speak Spanish. So unless he's using it for one of his debate arguments—"

"Whoa—what did you—"

"But there's a picture cut out of it."

"What page?" I said.

"Thirty-two."

I stood up and threw off the blanket. "Dan, the picture on the note that was thrown through my windshield was from that magazine, that page."

A stunned silence dropped between us. From within it, I heard Dan whisper, "God help us."

"Yeah," I whispered back. "Please."

God was showing off in Las Cruces at one o'clock Thursday afternoon when Sully walked out of jail. All of the aspens had turned October gold, and the sky was a crisp blue that beckoned his eyes upward to the brilliant flashes of two hot air balloons chuffing above the city.

Once he and Rusty Huff were beyond the reporters and the cameras that had blurred before him down the steps to Rusty's rental car, Sully let the window down on the passenger side and breathed in. Sagebrush, restaurant lard, the exhaust from some guy's Harley—he didn't care—they were the smells of freedom.

"Dude, I'm a happy man," he said.

Rusty glanced over from the steering wheel and nodded, but there was no real agreement in his eyes.

"Okay," Sully said. "Dish."

Rusty ran a hand over his clean-shaven head. "You want to grab something to eat first?"

"I'm not excited about going into a restaurant with this ankle bracelet on. The judge actually sees me as a flight risk?"

"I guess $500,000 doesn't talk as loud as we thought. How about a drive-through?"

Sully wasn't hungry, but he nodded. "Let's take it to the clinic and eat. There must be a lot of damage control to do."

Rusty jittered his fingers on the steering wheel. "I don't think that's a good idea. We all know you're innocent, Sully, but we feel like it's the best thing for you to stay away from the clinic until this whole thing is cleared up. Besides . . ." He frowned as he looked back to change lanes.

"Besides what?"

"You look like death. You've got to get yourself put back together again physically, my friend. Why don't you take some time to get your head straight?" He pulled the car into a Taco Bell driveway. "You want a couple of burritos?"

"Sure," Sully said.

Get his head straight. How was that going to happen? He wasn't sure he should call Porphyria. He'd like to run things by Kyle, but if he wasn't supposed to go near the clinic, that was out. The one person he wanted to go to was Tess. He swallowed back a rise of anxiety. She had to have written him off by now. He'd gone over that ad nauseum in jail. She knew he was desperate to find Belinda. He'd insisted on going alone. Why wouldn't she buy what the police believed? He tried not to consider that she may have been the one who told them he was stalking the victim. But that meant not thinking about her at all, and that was impossible.

When Rusty left him at the house and went back to the clinic, Sully tossed two uneaten burritos into the trash, and after one glance at the evidence that his house had been searched, pulled a kitchen chair out to the front porch. He couldn't see the street for the overgrown bushes, but at least he was outside. He wasn't sure he could ever stay in an enclosed room again. He avoided entertaining the possibility that he wouldn't have a choice.

He was gazing up at the Organs, searching their crags for peace, when his cell phone rang. It was Harlan Snow.

"Sorry I didn't get to talk to you after the hearing," he said. "Things got stacked up. How are you doing?"

"I don't know," Sully said.

"That's to be expected. Listen, Sullivan, we have some time before your case goes to trial, so I'm going to continue to flesh this thing out."

Sully waited.

"Aside from the fact that they found nothing on the clothes they took from your house, the DA has a strong case. Hernandez has a good track record, but I don't think she can knock down extreme emotional distress as a defense."

Sully let that sink into a cold place in his brain. "You think I did it."

"I didn't say that. But I have to be prepared if this thing starts to go south."

There was no way Sully could process that right now. "I'm going to get some rest," he said.

"Do it. I'll call you tomorrow."

Sully hung up and dropped the phone into his lap. Extreme emotional distress. He hadn't been feeling it the night he walked up Belinda Cox's front walk, but he was getting there now.

A vehicle pulled to the curb, and Sully stood up to peer over the tops of the bushes, anxiety immediately pumping. God, please don't let it be Baranovic, coming to tell him there'd been a mistake about the bail.

It was a small SUV with the name of a courier service emblazoned on the side. The driver left the motor running and started up the path with a large white envelope in his hand. He stopped and squinted at the numbers on the mailbox and then at the package.

"Yeah, somebody lives here," Sully called to him.

"Sullivan Crisp?"

"Yeah," Sully said, but he wondered if he was going to regret this.

Palms sweating, he signed for the thing and waited for the driver to take off before he slit it open. Unwelcome possibilities flipped through his mind until he pulled out a white sheet with a line drawing penned across it.

For the first time in more than a week, Sully felt a grin spread slowly, deliciously across his face—the same grin, he was sure, that smiled up at him from the drawing. An expert had sketched him in caricature—short hair askew, eyes dancing, grin loping from lobe to lobe. It was Sullivan Crisp himself, right down to the too-wild Hawaiian shirt.

She'd signed it unnecessarily. No one else but Tess could have drawn it. But the note she'd written at the bottom he did need.

I did you in ink, it said.

Sully propped a foot on his opposite knee and spread the paper on his calf. When another vehicle pulled up and its motor died, he shook his head. *Leave me alone,* he wanted to call to it. *I'm falling in love.*

I practiced my spiel all the way up the ragged front walk to Dr. Crisp's house: *I know I'm crossing some kind of therapist-client boundary, but I don't care. I had to see you face-to-face and tell you I don't believe you're any more guilty than Jake is.*

Tucking my laptop under my arm, I used one hand to part the bush that hung over the steps and jumped a foot when I saw Sullivan himself sitting on the front porch.

"I'm sorry!" we said in unison.

He stood up and put his hand down to me. I grabbed it and held on until I got the tears to back off. He didn't look like he needed anybody crying right now.

Even though I'd seen him earlier from afar, his appearance up close was a shock. His eyes seemed to have sunken into the dark crescents under his eyes, and the grin he was attempting now curved into gaunt cheeks. If he had eaten or slept in the last week, I would be surprised.

"I know I'm not supposed to be here," I said.

"Actually, I'm not sure what the rules are in this situation," he said, "so let's just make them up as we go along. Have a step."

I sank down onto the edge of the porch beside him and hugged my laptop to my chest to hold in the pain. I hoped I was keeping it off my face.

"Tell me about you," he said.

"You sure you want to hear, with all you're going through?"

"I do." He looked down at a folded piece of paper he was creasing over and over. "I'm so sorry I haven't been there for you."

"But you *have* been. I've been using everything you've taught me." I tried to smile. "I haven't destroyed any property since the last time we talked."

He tried to smile too. Neither of us made it work.

I lowered the computer to my lap. "I really came to tell you that I know what injustice feels like. For what it's worth."

"It's worth a lot."

"I'm just glad you got bailed out. We didn't have that option with Jake."

"I looked for him in there, but they don't let you mingle much."

"I told your colleague—what's his name? Kyle Neering?"

"You saw Kyle?"

"The night it happened, when I went to the scene to take pictures. I told him I'd help with bail, but he never called me."

Sullivan's eyes widened. "The night of the murder?"

"I didn't even know you were a suspect already, but he seemed to know what was going on. He was really concerned, and it scared me." I hunched my shoulders. "I guess rightfully so, huh?"

His attention seemed to have snagged on something else. I rubbed my hand across the computer.

"I'm not going to keep you," I said. "I do want to show you something."

Sullivan pulled himself back to me and nodded. I opened the laptop, pulled up the shots I'd taken earlier, and clicked on a close-up of his profile. His chin was lifted, his eyes focused and clear.

There was no downward slant of shame, no uncertainty around his mouth. It was the picture of a man anyone would trust.

"This'll be on the front page of the *Sun-News* tomorrow," I said. "I made a picture of an innocent man."

"I always said you were good."

"Just remember what I told you: I don't manipulate. I just photograph what's there."

"Thank you, Ryan. I mean it. This is . . . I can't even . . ."

"Don't try," I said.

I closed the computer and stood up. Only then did I see the KRWG van parked across the street.

"I think you should go inside and close all your shades," I said. "I've given you all the coverage you need."

Despite his vow never to be closed in again, Sully did what Ryan suggested—though not only to get away from the reporters. He had to get a handle on what else she'd told him.

He closed the last set of curtains in the kitchen and leaned on the sink, forcing himself to line up the facts in a mind that was running in a frantic circle.

He saw Kyle the day of the murder, Wednesday, just before he talked to Porphyria. He had a duffel bag in his hand, and he told Sully he was going back to Little Rock for a few days to finalize the sale of his house.

Kyle had been shocked when he got back to town and found out what happened—Sully was sure that was what Rusty told him when they talked Saturday morning.

Sully cocked his head back and searched the cracks in the ceiling. Ryan had just told him she saw Kyle at Belinda Cox's the night of the murder.

All right—so he hadn't left town yet. Then why the big surprise when he got back?

That part might be explained by a blurring of somebody's memory. But not the other thing. Not Kyle's concern for Sully before he was even arrested. For that matter, before the police had even questioned him.

The doorbell rang.

"Channel 6 News, Dr. Crisp," someone shouted. "We'd like to ask you a few questions."

Sully shook his head in the empty kitchen. No. Not until he asked a few of his own.

CHAPTER THIRTY-SEVEN

I didn't need coffee to wake me up the morning the trial resumed. I hadn't slept all night.

But I rethought that when I arrived thirty minutes before they opened the courtroom doors and had nothing to do with my hands as I stood in the corridor waiting. The stuff they sold in the kiosk downstairs tasted like engine sludge, but holding a cup might keep me from taking a swing at Ian if I saw him. I turned to the steps and ran almost head-on into Elena Sanchez.

I'd managed to avoid her on Monday, and our eyes hadn't met in the courtroom. She may have watched me from across the aisle, the way I had studied her, and made the connection that I was Jake's mother; I didn't know. Now, as delight replaced the grief in her eyes, I hoped she hadn't.

"Grafa!" she said. Her warm hands grasped mine, and her eyes went to my chest, where in her presence my camera always hung. "No pictures today?"

My hope was realized. But as she gazed at me, smiling and trusting, I couldn't let it go on.

"I'm not here as a photographer today, Elena," I said. "I'm here as Jacob Coe's mother."

I let the truth sink in, watched the disbelief and the disillusion rise to the surface. She withdrew her hands and stepped back from me, and in her eyes I saw what might have been slip away.

"Ryan," a male voice said behind me.

I turned to face Will and felt Elena brush past as she hurried away.

"I don't think it's a good idea for you to be talking to her," he said.

I shook my head. "Don't worry. It won't happen again."

I couldn't think about Elena Sanchez once Jake was brought in. He smiled at me when I said his name, and he even let Will put his arm around him and pull him closer for a conference.

"He seems good, doesn't he?" Dan whispered to me.

"Almost." I looked around him to the empty seat on his other side. "Where's Ginger?"

"Out in the hall with Ian. He can't come in until it's time for him to testify, so she's waiting with him."

"So . . ." I said.

"I gave the magazine to Will," he said.

I wasn't completely satisfied with that and was about to say so when Will patted Jake on the back and swiveled toward us, eyes drooping at the corners. "I couldn't get the magazine into evidence," he said.

"Why not?" I said.

"An issue of relevance. But I can still use what you've told me on cross."

I started to protest again, but the bailiff told us to rise. My hope didn't.

With the usual preliminaries out of the way, Nina Hernandez stood up as if she were about to announce an Academy Award winner and called Ian Iverton to the stand. My old anger went right up my spine and, I knew, into my face. Will had instructed us not to make any audible responses, no matter what happened, but he hadn't said anything about curled lips and squinty eyes.

Ian approached with a confident stride, wearing pressed khakis and a crisp white oxford shirt and a necktie he must have ripped off some prep school kid. He took his oath to tell the truth soberly, while I, to use Alex's word, tried not to puke.

When I stole a look at Jake, however, he was watching Ian with the same rapt attention he always gave the boy. He sat upright at the table, neck straining forward, the picture of eager anticipation. Will said he'd told Jake everything Alex reported to me and informed him of our suspicions that Ian had planted the bomb as well, but Jake still refused to talk—so what was this? What was Jake expecting Ian to say?

What Nina Hernandez expected him to say was apparent right after she established Ian's relationship to Jake and how, because Ian was a school leader, a star athlete, and an honor student, he could assess a situation intelligently.

"Were you aware of the relationship between Jacob Coe and the victim, Miguel Sanchez?"

Ian sighed deeply and said yes.

"And how is it that you know about their friendship?"

"It wasn't a friendship," Ian said. "Jake hated Miguel."

"Objection. Hearsay," Will said.

The judge overruled him and nodded for Hernandez to proceed. Dan put his hand on my arm. That and that alone kept me in my seat.

"Did Jake *tell* you he hated Miguel?" she asked Ian.

"All the time." Ian made a pained face. "But he didn't have to tell me. I saw it."

"Saw it how?"

"When we were playing soccer, Jake was always making racial slurs, calling Miguel a bean eater, among other things. He was extremely upset when he found out Miguel was trying out for the select team."

"Did he do anything to stop him?"

Ian shook his head. "He wanted to, but I told him no—everybody has a right to take their shot."

I had to plaster both hands across my mouth. Jake was perfectly still at the table, staring at Ian, all color gone from his face.

"Did Miguel make the team?"

"Yes, ma'am. So did Jake."

"Was Jake upset about that?"

Ian looked down at his lap, something I had never seen him do.

"Ian," Hernandez said. "I know Jake Coe is your friend, but you've got to tell the truth."

He made a show of swallowing and finally said in a half whisper, "He was beyond upset. He said he was never playing soccer with that Mexican—"

And Ian let out a string of words I knew had never come from my son's mouth. I jerked my head toward Will, certain he would stand up and object to this obvious perjury. But he was turned toward Jake, who was whispering into his ear.

"Ian," Hernandez said, "did you know Jake Coe planned to attack Miguel Sanchez in the alley that day?"

Ian pulled his neck up indignantly. "Absolutely not. If I had, I would have told someone. Friend or no friend, I wouldn't have let something like that happen."

"One more question." Nina Hernandez pressed praying hands against her lips before she went on. "If you and the defendant were such close friends, why wouldn't he tell you about his plan?"

"I guess because he knew I wouldn't have anything to do with killing somebody."

The room went black around the edges, and I could hear myself gasping for air and sanity. Will put a hand back toward me and stood up, all in one fluid motion.

"Your Honor, I would like to request a recess to confer with my client," he said.

The judge looked pointedly at his watch. "We've only been in session for a half hour, Mr. Yarborough."

"The prosecution was granted four days, Your Honor. I'm only asking for twenty minutes."

"All right. Make it thirty." The judge looked at Ian. "You will take the stand again for Mr. Yarborough's cross-examination after the recess, Mr. Iverton. You remain under oath."

Ian stepped obediently from the stand. In the midst of the gavel pounding and the buzzing of voices, Will conferred with a guard and took Jake up the side aisle and out into the hall.

"Where are they going?" I said to anyone who would answer.

The guard jerked his head toward the door. "Conference room."

I took off.

"You can't go in," he called after me.

I didn't ask him what army was going to try and stop me as I charged up the aisle and shoved my body against the heavy wooden door that swung out into the corridor. I nearly mowed Elena Sanchez down with it.

"Grafa," she said.

"I'm sorry, Elena," I said. "I'm sorry I misled you. I'm sorry for everything—but I have to go to my son."

"No. *Grafa,* you must listen."

I was backing off from her, pushing away her reaching hands. "I will," I said. "Later."

"Now. Please."

She pulled me to the other side of the corridor, then took my face in her icy palms and forced me to look at her.

"Everything that boy said was a lie, Elena." My voice was loud and shrill, and I couldn't stop it. "But everyone believes him, and I have to—"

"I do not," she said.

"What?"

She put her finger to my lips. "That boy—Ian. I know his voice. He call for Miguel that day, on the telephone."

I stared at her.

"I am home from work, sick, and I answer the phone. *That* voice ask for Miguel. *That* boy." Elena pulled her hands to the sides of her own face, as if to stop it from collapsing in her pain. "I told him where is Miguel. *I* told him. I lead him to my son, so he can kill him."

She did collapse then, into my arms.

Sully had paced and he'd prayed and he'd planned. He was ready at nine thirty Friday morning when Harlan Snow returned his call from the evening before.

"Sullivan, I haven't gotten much further with your case than I was yesterday," he said before Sully could get past hello. "You have to understand, this takes time."

"I just have one question for you."

Sully detected a sigh, but Snow said, "Shoot."

"I've been thinking about this severe emotional distress idea."

"*Extreme* is the word," Snow said. "Extreme emotional distress. And we haven't decided to go that route."

"I'm just trying to think ahead, in terms of who could testify to that."

Sully heard papers being shifted.

"Did you have anybody in mind?" Snow said.

"Detective Baranovic said someone at my clinic told him I was under a lot of stress. That was probably Martha Fitzgerald."

Sully waited, holding his breath and with it his hope that all of his conclusions had been wrong.

"I don't see her name on the report," Snow said. "It says that information came from a Kyle Neering. But listen, Sullivan, we'll put our heads together on that down the road. You let me . . ."

Sully missed the rest of it. He wasn't even sure he said good-bye before he hung up.

He sagged against the refrigerator. He'd known it since he talked to Ryan. Formed a plan around it. But he'd also had hope that he wouldn't have to follow through.

Only the alternative made him open his phone again, punch in the number for the clinic, and pray shamelessly that Rusty wouldn't answer.

Olivia did, sounding like an orphaned waif.

"Hey, Liv," he said. "You okay?"

"Dr.—"

"Yeah, it's me. Just checking in."

After a tiny pause, she said, in a voice that tried to sound formal, "Mr. Huff isn't here. He's not coming in until noon."

"Ah."

Again a pause. And then she broke into babbling. "He doesn't need to. We don't have any clients this morning. Everybody canceled, which is stupid because anybody who's ever even seen you knows you didn't kill somebody."

Sully pulled away from the fridge and straddled a chair. He should have known he could count on Olivia to tell him more than he needed to know and at least some of what he did, without even having to ask.

"Kyle's not here either," she was saying. "And that is just fine with me."

"Oh?"

"He's supposed to be in charge when Mr. Huff isn't here, and at first I was all happy about that, even though Martha got all pouty and would hardly even come out of her office." She went into a whisper. "I don't think I'm supposed to tell you this. Kyle said to leave you alone because you're so stressed out—but you don't sound that stressed out to me."

"I'm okay," Sully said. "Dish, Liv."

"See? You sound just like you always do. I wish you were here. Kyle isn't doing a good job, and I won't even care that much now if he does leave."

Sully's breath caught in his chest. "He's talking about leaving?"

"Yes. He said not to tell anybody, but I don't care about that either. You're the real boss, and you need to know. I think they should let you be here."

"Maybe soon," Sully said, finger already on the End button. "Hang in there, Liv."

"I totally think I can now."

Sully barely closed the phone before he opened it again and searched for Martha's mobile number. Renewed urgency coursed through him. This had to happen before Kyle disappeared and took Sully's innocence with him.

I stood against the wall opposite the door being guarded by a deputy who seemed to expect Jake to break out and make a run for it. When Will and Jake emerged, I was going to be there with the first real hope we had. Before Cecilia Benitez had come to take Elena Sanchez from my arms, Elena promised me she would testify, and I was hanging on to that.

"Do you know where Dan is?"

I pulled my gaze from the door and stared at Ian. He stopped a few feet from me, hands on his hips.

"Are you talking to *me*?" I said.

"Look, I don't want to get into it," he said. "I know you probably hate me right now, and I totally understand that. I'm just looking for Dan."

"No, you do *not* understand." I was too stunned to slap him across the face, but I was getting closer to it. The sympathetic lean of his head made my hand twitch at my side.

"I understand what it's like to find out somebody's not who you thought they were," he said. "It has to be even worse when it's your own son."

"Are you *serious*?"

"You couldn't see it, but he's probably changed a lot since you and Dan split up and you took off."

"Shut up," I said. "Just shut—"

"Ryan."

My head snapped to the conference room door. Jake stood just outside it, Will behind him, the deputy reaching for his arm. Will frowned at me, but I looked away, back to Ian, who was shaking his head sadly as if his heart ached for Jake.

I didn't have to listen to Will Yarborough. I could take this boy down, eviscerate him one organ at a time. There were no words too heinous, and I was capable of slicing him open with every one of them.

But when I looked at Jake again, I bit them back. He struggled visibly to hide the betrayal that stabbed at him. I could do this for him, and I could do it well. Or I could set him free.

Taking a step back but keeping my eyes trained on Ian, I said, "He's all yours, son."

Will put a hand on Jake's shoulder. "This is all going to come out in court now, Jake. Let's save it for the judge."

Jake shrugged his hand away, and the deputy went for his arm again, but Will shook his head at him. Neither of them moved away from Jake, but he seemed to stand apart as he shifted his gaze to Ian.

"It's good to see you, man," Ian said.

"You lied."

Ian's eyes startled only slightly before he turned his head to the side. "I don't know what you're talking about."

"In there, just now. That was all lies. *You* hated Miguel, not me. *You* were mad because he beat you at soccer—and debate. Not *me*."

Debate. Whereas. Inalienable rights. Pieces clicked into place almost audibly in my head.

"*I* didn't make up a plan to force him to drop out of soccer." Jake jabbed his finger. "*You* did. I just went because I thought I could change your mind."

"Come on, buddy," Ian said. "That's just wrong and you know it."

"And I thought when Miguel's mom said he was doing dishes at the restaurant, you wouldn't make some kind of big scene there."

Ian smiled like he was looking at a five-year-old. "I don't make scenes, Jake."

"No—you made sure there wasn't anybody else around. And you didn't even talk to Miguel about soccer, like you said you were going to." Jake's voice broke, but he pushed on, through the chasm I knew had to be splitting his heart. "You said we were just gonna take a ride in his truck—and I was so stupid I believed you."

Ian put one hand in his pocket and held up the other. "Look, knock yourself out," he said. "I gotta get back in there."

"No!" A vein bulged in Jake's forehead. "I had to sit there and listen to you lie. Now you're gonna hear me tell the truth."

"Jake," Will said.

"I still believed you when you said there was something behind us and Miguel better get out and move it before he ran over it. And then you ran over *him. You,* Ian, not me. And then I believed it when you said you were gonna help him, that I had to pull the truck forward while you pulled him out. I was so *stupid,* I believed it when you said you were gonna go get help even after I told you I already called 911 on that cell phone. You took off with it, and I waited for you to come back. Only you never did."

Jake was sobbing now, but I had never seen such courage in a face. His eyes never wavered from Ian.

"Does anybody believe this?" Ian said.

He spread out his free hand toward the knot of people who had gathered. Two deputies. Someone from the prosecutor's table, who turned and scurried into the courtroom. Dan.

"Dan, dude." Ian's voice caught on a high-pitched edge. "I know he's your kid, but come on, you know me."

"Do I?" Dan said.

"Look, he's messed up. We didn't go there to kill that kid. We were just gonna knock him down, scare him."

"Not *we*!" Jake said. "*You!* And then you said you were gonna fix it—you weren't gonna let me go down for it."

"I didn't think it would ever get this far. Who knew everybody would get all freaked out over an immigrant?"

"You never said that! You said for me to wait and let Miguel tell the truth when he woke up. And he didn't!"

"Like I knew he was going to die. Come on."

"Your mom said you were gonna tell the truth when you got up on the stand."

For the first time, Ian seemed brought up short. "My mom."

"She came to the jail and told me not to worry because you were gonna tell the truth today. I was counting on that."

Ian's incredulous mask slipped. "Dude, when did you ever know my mother to tell the truth? She's kept her mouth shut all this time. Why would she start talking now?"

"Ian—stop." Nina Hernandez sailed down the corridor toward us, hand up, all but blowing a whistle. "Don't say another word. Yarborough, what were you thinking?"

I left them to yammer at each other and stepped around the now-frozen Ian so I could see Jake. The deputy gave me a warning look, but I didn't need to touch my son to know that he was okay—more than okay. Even with sobs swelling his face and the crumbling of his idol still lingering in his eyes, he raised his hand to his ear and tugged at his lobe.

I tugged at mine too.

CHAPTER THIRTY-EIGHT

Martha Fitzgerald had always seemed nervous when she came into Sully's office. Coming into his home made her a veritable candidate for anxiety medication.

She made a valiant effort to hide it, crunching her hands tightly in her lap and fixing on a stiff variation of the smile as she perched on Sully's couch.

"Thanks for coming here," Sully said. "I'm limited in where I can go."

Her eyes darted to the bracelet on his leg, and her face cracked like an eggshell.

"Martha, I'm sorry," Sully said. "I didn't ask you here to upset you. Here, let me get you a Kleenex."

She shook her head and mysteriously produced one from inside her jacket sleeve. "I'm on overload," she said. "It's okay—you said you needed my help."

Sully leaned on his knees. "First of all, I want to apologize for blowing you off when you came to me about Kyle. I was wrong on every level I can think of."

"If it's all the same to you, I don't want to talk about Kyle right now. What can I do for *you*?"

He winced. "What you can do is talk about Kyle. I can't really tell you why. Holy crow, I don't even have the right to ask you to trust me on this."

"What do you want to know?" Her eyes were dry again, her voice solid. "If it helps you, I don't need to know why."

"I just need you to tell me what you've found out about him. I know you've looked into his background."

She nodded. "I just couldn't get past all the diagnoses of suicidality. You thought I was overreacting, but I know now that I wasn't."

"How?"

"I suspected that something happened, maybe to a patient, possibly when he was in grad school, so I looked up reported suicides in Little Rock over the past five years, and a Hayley Neering came up."

"Kyle's wife?"

"She took her own life a year and a half ago. That had to have played a part in his wanting to hospitalize everyone who came in depressed, but—"

"Suicide," Sully said. "You're sure?"

Martha's face softened. "He really didn't tell you? You two seemed to talk a lot. I thought maybe you knew, although I couldn't imagine that you—"

Sully closed his eyes.

"What is it?" she said.

"Kyle told me his wife was in an accident."

"Maybe he thought you wouldn't consider him a good therapist if you knew."

"He had every reason *to* tell me. Martha, would you be willing to find out more about Hayley Neering if you can?"

"With or without Kyle knowing?"

"Would it bother you if I said without?"

She looked him straight in the eyes. "No, Dr. Crisp," she said. "Not in the least."

For a bunch of people whose life's work was law and order, no one in the courthouse corridor seemed to be able to create any. Confusion reigned as the deputy took Jake back into the conference room to wait for Will while he argued with Nina Hernandez in legalese. I could only assume that the "recess" had been extended when Levi Baranovic showed up and went off into a corner with Hernandez, and Will returned to Jake. The deputy emerged and planted himself pointlessly in front of the door.

With one eye on Baranovic, another deputy hovered near Ian, but he needn't have worried that the kid was going to make a break for it. Even from a discreet distance, I could see that Ian's only focus was Dan. He sliced through everyone to get to him, hands already shaping an explanation.

"I never meant it to go this far," he said. "I really thought he'd get out of it. You had that Jew lawyer—"

Dan turned his head away, one hand up, eyes closed. "Ian, stop. You're only digging yourself in deeper."

But Ian went on, in a voice careening toward panic. "I thought Jake would get out of it and you wouldn't have to know it was me. I didn't want to screw things up between you and my mom. I just want you to understand—"

Dan's head snapped back to him. "You killed a boy and let my son take the rap for it. Period. What is there to understand about that, Ian?"

"You're just the only one who ever understood me."

The boy was so shameless I wanted to laugh—except for the pain that etched Dan's face.

"I thought I did," Dan said quietly. "It turns out I was wrong about a lot of things."

"Ian Iverton."

Heads turned to Levi Baranovic, who approached them with the deputy. Automatic anxiety gripped my stomach.

"We need to take you down to the precinct and ask you some questions."

Ian set his jaw, all begging for "understanding" gone. "You can't question me without a parent present."

"Where's your mother?"

"I don't want her. I want Dan."

Dan shook his head. "I'm not your parent."

"You almost are."

"No," Dan said, "I'm not." He stared at Ian until the boy's bravado melted.

"Almost doesn't count anyway," Baranovic said. He looked, inexplicably, at me. "Anybody know where this boy's mother is?"

I, in turn, looked at Dan, but Ginger herself appeared at the top of the stairs, hair and eyes wild.

"Someone said you're arresting my son!" Her voice echoed through the corridor like the cry of a woman gone mad in a horror film.

"We're not arresting him," Baranovic said. He nudged Ian toward the stairs. "We're just going to question him. You'll need to meet us at the precinct."

"I want a lawyer." Ginger gathered a handful of Dan's sleeve into her fingernails. "Dan—we need legal representation."

Dan pulled his eyes from Ian to her and peeled her fingers away. "You knew Ian was involved in this?" His voice was so dead it made even me shiver.

Ginger went white. "All I did was go pick him up from the alley when he called and bring him back to the house."

"You *what*?"

Ginger shrank back as I took a step toward her. It was the only uncalculated move I'd ever seen her make.

"All this time you *knew*?" I said.

"I only knew what Ian told me—"

"Which was what?"

She shook back the curls, tried to tilt up her chin, but her eyes wavered.

"*What?*" I said.

"He said it was an accident—he only meant to scare the kid."

"*He.* Not Jake."

"I was so stressed out, I don't know what I heard, okay?"

"But you heard something, and you never came forward."

"I had to protect my son!"

"And now I'm protecting mine."

I could hear the menace in my own voice. It was one thing to let Jake stand up for himself, but this part of the battle belonged to me.

Ginger groped backward until she found Dan. "She's scaring me," she said.

Dan swatted her hand away, his eyes on me. "You should be scared, Ginger," he said. "You deserve whatever she hits you with."

His nod to me was as subtle as a breath. He was giving me permission—to be who I no longer wanted to be.

Anger still pumped in my temples, but I shook my head. "You aren't worth it, Ginger," I said. "I'm going to my son."

I turned away from her and headed toward the conference room. The deputy's eyes startled wide and, inexplicably, he lurched toward me. Something slammed into my back and clenched me like a vise.

Before the deputy could get to us, Ginger's body was yanked from mine, and I stumbled to catch my balance. When I turned, she was clawing Dan's chest with her talons.

"Just go back to Ryan now!" she screamed at him. "Go back and let her beat you down again!"

Dan caught one of her wrists, then the other. She dissolved into wails.

"Dan—I'm sorry. Please, I can't handle this alone. I need help!"

Dan observed her the way I'd seen him observe a piece of artisan stone he was seeing for the first time. "I can't help you, Ginger," he said. "You need a professional."

I steeled myself for more shrieking and fingernail clawing as she pulled away from him, but she thrust her hands into the hair on the sides of her head and closed her eyes.

"I know," she said. "I know I do."

"Good," Dan said. "I really hope you find it."

Baranovic was at her elbow by then, showing even less pity than Dan. It was the first time I'd ever liked him.

"Let's go, ma'am," he said.

Ginger collapsed against him, face buried in her hands so that the detective had to half carry her down the steps. Ian's face, on the other hand, was a mask of pure contempt—broken only when he looked back over his shoulder and gave Dan one last longing look.

I wanted to spit in disgust, until I saw Dan's face. Until then he'd maintained more composure than I had achieved in a lifetime. Now that they were gone, he sagged against the wall.

"You okay?" he said to the floor.

"I'm fine." I waited for the *I could have told you that was going to happen* to rise to my lips. It didn't come.

"I'm sorry," I heard myself whisper.

"Don't be." Dan smeared his forehead with the heel of his hand. "It was over before this."

"I'm talking about Ian."

He looked up, face flickering surprise. "Our son almost went to prison because of him."

"I know." I closed my eyes—and the words were there, like a God-image. Words I never thought I'd say.

"Look, Ryan," Dan said. "Go ahead and blame me. It *is* my fault—"

"No." I opened my eyes and looked up at him. "No. I just think it would have been different if Ian had had a father like you."

Sully had the phone open and up to his ear before it stopped ringing.

"I have some more information," Martha said.

"Tell me."

"Hayley Neering slit her wrists, evidently right after Kyle left for work one morning. He found her when he got home that night."

Sully's stomach turned over.

"I can't even imagine how horrible that was for him," Martha said. "No wonder he's afraid every patient is going to meet the same fate."

"Were you able to find out why?" Sully put up a hand she couldn't see. "I don't even want to know how you found out this much."

"It's not as hard as you'd think. And yes, I did get something on that. The poor girl had just delivered a dead baby two months before the suicide. Full-term stillbirth. I can't imagine much that's more heartbreaking for a mother—or a father."

Sully stopped breathing.

"She *was* getting help, though," Martha said.

"They let you get into her medical records?"

"I got it from their online church newsletter. They did a little memorial to Hayley, and the church counselor was quoted in there as saying she did everything she could for her, and the congregation now had to pray for Kyle and for Hayley's family." Martha made a huffing sound into the phone. "You know, if she was suffering from that kind of loss, I can't understand why Kyle didn't have her seeing someone with more expertise in that area. Maybe that's why he's so—"

"Martha, did it give the counselor's name?"

"Yes—let me look it up again."

Sully pressed the phone to his forehead. Dread pressed down on him like a hand holding him in place, making him listen.

"Oh, by the way," Martha said. "While that's loading, I forwarded you an e-mail I sent Rusty this morning, before you even called me."

Sully pulled the phone back to his ear and clicked into his mail on his laptop.

"It says Carla Korman in the subject line," she said.

"Got it." Sully opened it and moved his lips soundlessly as he read. *Dear Mr. Huff,* blah blah blah, *after researching this matter,* blah blah blah, *the only complainant whose contact information did not lead to a disconnected phone number or defunct e-mail account was—Kyle Neering. Who was never a client of Carla Korman's.*

Sully ran his hand down the back of his head. "Martha."

"Here it is. The counselor's name is Belinda Cox."

The air went dead.

"Isn't that the name of the woman who was murdered?" Martha said.

"Yeah. It is." His mind raced toward panic, but he got up to walk it off. "Okay, if Kyle has any clients scheduled, cancel them. All of them."

"Got it."

"Don't tell him about anything we've talked about."

"Absolutely not."

"Or Rusty Huff either. I want to go over this with him myself when I've had a chance to sort it out."

"You have my word."

She was silent for a moment, long enough for Sully to picture Kyle standing over Belinda Cox's bleeding body, watching the life ebb from her the way it had from Hayley. And from Lynn. And from baby Hannah. Sully had never thought of murdering her. But as he felt Kyle Neering's pain course through his veins with his own, he knew why Kyle had.

"I never thought you murdered that woman, Sullivan." Martha's voice was thick. "And if there's anything else I can do to help prove your innocence, I want you to call me."

"You've given me a lot already," Sully said.

More than he wanted to believe. When they hung up, he stared at the e-mail. Kyle must have known about Sully's quest before he applied for the job at Healing Choice—a job he created by driving Carla Korman out with bogus complaints. If he killed Belinda Cox, it wasn't in a moment of rage. He'd planned for months, at least—and not only to murder her, but to set Sully up to take the fall.

Sully pressed his hand to his head and tried to think what to do. Call Snow. Enough with the extreme emotional distress. He could use that to defend Kyle.

Sully punched in the attorney's number and listened to it ring until his voice mail picked up. He didn't leave a message. Snow had little enough faith in his innocence as it was. If he heard Sully babbling about somebody's plot to frame him, he'd probably go for an insanity plea.

It occurred to Sully as he tossed his phone that it was Kyle who'd recommended Harlan Snow in the first place. Paranoid as it seemed, he could picture Kyle and Snow shaking their heads over their crab dip at what a shame it was that a guy like Sullivan Crisp was going down. If *he* couldn't control his emotions, what hope was there for the rest of us?

The anxiety stopped racing. Hope for the rest of us. Wasn't that what this whole quest had been about? His drive to keep a person like Belinda Cox from hurting anyone else, from letting another agonized client plunge to her death? Kyle Neering was a therapist, too, a therapist who had played God—just like the woman he'd killed.

Sully snagged the phone from the edge of the table where it teetered. There was one more number he could call.

CHAPTER THIRTY-NINE

I like what you've done with the place," Kyle said. He looked up at Sully, the glow of the fire in the outdoor kiva playing across his cheekbones. "I guess this isn't the time for humor."

Sully shrugged and lowered himself to the edge of the other chaise lounge. "Maybe it is. The whole thing is ludicrous."

"You're handling it better than I would be."

The irony of that sank its teeth into Sully, and he tried not to grit his own. He was depending on acting skills to get through this. Too bad he didn't have any.

Kyle, on the other hand, was giving an Oscar-worthy performance.

He'd accepted Sully's invitation to come over with tears in his voice. At the front door, he'd grasped Sully's shoulder and shaken his head—done everything but say, "I love ya, man." Sully had studied him as he opened the Frappuccinos Kyle brought and showed him out to the patio, where a breeze was blowing the stars around. There was nothing telling in his face. The concerned pinch between Kyle's eyebrows only etched deeper as he listened to Sully talk about gangbangers spitting into his cell and reporters staked out in his driveway. If there was murder tucked under his nods, Sully still couldn't see it.

Not until he looked at Kyle's hands. He had set the untouched Frappuccino on the table and sat with his palms on the arms of the chaise. Even as he watched softly with his eyes, his hands tightened and opened, the knuckles whitened and released, the muscles pulled and let go. Kyle hadn't killed Belinda Cox with his face. He'd taken her life with his hands. Sully kept his eyes on them as he spoke.

"I know, Kyle."

The hands squeezed shut until they were bloodless. "You know—what?"

"I know it wasn't fate that brought you to Healing Choice."

The relief was visible. "Since when do we believe in fate? That was all God."

"What about Carla Korman? Was that all God?"

Kyle formed the name silently on his lips and shook his head. "Who's Carla Korman?"

"You took her place."

"Oh." Kyle tilted his head. "You okay, Sully? I mean, of course you're not okay—but you're looking—"

"And evidently you were a client of hers."

"Now *that* I would remember."

"You don't recall filing a complaint about her to the main office?"

Kyle pulled himself up in the chair. "I'm not following you."

"I'm probably not going anywhere. Forget it—I guess I got some bad information." Sully inhaled noisily. "I think this whole thing is messing with my head. Like, I thought you told me Hayley died in an accident."

"Okay. I still don't know where we're going with this."

"But then I found out she committed suicide. Did I hear you wrong that night at the restaurant? I mean, I think I would have remembered that."

Once again relief relaxed Kyle's mouth. Relief where there should have been shame. At the very least, embarrassment.

"You didn't hear wrong, Sully. I should have told you straight out. I just thought you'd think I was a lousy therapist if I couldn't even keep my own wife alive."

That sliced at Sully, but he didn't have time to determine whether the swipe had been deliberate.

"I told you about *my* wife," Sully said. "Seems like that would have been the perfect opening for you."

"All right—bad judgment on my part. I'm sorry."

Kyle looked slightly less than contrite. The act was slipping. Sully put his hand in the pouch of his sweatshirt and flicked the switch on the mini-recorder.

"Look, Sully." Kyle swung his legs over the side of the chaise lounge and sat facing him. "It has to be hard to sit here with a murder charge hanging over your head. I think it's natural that you'd want to focus on somebody else's mistakes, distract yourself. So—we can talk about anything you want to. I'll take a hit for the team."

He didn't blink. Didn't look away. That was how he'd gotten Sully to trust him in the first place. And that was the only chance Sully had now.

"Then let me ask you something," Sully said, "because this has been niggling at me. I just want the air cleared if I'm going to count on you for support through this thing."

"Sure. Go ahead."

"I don't know, it just doesn't make sense to me that you didn't tell me Belinda Cox was a counselor at the church you went to in Little Rock."

Kyle hesitated no longer than a nanosecond before he widened his eyes at Sully. "I didn't tell you because I didn't know. Are you serious?"

Sully nodded. "Small world, huh?"

"No doubt! But I don't get why all of this is coming up now."

"Rusty Huff. He's main office, you know. I guess he doesn't have enough to do here, so he's going through everybody's files."

Sully took a long draw from the Frap bottle. He'd never been a good liar.

Kyle watched him, his eyes now sharper. "Belinda Cox must have come after . . . I didn't go back to that church after Hayley died."

"How did she kill herself?"

Kyle's face hardened almost imperceptibly. Sully might not have seen it if he hadn't been waiting for it.

"I take it back," Kyle said. "We can't talk about anything you want to."

Sully set the bottle on the ground. "Man, I'm sorry. I forget you're still so close to it. It took me over a decade to be able to say Lynn deliberately drove off a bridge with our baby because Belinda Cox told her she needed to renounce her demons."

"Right. So is the air cleared?"

Sully nodded. "Did you ever get that fan belt fixed?"

Kyle spat out a laugh. "I'm sorry—that's so random. No, I didn't."

Which was why the night of the murder, Angelina had gone to her window and looked out to see who was making all the noise. It wasn't much, but it did differentiate his Mini Cooper from Sully's.

Kyle sat back on the lounge and picked up the Frappuccino, but he still didn't drink it. "What else you got?"

Sully closed his eyes. The Light was still on, but he could only see one step ahead. He had to take it now, before the tape ran out and Kyle left him with nothing.

"I just keep thinking about Belinda Cox," he said. "I still hold her responsible for Lynn not getting the help she really needed, but holy crow, she was a human being. Nobody should die like that." He shuddered. "You should have seen what the killer did to her. He must have been a monster. Either that, or he was just so crazed with . . . I don't know . . . what would it take to cut a woman's throat with a steak knife?"

Kyle's hands squeezed the bottle.

"You know what's ironic?" Sully said.

"What?"

"When I was walking up to her house to talk to her that night, I was thinking that what she really needed was help. I mean, that's what we do, right? We try to lead people to healing. How was she any different from anybody else who's a total mess?"

"So what were you going to do, go in there and counsel her?" Kyle's voice took on an edge. "She screwed people up—drove women to kill themselves, for God's sake!"

"I only know of one woman," Sully said.

Kyle flung out a hand. "There were probably others—she had thirteen years after Lynn. She got worse through the years."

"How do you know that?"

"You told me," Kyle said, but not without tripping over it first.

Sully wasn't sure if he had or not. He had to move on.

"Here's the thing," he said. "Belinda made mistakes, but ultimately Lynn and Hayley made their own choices to end their lives. Who's to say anybody could have done anything to stop them?"

"I'll say it!" Kyle lurched up and kicked his feet to the patio. The bottle slammed to the table. "She could have stopped them. It was her fault, not theirs. You don't tell a woman who has given birth to a stillborn baby that the sins of the fathers are being visited upon the generations and that she has to sacrifice her life to God if she wants to stop the vengeance of Satan!"

"Is that what she told Hayley?"

"Yes!"

"And that's why you killed her."

Kyle's face froze.

"Like I said when we sat down here, Kyle: I know."

Everything slid away—the concerned pinch, the encouraging nods, the empathetic softness in Kyle's gaze. Something more real took its place.

"You do know," he said. He searched Sully with frantic eyes. "And you know the only way to stop her was to get rid of her. All this about helping her—it's bogus. She was a killer."

"And you're not?"

"Yeah, I am. And you know what's really lousy about it, Dr. Crisp?"

Sully watched his eyes swim and shook his head.

"Now that I've done it, I don't feel any better. You and I, we're never going to get over what happened to our wives. There *is* no healing from it, no matter what choice we make."

Sully pulled away from that. There was more he had to get on the tape before Kyle fully realized what he'd just done.

"How did you know I was looking for her before you came here?" Sully said.

"You said it yourself. You came to the church in Little Rock trying to find her. I got wind of that, put together from your podcasts that something major had happened to you. When I decided to come here and saw that you were here too—it just worked. What did you call it? 'All God'?"

Sully was chilled. "I take it you don't believe in 'all God.'"

Kyle stood up and sent the chaise lounge sliding across the tile. Sully rose and moved toward the door to the house and stood with his back to it. Kyle stared into the fire.

"I grew up being told that God has some vast eternal plan for our lives. When he didn't protect Hayley from Cox, when he let her kill herself and let me find her in the bathtub swimming in her own blood, I figured I better come up with my own plan."

"It was a pretty thorough one," Sully said. "Did you have it all mapped out before you came?"

"I was just going to let you lead me to her. But then when I saw how much alike we are . . . same build, same coloring . . ."

"Same car."

"I bought that when I saw yours."

"How did you get my fingerprints on the murder weapon?"

Kyle looked at Sully over his shoulder. His eyes were dark voids. "I took you out for a steak dinner. Look, I knew you could afford a good lawyer. I even recommended one. He'll get you off."

"He doesn't have to get me off," Sully said. "You just confessed."

Kyle turned to face him. "You don't have any proof of that."

Sully didn't answer. Kyle's eyes came down to pinpoints on Sully's sweatshirt pocket.

In an explosion of profanity, he hurled himself at Sully and threw his arms around his waist. Sully pulled his hands from the pouch, but he was already too off balance to stop the backward smash into the wall. He heard his own breath groan from him. Gasping for air, he clutched at Kyle's sleeves as Kyle flung him to the patio floor. Sully's neck snapped back, and his head smacked on the concrete. Even as the pain blinded him, Kyle drove his forearm into Sully's throat and groped in the pouch. Sully felt the tape recorder being pulled away. Kyle's sweat dripped into Sully's face.

"I had to pin it on somebody. I'm sorry it had to be you." With one hand still at Sully's neck, he pitched the tape backward into the fire, and with it Sully's hope. "Now it's just your word against mine."

"And mine."

Sully closed his eyes. From the open gate, the voice of Levi Baranovic settled over him like a prayer.

In a surge of energy that lasted no longer than ten seconds, Kyle was pulled off Sully and planted against the wall, face smashed to the stucco. Two uniformed officers searched him roughly and pinned his hands into cuffs.

"I want a lawyer," Kyle said.

Sully barely recognized his voice.

"Fine," Baranovic said. "I've already got your confession right here." He tapped his forehead and waved his other hand toward the gate. "These gentlemen are going to take you in. You can call your lawyer from there."

As the uniforms took a silent Kyle out through the gate, Baranovic put his hand down to Sully.

"You okay?"

"I've been better," Sully said.

Baranovic shook his head. "When I told you on the phone I couldn't use a tape in court, I didn't mean for you to let him throw it in the fire."

Sully sank onto the chaise lounge. "How long were you out there?"

"We tailed him here." He shrugged. "You give us a tip, we're going to follow up. Besides, I knew you weren't going to be able to pull off a recording."

"How'd you know that?"

"Because, Dr. Crisp"—Baranovic smiled—"you're not a criminal."

CHAPTER FORTY

Cade misses Alex," J.P. said.

I looked at her through the steam rising from my coffee. "*You* miss Alex, because he's the most adorable ten-year-old boy who ever lived. And no, you can't have him back."

Poco squeezed my hand, hers still warm from cupping them around her mug of mocha-Valium-double-latte, or whatever it was she was having.

"But *you* have him back," she said. "That has to feel good."

"We're doing joint custody for right now."

"A-*ha*!" J.P. said, jolting Victoria from her current reverie. "For right now. That means there's a later. You and Dan?" She poked me with her teaspoon. "Come on, you know we're going to get it out of you."

"You don't have to get it out of me," I said. "Why wouldn't I tell you? You're my best friends."

"Face it, we're your only friends. Spill it."

Even Victoria was now wide-eyed and pulling her mass of hair out of her face.

"Dan and I are talking," I said.

"About . . ."

"J.P.," Poco said. "Maybe it's private."

"I'm not asking for bedroom details."

"There *are* no bedroom details!" I said. "We're just talking through what went wrong and how we're different than we used to be and whether that means anything for us."

"How was White Sands Sunday?" Victoria asked.

"Good. We rented those sled things and we all slid down the dunes. Alex loved it. I don't think Jake is loving doing anything yet. He has a ways to go."

"Of course he does," Poco said.

"Dan and I took turns just sort of being there with him while the other one went screaming down the slopes with Alex."

"So I take it"—J.P. formed invisible breasts the size of cantaloupes in front of her chest with her hands—"is out of the picture."

"She's in the hospital, actually. The minute they started to question her, she had a complete breakdown."

"At least she's safe from Ryan in there." J.P. shook her head before anyone could protest. "Just kidding. But admit it—didn't you just want to strangle that kid when you found out what he did?"

I took a hot sip and considered that. Although for the most part I had concentrated on Jake, I'd definitely had my moments in the last four days when I wanted to do nothing more than take Ian's neck in my hands and squeeze it. Ginger's too. That was part of the reason I was bent on keeping my appointment with Sullivan Crisp. I glanced at my watch. He said he was leaving town this afternoon, but he wouldn't go before we had a session.

Still, it was hard to leave Milagro with the three of them around me, nudging out my personal information and holding it in their pretty smiles and their girly chatter and their womanly wisdom. How had this happened? How did I end up part of something only a group of females could be?

"Ryan, are you crying?" Poco said.

"No," I said.

"Liar," J.P. said.

Victoria gave me a misty look. "Crying is God's way of cleansing your soul."

"Then my soul ought to be pretty well scoured out. I've gotta go."

"See you at practice this afternoon," J.P. said. "We're getting down to the end of the season."

"We are?" I said.

"Well, yeah. It doesn't go on forever." J.P. shook her head at Poco. "Five weeks of soccer, and she still doesn't know a thing about it."

I gave her an eyebrow and started toward the door. When I turned back around, they were all watching me.

"You know what?" I said. "I think this is the body of Christ."

Poco was right about one thing. Some of the details of my time with Dan since Friday were private, for the most part because I was afraid that saying them would put them out there where someone else could tell me they didn't mean what I thought they did.

I pulled into the parking lot at the clinic and let the dependable New Mexico sun warm me through the windshield—and went over the scene for the twentieth time, at least.

The boys were exploring the gift shop at the White Sands monument Sunday, Alex with more enthusiasm than Jake. Dan and I opted for a bench out front where we could watch them through the window and count our sledding bruises. Dan had fallen into a ponderous silence, and I couldn't tell whether he was pulling away from me or gearing up to get closer. There was so much I didn't know about him. So much that perhaps I'd never known.

"This whole thing with Jake isn't the only reason I can't be with Ginger," he said suddenly.

"Did you figure that out before or after you got engaged to her?" I put my hand up. "I'm sorry. Old habits die hard."

He blinked at me. "Engaged? Who said we were engaged?"

"She did. The afternoon I came by your house after the bomb."

"You came by the house?"

I felt myself squinting. "She didn't want me anywhere near you, so she shut you down for the weekend. It's a done deal. Why do we need to hash that all out now?"

"Because I want you to know I found out I couldn't marry her."

I hid my relief behind a shrug. "Okay. Good. You know a crazy lady when you see one."

Dan ran his hand through the hair on the side of his head. "Ryan, would you just shut up and let me say it?"

I put my hands to my mouth and nodded.

"I thought I could—I mean, she made me feel—"

Sexy and desirable? I smashed my fingers harder into my lips.

"But when you came here, and we went through all this and I saw you—" He swallowed down the thickness in his voice. "I knew I couldn't marry Ginger or any other woman." He looked at me and into me. "Because none of them are you."

Alex had burst from the gift shop then with an oversized rubber white lizard, and Dan and I hadn't returned to the moment yet. I wasn't sure what to do when we did. I knew what I wanted to do. I just didn't know if I could.

That was the other thing I wanted to discuss with Dr. Crisp.

The clinic was quiet when I went in. There was something at once peaceful and sad in the air, and I had a fuzzy image of Sullivan emerging from a cell, arms outstretched to embrace a cloud.

"Dr. Crisp will be right with you," someone said timidly.

I looked up to make sure the same receptionist was at the desk. She had the usual I-just-got-out-of-bed look, but the lilt was gone from her voice.

"That's okay," I said. "I'm early."

She stared at me like I'd grown an additional head.

I settled onto a couch, striped by the sun through the blinds. I realized I'd never actually sat down in there before; I'd always been too busy pacing a furious path into the rug.

I pulled my yellow legal pad out of my bag. When the trial was over, I'd asked Will Yarborough if I could have it back—just because.

Jake's journey was still in black, Alex's in red. I uncapped a blue gel pen and wrote into the gaps Jake had filled for me over the last few days.

- I never had anybody like Ian since you and I used to talk. Then you left.

That one was hard to write down. But then, we were all facing the tough truths now.

- The day it happened—with Miguel—I wouldn't talk until I could see Ian and find out why he left me there. I wouldn't go home with you because I knew you could get me to tell, even though I was already mad at you for leaving Dad. And I couldn't tell—not without Ian. I knew there had to be a reason he ditched me.
- When I got home to Dad's, Ian said not to talk to you. I was going to anyway, but Alex said Ian would hurt him if he said anything about what he heard. I didn't believe it. Alex makes stuff up sometimes. But just in case, I had to be mean to you in front of Ian so he would know I wasn't telling.

I paused, squeezing the pen. There were moments when the urge to smack Ian was almost overwhelming.

- When you got too close to the truth, he said I shouldn't talk to you at all. Period. He kept saying he was working it out for me, that I'd never have to go to jail. He said Miguel would wake up and say it was an accident.
- I told him one day I thought you were right—that we ought to just tell the truth. Then he got really mad—like he was the day it happened. He said, "I maimed one kid. What makes you think I won't do it again?" He wouldn't even come over to the house. That's why I had to go to the debate tournament and see him, to make him believe I wasn't going to tell. I was afraid he'd hurt Alex.

- When I got caught, I picked jail so he wouldn't think I was talking to you. But I couldn't take it in there. Some guy was an epileptic or something, and they didn't give him his medicine. He had this huge seizure, and nobody even did anything to help him. Stuff like that just gets to me. I was still scared Ian was gonna hurt Alex, but I had to get out of there.
- And then I went on assignment with you, and I saw what Miguel's people were like, and I didn't want to be connected to that crime anymore. I didn't want anybody thinking I'd hurt them. Then we found out Miguel wasn't going to wake up, and I knew Ian was wrong. I was also figuring out I could trust you because you were different than you used to be. That day you left me at home, I was planning how I was going to tell you when you came back, and then Miguel died. I knew it was too late—nobody would believe me.
- Then when the lawyer told me the soccer field was bombed and you got threatened, I had to protect Alex. I had to find a way to make it work in jail because I was probably never coming out. You said to imagine God, and that's what I did.

My throat was as tight as it was every time Jake and I'd talked about this. I saw it all when it was happening, and yet I'd truly been powerless to change it.

- It tore me up that Ian was letting me take the blame for everything. I thought if *you* figured it out, without me telling you, he wouldn't hurt Alex because it didn't come from me. I gave you hints, like that I was the one who called 911.
- And then Ginger came to see me in jail and told me that Ian was going to testify and tell the truth. That's when I wrote you that note, so you'd know it was going to be okay. I know it was stupid, but I thought his conscience got to him.

> Ginger said Dad and her were getting married, and I thought Ian would do it so Dad wouldn't find out later and be mad. I wanted to tell him that Dad didn't *get* mad—that he would have helped Ian if he'd told the truth in the first place. He just didn't get that. He's never had any other dad except mine.

"Ryan? You ready?"

I blinked and nodded at the blurry figure in the doorway. "Ya think?" I said.

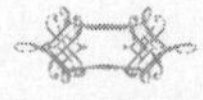

She climbed into her chair and looked around. "Where's my sandbox?"

Sully shook his head. "The police took it in their search, and I haven't gotten it back."

"What did they think they were going to find in there?"

"You got me."

"Never mind. I think both of us have about had our fill of the police department."

"I kind of have a soft spot for them right now," Sully said.

"I'm not there yet." She looked at him almost shyly. "I know we're not supposed to talk about you in here, but I'm glad you were cleared."

He grinned. "That's okay. It's my new favorite subject."

"I hear you." She pulled her feet up and hugged her knees. "I guess I'll have to manage without the sandbox."

"Are you in need of some calming down?"

"I already went to White Sands, for real—with my boys—and my ex-husband."

"Was that a good thing?" Sully asked.

"That's one of the two things I want to talk to you about. We should get started."

Sully let another grin spread across his face. Just when he was seeing the changes in her, she reminded him that some things would always stay the same.

"What?" she said. "Am I amusing you?"

He sat back and crossed his ankles. "Cut to the chase."

"Dan and I are talking. About us. We haven't actually used the word *us.* We're kind of tiptoeing around it." She stopped and shrugged.

Sully tilted his head. "I thought we were cutting to the chase."

"I don't know what I'm chasing."

"What are the possibilities?"

Up came the goalpost hands. Sully pulled a leg up across his knee. He wasn't sure before she came in if he had the spirit for this right now, but she was bringing it back.

"I think there are two," she said, focusing between the posts. "One, we're doing pretty well just being our boys' parents together. It's actually sort of comfortable. That could be all it will ever be."

"And the other possibility?"

"That maybe we belong together after all, and we can put the past behind us and start over."

Sully let out a buzz.

She squinted at him. "I thought you weren't going to do that with me."

"Sorry. Conditioned response."

"To what?"

"To the idea that we can ever completely put the past behind us."

"Huh," she said. "You've made me dredge it up and look at it until I want to punch it in the face—to use my younger son's phrase."

"And has it helped?"

"Okay, yes. But I know what happened with Dan, at least my side of it. I think I have a pretty clear idea of his side too. Are you saying I can't just move us forward?"

Sully lowered his foot to the floor and leaned on his knees. She leaned on hers, too, and opened her eyes to him. He'd once thought she was the most challenging client he'd ever had. But she might also very well be the most eager to find the path.

"Are you listening to yourself?" he said.

"What am I saying?"

"*You* know what happened with Dan, both sides of it. *You* want to move the two of you forward."

She dropped her forehead to her knees. "There's my answer. I am always going to be a control freak, so I might as well give up the idea of getting back together with Dan and having the life I've started thinking we could have."

"*Is* that your answer?" Sully said. "Or is it just that you have more work to do?"

"How much more? I don't even think I've gotten anywhere." She brought her head up. "No offense to you."

"None taken," Sully said. "But what about to you? Don't you think you're being a little hard on yourself?"

"No. I mean, I thought I was over wanting to hurl projectiles at people, and then sometimes I think about Ginger, and about Ian and what he did to Miguel and to Jake and to Alex—to himself—and I just want to flush him down the nearest toilet."

"Of course you do. But you haven't done it, have you?"

"No."

"Have you done anything else with that anger? Punched anybody in the face?"

"No."

"Then there's your progress, Ryan. There isn't a mother in the world who wouldn't get those surges of anger after what's happened."

She gazed at the painting on the wall, though he wasn't sure she was seeing it. When she looked back at him, her eyes brimmed.

"What you're feeling is righteous anger," he said. "It's the Jesus anger—turning over the tables in the temple."

"Telling the Pharisees they're a brood of vipers. I've always liked that passage."

Of course she had.

"I think what you're really chasing is righteousness," Sully said. "And the question you've been struggling with is: when do you fight, and when do you surrender? I think you've come a long way in learning how to discern that."

She looked again at the painting, this time with focus. "I hated that place when I first saw it."

"What—White Sands?"

"Yeah. I couldn't believe it the day I walked in here for my first session, and you had it right there in my face. It was like you knew what was going to tick me off."

Sully put up both hands. "I'm a lot of things, but I'm not clairvoyant."

"But now—I've figured out what it is that draws people to it, or at least me." She glanced at him. "We've already established that I can't speak for everybody on the planet."

"I said you were making progress."

Her eyes went back to the Sands. "There's nothing out there—except that it's so beautiful there has to be something. I think it's God, in a form you can't miss like you can everywhere else, with all the noise and people's stuff. So I guess the reason it gives me so much peace is because there's nothing but me and God. The images start coming to me, and I know things that I need to do—not the whole picture, which I would prefer, trust me."

She put up the goalpost hands again. "What I see is about this much. And so I guess that's all I'm supposed to see at any given time. What's *that* called?"

"Are you going to throw something at me if I tell you?"

She looked at him. "You're going to say surrender, aren't you?"

Sully nodded. "Sometimes we fight in righteous anger. Sometimes we let it go. But the surrender to the way God sees it always has to come first."

"And it's right here." She let her hands drop. "But sometimes I still don't see it. It's like anger blinds me."

"And you're getting to the bottom of that anger."

She gave him a squint. "Getting. As in I have more work to do."

"Let me tell you something my mentor always says to me." Sully closed his eyes, saw Porphyria—felt his throat clench. "She says, 'Sully, until you're dead, you're not done.'"

"That sounds like something my mother would say."

Sully opened his eyes and tried to grin. "And we haven't even gotten to her yet."

Her eyes filled again. "I just wish you weren't leaving. I want to work on this stuff. Dan and I could have couples counseling even."

"Who said I was leaving?" Sully said.

"You did."

"Not for good. I'm only going to be gone until—well, until I see to a personal matter."

"And then you're coming back here? To live?"

"That's my plan," Sully said.

He didn't add that there was one important piece that was going to have to fall into place for that to come to fruition. He just grinned at Ryan.

"What?" she said.

"I'm just thinking about you *wanting* therapy."

"It's not funny. Try to keep me out of here, and it won't be pretty. Trust me."

"Oh, I do, Ryan," Sully said. "I do."

CHAPTER FORTY-ONE

Sully checked his calendar one last time before he shut the computer down. There was no doubt Martha would handle things flawlessly while he was away, but the specter of things unfinished still haunted him. He was getting a little paranoid about missing the obvious. Another topic he wanted to discuss with Porphyria.

He slid the laptop into its bag and did a final eye-sweep of the office. His gaze fell on the picture on his desk. Automatically he picked it up to pack it as he always did when he traveled, but the frame felt too heavy in his hand.

"What's wrong, girls?" he said to it. "Tired of being on the road?"

Lynn and Hannah did not, of course, answer. They simply continued to delight in each other, unaware of what he had tried to do for them, and untouched by it. It didn't matter to them.

Perhaps it never had.

A prim knock brought him back and pulled a grin out of him.

"You'd *better* get yourself in here and say good-bye to me, Martha."

She pushed open the door—the hair, the pantsuit, and the portfolio all in their usual order. But today's variation on the smile appeared to be the real one.

He nodded her to a chair and took the other one. "Frappuccino?" he said.

"What in the world *is* a Frappuccino, anyway?" She shook her head at him, hair still immobile. "No, thank you. I just wanted to see if there's anything else you want me to do while you're gone."

"Just the interviews."

"I wish you'd let me wait until you get back, and we'll do them together."

"Since I did such a great job last time?"

Martha folded her hands on the portfolio in her lap. "I hope I'm not overstepping my bounds by saying this."

"Jump right over them, Dr. Fitzgerald. Matter of fact, it's time we knocked them down anyway."

"I just think you're being too hard on yourself about Kyle. He was very convincing."

"He didn't convince you. Which is why you should be the one to hire his replacement. Have you gotten in touch with Carla Korman?"

"I just talked to her."

"And? Is she interested in coming back?"

"She said she'd think about it. She's pretty gun-shy."

"We can't blame her. I think if anyone can convince her, though, it's you."

Martha's face colored to a proper pink. "So what time is your flight to Nashville?"

"Tomorrow morning at six."

"Ouch."

"I have a room in El Paso for tonight. I'll head down there after I take care of a few things." Sully leaned onto his thighs. "Listen, I just want to thank you again for all you did to help me."

"There's no need, Sully. Just come back, that's all I ask."

"I intend to. Meanwhile, I have no worries about you holding down the fort here. Oh, and by the way, if you feel like it's time to let Olivia go, I trust your judgment on that."

Her eyebrows shot up. "Olivia? I would have gone completely over the edge if she hadn't been here while all of that craziness was going on. I'm working with her on developing some decorum. She'll be all right."

Sully grinned. The image of Olivia becoming a mini-Martha was the most delicious thing he'd thought of in days.

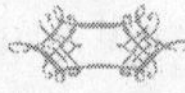

It was close to noon by the time Sully pulled into Tess's street, but he slowed down before he reached the house. If he didn't get it together, he really was going to stutter like Porky Pig when he saw her.

He'd called a few hours after Kyle was arrested and her voice had sounded just as he remembered it—like a bright silk scarf slipping across his soul. It was afterward that he dissected it. Of course she was happy he'd been cleared. So was the barista at Milagro, for that matter. But hadn't she seemed a little guarded? Not quite as—something?

The longer he'd stewed over it, the less sure he was that she wanted to hear from him again, much less pick up where they'd left off. He finally resorted to an e-mail to let her know he'd be going out of town. She'd replied within five minutes with an invitation to lunch.

He was now in front of the house, which meant he had to either get out and go to the door, or drive around the block again. He didn't have much faith that that would make him sound any less like Porky anyway.

And then the door opened, and she was there. Silky and smiling.

"Are you afraid you're going to get stopped for speeding, Crisp?"

"I'm sorry?"

"If you'd driven down my street any slower, you would have been going backwards," she said as she nodded him inside. "Was it something I said?"

"It was everything you said."

"About what?" She closed the door behind them and slid her hair back to look up at him.

"You really want to do the whole small talk thing?" Sully said.

"You don't want to know what we're having for lunch?"

"What are we having for lunch?"

"Steaks. Well done." She put her arms around his neck. "Now, where were we before they carted you off to jail?"

"A lot's happened since then. You might want to refresh my memory."

"I can do that," she said.

She kissed him, and proved him wrong. She wasn't guarded. She wasn't anything—except in love.

Porphyria opened her eyes the moment Sully entered the room. Winnie had told him not to expect much response, but her voice was stronger than it had sounded on the phone, and the expression that greeted him when he got to her bedside was vintage Porphyria—marvelous lips in an almost-smile, eyes knowing everything. She even managed to look queenly in a hospital gown. Winnie said Porphyria had eschewed the tangle of hanging bags and tubes and beeping machines. Nobody had argued.

"My, my, Dr. Crisp," Porphyria said. "I think you've fallen in love."

Sully grinned. "My lady love says I'm translucent. She must be right."

"No, I just know you."

"Yes, you do. Like no one else does."

"Except maybe you yourself."

She closed her eyes, and for an instant Sully thought she had drifted off. He curled his fingers around her hand, cool against his own sweaty palms.

"Tell me what you found out about yourself," she said.

"That I am not, nor will I ever be, perfect."

Her eyes opened. "You're going to have to go deeper than that, son. I don't have time to fool around."

Sully held on harder. "I prided myself on being a good judge of character, but I can't trust only that now."

"Go on." She licked at her lips.

"Do you want an ice chip?"

"I want you to tell me what else you've learned."

"I have carved a life out of helping people choose healing, and now I know how hard it is to make that choice."

She nodded, wise old-soul eyes still on him from a place already far away.

"That's what I know," he said.

"Mm-hmm."

He was fine until she did that. Now he could feel his face struggling. "What mm-hmm?"

"That's what you know in your head, Dr. Crisp." She pulled her hand, still wrapped in his, to her chest. "What do you know here?"

"That I don't want to be alone anymore."

She squeezed, her hand so weak it tore at his heart.

"And that I don't have to be."

"Mmm."

"And that I'm not." He brought their hands to his lips. "And I never was. It was all God, all along, wasn't it, Porphyria?"

"Still is, Sully. It's always about surrender. I've spent my whole life learning to succumb to it. It's the hardest thing God asks of us." She pulled her mouth slowly, painfully, into her magnificent smile. "But you know what I always say, son."

Sully closed his eyes and nodded. "Until we're dead, we're not done."

"And you know something, Sully? Look at me, son."

He did.

"I think I'm about done."

"No—"

"I waited for you, but now you have to let me go. That's what I've always done for you." She gave their hands a weak shake. "Do it, son."

Sully unwrapped his fingers from her hand, obedient as a boy, and laid it on her chest.

"I'm going to rest now," she said. "You, though—you go on." The magnificent smile lit up her face. "Because you're healed, Sullivan Crisp. But you aren't done."

"Far from it, Dr. Ghent," Sully said. "I still—"

He stopped. There was no *mm-hmm* on her lips. No *Talk to me, son* in her eyes. The soft lids closed. A peace beyond him slipped over her face.

"I'm not done, Porphyria," he whispered. "It's all God now."

READING GROUP GUIDE

Our biggest fear in providing questions is that they'll come across as an "assignment." We really just want to provide you with springboards for thought and, possibly, discussion over coffee. If you'd rather just savor the story (and the coffee), please do so without hesitation.

Blessings,
Nancy Rue and Steve Arterburn

About Anger

1. Nobody can deny that Ryan is our angriest character so far. Even if you've never wanted to throw pieces of sculpture across a studio, could you relate at all to her frustration and rage? Ever come close to that in your own life?
2. Sully muses that "innumerable expensive studies had shown that angry people who already knew they were ticked off didn't feel better after they punched something out. That only worked for people who weren't in touch with their anger—and that didn't describe Ryan Coe." What *did* describe Ryan's anger? What describes yours, if you have any (i.e., if you are human . . .)?
3. Ryan had to learn when to express anger for the sake of her sanity and when—and how—to get a handle on it. In reading *Healing Sands*, did you find a rule of thumb for that?
4. How do you know when to take action based on valid anger, and when to let a situation go? How does the answer to that play out in Ryan's situation? In Sully's?
5. Several other characters in the novel have their own issues with

anger. It might be interesting to discuss where theirs came from and how it influenced their behavior.

Kyle
Ginger
Jake
J.P.
Ian
Martha

On Faith

6. In each of the Sullivan Crisp novels, we've shed light on a concept of Christian faith that misinterprets the Gospel. We tackled legalism in *Healing Stones* and the toxic name-it-and-claim-it approach in *Healing Waters*. What twisted version of Christianity shows its face in *Healing Sands*?
7. Can you follow the thread of Ryan's faith as it grows in the course of the novel?
8. What about Sully's? Over the course of the three, if you've read them all?
9. What about yours?

Ah, Love

10. Before *Healing Sands* was even released, readers were e-mailing us, saying, "Isn't it time Sully had a relationship?" We thought the same thing. Sully was the only one who wasn't sure. What do you think about Sully and Tess? Is he more ready at the end of the book than when he first meets her? Do you think they can have a life together?
11. What do you think the future holds for Ryan and Dan? How might Sully approach his work with them?
12. An editor asked us why Dan ever got involved with Ginger in the first place. What's your take on that?
13. Moving to a different kind of love—how does Ryan's association

with the soccer moms influence the changes in her over the course of the story? Do you agree with what she says near the end, that together they are the body of Christ?

14. And then, of course, there's mother love. How does Ryan transform as a mom? What do you think lies ahead for her and Jake?
15. Finally—Sully and Porphyria. Can you define their relationship? Do you have that kind of spiritual companion in your life?

In Therapy

16. Ryan is by far Sully's most difficult client. Could he have avoided her walking out on their session when she did, or do you think that was a necessary part of their journey?
17. If you've read the other two novels, did you miss the Game Show Theology in this one? Would it have worked with Ryan?
18. What (if anything) in the therapy sessions resonated with you? Is there anything you could apply to the challenges you personally face?
19. One of our consultants told us after attending a conference for Christian psychologists that "Belinda Cox is alive and well." Do you agree that there are counselors who use Scripture incorrectly, if not dangerously, in their work with troubled people? Do you think Sully is "biblical" *enough*?

In Life

20. Sully points out that we are all born with certain neutral qualities. Sometimes they serve us well and sometimes they don't. That is certainly true for many of our characters. It might be interesting to discuss what those traits are in these people, and how they both enhance them and cause them to stumble—if not fall flat on their faces.

Ryan
Dan

Alex
Jake
Ian
Ginger
J.P.
Sully
Kyle
Martha
You

Did *Healing Sands* reveal anything else to you? Get you to consider anything differently than you did before? Confirm what you know? Make you want to call us up and tell us we need some therapy from Sullivan Crisp ourselves? If any of the above applies, we would love to hear from you.

nnrue@hughes.net sarterburn@newlife.com

An Excerpt from *Healing Waters*

CHAPTER ONE

I had done everything on my list. Everything but the last item. Neat black checks marked the first five to-dos:

✓ *paint bathroom*
✓ *put last layer on torte*
✓ *redo makeup*
✓ *call modeling agency—say NO*
✓ *shave legs*

Before the traffic moved again and I made the turn into tiny Northeast Airport, I put a second check beside number five. I'd shaved twice. Chip liked my legs hairless as a fresh pear. Not that I expected him to be interested in them or in any other part of my ample anatomy, but it couldn't hurt to be prepared for a miracle. In truth, I'd probably broken out the razor again just to procrastinate—because I wasn't sure I could do the sixth thing on the list.

I snatched the paper from the seat next to me and folded it one-handed as I pulled up to the gate marked *EXECUTIVE AIRPORT PARKING.* I was still trying to stuff the thing into my purse when an attendant marinating in boredom slid open the window in the booth. She drew sparse eyebrows together and mouthed something I couldn't hear. Of course. My car window was still up.

I pushed the button and felt like I'd just opened an oven door. As the aroma of jet fuel joined the July heat, the makeup melted from my face.

"Help you?" the woman said.

"I'm meeting my sister's private jet," I said.

"Name."

"Lucia Coffey. Oh—did you want my name or hers?"

"Don't need your name."

Staring vacantly at some point beyond me, she smeared her wrist across her forehead and produced a damp cuff. My mascara gathered in puddles at the corners of my eyes. I didn't even want to think about the damage in my armpits.

The woman shifted her gaze to a computer screen. "Who's it you're meeting?"

"Sonia Cabot," I said. "Abundant Living Ministries?"

The attendant's colorless eyes met mine for the first time. "She that woman on TV? Does the show for people got somebody dyin'?"

I gave my watch a surreptitious glance. I would be the one dying if I had to run from the car to the terminal to meet them on time. Just sitting there I was already dissolving like a pat of butter in a skillet.

"She's your sister?"

I looked up, unsurprised at the sudden interest on Apathy Woman's face. The tinge of suspicion didn't shock me either. I waited for the usual next question: *Are you sure?* To be punctuated with: *You don't look anything like her.*

I was tempted to save her the trouble and say, *Sonia's adopted,* which wasn't true. Or, *Usually I look more like her than this, but I'm pregnant,* which wasn't true either. The bulge hanging over the elastic in my pants resulted from pure mashed potatoes and gravy.

"Where do I park?" I said instead.

She perused the clipboard and, the epitome of servanthood now, pointed. "Just to the left of that building. Door's on the end. You better hurry. Plane's due in about five minutes."

I resisted blurting out a *No kidding?*

She knew who Sonia was, which meant I should be careful not to smudge the image. Besides, as I headed for the small, unimpressive terminal building, I had other things to deal with. Like the fact that my hands were now sliding off the steering wheel and my face felt like I'd baked it in the aforementioned oven.

When I parked, a glance in the rearview mirror confirmed it. My cheeks were the color of a pair of tomatoes. I pawed in my purse for Kleenex, found none, and grabbed the list. I tamped it against my forehead, my vine-ripened cheeks, my neck, and then viewed the half bottle of L'Oreal foundation I'd spread on them so carefully just an hour before. So much for the 'do as well. Dark curls, the only thing on me that I *wanted* to be plump, had flattened to my head in strips.

A jet taxied in already, white and sleek, the sun glinting from it like an insult as it made a ninety-degree turn to come perpendicular to the terminal.

The hair was hopeless. Ditto for the sweat situation. My black tunic, permanently glued to the Spandex shaper beneath, cooked my skin and did little to keep the fat under control. I dabbed at my raccoon eyes with my fingers, wiped them on my black pants, and climbed out of my PT Cruiser.

The list dropped at my feet and I would have abandoned it, except that all I needed was for Sonia or someone from her entourage to see it when we got back to the car. Especially the last entry:

- *tell Sonia I want my husband back*

ABOUT THE AUTHORS

Nancy Rue is the best-selling author of books for teens and adults, including the Christian Heritage series and the Lily series. Nancy has been an English teacher, a public speaker, and a contributor to several publications. Her books have sold more than a million copies. She and her husband, Jim, live in Tennessee.

Stephen Arterburn is the founder and chairman of New Life Ministries, the nation's largest faith-based broadcast, counseling, and treatment ministry, and the host of the nationally syndicated *New Life Live!* daily radio program heard on more than 140 radio stations nationwide—including Sirius and satellite radio. Steve is also the founder of Women of Faith® conferences and has written over seventy books, including the best-selling Every Man's series.